HENDERSON HOUSE

A Novel

Caren Simpson McVicker

Published by Inkshares, Inc., Oakland, California
www.inkshares.com

Edited by: Avalon Radys and Pam McElroy
Cover design by: Tim Barber
Interior design by Kevin G. Summers

ISBN: 9781950301553
e-ISBN: 9781950301560
LCCN: 2022952065

First edition

Printed in the United States of America

In loving memory of Aunt Boo Boo
and Grandma Simpson.
And for sisters everywhere,
no matter how similar or different we are.

Beulah Taylor Allen
Born: Indian Territory, January 28, 1896
Died: Bartlesville, Oklahoma, February 5, 1995

Lelah Taylor Simpson
Born: Indian Territory, December 18, 1897
Died: Tulsa, Oklahoma, September 28, 1986

MONDAY
MAY 19, 1941

CHAPTER ONE

Mrs. Henderson

LOUIE BARKS THREE times. I glance up from my son's letter and note the hour on the desk clock. Mr. Davis is five minutes early for his interview. Louie jumps off the settee and trots into the foyer. I set the letter on the side table and follow him. The memory of one of my mother's favorite maxims floats through the entryway on the back of the afternoon sun: *Five minutes early is on time, on time is late, and five minutes late is inexcusable.*

"Oh, Louie, on time or not, is it wrong to interview a new lodger today? Perhaps room number one should remain empty until I make up my mind?"

Louie answers by swishing his tail impatiently on the marble floor.

"Yes, but if I'm seriously considering—"

The bell rings. No time for debate. I smooth out my dress and open the door to the kind face of Frank Davis.

Mr. Davis appears to be in his mid- to late forties. He's not as tall as I am, but he's well proportioned—a complete man in a small package. A delightful yellow glow rises from his cheerful smile and wire-rimmed glasses. It's not a sunshine yellow but more the shade of a ripe yellow summer squash. I often need more time with a person before their color reveals itself. An immediate connection such as this could be the sign of a humble man who wears his heart on his sleeve. Then again, it might indicate an overconfident man, working to impress. My gut tells me it's the former.

When I was a little girl, I thought everyone saw people and colors the way I do. I never mentioned it to anyone because, to me, it was normal. A shimmer of color around someone's head and shoulders was part of their personality and a signal for how they were feeling. When my mother found out about my special ability, she made me promise I would never tell another living soul. She worried it would tarnish our family's good name and ruin my marriage prospects. In her opinion, my gift could cause nothing but trouble. But my intuition has helped me avoid trouble most of my life. An extra dose of insight is particularly useful when evaluating new lodgers.

In the richness of Mr. Davis's yellow, I sense joy and grief tumbling over one another, wrestling to see which will wind up on top.

"Welcome, Mr. Davis. I'm Mildred Henderson. Please come in," I say. "May I take your hat?"

Mr. Davis looks dapper in a double-breasted gray suit with a freshly pressed white shirt, a blue and maroon striped tie, and a coordinating pocket square.

"Thank you, Mrs. Henderson. I must say, this is a fine home." Despite his big-city attire, there's an amiable Midwestern lilt to his voice. I doubt he's from San Francisco originally.

"And who do we have here?" he adds, looking down at the beagle.

"My second in command, Louie."

"Nice to meet you, too, Louie." Mr. Davis bends down to rub the top of the dog's head. Louie presses his snout up into Mr. Davis's hand, thumping the white tip of his tail on the floor.

The air in the foyer warms and buzzes, murmuring with possibilities. Rarely does Henderson House give a stranger such an enthusiastic greeting. Curious. The house's ready acceptance of Mr. Davis reminds me of its response to my first lodger, Bessie Blackwell, some twelve years ago. The similarity in the welcome is startling—an open invitation brimming with giddy anticipation.

My ability to sense houses didn't emerge until I was a teenager. After my fourteenth birthday, Mother began asking me to accompany her to various committee meetings and afternoon teas—a thinly veiled attempt to strengthen my friendships with the daughters of each hostess. "Just think, you'll be debutants together," she would say, as if that was a selling point.

One autumn afternoon, we arrived at the home of Mrs. Edward Gould. When Mother and I entered, I felt the inside of the house flutter like a bird's wings. At first, I thought the sound and sensation might be an extension of Mrs. Gould's peachy color, but then I realized it emanated from the structure of the building itself. The house was happy to see us. After that, I paid close attention to every home we visited. Of course, I never said a word about the houses to my mother. An only daughter with two special gifts might have caused her to take to her bed.

So far, Mr. Davis has met the first three requirements on my interview checklist: He has a nice color, Louie trusts him right off the bat, and the house welcomes him like an old friend. We move as a threesome into the living room. The silver tea service glimmers on the coffee table. A tiny plate of shortbread cookies rests between the teapot and two cups and saucers. The final test. I'm hesitant to rent a room to anyone who won't accept a cookie over tea.

"I'm very interested in the history of this beautiful home," Mr. Davis says, taking a seat on the sofa as I settle into my favorite chair across from him. "How long have you lived here?"

"My husband, Dr. Charles Henderson, and I moved to Bartlesville from St. Louis in 1922, when he accepted the chief surgeon position at Memorial Hospital," I say.

Charles brought home a dozen red roses the night he told me he wanted to move the family to Oklahoma. He was hoping to soften the blow. Little did he know, the move was the answer to my prayers. Finally, a life of our own—free from the demands of my mother and high society. I remember the surprise in my husband's eyes when I cheered, threw my arms around him, and smothered his ruddy cheeks with kisses.

"I'm a Missouri boy myself. Born and raised in Joplin," Mr. Davis responds, cutting through my reverie and confirming the source of his accent.

"My husband and I completed the construction of the house in 1923." I pause to swallow. "He died unexpectedly six years later."

"I'm sorry for your loss," Mr. Davis says, and I believe him. "Was it an accident?"

"No. Charles went out for a walk, had a heart attack, and dropped dead." I sigh out loud, and the house sighs in sympathy. "All four of my boys traveled home for their father's funeral. Robert, the oldest, began nudging me to sell the house and move to New Jersey, where he was opening a law practice."

I don't normally dish out personal information during a lodging interview, but I'm comfortable sharing with this man. The same way I was comfortable sharing with Bessie during her interview all those years ago.

"Every night during my sons' visit, Robert and his brothers gently made their case for me to move on from this house and move closer to them," I continue. "The funny thing was, the more they sold me on a new life back East, the more I realized how much I loved living in Bartlesville. My life was here in this town, with or without Charles. I wasn't ready to leave; however, I couldn't imagine staying if Henderson House was empty. So, I told my boys I wanted to turn their grand family home into a boarding house."

"And what did your children think of your plan?" Mr. Davis asks, one eyebrow raised.

"To say they were not receptive to the idea would be an understatement." I chuckle as I remember. "My youngest, Artie, turned purple at the dinner table trying to keep his voice calm. Overall, I think their reluctance was a mix of concern and embarrassment. I made my case to them point by point, with the alternative being that if it did not work out, I could always sell Henderson House and move to New Jersey." My thoughts turn to Robert's letter. His latest offer is the strongest yet. But I'm still waiting for a sign to help me decide.

"I'm fairly sure that, in the end, my sons agreed to let me try my hand at being a lowly landlady because they were tired of trying to convince me otherwise," I say. "They were ready to return to their work and studies. As I waved goodbye to their train at the station, I dried my tears and began planning the reinvention of Henderson House."

"Did you make many modifications to the building?" he asks.

"A few. When we tour the house, I'll be sure to point out the changes to the original floor plan," I offer. "Now, Mr. Davis, I've monopolized the conversation long enough. Please, tell me what brings you to Bartlesville."

"I'm sure it's a story you've heard a hundred times—a job at Phillips Petroleum." Mr. Davis shrugs. "I've wanted to work for Phillips for as long as I can remember. Finally, the right position opened."

I catch the humility in his response. My friend who referred Mr. Davis for the open room said he's a top petroleum engineer and recently started as a high-level executive in the Phillips research facility. She told me that Boots Adams, the president of the company, had personally recruited Mr. Davis away from Shell Oil.

"Yes, we've hosted many Phillips employees over the years, but none as dedicated as Bessie Blackwell. She was my first lodger when I opened the house in August of '29," I say.

Sweet Bessie, she's always so uncomfortable around a new male lodger. When Mr. Clark moved in, she barely spoke for a week. Perhaps she won't be as nervous with Mr. Davis. He's quite companionable.

"And what did Bessie Blackwell do for the company?"

"Oh, she still works at Phillips. She's the queen of the office machine room. Handles the duplication needs of every department." I glance down at the tea tray. "Goodness, here we are chatting away, and I haven't offered you a cup of tea. Milk and sugar?" I ask, filling his cup.

"Just a little milk, thank you."

"Would you like a cookie before we take our tour?" The final hurdle for Mr. Davis to clear.

"Yes, please. I can't remember the last time I had home-made shortbread. Thank you." Mr. Davis adds two shortbread cookies to his saucer—a perfect score.

We eat our cookies and finish our tea while Mr. Davis tells me about his drive from California and his sister, Helen, and her family in Joplin. His mother still lives in Joplin, as well. He's looking forward to planning a visit to Missouri soon.

"Are you ready to see the available room, Mr. Davis?" I ask once he finishes a third piece of shortbread.

"Yes, ma'am," he says, rising from the sofa. "Lead the way, Louie." The dog springs to attention at the sound of his name, strutting back into the foyer as our guide.

"As luck would have it, when I was ready to begin making modifications to the building, my housekeeper, Edna, married an excellent handyman. We began by converting the downstairs parlor into my private suite."

I swing the door to my quarters wide open to reveal my sitting area. I moved one of my favorite oriental rugs from upstairs to define the space. The striped damask settee looks out across the deep covered front porch through two large windows. My slant-top desk fits perfectly between them. I deliberately avoid glancing in the direction of the letter on the side table. I'm not ready to let go of this place. Not today. But I do sense change in the air. Change always smells like the roses Charles brought me that evening long ago—the moving roses.

"We constructed two doorways," I continue. "I can enter and exit my quarters through the foyer or the kitchen. My sleeping area and a new private bath are around the corner."

"Was there already plumbing on this side of the house?" Mr. Davis asks, sounding like an engineer for the first time today.

"Yes. My bath is located directly underneath what used to be the master bath upstairs. The pipes were right where they needed to be." We turn back toward the staircase. "When Charles and I designed Henderson House, we longed to have an open staircase reminiscent of the historic homes of St. Louis. It's still one of my favorite features of the house."

"It's spectacular," Mr. Davis says.

"We serve breakfast daily, and supper is at seven p.m. every weeknight except Wednesday," I say as we climb. "On

Wednesday evenings, you are welcome to join us for the Wednesday Night Supper at the Baptist church, or Edna can leave a cold plate for you in the kitchen. Supper is served one hour earlier, at six p.m., on Saturday evening, which leaves time to attend the cinema. Sunday dinner is around two or three, depending on the length of Pastor Harper's sermon."

We turn left at the top of the landing and left again to walk back along the open hallway, with bedrooms on our right and an ornate wrought-iron balustrade on our left. Mr. Davis pauses to peer over the railing down to the foyer below. I open the door to the corner bedroom on the front of the house. The room is cozy but not overcrowded with a full-sized brass bed, bookcases, a small desk with a lamp, a black-and-white-checkered reading chair, and lace curtains in the windows.

Mr. Davis walks in and takes stock. "What a finely appointed room," he says.

"Thank you. Corner rooms always bring in the best light, don't they? When it belonged to my son Walter, it was filled to the brim with trophies, awards, and books."

I removed every trace of Walter's personality years ago and yet, as light flickers through the window, I can almost see him scrunched up in the overstuffed chair, devouring *Doctor Dolittle*. Walter has two boys of his own now. I don't know what books they are reading. I see my grandchildren once a year. Louie and I travel to Spring Lake, New Jersey, every August. Robert rents a house big enough for the whole family to enjoy a month by the sea.

"I'll take it!" Mr. Davis declares.

"It's yours," I respond without a second thought. Frank Davis belongs here. Even if I do decide to move to New Jersey this August and never come back, Mr. Davis should be here now. A rustling of the curtains confirms my assessment. "Before we get to the paperwork, I'll show you the rest of the house and fill you in on your fellow residents." We exit room number one and start back down the hallway. "Mrs. Stanton rents room number two. She's a widow and is currently in Oklahoma City helping her daughter, who just had twins."

The air in front of Mrs. Stanton's door presses heavy and damp against my skin. The house doesn't like having empty rooms. This side of the house was as cool and musty as a root cellar once all the boys left for college.

"I think Mrs. Stanton is hoping her daughter will ask her to move in with them. But, for now, it gives her peace of mind to know her room will be ready and waiting if she returns," I explain, as much to the house as to Mr. Davis.

At first, I thought Mrs. Stanton leaving to be with her children was the sign I've been waiting for—a sign that it was time for me to leave and live closer to my own children and grandchildren. But her departure hasn't made my vision of the future any clearer.

I lower my voice as we walk farther down the hall: "Professor Albert Rutledge lives in room number three. He's a poetry professor by vocation but currently works as a night-time security guard at First National Bank. He leaves for work about the time we sit down to supper. You may not have an opportunity to chat with him until Saturday."

Louie plops down in front of the professor's door and sniffs along the threshold.

"Sorry, Louie, you might not see him until Saturday, either," I whisper.

"Is the professor Louie's favorite?" Mr. Davis whispers in return.

"Oh, Louie loves all the lodgers, but lately we've been enjoying spending our Saturday afternoons with the professor," I say.

My growing fondness for Professor Albert Rutledge isn't making my vision of the future any clearer, either. Recent variations in his color make me wonder if he will play a part in my decision, though I'm not sure what his role might be. Mr. Davis and I turn the corner and head along the backside of the house.

"Eddie Blackwell lives in room number four," I say. "He's a taxicab driver. Eddie is the younger brother of Florence Fuller and Bessie Blackwell who live in rooms five and six."

"Wait, the same Bessie Blackwell who's the queen of duplication at Phillips?" Mr. Davis asks.

"One and the same. Here is the first shared bathroom." I open the door to the black-and-white-tiled room. "Typically, this bath is shared by the residents of rooms one, two, and three. So, you'll practically have it all to yourself, given Mrs. Stanton's absence and the professor's odd schedule. We converted the original master suite into rooms five and six with a shared bath," I say, pointing toward the other wing of the upstairs. "We call it the Blackwell family bath now."

"So, Bessie Blackwell and her brother and sister all live here with you?"

"Yes. Miss Blackwell's sister, Florence Fuller, and her thirteen-year-old son, Johnny, live in room number five. Mrs. Fuller is also a widow and works at Linn Brothers, the men's department store downtown. Johnny is a charming young man. Very athletic. Florence and Johnny moved in about nine years ago . . . yes, that's right because we had Johnny's fourth birthday party here. Eddie joined them more recently."

If change is coming, what will it mean for the Blackwell family? Where will they go if I sell the house and move? Henderson House is the only home Johnny's ever known. Making this decision is like trying to finish a jigsaw puzzle. If only I could put a few important pieces into place, I'm sure the rest would come together quickly.

Mr. Davis cocks his head to one side. "I want to make sure I've got this right, Mrs. Henderson," he says, "Miss Blackwell's family has lived here with her for nine years, and Miss Blackwell has lived here ever since you opened the boarding house twelve years ago?"

"Precisely."

"Isn't that a little out of the ordinary?"

"Oh, Mr. Davis, there's nothing ordinary about Henderson House. You'll see what I mean when you meet the Blackwell family at supper this evening."

"Mrs. Henderson, I can hardly wait," he says with a laugh. The air in the hallway pops and crackles. The house is looking forward to supper as well.

CHAPTER TWO

Bessie

I SHUT THE tall office windows one by one. The chain and pulley systems groan as each sash settles with a satisfying *clunk*. The scent of fresh ditto copies rushes to fill the enclosed space. Damp purple pages sit in perfect piles on the long worktable.

"Ready for collating in the morning," I say to the empty room.

My new assistant, Doris, clocked out at five on the dot. I'm sure she has places to go and people to see. Assistants pass through the office machine room as if through a revolving door. Most work until they get married. Occasionally, one stays until the first baby comes along.

Securing the dust covers over each duplication machine and typewriter, I tuck the room in for the night.

Dear Lord, thank you for Phillips Petroleum and Bartlesville, Oklahoma, I pray. *You have provided for my every need, and I am truly grateful. Amen.*

When I arrived at Phillips Petroleum more than a decade ago, I had limited experience with business machines—barely enough to garner a reference letter from my previous employer. I'll be forever grateful for that letter. A fine reminder that a single act of kindness can change the course of someone's life. Over the years, I've learned how to keep old equipment running up until its final breath and collected enough experience to operate new models in record time. I know the intimate details of every contraption in this room—their quirks and weaknesses, their sticky drums and messy trays. My sister teases that I've never married because I'm in love with my machines. She's not completely off base. While the equipment in this room cannot return my affections, it is also incapable of breaking my heart.

"Hey, Miss B. You taking the bus home this evening?" Young Martha Williams's voice rings from the doorway. She works down the hall in accounting.

"Hello, Martha. You know, I'm thinking about walking home. Doesn't look like we're going to get any rain."

"Sure doesn't. Well, I just want to thank you for your advice last week. I've been asking my mother-in-law tons of questions about Daniel—questions about when he was little, holiday traditions, and favorite foods. And then I've been listening to her. Just listening like you told me to. We're getting along so much better; it's like a miracle."

"I'm glad to hear it," I say.

Martha got married in March, and her mother-in-law arrived last week to stay through Memorial Day. Being the wife of someone's only beloved son can't be easy. My sister, Florence, is raising a boy. Johnny is the apple of her eye. It's not hard to imagine her making life difficult for a daughter-in-law someday.

"Have a pleasant walk home, and thanks again for your help. You're the best," Martha says.

"Anytime. Good night." I say another prayer while tidying up my desk.

Dear Lord Jesus, spread your glorious blessings of love and faith on Martha Williams and her husband, Daniel. Grant them wisdom and patience as they grow to know one another and grow in your love. Amen.

I push my eyeglasses back onto the bridge of my nose.

Oh, and help me get used to wearing these new glasses. Amen, again.

"Another satisfied customer?" My friend Anna Porter pops her head around the doorframe.

"Why do they come to me?" I shake my head.

"You give great romantic advice. Remember what you told me when I was worried Wyatt would never propose?" Anna asks, walking into the office.

"Sort of," I say, trying to recall our conversation all those years ago. Anna and Wyatt celebrated their tenth anniversary last month.

"You told me to tell him the truth. To tell him how I was feeling and let him know I'd been thinking about the future, and that I couldn't imagine it without him."

"Sounds like something I'd say."

"Worked like a charm." Anna pauses. "Face it, counseling young lovers is in your blood. You've told me a million stories about growing up over that little store in Indian Territory and how your mother was constantly handing out advice to the lovelorn."

"If only my mama could have saved some for herself," I say. Not a day goes by that I don't miss my mama and wonder how things might have turned out differently for her, for all of us, if our family had been able to follow her simple rules. "As I recall, Mama's advice usually fell into one of four categories," I continue, "listen with love, tell the truth, don't dwell, and forgive. Oh, and sometimes the person you need to forgive is yourself."

Anna chuckles and leans against my desk. "This is new information. So, your advice to me about Wyatt came from the 'tell the truth' category?"

"Exactly. If my mother had charged as much for wisdom as she did for flour and sugar, we'd have been the richest family in Indian Territory." I take my pocketbook and gloves out of the bottom desk drawer.

"And your recent advice to Martha Williams?"

"I encouraged Martha to ask her new mother-in-law questions and then listen with love. Just following my mother's recipe."

"Well, your family secrets are safe with me. Are you taking the bus home tonight?" Anna asks.

"Nope. Feel like walking," I say, putting on my gloves.

"Mind if I join you?"

"I'd love that."

"By the way, you're quite the dish in those new specs," Anna remarks as we walk to the door.

"My vision is going. Florence says that's the way it is over forty. Everything starts to go." I turn out the lights and head down the first-floor hallway with Anna by my side. It takes two of my quick, little steps to keep up with one of her long, effortless strides.

"Those glasses look great on you. I love the little gems in the pointy corners at the top."

"In a thousand million years, I never would have bought these for myself," I reply.

"Did Florence pick them out?"

"Of course she did. When she found out I needed glasses, she bought five magazines and did research for a week."

"Why do you let your sister handle these important decisions for you?" Anna asks.

"Oh, it makes her happy."

"What else did she discover in her extensive research?"

"Turns out, if you have a round face like I do, you should avoid round glasses, as they can make your face appear chubby," I report. "The cat-eye style is the most flattering option for my facial shape."

Anna's shoulders shudder with silent laughter. "Did she share any other fashion tips with you?"

"Let's see. I shouldn't consider my eyeglasses a beauty handicap. Oh, no! I should embrace them as I would a fine piece of jewelry, employ them as a new tool to help augment my overall image." We're both giggling now. "I am also supposed to wear my hair pulled back low and loose around my shoulders whenever I need to create a glamorous effect."

"Florence sure loves to boss you around. But you have to admit, those pink frames look dynamite," she says, her laughter subsiding.

"Thank you. I get compliments on them every day."

"You don't sound happy about the attention." Anna pushes one of the heavy entrance doors open, and we step out into a beautiful May evening.

"Picking out eyeglasses may have been a fulfilling side project for my sister, but it's left me feeling old."

We merge into the flow of people walking toward South Johnstone Avenue. The sidewalk bustles with skirts and suits as people pour out of the downtown offices.

"Now that I'm forty-three, I've decided I'm no longer going to think of myself as an old maid. Instead, I'm going to refer to myself as a spinster."

"Hmm, yes, spinster certainly has a more glamorous effect," Anna says with another laugh. She links her arm in mine. "Listen to me, my friend. You're no spinster. You're incredibly patient, that's all. You're still waiting for Mr. Right to come along and sweep you off your feet."

"Ever the optimist." I bump my hip into her thigh.

"One of these days, you're going to plop down next to me in the cafeteria and say, 'Anna, I've met someone.' I'll bet you two bits."

I roll my eyes. "Trust me. If I meet Mr. Right at this late date, I'll be happy to pay up."

"You'd better," Anna says with a huff. "How's life at Henderson House?"

"Oh, fine and dandy. Mr. Clark moved out over the weekend, took a job in Texas. Mrs. Henderson asked Eddie if he wanted to switch rooms. Mr. Clark was in room number one, the big sunny one, but my brother said he was 'as happy as a clam in high water' in room number four. Mrs. H already had an interview lined up for today—another engineer."

"Let's hope he has more personality than Mr. Clark."

"At least the engineers are quiet. The salesmen are too chatty for my liking."

My stomach churns at the thought of stammering through polite conversation with a strange man at the dinner table tonight. The new engineer will probably ask me questions, if only to be polite. But chances are, I'll seize up and stutter when I try to answer. I didn't start stuttering until I was a teenager. My daddy used to make fun of me at supper. He was merciless about peppering me with questions and mocking my halting responses. I can go weeks or months now without tripping over a word, but a strange man interrogating me over supper is the perfect setup for disaster. My churning stomach ties itself into a knot.

"A vacant room at swanky Henderson House won't last for long. He'd be a fool not to take it," Anna says.

"He'll have to pass Mrs. H's rigorous interview process first. Maybe he doesn't like cookies," I say with a raised eyebrow, secretly hoping this new engineer failed his interview this afternoon so I won't have to meet him at the table tonight.

"Mildred Henderson is an odd duck. They broke the mold when they made her." Anna shakes her head. "I'm crossing here—need to pick up something for Wyatt at the pharmacy. Hope to see you tomorrow. And, really, you look fabulous." Anna blows me a kiss and starts for the crosswalk.

Anna and Wyatt never had children. It's a shame. She would have been a wonderful mother.

I peek through the front door at Linn Brothers, the men's clothing store where my sister works. No sign of Florence in action, but her talent shines in the new window displays. She's arranged the lightweight men's suits, casual wear, and summer hats in a picnic setting. A red-and-white-checkered blanket, wicker basket, and a stack of books occupy the center, with fishing gear and canoe paddles framing either side. I admire the scene for a moment before continuing on my way. The walk from downtown to Henderson House takes less than thirty minutes, and, I must admit, these stack-heeled, lace-up oxfords Florence picked out are mighty comfortable. We're practically the same size and can shop out of each other's closets, mixing and matching. When we were children, people thought we were twins. Florence was quick to point out that I was the older sister—if only by fourteen months.

I walk one more block through town and head south. Almost immediately, the brick storefronts turn to houses and tree-lined streets. Rows of elms create a tunnel of shade this time of day. Flickering patterns of sunlight dance on the sidewalk. I take in a stray whiff of honeysuckle before the smell of peonies hits me. A mass of blooms erupts in front of the house on the corner every spring. The enormous blossoms are such a deep pink you could almost mistake them for red—the same dark, reddish pink of an Oklahoma sky the morning before a storm.

As I get closer to Henderson House, I hear the thump of a baseball landing in a glove, a pause, then the thud of the ball landing in another glove. The front section of the yard comes into view, and I see my tall, skinny nephew. Johnny is nothing but legs and elbows all of a sudden. He's in such an awkward phase. "No longer grass and not quite hay," my mama used to say. I'm still on the fence about his new haircut. It's clipped short on the sides and longer on the top so he can part it and comb the center section over. It's a complicated haircut for a thirteen-year-old boy, but Florence likes Johnny to appear fashionable, and with this style, I suppose he does. Johnny's high cheekbones and strong nose make him look far more Cherokee than the rest of the family, which is the other reason for his fancy hair; Florence doesn't want Johnny to look like an Indian.

Somewhat eager to discover who Johnny's roped into playing with him, I quicken my pace. I doubt Tommy Westfeldt would be over on a Monday evening, though Johnny and Tommy have been thick as thieves lately. Florence constantly tries to connect Johnny with the top families in Bartlesville, and she's hit a home run with the Westfeldts.

I walk around the neighbor's large privet hedge, and the man at the far end of the yard comes into view. He's a stranger, yet there's something familiar about him. Is it the tilt of his head? The way he leans forward as he throws the ball?

"Nice catch," the stranger says to Johnny.

"You've got a natural slider working there," Johnny replies.

"I'm just happy the ball made it to you," the man jokes. "It's been a long time since I threw a baseball. Now, how about you give me another one of your Danny MacFayden specials?" The man crouches down into a catcher's stance.

"One Deacon Danny sidearm surprise coming up, Mr. Davis," Johnny says as he prepares to throw. The ball zings through the air and lands in the man's glove with a loud smack.

Mr. Davis. This must be the new engineer. Guess he passed the cookie test. Suit coat draped over the porch railing, shirt sleeves pushed up, and tie flapping in the wind, he appears to be a young man in his thirties. His gray fedora teeters on top of his wavy brown hair as if it's ready to take flight.

"Ooh, wee! That's quite an arm you've got there, young man." Mr. Davis stands, fans his gloved hand back and forth, and blows on it as if it's on fire.

His overacting makes me smile, and Johnny laughs.

"Good evening," I say, coming up the walk and interrupting their game.

"Aunt Bessie!" Johnny puts down his glove, grabs my hand, and drags me across the yard to meet Mr. Davis. "Aunt Bessie, this is Mr. Davis. He moved in today—all the way from San Francisco. Mr. Davis, this is Aunt Bes—my aunt, Miss Elizabeth Blackwell." I sure love it when my boy uses his good manners.

"Nice to meet you, Mr. Davis," I say.

Now that I'm standing close to him, I see wrinkles around his eyes and the slightest hint of gray at his temples. Mr. Davis is at least my age, maybe a little older. His compact stature and athletic build make him seem younger than he really is.

"And it's nice to meet you," he says. "Johnny's been giving me the full rundown on the family."

"Oh, he has, has he?" I glance sideways at Johnny.

"I didn't mean to pry," Mr. Davis offers in Johnny's defense.

"I'm sure it didn't take much prying," I say, and Mr. Davis chuckles. It's a sweet, melodic laugh, like water bouncing off stones in a stream.

"I'm genuinely interested in the backstory of how your whole family ended up at Henderson House," he says.

I wait for the familiar apprehension to settle in my stomach with his line of inquiry, but it doesn't come. No nausea. No jitters. Nothing.

"I leave the family storytelling to my brother, Eddie. I'm afraid your curiosity will have to wait until supper, Mr. Davis." I don't stumble over any of the words or stutter like I usually do in front of a man I've just met.

Mr. Davis smiles at me, and I smile back. I like his round wire-rimmed glasses. They don't make his kind, round face look chubby at all. They suit him perfectly. I can't say whether his eyes are brown or green. They must be hazel. Realizing I'm staring, I turn my attention to my nephew.

"I'm going upstairs to change out of my office clothes, and then I want to check on the flower project before supper. Will you join me, Johnny?"

"Sure, Aunt Bessie. Can Mr. Davis come, too?

"Mr. Davis, you are welcome to join us if you're interested, but please don't feel obligated," I say.

The breeze kicks up and blows Mr. Davis's fedora off his head. "Whoa!" he exclaims, stretching out to catch his hat with a flourish of his right hand. He runs his other hand through his curls, and I notice a long, faded scar below his hairline. Mr. Davis fluffs his hair back over his forehead and replaces his hat firmly with an exaggerated grimace of determination.

As Johnny and I laugh, the word adorable pops into my mind. This man is one hundred percent adorable. My belly quivers, only it's not my customary discomfort around a stranger. It's something I haven't felt for a long time. This flutter is deep and warm. And that's even more terrifying.

CHAPTER THREE

Florence

I ADJUST THE nozzle on the garment steamer. I swear, the manufacturer must iron these wrinkles into the suits as a cruel joke before they ship them to us. It's taken me the entire afternoon to get through this box.

The steamer sputters: time for more water. I switch off the appliance, but the humming continues in my ears. The shopkeeper's bells jingle out front. No matter—Jordan Linn, my manager, is on duty. Jordan is the youngest son of Nathan Linn, the store owner. Everyone at Linn Brothers calls Jordan by his family nickname, Sonny. All the employees, except for me, are members of the Linn family either by birth or marriage. I'm the outsider. At first, I called him Jordan. I wasn't sure it was proper for me to use his nickname, but Jordan insisted I was part of the family and should call him Sonny, so I do. Of course, when customers are present, I refer to him as Mr. Linn.

Sonny took over as store manager a year ago—about two seconds after he graduated from the University of Tulsa. He turned twenty-two last month. Must be nice to be the boss's son and go straight to the top.

From out front, Sonny's smooth voice seeps through the heavy red curtains separating the workroom from the show-room floor. I can't make out the conversation, but his tone is charming. You can always tell when Sonny's talking to a cus-tomer of the female persuasion. I pick up the small pitcher to refill the steamer and head over to the utility sink. Sonny parts the drapes and sticks his head into the workroom.

"I hate to interrupt you, Florence, but Mrs. Spencer is out front, and she's asking for you specifically." He looks me up and down. Sonny's penetrating gaze, accompanied by a wry smile, makes my chest ache. "Hmm, and I can't blame her," he adds, sauntering through the curtains toward me. "You look lovely today, Miss Florence, and a little steamy yourself."

Sonny's sweet talk tightens the sensation in my chest, and I sense a headache coming on. I set the pitcher on the lunch table and walk back toward the alterations platform to put some space between us.

"Give me a second to freshen up," I say, inspecting myself in the three-way mirror.

"You helped her once before—right after I started work. Where did the family go on their vacation last summer?" he asks, checking himself in the mirror, too, and straightening his tie.

"Chicago. The Spencers spent two weeks in Chicago. She outfitted her twins from head to toe. The boys graduate from College High this week." I attempt to tame my frizzy hair.

Ugh, I look like a head of overcooked broccoli.

Most days, I'm grateful I look Irish like my mama instead of Cherokee like my father, but I'd take my late sister Rachel's perfectly straight black hair on a day like today. I always envied how unruffled she looked, even in the heat of summer. Sonny stands behind me and stares as I rearrange the bobby pins in my hair. Is he gonna give me a few pointers on how to pull myself together?

I speak to his image in the mirror. "Please tell Mrs. Spencer I'll be right out. You never want to leave an important client alone on the floor, Sonny." I shoo his reflection out of the workroom.

When Sonny started at Linn Brothers, I trained him. We spent long hours together. He was eager to learn and took to the business like a natural. At first, his attention and compliments were flattering. He's a handsome young man, taller than his father, slender with a thin nose and eyes the color of a strong cup of tea. I never considered Sonny's kind remarks or a grateful hand on my shoulder to be flirtatious; I'm old enough to be his mother, for goodness' sake! As our working relationship progressed, I suppose I encouraged his behavior and teased back in my own way. It was fun and harmless. Or so I thought. A couple of weeks ago, his hands started landing places other than my shoulder.

Last Saturday, when we were closing the store, Sonny snuck up behind me while I was straightening the dressing room. He put his hands on either side of my waist, and I screamed like I'd just seen a rattlesnake.

"There's no reason to be alarmed," Sonny had said.

"You're the one who should be alarmed," I shot back at him. I turned around and pushed his muck forks off of me. "Get out of this dressing room immediately!"

Sonny stood his ground. I felt his hot breath on my forehead and smelled the late-day remnants of his face lotion—Aqua Velva. He smiled and brushed a strand of hair out of my eyes.

"Do you have any idea how sexy you are?" he asked.

"Do you have any idea how ridiculous you are?" I responded.

He turned away and laughed. Something in Sonny's laughter reminded me of the way my daddy used to laugh whenever I tried to talk my way out of trouble. It was the confident laugh of a man holding all the cards. Since the dressing room incident, my chest hurts every morning on the way to work.

If this were any other job, I'd complain to the owner or quit and move on. But I'm not sure what I'd say to Sonny's father, and it's not just any other job. I've worked at Linn Brothers for eight years. C.R. Anthony's would never pay as much, and I can't take a pay cut now. We're close to having enough in the family savings account to go house hunting. I've got my heart set on Johnny starting high school when we're living in a home of our own, not a boarding house. Besides, Linn Brothers is by far the nicest men's clothing store in Bartlesville. I've worked too hard to let Sonny's wandering hands force my career to take a step backward. There has to be another way out of this unfortunate situation.

Oh, but Mrs. Spencer is waiting. I tuck in my blouse and smooth my hair again—not much more I can do. I take a few deep breaths before walking through the curtains into the glow of the showroom. My temples throb, but I stride as cheerfully as possible to the front of the store, where Mrs. Spencer browses the summer suits.

"Mrs. Spencer, what a pleasure to see you again," I say.

She's decked out in a pastel-colored print dress with a wide pink belt, coordinating pink gloves, and a matching skimmer hat—dressed to impress.

"Thank you, Mrs. Fuller. You were such a doll when you helped me outfit the boys for our trip to Chicago last summer. Are you up for a repeat performance? We're spending two weeks at a private estate on a lake in upstate New York. They call it a 'camp,' but you should see the photographs. It looks divine. The height of old-world charm." She gestures broadly with her hands as if speaking to a large audience.

"How delightful. Are the boys excited about graduation?" I ask.

"Oh, yes. We all are. We're hosting dinner for forty people on Saturday! Did you know both boys are heading to Oklahoma State next fall?"

"No. I hadn't heard. Congratulations, Mrs. Spencer."

Enough small talk, I coach myself. *Time to get down to business.*

"So, a private estate on a lake. Can you tell me a little more about your planned activities and dress expectations?" I ask.

I learn they will dress in a jacket and tie for dinner every evening except for the two Saturday evenings, which will be black tie. Mr. Spencer has a tuxedo, but the boys don't. They will need attire suitable for boating and tennis as well. The twins have outgrown all their clothes from last summer. Must be nice to buy your family a new wardrobe for every vacation. Then again, it would be nice to go on any vacation at all.

Sonny assists me as I move around the perimeter of the store, pulling options for the twins from almost every department—suits, separates, shirts, ties, and casual wear. Then we head down into the center section, which is three steps lower than the main showroom, to look at formal wear. Surrounded by a polished brass railing, the sunken midsection has wide entrance steps on either side. In addition to formal wear and outerwear, a glass case displays aftershave, cologne, cufflinks, wallets, and a few other gift items.

I present potential outfits to Mrs. Spencer while she sits on the small sofa outside the dressing rooms. The dressing rooms and restroom are in the back left corner of the store, the entrance to the workroom sits behind the checkout table, and the staircase to the offices occupies the back right corner. It's a well-organized if modest-sized department store. Sixteen-foot ceilings make the showroom feel larger than it is, and the round crystal drop chandelier is a showstopper.

Sonny brings Mrs. Spencer a glass of water. She rejects the items she doesn't like with a dismissive wave of her hand, a roll of her eyes, or a slow shake of her head. I combine the remaining pieces of clothing into outfits for her twins. From the stories my son, Johnny, tells me, Mrs. Spencer's boys are just as snooty as she is. In less than an hour, the checkout counter overflows with a mountain of approved items.

"Mrs. Fuller, you are a miracle worker," she says as I ring up her purchases. "You have such a knack for fashion. The boys are going to look wonderful." She glances over her shoulder at Sonny. "You'd better hang on to her with both hands, Mr. Linn."

"Oh, I'm planning on it, Mrs. Spencer." Sonny gives me a wink. My head pounds.

"Thank you, Mrs. Spencer. It is always a pleasure to help you." I smile.

Mrs. Spencer is right. I have always had a knack for fashion. Mama and I used to pore over the latest magazines, trying to figure out how we could recreate a look using whatever remnants and notions we could find in Daddy's store. We sewed together almost every evening, just the two of us.

When I was fourteen, I played the role of the angel in the Christmas pageant—not the one who told Mary she was on the nest, but the angel who appeared to the shepherds watching their flocks by night and told them to be not afraid. I made my own costume. There was no way I was going to wear one of those old sacks with a sash from the church attic. Oh no, my costume was a lovely, simple gown with an empire waist, bell sleeves, and a long, flowing skirt. Instead of a cheap wire-framed halo, I wore a wide headband made of fabric with real gold thread running through it.

The night of the pageant is one of my happiest memories of growing up. John Fuller made eye contact with me that night—you know, the real "I like you" kind of eye contact. We didn't start going steady for another two years, but my angel costume set the wheels in motion. I never imagined that sewing project would land me in this role—a widow living in a boarding house with her brother and sister, doing her best to raise a teenage boy, and working for a letch.

Movement at the back of the store pulls me out of my daydream. Mr. Linn's assistant, Peggy, stands at the foot of the staircase, waving like a homecoming queen. Practically Perfect Peggy has the figure of a pin-up girl and the bubbly personality to go with it. She works in the office upstairs and occasionally helps on the sales floor. Whenever she needs to speak with me, she waves before beckoning with her index finger to "come here." And there's the beckoning finger, now. I hope she doesn't want to change the schedule for next week. I've worked every angle I could to finagle three days off in a row. I need a mini vacation, even if three days at home in Bartlesville isn't exactly the height of old-world charm.

"May I help you to the car?" Sonny asks Mrs. Spencer as we finish wrapping up her purchases.

"Yes, thank you, Mr. Linn." Mrs. Spencer struggles to hand him two of the large bags.

Loaded down with a complete summer wardrobe for two, they head to the door.

"Thank you, again, Mrs. Spencer. I hope you and your family have a marvelous vacation. Don't forget to have the boys make an appointment with Clara if they need any alterations. She's here Thursday and Saturday next week," I say.

"Oh, thank you, Mrs. Fuller!" she responds. Mrs. Spencer steps out of the store and into the evening light, Sonny at her heels.

Practically Perfect Peggy clears her throat.

"My, my, Betty Jo Spencer. What a shopping spree. Nice job!" she exclaims.

"Thank you, Peggy," I say, taking a small bow.

"Mr. Linn would like to speak with you in his office as soon as possible."

"Of course," I respond, even though I'm more than ready to clean up and call it a day. "Give me a moment to powder my nose."

"I'll see you upstairs." She twirls around and bounces back up the staircase. Her blonde hair bobs in rhythm with each step.

I grab my purse out of the drawer under the cash register and head to the restroom to freshen my lipstick. You'd think Sonny would direct his youthful advances toward Peggy over me, but she's married to his cousin, so I guess she's off-limits. Lucky girl. Also, an older widow is an easy target. Mr. Linn wouldn't believe me if I told him Sonny's behavior was making me uncomfortable. He'd say I was overreacting, that Sonny was being kind, and I should feel flattered. After last Saturday, I don't feel flattered anymore.

I step into the small restroom and close the door. Why does Sonny's father need to speak with me as soon as possible? Have I done something wrong? I rub my forehead, but it does nothing to relieve the pain. My chest burns in sympathy.

Calm down, Florence. He's probably just adding another family member to the staff.

I'm not sure I have the energy to train another nephew or niece who doesn't know poplin from gabardine. Well, what else can you expect when you give your heart and soul to a family business and you're not a member of the family? I shouldn't complain about working for the Linns. They've been good to me, and they are a genuine success story—a Jewish family fleeing Russia to pursue the American dream and all. They even changed their name from Fabelinsky to Linn. But family is family.

I carefully reapply my favorite shade of lipstick, Red Letter Red, and smack my lips together a few times—no reason to look as worn out as I feel. I exit the restroom and drag myself up the oak stairs to Mr. Linn's office. My heart races and I'm gasping for breath by the time I reach the top. I don't know why I've been tiring so easily lately. My mini vacation can't come soon enough. Practically Perfect Peggy waits eagerly for me at her desk, drumming her manicured fingers on her coffee cup.

"He's expecting you, Mrs. Fuller." She flashes her glamour-girl smile. I smile in return and knock lightly on Mr. Linn's door. Here we go.

"Come in," he responds in his even-toned, mellow voice. I turn the handle and push the door open. "Ah, Mrs. Fuller, please take a seat."

He stands briefly and gestures to the leather chair across from his oversized wooden desk. Mr. Linn's custom-tailored suit in worsted wool is an excellent choice for this time of year. The light tan windowpane plaid complements his small, dark angular features and graying hair. Mr. Linn smiles. It's a kind smile. The tightness in my chest relaxes, but my head continues to throb.

"Good afternoon, Mr. Linn." I settle into the chair and my legs tingle with relief.

"My dear Mrs. Fuller, please let me start by telling you what an asset you have been to Linn Brothers over the years," he says in his usual steady and deliberate style.

"Thank you, Mr. Linn. I thoroughly enjoy working for you and your family."

Except for your son, who is a groping menace.

"Yes, yes, and you are quite good at it, Mrs. Fuller. I have to say, you have an innate talent for men's fashion and a wonderful way with the customers—not to mention how you've increased sales with your window displays."

When I took over the window displays a few years ago, I insisted we have a seasonal section at the front of the store to correspond with the items featured in the windows. It's been an effective sales technique. If a customer spots something they like, they can walk right in and buy it.

"I'm impressed," Mr. Linn continues. "So much so, I've recommended you for a management position at our flagship store in Tulsa," he says, clasping his hands together in front of his chest.

"A management position?" I ask.

"Yes, ma'am. Management. If it all works out, you'll be the new manager of the Tulsa store."

"Manager of the Tulsa store," I repeat.

Florence, what are you, a parrot? Pull yourself together, girl.

"This is probably a lot to take in. I'm sure you and your family weren't thinking about leaving Bartlesville, but it would mean a significant pay increase for you and lots of new opportunities in a larger city. I've seen your son play ball, and Tulsa Central High School has the best sports program in the state," he says.

"I'm speechless, Mr. Linn. I'm not sure what to say." It's all I can manage.

"Well, I can only recommend you for the position. You'll need to go down there and close the deal on your own," he says, patting his desk. "My Uncle Aaron, at the Tulsa store, would like to meet you in person. Peggy has agreed to work your hours this Wednesday, and the company would be more than happy to cover bus fare and expenses for your trip to Tulsa."

"How generous of you, sir. Thank you. I would enjoy meeting your uncle and seeing the Tulsa store."

Much better, Florence.

"Now, I want to be clear on one point, Mrs. Fuller. If Uncle Aaron offers you the position and for any reason you are not interested in accepting it, please know you are welcome to stay here in your current role at the Bartlesville store. I don't want you to feel any pressure about this decision. Sonny and I would love to keep you right here." He pats his desk again.

"Thank you, Mr. Linn. I appreciate your assurance a great deal. This is such a surprise. I still don't know what to say." I shake my head in disbelief.

A job in Tulsa would solve all your problems, Florence. This is just what the doctor ordered.

"Well, you're the best candidate for the job. And it is, after all, still in the family." He grins. "Now, check with Peggy about the bus ticket and a little lunch money. She'll help you get your travel plans squared away for Wednesday." He walks around his desk and leads me toward the door.

"Yes, I will, Mr. Linn."

My mind churns with all the possibilities of a new job in a new city. I always imagined we'd go house hunting in boring, old Bartlesville, but the thought of finding a house in Tulsa is far more enticing. I'm more than ready to stop sharing a bedroom with Johnny and have some privacy. Plus, I'd be a manager. Maybe I'd even get paid vacation time, and we could go on a real holiday. To top it all off, I'd be rid of Sonny.

"Remember, if it's not a good fit for you in Tulsa," Mr. Linn says, "everything can stay exactly the way it is."

My heart sinks, and I put a hand to my chest. No. Things can't stay exactly the way they are.

"This is one hundred percent your choice, Mrs. Fuller."
Mr. Linn points at me, emphasizing the words "your choice."
The office door clicks shut behind me. Practically Perfect Peggy
flashes her glamour-grin once more from behind her desk.

"I couldn't wait for you to come up and talk with Mr. Linn.
Isn't it just so exciting? A business trip to Tulsa and a possible
management position. You must be thrilled, simply thrilled!"
Peggy gushes.

"I am thrilled, simply thrilled," I reply, matching her pitch
and inflection.

Parrot again.

You'd think they were flying me out to Hollywood for a
screen test given her enthusiasm. I'm not sure how enthusiastic my family is going to be. It won't take much convincing
for Eddie to agree to a change of scenery, but I'm not so sure
about Bessie. My sister adores Bartlesville, her job, and that
darn church. Not to mention Mrs. Henderson.

But Bessie won't want to be separated from Johnny.

True. She promised we'd raise him together. After all, family is family.

CHAPTER FOUR

Mrs. Henderson

"BESSIE? IS THAT you?" I call through the open door of my suite.

"Yes, Mrs. Henderson. Just running upstairs to change before heading out to the garden."

"Pop your head in for a minute, dear."

Bessie appears in my doorway, clutching the handles of her black patent leather handbag in her tiny white-gloved hands. She's barely five feet tall with heels on and still has the slim figure of a girl. Her rosy glow flickers. She's flustered. I hoped she'd be comfortable around Mr. Davis. Then again, flustered is different than uncomfortable. I opened my windows this afternoon and heard laughter in the front yard. When I took a quick peek, I saw something connecting Mr. Davis's and Bessie's colors—a compatibility of sorts.

"Did you meet Mr. Davis?" I ask.

"Yes, I met him out front when he was playing ball with Johnny." She shifts her weight from one foot to the other, her color pulsing.

"He's a fine fellow, don't you agree?"

"It appears so."

"I know sometimes you're nervous when a new man moves into Henderson House, at least until you get to know them, but I have a good feeling about Frank Davis. You know me and my feelings." I trail off.

"Yes, ma'am. There is no disputing your God-given intuition." Her high-pitched voice quakes a tiny bit.

"Louie likes him, too. Took to him right off the bat." I rise and walk toward the back door of my suite, the one leading to the kitchen. "I'm curious." I turn back to Bessie. "What word would you use to describe him?"

Bessie pauses for a moment. I can almost make out the word on the tip of her tounge. She casts her eyes downward. The edge of her glow turns a darker shade of pink. "I'm not sure yet," she says before heading upstairs, her gait a little unsteady.

I smile down at Louie. "Oh, but she is sure; she's just not telling. I have a good feeling about those two." The moment I push open the kitchen door, the hearty aroma of slow-cooking beef wraps itself around me like the arms of an old friend. I close my eyes and take in the scent.

"You know what this smells like, don't you, Louie?" The dog looks up at me with his soulful brown eyes and I half-expect him to answer. "That's right—freedom," I say. Louie trots over to his usual spot under the red and white dinette while I continue to reminisce. "I had to hide my cooking in St. Louis—lied to my mother about it." Louie listens attentively, even though he's heard this monologue before. "She thought a proper woman's place was at a committee meeting, not in the kitchen." The dog shakes his collar. "I agree. She'd be mortified to see me in this apron." I take my red gingham apron off the wall and tie it on over my day dress.

I never understood why people called dogs "man's best friend" until Louie came into my life four years ago. He was a gift for my fiftieth birthday. My grandchildren named him St. Louis after my hometown, but he was Louie before the day was out. He's a fine-looking beagle with long brown ears, a white snout, soft black markings on his back, and a fluff of unruly white fur on the tip of his tail.

"Well, this seems like a mighty fancy supper for a Monday night," Edna comments as she enters from the dining room. She gestures to the mound of fresh peas and an open bag of potatoes on the counter. "Is something on your mind, Mrs. H? I know how you like to cook up a storm when you're trying to work something out." Edna puts her blue apron on over her white housekeeper's uniform. She wears her long strawberry blonde hair, recently streaked with silver, piled on top of her head in a flat bun. It always reminds me of a Scottish hat of some kind. "You still chewing on the letter you got from your boy Robert?" she asks, her blue eyes flashing in my direction.

"I'm not trying to work something out," I reply. "I'm making a nice welcome dinner for our new lodger, end of story." I start peeling potatoes. "Besides, it's just a pot roast."

"Hmm," Edna grunts under her breath. "This is way more than just a pot roast. Looks like we're making peas and mashed potatoes, and do I smell fresh rolls?" She takes her place next to me at the counter.

"Baked them this afternoon. I was hoping you'd cream the peas. Johnny sure loves your creamed peas."

"A nice welcome dinner," she says. "So, this is about Mr. Davis. I bet you have a feeling about him." She shakes a pea pod at me.

Edna is more than my housekeeper; she's also my closest friend. She was nothing but a skinny country girl with freckles and a single letter of reference when she first showed up at my kitchen door in 1923. Henderson House still smelled of fresh paint and wallpaper glue the day she arrived. It's strange to think Edna and I have been dancing around each other in this kitchen for almost twenty years.

"Oh, Edna, you know I have a feeling about everybody," I say, picking up another potato.

"Well, what are you feeling about Mr. Davis?" She starts shelling peas.

"He's going to be a good fit at Henderson House, that's all."

"No, that's not all, Mrs. H. I can tell when that's not all. Come on, spill the beans. What happened during the interview?"

"First, he introduced himself to Louie and bent down to pet him. Not only did Louie wag his tail, but he pressed his muzzle up into Mr. Davis's hand. And the house perked up the minute he walked through the door."

"A strong start." Edna deftly unzips another pod and deposits the peas into the small pot in front of her. "What color did you see around him?" she asks.

Edna is the only person alive who knows I see colors. I kept my promise to my mother and never told another living soul—not until the day my husband, Charles, died. When news arrived of his collapse, I was in the kitchen with Edna. I was distraught not only because I had lost my wonderful husband but also because my gift had failed me. Nothing in Charles's color that morning had warned me about his health. I had no idea something terrible would happen to him. I sat in the kitchen and bared my soul to Edna. I told her how the colors spoke to me and helped me understand people. Amid such utter sadness, a weight lifted. Someone knew. After all the years of hiding, someone I trusted knew my secret. Edna wasn't scared or nervous or uncomfortable. As I recall, she only replied, "Well, that explains a lot." My wonderful Edna.

"Yellow," I report. "Yellow glows all around him. It's not a sunshine yellow. It's the shade of a ripe yellow summer squash, like that cute patty pan squash we grew last year." I continue peeling potatoes. "I sensed nothing in Mr. Davis's color except good health and a pleasant disposition."

Once I become familiar with someone's color, I can tell when it's a little off. Changes in the shade might mean someone is lying, a topic of conversation is difficult, or they're feeling under the weather.

"Did he take a cookie with his tea?" Edna asks.

"Yes, he took two and then a third while we were talking," I reply.

"Hmm. A solid four out of four—dog, house, color, and cookie," she says. "Is Mr. Davis originally from California?"

"No, he's from Joplin, Missouri."

"Now we're getting somewhere. He's from your home state—a Midwesterner at heart. What else did you learn about him? Married, widowed, divorced?"

"We didn't discuss his marital status, but he's not wearing a wedding ring." I grab another potato.

Edna pushes a pile of empty pods to the side and pulls another pile toward her to shell. "What brings him to Bartlesville?"

"He said he's wanted to work for Phillips for a long time and was ready to move closer to family. I'm telling you, Edna, he's nothing like the other engineers who've stayed with us. He was simply a delight to chat with over tea."

"Remember Mr. Little? He could hardly string the words together to ask me about his laundry. I can't imagine chatting with him over tea!" Edna laughs.

"Well, Mr. Davis is different. Wait until you meet him. He's quite charming." I move on to slicing the peeled potatoes and toss the chunks into a large pot of water.

"So charming he deserves a Sunday dinner on a Monday night?" She stops shucking peas and looks at me. "What are you up to, Mrs. H?"

"Nothing," I protest.

Edna wipes her hands on her apron, placing them on her hips, then stares me down.

"All right, all right." I give in. "The way the house welcomed Mr. Davis was almost exactly the way it welcomed Bessie a dozen years ago. So, this afternoon, when I overheard Bessie and Mr. Davis laughing in the front yard, I walked to the window to have a look."

"And . . . " Edna encourages.

"And, when I saw Bessie's rosy color next to Mr. Davis's yellow, I felt an overwhelming sense of compatibility between them."

"Compatibility between Mr. Davis and Bessie—well, I'll be darned, you're matchmaking!" she exclaims.

"Hush now, Edna. I'm doing no such thing. I'm just cooking a nice welcome supper for our new lodger." I light the burner and put the potatoes on the stove to boil.

"Yup, you said that before, and I'm not buying it. Give me the whole story, Mrs. H," she presses.

"I don't have the whole story, yet." I sigh. "Compatible. That's the word that keeps popping into my head. A nice big supper might encourage folks to linger around the table and talk. There's nothing like a good meal to help people open—"

"Howdy, Edna. Mrs. Henderson." Johnny interrupts our conversation as he and Mr. Davis enter the kitchen. "We're just passing through on our way to the garden."

"And am I glad. It smells incredible in here." Mr. Davis looks around, taking in the activity on the counters. "This is quite a well-designed kitchen, Mrs. Henderson."

"Thank you, Mr. Davis. When I updated the appliances a few years ago, I installed new cabinets and this peninsula. The continuous counter space makes such a difference—especially with two cooks in the kitchen most evenings."

I glance at the cheerful red linoleum countertops and smile as I make eye contact with Edna. She raises her eyebrows.

"Goodness me, you two haven't met," I say. "Mr. Davis, I'd like to introduce our housekeeper and my dear friend, Edna Anderson."

"Pleasure to meet you, Mrs. Anderson. My room was in absolute perfect condition when I moved in today. Thank you so much," he says, looking directly at Edna. She beams in response.

"Please call me, Edna, Mr. Davis. Everyone does. Welcome to Henderson House."

"Is the house happy with Mr. Davis's arrival?" Johnny asks. "Mrs. Henderson talks about the house like it has feelings," he says behind his hand to Mr. Davis as if whispering a secret.

"Mmm mmm, she sure does," Edna murmurs.

"Well, I have a theory about houses," I admit.

"I'd love to hear it," Mr. Davis responds.

"Oh, I'm sure Johnny and Edna are tired of hearing my theories after all these years."

"Not really, Mrs. H. I think it's neat when you talk about the house," Johnny says, taking a seat on a stool under the peninsula.

"Oh, me too," Edna says as she begins collecting the ingredients to make the sauce for the peas.

"Well, I have a special sense about houses," I say. "I believe some houses need people more than others."

"Houses need people?" Mr. Davis asks as he takes a seat next to Johnny.

"Yes. While it would satisfy some houses to have a single owner or perhaps an old couple puttering about, others crave a variety of human stories playing out against their walls and windows," I say, turning to check on the potatoes.

With his elbows propped on the counter and his chin resting on his fists, Mr. Davis looks more like one of Johnny's friends than a grown-up.

"Did Henderson House respond when I entered today?" Mr. Davis asks, turning his face upward and looking around the ceiling.

"Yes, it did. Houses that need people celebrate your entrance," I say. "They are hungry for a cast of characters to pass through every day in order to feel satisfied. I guess that's why I was so excited to move to Oklahoma. I was hoping we might build a house that needs people. There was no way to be sure while we were constructing Henderson House whether it would need people. We designed, we built, we decorated. The first evening we had dinner here as a family, I heard it."

"Heard what?" Mr. Davis asks.

"I heard the house humming."

I wipe my hands on a dishtowel next to the sink. Mr. Davis looks intrigued by my story, not frightened. I have scared away a few people over the years with my talk about the house. Can you imagine if everyone knew I saw colors around them, too? Thank heavens Edna is such a good secret keeper.

"From the beginning, Henderson House was happiest with a full crew," I continue, "the more the merrier. While I could have hired a full-time cook in addition to Edna, I preferred to do most of the cooking myself." I lean across the counter and whisper. "A fact that annoyed my mother until the day she died."

Mr. Davis laughs. It's a lovely, playful laugh. I wonder whether he has a nice singing voice.

"I smile with deep satisfaction every time the dining table overflows with food and friends. And this house smiles back." I turn the flame under the potatoes down a notch to keep them at a perfect simmer.

"Now I understand why you told your sons you wanted to turn Henderson House into a boarding house," Mr. Davis says.

"You do?" Edna asks. I imagine she's surprised he knows that bit of history already.

"Because the house needs people," he says.

"Exactly!" I exclaim.

"And Aunt Bessie was her very first lodger," Johnny says proudly. "Speaking of Aunt Bessie, she's gonna be down any minute. Let's get outside and check on the flower project."

Johnny hops off his stool and heads to the kitchen door. Mr. Davis follows.

"Thanks for telling me about the house," Mr. Davis says to me. He scans the room with his eyes. "And thanks for celebrating my entrance," he says with gusto.

I laugh and the house bubbles in rhythm with the potatoes on the stove.

"Okay, so, he's not your typical engineer," Edna says once Johnny and Mr. Davis are out the back door. "When he thanked me for the condition of his room, I could feel his genuine admiration, right here." She pats the center of her chest. "Most men don't know how to deliver a proper compliment." She adds flour to the melted butter. "And he wasn't uncomfortable with your house feelings at all."

"No, he wasn't. I think he's got a nice sense of humor, don't you?"

Edna nods in agreement as she stirs the sauce briskly. "Do you really think there's the possibility of a romance between Mr. Davis and our Bessie?"

"I don't know, Edna. But I will say this: if anyone on God's green earth deserves to find true love, it's Bessie Blackwell."

CHAPTER FIVE

Bessie

I STARE AT the contents of my closet. My sister frowns upon my frumpy after-work clothes. But why risk spoiling an expensive outfit once I'm no longer at the office? I hang up my jacket, blouse, and skirt from the day and pull out my brown housedress. Swinging back and forth on its hanger, the dress resembles an oversized potato sack. Once again, Florence is right. Where's the other dress I sometimes wear after work? There it is—a soft blue shirtwaist dress with white buttons and white piping around the collar. I hang the brown dress back in the closet and slip on the blue one instead. I step into my everyday brown low-heel pumps, tuck a few wayward strands of hair back into place, and adjust my glasses. All ready to check on the flower project.

On the way downstairs, I remember the ease of my conversation with Mr. Davis in the front yard. I can't believe I lied to Mrs. Henderson. There's no getting around the truth with her. Does she already know I think Mr. Davis is adorable? My legs tremble. I probably need a glass of water after my walk home. I head through the dining room and into the kitchen.

"Mmm. What's for dinner?" I ask Mrs. Henderson.

"Oh, just a pot roast," she says.

"It's way more than just a pot roast," Edna complains. She glances up at me. "I like that blue dress on you, Bessie."

"Thank you, Edna. It's such a pleasant evening; I thought it might be a nice change."

I pour myself a glass of water and down it quickly. According to family legend, pots boil over and cookies burn if I so much as walk past the stove, so I limit my time in the kitchen.

"Johnny and Mr. Davis are already out back." Mrs. Henderson pulls the potato masher out of one of the kitchen drawers. She's wearing her old red gingham apron over an elegant summer dress. Mrs. Henderson still prefers the long-flowing styles of the 1930s. Florence constantly tries to get her to embrace shorter skirts and tailored blouses. But I like the way Mrs. Henderson looks in her ankle-length floral dresses with flutter sleeves or bertha collars, graceful and refined.

"I'm heading out to the garden now," I say. "Everything smells heavenly."

I put my empty glass in the sink. I don't think the pot roast burst into flames during my visit, though I glimpse Edna checking the oven just to be sure. My legs feel better as I walk out the back door.

Mrs. Henderson and I started the kitchen garden during my first spring in Bartlesville. It's not large, but it has enough room to grow a variety of herbs and a few vegetables. A few years ago, Edna's husband built the sweetest white picket fence around it with an arbor over the gate. The flower project lives in several old soda crates Johnny and I got from Lonnie's Ice Cream Parlor.

"The flower project is pretty involved," I hear Johnny explaining to Mr. Davis. "We grow specific flowers or colors of flowers for specific people. Then we plant the flowers in the cemetery in Claremore on Memorial Day. Only this year, we're going to the cemetery a week early. We're going this Saturday instead of on the holiday next Friday. And I'm not going at all because my friend Tommy's dad helped me get a job as a caddy at Hillcrest Country Club. I start this weekend."

I swear, that boy could talk for an hour without coming up for air.

"Who are these flowers for?" Mr. Davis asks.

"Those are for my aunt Rachel," Johnny says. "This flower's called 'Love in a Mist.' She loved the color of lilacs, and it's tricky to find flowers with the right shade. Most are too blue."

"Did you know your aunt Rachel well?" Mr. Davis asks him.

"No, sir," Johnny replies. "I think maybe I met her when I was a baby, but I don't remember. She died when I was pretty little. Come to think of it, I never met any of the folks buried in Claremore. I know all their favorite colors, but I never knew them."

"All right, gentleman, how are our young flowers coming along?" I pass under the glorious arbor smothered in deep blue clematis. "Yes, yes," I say, looking over the crates. "We should be ready by Saturday, don't you think, Johnny?"

"Well, I was a little nervous about the marigolds when Mom wanted to move things up a week, but I think they'll be big enough to plant in another five days," he replies.

"Did you tell me why you all are going this Saturday instead of on the holiday next Friday?" Mr. Davis asks Johnny.

"My mom has the next two Saturdays off from work," Johnny begins, "so if the family visits the cemetery this Saturday, she will have three days off in a row next week—the holiday on Friday, then Saturday and Sunday. She says it will be like a mini vacation. She works really hard. If anyone deserves a vacation, it's my mom."

A twinge of envy digs in when Johnny speaks so sweetly about Florence. He cares for me, too, but nobody loves an aunt the way they love their mother.

"Makes sense. I'm trying to keep up. You're a busy family. This is a fine operation, Miss Blackwell," Mr. Davis declares as he waves his hand over the flower project.

"Thank you, Mr. Davis. We take our Decoration Day flowers seriously around here."

"You most certainly do. What's your favorite flower?"

"Yeah, Aunt Bessie, I don't know yours," Johnny says.

"It's hard for me to pick a favorite but, growing up, I loved the wild black-eyed Susans that covered the meadow next to your grandfather's store," I say, nodding to Johnny.

I'm surprised once again at how easy it is to talk with Mr. Davis. I usually struggle to answer even the simplest question when it's posed by a stranger.

"What kind of store did your father own?" he asks.

"Oh, tell Mr. Davis the story about Grandpa's store," Johnny says.

A dry lump forms in my throat and I have trouble swallowing.

"I already told Mr. Davis I leave the storytelling to Uncle Eddie," I protest.

My heart pounds as I imagine stuttering my way through the story and making a fool of myself. But an unfamiliar confidence settles over me and, for a moment, I feel as though I could tell this man anything.

"Please?" Johnny asks, staring up at me with his big brown eyes. My sister's eyes.

"Okay, I'll do my best," I say. I don't want to disappoint Johnny.

"The first thing you need to know," I say, then pause and swallow one more time, "is that my father was a notorious

storyteller. Come to think of it, he may have been a better storyteller than store owner. I've often wondered if the reason he
opened a general store in the first place was simply because he
needed an audience daily." I pause again and take a breath.

Mr. Davis seems engaged. So far, so good.

"The story goes something like this: Daddy won the
building from Old Man Bushyhead in a late-night card game.
When he showed up the next day ready to move in, Old Man
Bushyhead refused to budge, so Daddy took dead aim with his
shotgun and gave Mr. Bushyhead ten minutes to pack and run
over to his son's place down the road."

Mr. Davis smiles, and the delightful little wrinkles around
his eyes deepen. His gaze never strays from me. The attention
is both affirming and unnerving at the same time. I lean back
against the gatepost to steady myself. My legs are still wobbly. I
hope I'm not coming down with something.

"There weren't many wooden buildings in Oologah back
then," I continue. "Most folks still lived in log cabins or
dugouts."

"Dugouts?" Mr. Davis asks.

"A type of house built by digging out a section of a hill.
They usually had one front wall made of logs. Some had partial
roofs, but most were underground. There wasn't much milled
lumber in Indian Territory until after the turn of the century.
I suppose Mr. Bushyhead's wooden house looked mighty fine
sitting nice and close to the big road. It had a porch, a large
front room, and a small kitchen and sleeping room in the back.
After he moved in, Daddy turned the front room into the store
and lived in the back. He planned to provide necessities so
folks wouldn't have to travel into Claremore all the time. He
carved the words 'Blackwell's Store' into a piece of wood and
burnished it with charcoal. Our Cousin Wahya helped him put
up a post and hang the sign out front. But in all my days, I

never heard anyone refer to it as 'Blackwell's Store.' Everyone in Indian Territory called it the 'Pack and Run' after the story about Old Man Bushyhead's expedited shotgun departure."

Mr. Davis laughs softly, and I hear water falling down a creek again.

"For someone who doesn't see themselves as a storyteller, you did a marvelous job," he says. My cheeks warm with his compliment.

"Of course, there's the story that gets told and then all the stories that get told after it," I say. "I've heard that my father tricked Old Man Bushyhead into thinking he had lost his house in the card game—that he took advantage of the aging gentleman's failing memory and tendency to drink too much whiskey when it was offered to him. I also heard one that Daddy had been eyeing the property for quite some time and had been waiting for an opportunity to force Old Man Bushyhead out so he could lure a wife to Oologah with the promise of a store and a wooden house!"

"Which one do you think is true?" Mr. Davis asks.

"Oh, knowing my father, they could all be true. He was always working a plan to get something he wanted. While my brother Eddie gets his storytelling genius from my dad, my sister Florence appears to have picked up the planning piece."

"Did you ever ask Grandma if Grandpa lured her to Oklahoma with the promise of a store and a wooden house?" Johnny asks.

"You know, sweetheart, I never did." I pause. "Your grandfather could be quite charming when he wanted to be."

It's not a lie. My daddy could be charming when he wanted, then cruel as soon as he stopped being charming. Johnny doesn't need to hear any of those stories.

"Well, Mr. Fuller," I say, changing the subject, "let's get everything watered and head inside to wash up before supper. We don't want Mr. Davis to be late for his first meal at Henderson House."

"Yes, ma'am," Johnny replies as he grabs the watering can and heads out of the garden and over to the water barrel on the other side of the garage.

Mr. Davis and I walk together under the arbor. He stops just outside the garden, so I stop, too. There's plenty of shade this time of day. A warm and windy day has given way to a pleasant evening with a slight breeze.

"He's a swell kid," he says.

"Yes, he is, isn't he?"

"It's nice you two are so close. I've been away from my nephews for so long, I'm not sure I could pick them out of a crowd."

"Where do they live?"

"In Joplin, Missouri."

"Is that where you're from?" I ask.

"Yep, it's where I grew up. My mom still lives there, and my sister, Helen. She's married with two boys. I guess they're about fifteen and seventeen now—a little older than Johnny. It's one of the reasons I'm excited to be back in this part of the country. Bartlesville is only a couple of hours from Joplin by car."

"Are you planning a visit soon?"

"I'd like to go for Independence Day. It's been a long time since I've been to a good old-fashioned Joplin Fourth of July celebration."

"What makes a Joplin Fourth of July special?" I ask.

"Oh, the usual. A parade, marching bands, fireworks, and tons of ice cream." He grins like a little boy. "Other than flowers, what makes a Memorial Day in Bartlesville special?"

"Do you like to fish, Mr. Davis?"

"It's been a while, but as a matter of fact, I do."

"Well, you've moved to the right place. Bartians love the Memorial Day Fishing Derby."

"Bartians?"

"Yup. You're a Bartian, now. The newspaper sponsors a fishing derby every Memorial Day out at Bar-Dew Lake."

Mr. Davis raises an eyebrow.

"It's a lake between Bartlesville and Dewey—Bar-Dew," I explain.

"Gee, it's good to be back in the Midwest," he says with a snicker. "Folks in California just don't have the same no-nonsense approach to naming their lakes. Tell me more about the fishing derby."

"Well, this year, the starting shot will sound at 12:01 a.m. Friday morning, and the contest will run until Sunday night at midnight."

"Do people really go out fishing in the middle of the night?"

"Absolutely. Over five hundred people competed last year. And there are plenty of prizes," I say as Johnny returns with the watering can.

"Are you gonna enter the fishing derby, Johnny?" Mr. Davis asks.

"Oh, no, Mr. Davis. I start my new job this weekend."

"Right, you're working as a golf caddy this summer."

"Yes, sir. If there's one thing Bartians love almost as much as fishing, it's golf!" Johnny says. "Besides, Aunt Bessie's the best angler in the family. She won top prize for a woman two years ago." Johnny continues watering.

"Really?" Mr. Davis asks.

"Caught a seven-pound largemouth bass," Johnny calls over his shoulder.

Mr. Davis glances back at me. I smile and shrug.

"No offense, Miss Blackwell, but you don't look big enough to pull in a seven-pound bass all on your own," Mr. Davis says in a gentle, teasing manner.

"Oh, Mr. Davis, I may be small, but I'm mighty." I'm immediately embarrassed by my boldness and add, "And the bigger fish don't fight you for nearly as long."

Johnny heads back around the garage for a refill.

"What did you win?" Mr. Davis asks.

"Three dollars' worth of Hawaiian wigglers."

Mr. Davis pushes his fedora off his forehead in disbelief, and I catch sight of his scar again. A scar like that must have a story to go with it. I have the strangest urge to reach out and trace the length of it with my fingers. I stick my hands in my dress pockets instead.

"That's all you got for a seven-pounder?" he asks.

"That's all. First place for the derby was a gold-plated trophy, a case of Budweiser, and a three-dollar tackle box. It went to Horace Cheney. His catch was only six pounds four ounces, but women have to compete in a separate category." I pause. "What would I do with a case of Budweiser, anyway?"

Mr. Davis laughs. It's a full-body laugh, and it's contagious. As the sound of our voices mingles, I'm overwhelmed by the same familiar sensation I had when I first saw him in the yard with Johnny.

"Mr. Davis, have we met before?" I ask, peering into the hazel eyes behind his glasses.

"I don't see how we could have," he replies.

"No, of course not." I look away.

Oh, dear. My question must have come across as forward. What's gotten into me? Mr. Davis is a stranger. I force my gaze onto a clump of weeds in the center of the path, but something pulls my eyes back to his. This time, he looks away first.

"If I had met you before, I'd remember," he says, shuffling a few stones with his shoe.

My pulse quickens. I need to get out of here. Now. I head for the kitchen door, and Mr. Davis follows. In my hurry, I step awkwardly on a rock in the path. My ankle rolls over, and I collapse backward onto Mr. Davis. My shoulders land against his chest and he catches me. My head moves in rhythm with his breath. His heartbeat pulses in my ears. The embrace only lasts a few seconds, but it's long enough for heat to travel from where his arms were around me straight to my face. My cheeks are burning hot. I'm blushing. I'm sure of it.

"Are you all right, Miss Blackwell?" Mr. Davis props me back up on my feet.

"Flowers are all set," Johnny says, running up between us.

I keep my head down, looking for something I can pretend to brush off my dress, hiding my reddened face. Embarrassment courses through my veins. I may be able to give romantic advice to others, but when it comes to my own interactions with men, I'm a disaster.

"Good work, Johnny," I croak. I move slightly to keep Johnny positioned between us. "Why don't you show Mr. Davis where he can freshen up before supper?"

"This way, Mr. Davis. I can't wait for you to meet my mom. She should be home any minute."

Johnny ushers Mr. Davis inside, and I walk unsteadily at a safe distance behind them. Busy getting supper ready, Edna and Mrs. Henderson don't pay any attention to the three of us trespassing through their domain, but Louie gives me a curious glance. For once, I hope my presence does set something on fire. I need time to pull myself together before supper.

Johnny and Mr. Davis head upstairs, and I slip out the front door to the porch. I take a seat on one of the white rocking chairs and raise my hands to my cheeks. They're still warm. When we were teenagers, Florence used to scold me for being an open book. "Men like mystery," she would say, "and you're nothing but a silly schoolgirl who blushes at the first sign of romance. Where's the mystery in that?"

Dear Lord above, I'm not sure what happened out in the garden, but please, please don't let my sister see my face before it returns to its normal color. Amen.

CHAPTER SIX

Mrs. Henderson

EDNA BRINGS OUT the final platter with the pot roast, onions, and carrots, and searches for a landing spot on the crowded dining room table.

"Did we overdo it?" I ask, shifting the bowls of mashed potatoes, creamed peas, and baskets of rolls to make room for the serving platter.

"No, it's just a pot roast!" Edna teases. "It will be worth it if all this food gets Mr. Davis and Miss Bessie talking. I'll tidy up a bit in the kitchen before I head home, and you can bet your britches I'll be here bright and early tomorrow morning for a full report."

"Aye, aye, captain," I reply.

Edna heads back into the kitchen. Louie looks in her direction to bid farewell before settling in at his place next to my chair. Johnny ambles into the dining room. He sure looks tall all of a sudden.

"Evening, Mrs. Henderson. Is it time to ring the bell?" he asks.

"Yes, please. Supper is ready," I say.

Johnny picks up the old brass bell off the sideboard. He walks to the center of the foyer and rings the bell several times. The sound reverberates off the marble floor and bounces off the second-story ceiling. Johnny returns the bell to its designated spot and walks around the table to pull my chair out for me.

"What manners, Mr. Fuller."

"My pleasure, Mrs. H. And as Uncle Eddie likes to say, 'The roast smells very-good-delicious!'"

As if on cue, Eddie Blackwell strides into the room. "Evening, all."

He's changed out of his taxicab driver uniform and looks stylish in a pair of pleated tan slacks and a short-sleeved blue shirt with double chest pockets—thanks to Florence's discount at work, no doubt. Eddie's about ten years younger than his sisters and has the same round Irish face. He left his job wrangling cattle in Montana to help Florence after her husband died. But I suspect something else made him seek the safety of his sisters, and now he's not sure how to break away.

Florence and Bessie walk into the dining room next, followed by Mr. Davis. An afternoon of moving in, playing catch, and touring the garden has left Mr. Davis's sandy-brown hair a little curlier than it was this morning. He's put his suit jacket back on and spruced up his appearance for supper. I think he's even wearing a fresh dress shirt.

"Mr. Davis," Johnny says, "this is my uncle."

"Eddie Blackwell. Nice to meet you," Eddie says as they shake hands.

"Frank Davis. Nice to meet you as well," Mr. Davis replies.

Johnny continues in his role as master of ceremonies. "And this is my mother." Johnny gestures to Florence.

"Welcome to Henderson House, Mr. Davis. I'm Florence Fuller," she says.

"Nice to meet you, Mrs. Fuller."

"And this is my sister, Bessie Blackwell." Florence turns to introduce Bessie.

"Oh, I've already had the pleasure of meeting Miss Blackwell and the privilege of reviewing the flower project for Saturday," he says, beaming at Bessie.

Bessie's normal light pink color is a deep shade of rose this evening. She returns his smile, and her cheeks turn rosy to match.

"Mr. Davis, why don't you sit here on my left?" I gesture to the seat directly across from Bessie's spot at the table. "Johnny, will you say grace?" I ask.

We all bow our heads.

"Dear Heavenly Father, kind and good, we thank Thee for our daily food. We thank Thee for Thy love and care. Be with us, Lord, and hear our prayer. Amen."

"Amen," we respond.

"Mrs. H, you and Edna have really outdone yourselves for a Monday night. What's the special occasion?" Eddie asks as he serves himself some peas and passes the dish to Florence.

"I thought we should give Mr. Davis a proper Henderson House welcome," I say.

"Well, Mr. Davis," Eddie says, "my stomach is thrilled you've arrived. What brings you to Bartlesville?"

"It's sort of a long story," Mr. Davis says as he passes the potatoes.

"Looking at all this food, I'd say we have plenty of time for long stories tonight." Eddie reaches for a bread basket.

My plan to facilitate conversation is working. I settle into my chair, ready to watch and listen.

"All righty then." Mr. Davis puts his fork down. "My desire to work at Phillips dates all the way back to 1927 and the flight of the Woolaroc."

"The Woolaroc? That's the name of Frank Phillips's ranch," Johnny interjects.

"Did you know the word 'Woolaroc' is a portmanteau?" Florence offers.

"A portmanteau?" Mr. Davis asks.

"Yes, it means words packed together. The name Woolaroc combines the words 'woods,' 'lakes,' and 'rocks'—all of which make up the beautiful Osage Hills southwest of Bartlesville, where Mr. Phillips has his ranch."

"Gosh, in 1927, all I knew was it was the name of an airplane," Mr. Davis says. "You see, after Lindbergh flew across the Atlantic in May of '27, the Dole Food Company announced a prize of twenty-five thousand dollars for a plane that could fly from California to Hawaii."

"Twenty-five thousand dollars," Johnny repeats, his eyes widening.

"Yep, and Frank Phillips sponsored one of the pilots. His research team here in Bartlesville created a new high octane aviation fuel for the flight. I was there the day the planes left Oakland." Mr. Davis's yellow glows a shade brighter, energized by the conversation. "There must have been fifty thousand people cheering as eight pilots attempted to take off from the Oakland Airport."

"Whoa," Johnny whispers. He's hanging on every word.

"Rainy weather left the field wet and muddy. It was a mess. Only five of the eight planes took off successfully over the Pacific. And only two made it to Hawaii." He stops for a moment. "The remaining three airplanes and their crews were lost and never recovered."

Listening to his story, I remember reading about the success of the Phillips-sponsored pilot and the missing planes years ago.

"Arthur Goebel was the Woolaroc pilot," I recall.

"Yes," Mr. Davis confirms. "He made the two-thousand-four-hundred-and-thirty-nine-mile flight in just over twenty-six hours. Since that day, I've dreamed of working in the aviation fuel department at Phillips Petroleum. I climbed my way up through the ranks at the Shell Oil Company while studying at Berkeley. Shell was a terrific place to work—don't get me wrong—but finally the right position opened up at Phillips. Now, here I am in Oklahoma's first oil boom town, reporting for duty," he says with a mock salute.

Mr. Davis leans forward. "I believe the United States will officially join the war very soon," he says, his tone turning serious. "It's inevitable. And while we fought the Great War on the ground, in the trenches, this war will be won or lost in the skies. Developing the best fuel for our military aircraft will be a key to victory, and I want to do my part."

His eyes linger on Bessie for a moment. She doesn't look away.

"Well, I'm sure the team at Phillips is happy to have you on board," Florence says, pulling his gaze to her. "Do you have a wife and family who will join you in Bartlesville once you're settled?" she asks.

Florence's lack of tact often embarrasses me, but this evening I'm happy to let her coax the details out of Mr. Davis regarding his marital status.

"No. It's just me and my slide rule," Mr. Davis responds.

"Never married? Or not married now?" Florence asks.

"Really, Florence," Bessie interjects, "it's none of our business."

I'm not sure I've ever heard Bessie interrupt her sister at the dinner table. Given the furrowed brow on Florence's forehead, she's as surprised as I am.

"I'm sorry, Mr. Davis," Florence says. "Sometimes my curiosity gets the best of me. I didn't mean to pry."

"I was married once," Mr. Davis replies, "a long time ago." He runs his hand through his hair, and I notice a scar stretching almost the full width of his forehead. A wound that severe must have taken months to heal. No wonder he wears his hair a little longer than most men his age.

"Let me save you the trouble of asking a follow-up question," Mr. Davis continues. "I'm divorced. I married my childhood sweetheart and went off to fight in the war in Europe. When I came home, well, things were different."

The room falls quiet.

Mr. Davis's color darkens when he mentions his divorce. Since I don't know him well, it's hard to interpret the color change. My intuition tells me the divorce was difficult for him and perhaps still is. Getting into a relationship with a divorced man could be a serious roadblock for Bessie.

"Uncle Eddie," Johnny says, breaking the silence, "I asked Mr. Davis if he'd drive us to the Wednesday Night Supper and he said yes. Did you see his car?"

"See it?" Eddie responds. "Why, all that chrome practically blinded me when I walked up the driveway this evening!"

"Do you promise to give us a ride to the Wednesday Night Supper, Mr. Davis? Do you promise on the bones?" Johnny asks.

"I'm not sure what that means, but I promise," Mr. Davis says, looking to me for guidance.

"Ah, 'on the bones' is one of the many Blackwell family sayings you'll need to get used to around here," I say. "I think Eddie tells that story the best."

"All right then, Mrs. H," Eddie says. "My turn to talk so Mr. Davis can enjoy some of your fine cooking."

"I don't see how you tell the story the best, since you weren't even there." Florence groans.

"Well, I am the unofficial Blackwell family historian. Feel free to chime in, Flossie, if I miss any of the pertinent details."

"Oh, you know I will," Florence replies.

I can tell she dislikes it when her brother calls her Flossie. Of everyone in the Blackwell clan, the color around Florence says the most about her. A muddy green fog surrounds her head and shoulders most days. When she's upset or hiding something, it turns dark, like the color you'd find deep in the forest when night falls. Eddie and Johnny are also greens, but they carry a light yellow-green color, like the leaves of a red-bud tree in early autumn. Bessie stands out with her rosy glow whenever the family is together.

"'On the bones' began one summer afternoon when Flossie and Bessie were growing up," Eddie begins. "Bessie was ten and Flossie was a scrappy nine-year-old—"

"And you were a babe in arms, yet you're telling the story," Florence grouses as Eddie waves her protest away.

"Back in those days, our family ran a small general store just outside of Claremore—"

"The Pack and Run," Mr. Davis adds.

"Very good, Mr. Davis. Yes, the Pack and Run. On those hot summer afternoons, Flossie and Bessie would race to finish their chores so they could meet up with their friends at the nearby swimming hole. The swimming hole had a large rock outcropping at one end. There were plenty of tales about a cave at the top and that something terrible lived inside. All the kids knew that Willie Nunley had climbed up there one day on a dare. He fell back into the water, hit his head on a rock, and drowned. Parents for miles around warned their children to swim there with caution and to never climb those rocks under penalty of a good thrashing if they ever heard you'd tried. So, of course, one afternoon my sister Flossie tried to convince Bessie to climb up there and find out what was in that cave. Bessie was the best climber in all of Indian Territory." Eddie winks at his oldest sister.

"She was also the most annoying Goody Two-shoes," Florence quips.

"When Bessie refused, Florence figured out how to scramble up there on her own," Eddie says.

"What did you find?" Mr. Davis leans in and addresses Florence directly.

"Bones," Florence says, wiggling her fingers in a spooky gesture. "Human remains. Well, it was some sort of skeleton. At the time, I was pretty sure it was a human one."

"Ooh," Mr. Davis says, matching Florence's eerie tone and looking at Johnny, who nods in return.

"Flossie was so scared, she came clambering down those rocks like a black-tailed prairie dog with a coyote on its heels," Eddie continues. "When she got back to her friends in the water, she was sure afraid our daddy would find out and take his belt to her! She made all the kids swear their most solemn promise they would never, ever tell anyone that she'd climbed up there. Flossie made them all promise 'on the bones.' And that's how it started."

"Of course," Bessie speaks up, "Florence made us promise lots of things 'on the bones' from that point forward. And, as I recall, most of those promises were about us not telling our daddy certain things that might get her into trouble."

"Oh, really, Bessie," Florence tuts, "I can't help it if you never did anything against the rules your entire childhood!"

Mr. Davis chuckles. "Well, Johnny," he says, "I promise to drive you to the Wednesday Night Supper. I promise on the bones."

"Thank you, Mr. Davis. I'll hold you to it," Johnny replies.

"We'll be riding in style," Eddie says. "What a fine automobile, Mr. Davis. Did you buy it out in California?"

"Yes, I did." He smiles as if to himself. "It's sort of a good story."

"Please tell us," Bessie says in such a sweet voice it makes my eyes sting a little.

"I don't want to monopolize the dinner conversation," he says.

"Oh, Mr. Davis," I say, "dining at Henderson House with the Blackwell family is all about telling stories. I'm guessing we'd love to hear it."

"Absolutely," Eddie chimes in. "Take it away, Mr. Davis!"

"Okay, well, it all starts with my friend, Syd Carmichael. I met Syd during my early days at Shell. He grew up in New York City and is one of those street-smart fellers who's always looking to make a couple of extra bucks. Over the years, Syd built up a lucrative side business, helping San Francisco's high society dispose of their used cars so they could purchase the latest and greatest models. When I told him about my new job in Oklahoma, I asked if he knew anyone who was looking to sell a car. Boy, did he!" Mr. Davis's shoulders relax, and he becomes more animated as he settles into his tale. "Syd and I ventured out to Sea Cliff, one of the city's swankiest neighborhoods. We met up with a gent who lives in a mansion on El Camino Del Mar. It has to be one of the most beautiful streets in the world. The homes sit way up high and have panoramic views of the water," he says, moving his hand across an imaginary horizon. "Now, they all have views of the Golden Gate Bridge, too."

"How breathtaking," Bessie responds, never taking her eyes off Mr. Davis.

"Oh, it sure is," he says, smiling at Bessie before turning back to the entire table. "After some high-flying negotiations, mostly handled by Syd, I left as the proud owner of a 1939 Chrysler Imperial and with a much lighter savings passbook."

"Yeow! A 1939 Chrysler Imperial!" Eddie shakes his head. "Does it have Chrysler's 324-cubic-inch straight-eight engine and a semiautomatic three-speed manual transmission?"

"Yep," Mr. Davis replies. "You can shift into second and third gears just by letting off the gas pedal and shifting—no clutch required! She drives like a dream. I took my time making my way here from San Fran."

"Which route did you take?" Eddie asks.

"I drove south to pick up Route 66 in San Bernardino. Stopped in Arizona and New Mexico, staying at motels along the way and talking with the most interesting people. Traveling by car is the only way to go."

"Excuse me. I hate to interrupt such a lively dinner," Professor Rutledge says as he walks into the dining room.

Standing tall in his navy-blue security guard uniform, the professor looks stalwart and strong. But I know his secret. On the inside, he's a marshmallow—soft and sweet. I'm sure one reason I took to the professor so quickly is his color. The professor is blue like my dear Charles, though Charles was a sky blue and Professor Rutledge's shade always feels more like the sea. Using his color as a guide, my best guess is that Albert Rutledge took the night watchman job to hide from his grief after his wife died. Grief never seems to change someone's color; it takes the shine out of it, like tarnish on a silver pitcher. But lately, I see his true vibrancy breaking through.

"I wanted to offer my welcome to the newest member of the Henderson House family," the professor says, walking behind my chair to greet Mr. Davis. "Professor Albert Rutledge, at your service."

He extends his hand and Mr. Davis stands to shake it.

"Frank Davis, a pleasure."

The professor towers over our new lodger, but Mr. Davis carries a strength of his own. I sense that Mr. Davis has overcome great obstacles yet managed to maintain his optimism. I see his positive nature in the angle of his head while he listens and the gentleness of his ready smile.

"Please return to your feast and conversation," the professor says with a slight bow as he heads for the kitchen.

"Professor," I call. "I left a lunch pail for you on the counter. I didn't want you to miss out on Mr. Davis's welcome supper."

The professor smiles in my direction and bows a second time before disappearing into the kitchen. Oh, he does look handsome in that uniform.

"Mr. Davis, can you tell us more about San Francisco?" Bessie asks. "What was it like living in the Paris of the West?"

"Gosh." Mr. Davis pauses. "It was noisy—cars, trolleys, boats, people speaking different languages. To be honest, I'm happy to be back in familiar territory. Bartlesville's more like where I grew up in Joplin. I was never keen on San Francisco's nightlife—supper clubs and floor shows and all. For me, the greatest attraction was watching the bridges go up."

All the eyes around the table focus on him, waiting for another story.

"The Bay Bridge opened in 1936 and the Golden Gate the following year," Mr. Davis continues. "They were both incredible feats of engineering. I spent countless hours watching the construction and never ceased to be amazed at the brave men who built them. Twenty-eight men died building the Bay Bridge, but only eleven died in the construction of the Golden Gate," Mr. Davis explains.

"Oh, my, so many lives gone to building bridges?" Bessie shakes her head. Knowing her, she's probably praying for the families of the men who lost their lives building those bridges right now. God bless her.

"Well, the experts say you have to expect one death per million dollars of construction," Mr. Davis continues. "Now, considering that the Golden Gate Bridge cost twenty-seven million dollars, it is actually an impressive safety record. While

I agree it's sad to think of losing any workers, eleven sure beats twenty-seven."

Mr. Davis and Bessie's eyes lock. As if there is an invisible string pulling pink and yellow across the dinner table, their colors begin to overlap. It's an astonishing sight to behold.

Mr. Davis clears his throat and continues. "The length of the Bay Bridge is extraordinary—over four and a half miles—but the Golden Gate catching a few targeted rays of sunlight through the early morning fog is a sight I'll never forget."

Bessie and Mr. Davis continue to hold each other's gaze. They look so content to do so. It's as if we are all frozen in this beautiful moment with them.

"Well, I'm making a trip to a big city myself," Florence announces, breaking the spell.

"Really, Mom? Where to?" Johnny asks.

"Tulsa. My work with the window displays has been generating a great deal of business," Florence says, her color deepening. "Mr. Linn is sending me to the Tulsa store this Wednesday to share my expertise. The store is paying for my bus ticket and my expenses." Florence smiles at Johnny.

She's not telling the whole truth. I see it in the deep, dark green swirling around her. It's not an outright lie, but it's not the truth, either. What is Florence up to now?

"Wow, my mom's going on a business trip!" Johnny beams.

"Congratulations, Florence," Bessie offers. "I'm so pleased your hard work is being recognized."

"My trip means there's one more seat available in your Chrysler for the Wednesday Night Supper, Mr. Davis. I won't be back from Tulsa in time to ride along," Florence adds.

"And I'm on the late shift—no Wednesday Night Supper for me this week," Eddie says.

"Well, I guess it's my lucky day." I jump into the conversation. "Sounds like Edna and I might be able to hitch a ride." I motion with my thumb.

More laughter fills the dining room, and the house hums with a satisfaction I haven't heard in a good long time.

CHAPTER SEVEN

Florence

BALANCING ON THE edge of his rocking chair, my brother carries on with one of his favorite taxi-driver stories. "So, at that point, the argument in the backseat regarding German versus American potato salad gets serious. The new bride leans forward and says, 'Here, hold Pumpkin,' and hands *me* the tiny dog who's been whimpering louder and louder in sympathy with the increasing volume of the newlywed's disagreement." Eddie puts his left hand up as if it's on the wheel and braces his right arm like he's holding a football as he continues. "Now, I'm trying to drive one handed in a thunderstorm and calm this shaking little orange poodle under my arm, all the while knowing we still have ten miles to go!"

Eddie is a very physical storyteller. His wiry frame bends, twists, and stretches its way into every yarn he spins. After a vigorous night of swapping stories with Mr. Davis, Eddie's brown hair springs out in every direction from his animated, round, and reddened face. Bessie and I have heard the "Here, hold Pumpkin" story a million times, but this is a first for Johnny and Mr. Davis, and we're all in stitches. Johnny sits next to me on the front porch swing. The chain jangles, and the seat creaks in rhythm with our laughter.

"What happened in the end?" Mr. Davis asks once he catches his breath.

"Oh, this story ends the way most do," Eddie says. "The young husband agrees with his young wife. Yes, American potato salad is best. The young wife says something sweet in return, and they kiss. Pumpkin stops shaking and scampers over the seat into their waiting arms. As we arrive at our destination, the storm subsides, and the skies part. Then the happy couple tips their cabbie handsomely, and we all live happily ever after." Eddie bows his head to the audience.

We offer a quiet round of applause.

"Feels a little like Cowboy Coffee Hour, doesn't it, girls?" Eddie sits back in his chair.

"Yes, it does, I suppose," Bessie says from her rocker at the far end of our group.

"Minus the gossip," I chime in.

"Is 'Cowboy Coffee Hour' another Blackwell family tradition?" Mr. Davis asks.

"Sort of," Bessie says. "When Daddy started the Pack and Run, it turned out he was mighty good at making coffee. He brewed it on top of the wood stove in the back room, cowboy style."

"Some people said his coffee was so good because our well was spring fed and the water he used was fresh and crisp," I say.

"Others said it was because he waited to grind the beans until the last possible minute," Bessie adds.

"Still, some thought it was his special technique of stirring the brew with a long-handled spoon to extract the most flavor out of the grounds," I counter.

"Hmm," Eddie murmurs. "I've always thought it was because he added a spoonful of cold water just before serving, to help the grounds settle at the bottom of the pot."

"Oh, whatever the reason, his cowboy coffee helped put the store on the map," I say.

"He had a group of regulars who stopped by every morning for what the locals called "Cowboy Coffee Hour," Bessie explains. "By seven o'clock, the smell of coffee grounds and work boots filled the store to the rafters."

"Those men stood around yacking about everything under the sun—the weather, farming, tribal business, you name it. But mostly they gossiped. They were worse than a brood of hens," Eddie says with a soft chuckle.

"Some mornings, the sound of men clucking in the kitchen was so loud, Florence and I had to shout to each other upstairs while we got ready for school," Bessie says.

Mr. Davis cocks his head. "When did the Pack and Run get an upstairs?"

"Daddy built a second story after I was born," I say. "I guess two babies in the back room was too crowded. The second floor had a sitting area, a bunkroom, and a bedroom for our parents."

"Thanks for clarifying." Mr. Davis runs his fingers through his hair and smiles. "I'm doing my best to keep up."

"And you're doing a fine job," Eddie confirms.

"Is Cowboy Coffee Hour where you honed your storytelling skills?" Mr. Davis asks Eddie.

"Nope. Just something passed down to me from my daddy, I guess." Eddie looks out across the broad porch. A shadow crosses his face. He rocks slowly, back and forth. "I spent a lot of time telling tales around the campfire when I lived out west."

"Yes, by all accounts, our little brother is the only real cowboy in our Indian family," I say to Mr. Davis. "As soon as he turned eighteen, Eddie shook the dust of Oklahoma off his boots and headed out to Montana to ride the range and run cattle."

"What made you hang up your spurs?" Mr. Davis asks Eddie.

"Well, I got a letter from Florence." Eddie nods at me with a wink before returning his attention to Mr. Davis. "Her husband, John, died in an accident. Bessie invited her and little Johnny to move here. Turned out, there was a room for me if I wanted it. I felt it was important for Johnny to have a man around the house, so I traded my pony for a taxi," Eddie says, continuing to rock.

"My brother promised he'd stick around until I found another husband. Ha! Guess he didn't know he was signing up for a life sentence," I joke.

"Florence, really," Bessie interjects.

I wave off her protestation. "Finding another husband isn't exactly on the top of my list. I've dated off and on, even had a regular fellow a few years back, but in the end, men are all after the same thing—" I wait a couple heartbeats before delivering my punch line: "A housekeeper!"

Mr. Davis, Eddie, and Johnny laugh. Bessie does not look amused.

"Mom always says the last thing she needs is a man expecting her to quit her job and stay home to cook and clean for him," Johnny says. "She'd rather sell shirts than iron them."

"Exactly!" I pat Johnny on the knee. "And on that note, I've got shirts to sell in the morning, and you've got school. It's not summer yet. We should call it a night."

Johnny and I put our feet down to stop the motion of the porch swing and stand at the same time.

"Good night, everyone," Johnny says.

"Yes, good night," I say. "Are you coming, Bessie?"

"I'm not quite ready to turn in," she responds.

"Are you sure? You'll be tired in the morning," I warn.

Bessie smiles and stays put in her rocker. One more round of bidding us good night follows us to the front door, and Johnny and I head inside.

What's gotten into Bessie? I wonder as Johnny and I start up the stairs. *She interrupted me twice this evening, and now she's staying up way past her usual bedtime. Hmm. Must be nice to have the freedom to go to bed whenever you feel like it. She doesn't have to share a room with a teenaged boy.*

When Johnny was little, I could put him to bed early and then rejoin the grownups downstairs. Now, it's easier if we turn in at the same time. We've adopted a bedtime routine to maintain privacy. It means I have to go to bed earlier than I used to, but I've needed the extra sleep lately, to be honest. Seems I run out of steam at work by two or three every afternoon. Tonight, I stop at the top of the stairs to catch my breath. Johnny waits for me, and we continue to our room.

While Johnny is in the bathroom, I pace back and forth. Following our new plan, I use the bathroom to change into my pajamas and get ready for bed first. Johnny puts on his PJs while I'm out of the room. Thank goodness, Johnny's friend Tommy asks him to spend the night on Saturdays. I cherish my one evening of solitude each week and the opportunity to take a long bath and sleep in a little on Sunday mornings.

Normally, I start reading while Johnny washes his face and brushes his teeth, but tonight my mind's jumping around like a frog on a wet road. I keep pacing. My brain churns as bits and pieces of memories rise to the surface and then fall away—a frequent side effect of telling stories about the good old days. Which, when I stop to think about them, weren't very good for any of us. Those gossiping fools at Cowboy Coffee Hour got me into trouble on more than one occasion. But I don't want to think about the past tonight. I want to focus on the future. If only my mind would let me. I count my tiny steps—eighteen to the window and eighteen back to the foot of my bed. My slippers glide quietly across the rug, and the legs of my pajama pants flap against each other with each step. I concentrate on the details of my room to try to calm the chaos between my ears.

When Mrs. Henderson divided her original master bedroom into two smaller boarding house rooms, one ended up long and rectangular, the other perfectly square. Johnny and I live in room number five, the long rectangular room. It has one large front-facing window and easily accommodates two twin beds with a nightstand, a double-width bureau, a walnut Queen Anne writing desk, and a matching desk chair with one of those round needlepoint pads on it. An enormous blue and gold oriental rug with an intricate red floral pattern spans the entire width and length of the room. A rolled-arm reading chair with a round side table and an old Tiffany lamp occupies the front corner next to the window. Henderson House is, by far, the most elegant place I have ever lived. But, as nice as it is, none of this is mine. I'm still renting a room in someone else's house and pacing on someone else's rug.

When did you stop feeling grateful and start feeling stuck?

I know exactly when my dissatisfaction started—the day I turned forty. All the unfulfilled expectations of my life began staring back at me when I looked in the mirror. Every heartbreak, every betrayal, every broken promise has been recorded in the lines on my face. I start my route back to the bed.

As much as I like to complain about Mrs. Henderson and her oddball intuition, the years at Henderson House have been good for our little family. Living in one of the nicest neighborhoods in town helped Johnny make friends he otherwise might not have met. I'm thankful for our time here, but life is a series of chapters, and for the last year or so, I've felt it's time for us to turn the page and move on. Trust me, I don't plan on sharing a rented room with my son much longer. I always thought our next chapter would be buying our own home in Bartlesville. But if I can land this position as manager of the Tulsa store, our family may be moving in a completely new direction. And soon.

I turn and pace back to the window, thinking about Bessie's room next door. She chose room number six, the square room, when she arrived in Bartlesville. Johnny and I didn't join her here until after John's drowning accident. I always wondered whether Bessie picked the square room because she liked it best or because she knew the adjacent room would be perfect for me and Johnny if we ever needed it. Was she counting on my life falling apart? We weren't on speaking terms when she left Wichita, but true to form, Bessie welcomed us at Henderson House with open arms, and all was forgiven from her side. I wish I could say the same. Forgiveness has never been my strong suit.

I hear the door handle click and look up. Johnny saunters into the room and strikes a dashing pose as he flashes his pearly whites.

"Colgate Ribbon Dental Cream cleans your breath while it cleans your teeth!" he announces.

"If it's kissin' you've been missin'—" I say, playing along with the familiar radio advertisement.

"Do as I do!" we say together.

I walk over and put my hands on his shoulders. He bends down, and I get up on my tiptoes to give him a smooch on the forehead. All the heartache aside, this child has been a blessing. I can't imagine my life without him, and I can't imagine not being his mother.

"Time for bed, Mr. Fuller," I say.

"Mr. Davis sure is swell, ain't he?" Johnny says as he hops into bed.

"Isn't he," I correct.

"Isn't he swell?" Johnny asks again.

"Yes, he's a fine man," I agree.

"He's got almost as many stories as Uncle Eddie. He's gonna be a lot more fun to have around than boring old Mr. Clark."

"Mm-hmm."

"He and Aunt Bessie sure took a shine to each other, didn't they?" he asks, pulling his covers up under his chin.

"What on earth would make you say that?" I climb into my bed.

"Mom, you know Aunt Bessie's usually as nervous as a cat in a room full of rocking chairs when she's around a strange man. She rarely makes a peep until a new lodger has been here for at least a week. You wouldn't have recognized her out in the garden today. She was telling Mr. Davis stories and laughing with him about winning the fishing derby."

"Really?"

"Yup, and didn't you notice at dinner how she was encouraging him? 'What was it like living in the Paris of the West?'" Johnny imitates the trill in Bessie's voice and bats his eyelashes.

"Johnny Fuller, are you making fun of your aunt?"

"I'm not making fun. She likes him! Uncle Eddie thinks Mr. Davis likes her, too. He said there were sparks flying across the dinner table tonight."

"Don't you let your uncle put crazy ideas into your head. There weren't any sparks. Go to sleep. You've only got a few days of school left and then it'll be summer." I turn out the bedside lamp.

"Summer. I've got the entire summer at the golf club to look forward to. I can't wait. Good night, Mom," he says into the darkness.

"Good night, Johnny. Sweet dreams." I settle in under my quilt.

I guess I wasn't paying close enough attention during supper this evening—too busy strategizing how to tell everyone about my business trip without mentioning the job offer. I hope my decision to omit the potential promotion doesn't backfire. Why get everyone all riled up about moving to Tulsa until I have a firm offer in hand? Still, Mrs. Henderson kept giving me one of her funny looks. She makes me uncomfortable. It's downright strange how she knows when I'm up to something. With my attention on avoiding Mrs. Henderson's gaze and waiting for the right moment to make my announcement, I forgot to keep an eye on my sister.

Bessie did look a little flushed at the table. Was she blushing? Come to think of it, she had on her cute blue dress, not the frumpy brown one. Oh, dear! Was she trying to look nice for him? And she stayed out on the porch tonight, even though it was getting late. The last thing I need right now is a case of puppy love getting in the way of my plans. If Bessie falls in love, she might not want to move to Tulsa with us. Johnny is as much her responsibility as mine. After John's death, she promised me we would raise Johnny together. I need her to keep that promise.

Hold on, Florence, there's no reason to get wound up. Even if Bessie does like Mr. Davis, she doesn't know the first thing about starting a romance.

Bessie's never been lucky in love—that much is true. I'll never forget the Farmer's Picnic date disaster. Bessie must have been about sixteen at the time. Jake Haskell asked her to the picnic right after church and she accepted. Imagine saying yes to the first boy who asked you—Jake Haskell no less! Jake was a short, round boy with a pudgy, pockmarked face and stringy black hair. When we headed outside, Carter Moore was waiting for her by our wagon—the one and only dreamboat, Carter Moore.

He looked mighty fine. His blond curly hair shone in the afternoon sun. He had his big, strong hands hooked on the pockets of his dungarees, and he kicked his custom cowboy boots at the dirt while he waited for Bessie to arrive. When he asked her to the Farmer's Picnic, she politely declined. Said she was already going with Jake. Never even hesitated.

The whole ride home, I tried to explain how easy it would have been to say "yes" to Carter and let Jake know her plans had changed. We were talking about a date with Carter Moore. Could there have been any better occasion for bending the truth? But oh no, not for by-the-book Bessie Blackwell. She'd already promised Jake, and "a promise is a promise," she said. She even told Carter to ask her friend Joyce Simmons. Of all the crazy things to do!

Carter asked Joyce to the picnic. They ended up getting married and having a bunch of blond curly-haired babies. Bessie and Joyce continued to be friends for years—right up until we moved to Wichita. Joyce never liked me. I could tell. No matter. I never liked her either.

Carter inherited his family's lumber business, and he and Joyce are some of the richest folks in Claremore now. They've started a new construction company together. If only Bessie had known how to play her cards right, she could be Mrs. Carter Moore of Moore Construction instead of a never-been-married mimeograph machine operator blushing at the dinner table over a man she just met.

But Bessie doesn't know how to play her cards right. In fact, she doesn't even know the rules of the game. If she did, she never would have ended up in such a mess with Doc Jenkins. Did she honestly believe he wanted to marry her?

A chill runs up and down my spine, and I snuggle my head deeper into my pillow. Now is not the time to let myself be distracted by my sister's pathetic crush on Mr. Davis. If I want to manage the Tulsa store—if I want an easy way out of the whole uncomfortable Sonny situation, and if I want to improve our family's circumstances and start writing our next chapter—I need to put all my energy into this job interview on Wednesday. I close my eyes and run through potential outfits in my head.

"You asleep?" Johnny whispers.

"Not yet," I say.

"I'm still wound up after all those stories," he says. "What are you thinking about?"

"What to wear on my business trip on Wednesday. I want to look professional. That means a suit," I reply.

"Aunt Bessie said the weather's gonna turn warmer this week. Won't a suit be hot?" he asks.

"Johnny, are you really interested in my wardrobe decisions? Go to sleep."

"Keep talking, Ma. I like falling asleep to the sound of your voice."

"Well, my yellow suit skirt and matching collarless jacket with a white blouse would be bright and comfortable. On the other hand, my cotton gray-and-white-dotted Swiss suit with the three-quarter-length sleeves sends a more positive message about my fashion sense, and it's certainly appropriate for a warmer day at the end of May."

"You look swell in the gray one," Johnny says. "That's the perfect choice." And with that, my sweet boy yawns and drifts off.

Choice. Mr. Linn said this decision was one hundred percent my choice. Oh, Johnny, your aunt Bessie is the only reason I ever brought you here. After John died, we needed somewhere to land, and we didn't have any other place to go. Bessie's steady job and her good fortune drew us to Bartlesville and Henderson House. But I never chose any of this for us. Maybe it's time for my job and my good fortune to be the driving force in our family's future. Maybe this time, I get to choose.

CHAPTER EIGHT

Bessie

AFTER FLORENCE AND Johnny turn in, Mr. Davis, Eddie, and I rock on the porch in comfortable silence. My brother was in rare form tonight, and Mr. Davis certainly held his own. I sat in the rocking chair farthest from Mr. Davis—to see if a little space between us might keep me from blushing again. Worked like a charm. I still don't know how to explain my strange reactions to Mr. Davis in the garden. Mrs. Henderson has hosted dozens of male lodgers over the years, but not one of them ever made me tingle. The Kitchen Ladies at church have set me up with every widower in town. I've probably sat with fifteen different men at the Wednesday Night Supper, and I've never blushed or felt like my legs might give way. I was nervous when I dined with those men, but only due to my usual fear of stuttering. And a healthy skepticism of matchmaking in general. I shut the door on romance decades ago, locked it tight and threw away the key. I've built a life full of love and family—there's no room for blushing and tingling.

Maybe my feelings in the garden have nothing to do with Mr. Davis. Perhaps I'm coming down with a cold. The onset of an illness is a far more likely explanation than being attracted to a man I hardly know. I suppose I did think he was adorable when I first met him. But I studied Mr. Davis from a distance on the porch this evening with no unwelcome side effects. I watched the little wrinkles deepen around his eyes when he smiled, how he puckered his lips and furrowed his brow when he was concentrating. I noticed him squeezing his eyes shut to keep from laughing out loud. And how after he ran his hand through his hair, he fluffed the curls in the front to cover his scar. I took all this in without one sigh or flutter. Proof there is no attraction.

Eddie reaches in his pocket for a smoke and silently offers one to Mr. Davis, who declines. Eddie strikes a match and lights his cigarette as the crescent moon rises between two sycamore trees.

"I remember the first time I set foot on this porch as if it were yesterday," I say, breaking the silence.

"Mrs. Henderson told me you were her first lodger. How did you find her?" Mr. Davis asks.

"Through my friend Anna from work. I went to services at the Baptist church with her so I could meet Mrs. Henderson. Had my interview later that day."

"Did she have the tea waiting?" he asks.

"Of course." I smile.

"I never got the tea or the cookies," Eddie laments.

"She grandfathered you in," I reply. "When I arrived, I was sure I had written the address down incorrectly. This deep porch, the tall columns and wood trim gleaming white against the red brick. Well, it was the most beautiful home I'd ever seen. Nothing like the drafty old farmhouse where I'd been living with my aunt Maude in Wichita and certainly a far cry from the Pack and Run. I knocked on the door and when Mildred Henderson appeared, I knew I was in the right place."

"You sure were, sis," Eddie says. "Henderson House has been a sweet spot for us."

"I'm glad the receptionist in the engineering department knew she had a room available." Mr. Davis smiles and the tiny wrinkles appear. "She doesn't charge nearly what she could for room and board here. A place as nice as this would be three or four times as expensive in San Francisco."

"Mrs. Henderson isn't trying to support herself by taking in lodgers," I say.

"I figured as much," Mr. Davis responds.

"She says she charges enough to cover the grocery bill, Edna's salary, and Louie's treats."

"So, you've talked to her about the room rate?"

"Oh, yes, I've begged her to raise our rent several times, but she won't hear of it."

"It's been pretty easy on the old wallet for us to live here so long," Eddie says. "We've been pooling our savings. One of these days, we'll have enough to buy a house of our own."

"How soon will that be?" Mr. Davis asks.

"It's up to Florence," Eddie answers. "She's the only one antsy to leave the boardinghouse. She went on and on at supper the other night about how close we are to having enough in the savings account to go house hunting—urging me and Bessie to watch every penny. The next day she bought Johnny a new baseball glove."

"She loves to spoil our boy," I say.

"Funny how Florence's rules never seem to apply to Florence," Eddie says with a chuckle. "Her plan has always been for us to buy something before Johnny starts high school, so we've probably got another year at Henderson House."

"Florence is the planner," Mr. Davis states.

"You've got that right!" Eddie agrees. "What was it Mama used to say?" he asks me.

"You can try to take Florence out of the plan, but you'll never take the plan out of Florence," I recite.

"So, if Eddie's the storyteller, and Florence is the planner, what's your role in the Blackwell Trio?" Mr. Davis looks directly at me.

I freeze. My throat tightens, and I swallow hard. I honestly don't know my role. I've never thought about it before. I look frantically to Eddie for support. If I try to speak without having a solid answer, I know I'll stutter. Experiencing my normal variety of panic with Mr. Davis is somehow comforting.

"That's easy, Mr. Davis," Eddie says. "Bessie's the glue. She's the only thing holding this family together."

My brother winks at me, and I relax. How Eddie comes up with these witty sayings off the top of his head is beyond me.

"Well, 'the glue' is getting sleepy," I announce. "I'm heading up. Thank you both for the wonderful stories earlier. It's going to be an entertaining summer with you two going head-to-head on the porch."

"My pleasure, sis. It's nice to have a reason to trot out some of the old favorites." He inclines his head to Mr. Davis.

"The pleasure is mine. I haven't had an evening like this since . . . " Mr. Davis pauses, his gaze resting on me. "Well, not in a long while. I should turn in as well. I've got another big day tomorrow."

The two of us stand at the same time.

"Think I'll sit out here for a bit longer and finish my smoke," Eddie says. He winks at me for a second time. "Good night, sis. Sweet dreams."

Once inside, Mr. Davis and I climb the stairs in silence. I sway slightly on my way up and our arms brush against each other. In an instant, the tingling returns. Only, this tingling is different because it comes with heat—a deep, penetrating warmth building in my chest. The hot and prickly sensation radiates down my arms, all the way out to the tips of my fingers. I move farther to the right side of the staircase, hugging the railing. I make a mental note to take an aspirin before bed. If I am coming down with a cold, I might be running a fever. Mr. Davis and I reach the top of the stairs and stop.

"Good night, Mr. Davis," I say. "I hope you enjoyed your welcome party."

"It's been a wonderful afternoon and a wonderful evening," he says, then pauses as if weighing his next words carefully: "full of surprises."

The corners of his mouth turn up tentatively as he fixes his gaze on mine. In this light, his eyes are more brown than green—deep and inviting. I hear myself responding in a voice I hardly recognize.

"Good surprises?" I ask, cocking my head to one side. Heaven help me. I'm flirting with a man at the top of the stairs—a divorced man, no less. What on earth has gotten into me?

"Yes, very good," Mr. Davis whispers as he takes a small step closer.

The soft sound of his voice ignites the warmth in my chest like a battery of firecrackers. The heat explodes into a hundred sizzling flashes of desire. An unexpected ache of longing surges through my body and transports me deep into the memory of another night of fireworks. Evening breezes, stolen kisses, and nervous laughter turn urgent and hungry in a tangled web of rumpled clothes, tall grass, and hot breath.

Over the years, I've decided this is not a painful memory. Everything about that night was perfect, aside from the fact it was all a lie. The pain came later. Why this memory at this moment? Mrs. Henderson always talks about signs. Is this memory a warning sign? A beacon on a lighthouse, helping me steer clear of the rocks?

"Good night, Mr. Davis." I push each word through my lips with as much detachment as I can muster, but I'm breathless, and as a result, my voice sounds sultry when I was hoping for disinterested.

"Good night, Miss Blackwell. Until tomorrow."

I don't let his words penetrate my defenses this time. I turn away and start toward the hallway. I don't hear a sound from Mr. Davis at the top of the stairs. The thought of him watching me walk down the hallway sends another wave of trembling through me. It's all I can do not to break into a run. Finally, I hear his footsteps moving in the other direction.

Once I'm inside my room, I fall back against the wall, grateful for some support. I turn on the lamp next to my dressing table, and amber light floods a small section of the floor. I must regain my composure. Sticking to my routine is always the best medicine when something sends me sideways, and I am most certainly sideways this evening.

I slide the upholstered bench out from under my dressing table and take a seat. My evening routine starts here, at the only piece of furniture I own. As I run my fingers over the yellow and orange stripes in the wood, my breathing returns to normal. I bought this dressing table at a secondhand shop in Bartlesville the weekend after I moved into Henderson House. The drawer on the left holds my letters, prayer book, and Bible. The drawer on the right is home to my small collection of jewelry. The center panel lifts to reveal a mirror and a storage area that's perfect for organizing my hair and beauty aids—a place for everything and everything in its place. Yes. That's what I need to do. I need to put Mr. Davis in his proper cubby. He's another lodger at Henderson House, that's all. I will heed the warning sign. I will not crash into the rocks a second time. When I lift the center panel and lock the mirror into place, I'm shocked to see my rosy face and red, rash-like splotches on my neck. I close my eyes and pray.

Dear Lord in Heaven, I cannot keep secrets from you, for Thou hast possessed my reins and covered me in my mother's womb. Lord, I don't understand what's happening to me. I am attracted to a man I hardly know, having feelings and sensations I thought had long passed me by. And remembering people and experiences I put to rest years ago. Please, Lord, help me regain control of my senses and lead me to safety, for you are the true guiding light. In Jesus's name, Amen.

I look in the mirror again and put a hand to one of my flushed cheeks. My mind returns to the garden this afternoon: Mr. Davis's arms wrapping around me when I fell, heat rushing to more places in my body than just my face. Routine. I need to stick to my routine. I open the left-hand drawer, take out my dog-eared red leather notebook, and flip to the current page of my prayer list. After a moment of hesitation, I write the name "Frank Davis" under "Martha Williams" and my new assistant, "Doris Limbach." It's only right to pray for Mr. Davis as he starts his job at Phillips. I've prayed for every other new lodger who's come to Henderson House. Mr. Davis deserves the same.

Frank Davis. I look at the letters of his name. Frank Davis, I know so little about you. Maybe your divorce wasn't your fault. If your wife broke your marriage vows, you'd be free in the eyes of the Lord to remarry. Oh, what's the matter with me? I seem to have forgotten that I am the one who's not free. I promised Florence I would keep our secret about Johnny safe. I promised "on the bones" that I wouldn't say a word until Florence was ready for Johnny to know the truth. We argued about it again last weekend. I think we should tell him this summer, but Florence isn't ready yet. She's afraid of how Johnny will react. Until Florence releases me from my promise, I can't say a word. We agreed Florence would raise him. So, that's that. Even if I wanted to fall in love with Mr. Davis, I can't because I can't tell him the truth. It isn't love if one of the parties involved isn't completely honest. I learned that the hard way.

I leave the notebook open on the side of the dressing table and begin taking the bobby pins out of my hair. I place the pins neatly in their designated compartment. Once my hair is loose, I pick up my brush to begin my nightly ritual of praying for the people on my list while I brush my hair. But hard as I try, I can't start brushing and praying. Instead, my thoughts return to the top of the stairs, to Mr. Davis's eyes, the tingling, the memory. I turn the brush over and over in my hand.

"Oh, Mama," I whisper, "I'm a mess. I wish you were here to give me some of your good advice."

I close my eyes and picture my mama. We're cuddled together on the sofa in the sitting room above the Pack and Run. She's working patiently to get the knots out of my hair. Mama's young in this memory, maybe in her mid- to late twenties. I'm probably six or seven. Our house was happy then. Daddy hadn't started drinking yet. He was strict, but he wasn't mean. Mean came into the house with the whiskey.

Mama looks like a tiny angel in her white nightdress. She's petite, like Florence and I are. Her skin is fair with freckles on her nose and cheeks. Her green eyes dance in the lamplight while she brushes my hair. When I was little, my long, curly hair got tangled during my outdoor adventures. I used to love foraging for wild berries, especially huckleberries. Mama made the most delicious huckleberry bread. I'd come home with my hair looking worse than the bushes where I'd been harvesting.

Mama started an evening routine of brushing my hair and praying with me while she worked ever so gently on all those knots. We always started with thanksgiving—thanking God for everything we could think of. Then we would pray for the family, both in Oklahoma and Kansas. Next, we would move on to people who were struggling with illness or injury. On nights when my hair was particularly ornery, we would end up laughing as we tried to think of anything else we could pray for, like flower seeds or robin's eggs—anything to keep us praying while she worked.

When Mama could run the brush smoothly through every inch of my hair, she would kiss the top of my head and say, "Amen." This is the picture of her I hold in my heart. This memory always sets me to rights. I try not to think about how Mama looked when she was so sick with the Spanish flu. I try not to remember the eleven days when I brushed her hair. Both my mama and my baby sister, Mae, gone in only eleven days.

And God shall wipe away all tears from their eyes, and there shall be no more death, neither sorrow, nor crying. Neither shall there be any more pain, for the former things are passed away.

Yes. The former things are passed away. I close my eyes and take a few deep breaths. My shoulders rise and fall, rise and fall again. I open my eyes and return my gaze to the mirror. I am myself again. I am the glue. I look down at the names on my list. Frank Davis. A new lodger at Henderson House. I start brushing and praying, as I always do.

WEDNESDAY
MAY 21, 1941

CHAPTER NINE

Mrs. Henderson

"SO, MISS BESSIE didn't stick around to visit after dinner last night?" Edna says, filling the half sections of each hard-boiled egg with the precision of a surgeon.

Her deviled eggs have won more awards than I can remember, including the blue ribbon at the Washington County Fair last year. Her secret? She puts a little of her homemade sweet relish in the yolk mixture.

"No. She excused herself politely and went straight up to her room. Said she had some reading to catch up on."

I pull open the oven to check on my cornbread and hot dog casserole—not quite the golden color I like. A few more minutes should do the trick. This dish is always a hit with the kids at the Wednesday Night Supper.

"Hmm. She missed *The Pepsodent Show.* Everybody knows she loves listening to Bob Hope on Tuesday nights." Edna starts moving the eggs to a pan lined with wax paper for transport. "And you're sure there's something brewing between her and Mr. Davis?"

"In all my days, Edna, I've never seen two people's colors reach out for each other like I saw on Monday night."

"She stayed up late on Monday, settin' out on the porch with everyone having a good old time, right?"

"As good a time as I've ever seen. She was making conversation as if she'd known Mr. Davis forever. I think they went on telling stories for almost an hour after I turned in. I could still hear them laughing as I fell asleep."

I reach for the pot holders.

"Well, that's it then." Edna shakes her head.

"What's it?"

I transfer the large casserole dish out of the oven and onto the top of the stove. It looks perfect. I turn the oven off.

"She likes him." Edna reaches for the paprika and lightly dusts the tops of the eggs. "But—she—is—a—fraid—to—like—him," she says, emphasizing each syllable with a dash of red spice.

"I think you're onto something, Edna." I hang the pot holders back onto their hook. "On Monday evening, I got the feeling things were chugging along full speed ahead; now she's deliberately throwing the train in reverse." I move over to the sink. "I've always known Bessie carries a load of heartache behind her sweet smile—a difficult father, the loss of her mother and baby sister, then the unexpected death of her dear sister Rachel. But for the first time, I'm wondering if someone broke her heart."

"Like a lover?"

"Exactly. We've always assumed men make Bessie nervous because she has limited experience around them. But what if we're wrong? What if men make Bessie nervous because she's afraid she might fall in love again?"

"Oh," Edna says. Her eyes dart back and forth as she considers my new spin on the situation. "And she doesn't want to fall in love because the last man broke her heart." Edna opens the icebox and carefully places the full pan of deviled eggs inside. "But in all these years, Bessie's never mentioned an old flame to me," Edna says, challenging my theory. She wipes her hands on her apron and begins bringing the dirty bowls and utensils over to me at the sink.

"Nor to me. However, my gut tells me I'm right." I start washing.

"Your gut rarely makes a mistake. But you said Mr. Davis is divorced. Isn't that reason enough for her to distance herself?"

"The fact that he's divorced is troubling. If she knew the details of why his marriage ended and if it wasn't his fault, that might turn things back in the right direction."

"They need time alone to get to know each other," Edna declares. "Mr. Davis isn't going to tell her about his divorce right out of the starting gate."

"How do we get them to spend time alone when she's actively avoiding him?" I ask.

"When Mr. Davis drives us to the church, Johnny will want to sit up front so he can study all the dials on the dashboard. Bessie will naturally want to sit up front with Johnny. You and I will sit in the back with the food. Why don't you suggest the seating plan when we're heading out to the car, just to make sure?"

"Okay."

I watch her formulate her plan. She is one of the few people on this earth who can tell me what to do. Edna's color is so consistent—the same strong shade of purple, every day.

"But won't Johnny want to sit in the middle?" I ask as I visualize her seating arrangement.

"Yup, I suppose he will. When we get to the church, you'll ask Johnny to hop out and help us unload, and then you'll suggest Bessie rides with Mr. Davis, so she can show him where to park."

Edna grabs a fresh dish towel and takes her usual stance on my left—ready to dry.

"I see where you're going with this. They'll be alone in the car. But the walk from the parking lot isn't going to take more than a few minutes," I say.

"True, but we've got to help them start somewhere."

The gravel in the driveway crunches as a car pulls in.

"It's Mr. Davis. He's home from work."

A car door slams, followed by footsteps walking up the back path toward the kitchen.

"Howdy, Edna, Mrs. H. Is it all right for me to come in and out through the back door?" he asks.

"Absolutely, Mr. Davis. I want you to feel like this is your home, not a hotel. You don't need to use the front door unless it's more convenient for you," I respond, handing Edna the small blue and white mixing bowl to dry. It's my favorite, the one I always used to make a separate batch of egg salad for my son Will—with extra onions.

"Thank you. Your hospitality is much appreciated. My room in San Francisco never felt like home. It sure smells good in here. What are we bringing to the church tonight?" Mr. Davis peers at the countertops.

"Oh, just the usual," Edna begins, "Mrs. H's cornbread and hot dog casserole, my famous deviled eggs, and a nice plate of oatmeal raisin cookies."

"It's making me hungry already." He reaches for a cookie, and Edna tuts at him.

"Would you like a celery stick to tide you over?" I offer.

"That would be great, thanks."

I extend the celery plate, and he takes a stalk and settles in on a stool at the end of the peninsula. I study Mr. Davis for a moment. He looks as comfortable in my kitchen as someone who's lived here for three years, not three days.

"Is there anything I can do to help?" he asks.

"Oh, no. We're just tidying up a bit and then we need to put together cold supper plates for Florence, Eddie, and something for Professor Rutledge to take to work." I hand another knife to Edna to dry.

"Other than a quick hello at suppertime, I have yet to converse with the elusive Professor Rutledge. He seems like quite a character."

"Oh, he's a character, all right," Edna grumbles as she gestures with the knife.

"Edna is not as fond of Professor Rutledge as the rest of us." I begin putting the dishes away.

"Says someone who's growing very fond of him lately." Edna bats her eyelashes at me.

I wave her teasing away. I should have known I couldn't keep my deepening affection for the professor hidden from Edna. Saturday is quickly becoming my favorite day of the week, knowing I'll be spending it with him.

"Why doesn't Edna like the professor?" Mr. Davis asks me between celery crunching.

"Well, when he first arrived, he made a few, um, a few controversial remarks about some of Edna's cooking," I say.

"A few? A few?" Edna's voice booms. "Humph, it was more than a few. As if someone should ever serve chicken-fried steak with brown gravy instead of white gravy. Everybody knows you serve country-fried steak with brown gravy and chicken-fried steak with white. Ridiculous!"

Mr. Davis chuckles. "I'll file that away for future reference. Thanks, Edna. A poetry professor working as a night watchman is a bit unusual."

"I'll say. He graduated from Princeton and taught literature at the University of Chicago before moving to Oklahoma with his wife. She wanted to live closer to her mother in Sapulpa. He taught at the University of Tulsa for years before his wife passed on unexpectedly." I pull the tinfoil out of a drawer.

"I wonder how Mrs. Fuller's big trip to Tulsa went today," Mr. Davis says.

"I've been wondering about that, too. She may already be on the bus home."

I cover the casserole and then wrap it in a couple of large dish towels so it will stay warm and we can carry it out to the car without pot holders.

"How long is the trip?" he asks, taking another piece of celery.

"A direct bus would take a little over an hour. With stops, it could be longer," Edna answers.

"I'm sure she'll be here when we get back from the church, and she'll be dying to tell us all about it." I wipe down the counters.

"Yes, in great detail," Edna chirps.

"Now, Edna," I glance sideways at her.

"You know it's true, Mrs. H," Enda says and then turns to Mr. Davis. "Florence Fuller loves the spotlight."

"Florence has had more than her share of sorrow," I say to Edna. "We need to have compassion for her, even if she requires extra . . . " I pause, looking for the right word. "Attention." I walk over to the dinette and take a seat. It feels good to get off my feet.

Mr. Davis turns on his stool to face me. "Did you meet Florence's husband before he passed away? Did they ever come to visit Miss Blackwell?"

"No. I never met him. To be honest, I don't know much about John Fuller. For all the stories the Blackwell family loves to tell, they don't tell many about him," I say. "Florence ran away to marry John as soon as she turned eighteen. I guess her father didn't approve of the match. As newlyweds, they lived in Claremore and worked at a hotel owned by John's family."

Edna jumps in: "Then John went off to serve in the war. And when he returned, he wasn't, well, you know, he wasn't the same." She joins me at the little red and white table in the window.

"A lot of guys came home shell-shocked," Mr. Davis says solemnly. "It's a bonafide condition, no matter what anyone says."

"Who knows what plagued John Fuller? Florence has never confided in me."

"She never confides in anyone," Edna says under her breath.

"Bessie told me Florence's husband struggled to return to his former life working at the hotel. Sometimes he would go off on his own for weeks at a time," I say.

"He was drinking," Edna interjects while tipping her head and her hand back, as if chugging liquor.

"Perhaps. Anyway, at some point, Bessie, Florence, and their sister Rachel left Claremore and moved to Wichita to live with their aunt Maude."

"Their mother's sister," Edna clarifies. "Johnny was born there, not in Oklahoma." Edna pops up and heads back to the peninsula. She rarely sits for more than a minute.

"Florence's husband joined her and little Johnny in Wichita not long after the baby was born," I add.

"After they got settled, Bessie moved to Bartlesville," Edna adds as she wipes down the counters.

"I think Florence believed a baby would be enough to bring her husband back to his senses," I say.

"But it didn't," Mr. Davis concludes.

"I think it did for a while, but John continued to struggle." I sigh. "A few months before Johnny turned four, Florence got a telegram from the authorities in Topeka informing her that her husband had died in an accident."

"Drowned," Edna says. "He jumped off a bridge and drowned. He was probably drunk."

"It didn't say that he jumped or that he was drunk in the telegram, Edna. It said it was an accident," I point out.

"And that's when Florence and Johnny moved here?" Mr. Davis asks.

"Yes, that's when Bessie invited them to Henderson House," I say. "After the news of John's death."

"Wow, I sure feel for her. It's hard when you have a dream of things working out and then, well, things don't work out."

"Sounds like you might have some experience with heartbreak, Mr. Davis," Edna prods.

"Yes, Edna, unfortunately I do." He pauses. "I already told you I'm divorced. The fact of the matter is, putting an end to your marriage is easy—it's just paperwork—but putting an end to all the rest of it, all those little dreams about the future, that's the hard part."

A mix of dark and light yellow swirls around Mr. Davis—a soul in flux. Mr. Davis continues to surprise me. He's so forthcoming to have only known us for a few days. Then again, Henderson House has a way of opening people up.

"Is it ever too late for new dreams?" he mutters to himself.

"No, siree Bob. It's never too late," Edna answers without hesitation. "Is it Mrs. H?"

"Oh, no. Never too late," I agree.

"So, how long has the church been holding Wednesday Night Suppers?" He changes the topic of conversation and, once again, his color stabilizes almost immediately. Mr. Davis is resilient.

"Oh, we started the Wednesday Night Suppers back in the early thirties. Lots of folks were out of work by then, though the oil business helped Bartlesville fare better during the Depression than most parts of Oklahoma," I say.

"Everyone brought what they could on Wednesdays, and if there were times you couldn't bring anything to share, no one paid any mind." Edna walks over to the icebox. She starts pulling out leftover chicken, green beans, and cucumber-tomato salad to make cold supper plates.

"Yup, we stopped passing the offering plate during the service," I say. "Put a money box in the vestibule instead."

Bessie slips through the swinging door without a sound, spies Mr. Davis on the stool, and freezes. For a moment, I'm afraid she'll sneak back out before he sees her, but to my relief, she stays put. She presses her back against the doorframe as if to steady herself or to keep her distance. I'm not sure which. Maybe it's a bit of both.

"Wednesday nights became a wonderful time of fellowship and support for this community," Edna says.

When Mr. Davis turns to listen to Edna, he sees Bessie in the doorway and his face lights up.

"We found out more about who needed help at those suppers than we did at any other time during the week," Bessie speaks from her spot against the doorjamb, her gaze landing softly on Mr. Davis.

"How true, Bessie," I affirm. "Seems like over a meal is always the best way to find out what's really going on—who's sick, who's hungry, who's lonely."

"Amen to that," Edna nods.

With Edna standing at the counter, Bessie at the doorway, and me seated at the dinette, Mr. Davis's neck is getting quite a workout as he follows the conversation. There is a nervous energy in the room, and I sense that the house is thoroughly enjoying it. Mr. Davis's color is noticeably brighter since Bessie entered the room. And look at that—so is Bessie's. Let's keep this conversation going.

"We were still holding services in the basement back then," I say. "After the church experienced a second fire, we tore down the original building and made room to build a larger church with a basement, but since the economy was so slow, we made little progress. The basement was the only usable space in the new building."

"For years, everything happened in the basement," Edna says, and Frank turns his head to her. "Worship, Sunday school, weddings, Wednesday Night Suppers—all in the basement. Oh, there were architectural plans and plenty of meetings . . . "

"Lots and lots of meetings," Bessie contributes with a smile.

"But we had to keep pushing the start of construction back because we didn't have the funding," I continue. "Then, something wonderful happened. In 1937, an anonymous benefactor paid off the mortgages of the five major churches in Bartlesville—including ours."

"That's incredible!" Mr. Davis throws his hands up in the air.

"Yes, it was. Of course, everybody knew the anonymous friend was none other than Mr. Frank Phillips," Edna explains.

"He paid off the mortgages of five churches? No wonder people in Bartlesville love him so much," Mr. Davis says, his eyes landing on Bessie once more.

She returns his gaze briefly and then looks down at her skirt and starts fussing with a loose thread. More church talk. She loves to talk about the church.

"Yes, after he paid off the mortgage, we completed a large auditorium with a balcony," I say.

"And we installed a beautiful organ." Bessie looks up at Mr. Davis again. "We dedicated the new building with a week-long celebration, full of thanksgiving and wonderful music. The church has grown so much in the past few years. We have over fourteen hundred members," she reports.

"Fourteen hundred! Well, I hope the entire congregation isn't coming for supper tonight. I want to make sure I get one of those deviled eggs!" Mr. Davis exclaims, and we all laugh.

"Don't worry, Mr. Davis, I will make sure there's one left for you," Edna says, pointing at him.

"Thanks, Edna. I suppose I should freshen up. I wouldn't want you to be embarrassed by your driver this evening." He gets up and heads toward Bessie at the door.

She's motionless for a moment, standing directly in his path, and then she pushes the door open and skips out of the way, looking more like a teenager than a middle-aged woman. Eddie has told us countless stories about Bessie's adventures growing up in Indian Territory. Now, I believe them all. An adventurous, spirited girl is still in there, and Mr. Davis seems to be coaxing her out.

"Mr. Davis, do you mind knocking on Johnny's door before you come back down? We should plan on leaving soon. Edna and I like to arrive a little early," I say.

"Absolutely, I'd be happy to," he says, giving Bessie one more smile.

The door swings closed. Bessie stands staring at the spot where he passed.

"How was your day, Miss Bessie?" Edna puts the cold supper plates into the icebox.

"Oh, my day was fine," Bessie says. She wanders over to the dinette and takes the chair next to mine.

"Hmm, yes, and it's not over yet." Edna glances at Bessie out of the corner of her eye, and I watch Bessie smile. It's her teenager smile. I'm sure of it.

CHAPTER TEN

Florence

I DIDN'T EXPECT the Tulsa bus station to be crowded on a Wednesday evening, but people of all ages scurry about the terminal while departure and arrival announcements ring through the air. A young mother in line behind me struggles to hold on to her small valise and her squirming toddler. The line moves slowly through door number three, toward the Bartlesville bus. I don't envy her traveling alone with a child. The day I took Johnny on the train from Wichita to Bartlesville, I was afraid he would break away from me, get lost at the station, and I'd never see him again. I feared he might fall onto the tracks and get run over. No one tells you how terrifying it is to be a mother. The woman bumps into me, and I lose my footing for a moment.

"I'm so sorry," she apologizes.

"Don't you worry about a thing," I say. "You two go ahead, please." I step slightly out of line so she can proceed in front of me.

"Thank you." She offers me a weary smile as the little boy, who appears determined to get onto the bus by himself, refuses her help and resorts to climbing up the stairs on his hands and knees. He's ruining his traveling clothes.

I take a window seat toward the front of the bus, far away from the fidgeting boy and his frazzled mother. I hope no one chatty chooses the seat next to me. I have a lot of planning to do on the way home. If I pretend that I'm sleeping, perhaps no one will bother me. I lean back and close my eyes.

My thoughts are all a jumble. I met so many new people today. Aaron Linn officially offered me the position as store manager at our meeting after lunch. I asked him if I could talk it over with my family and give him my answer on Monday, but I already know I want the job and I want us to move. I loved Tulsa from the minute I stepped off the bus this morning. I could feel the excitement of the city right away. Tulsa is almost ten times the size of Bartlesville—over one hundred and forty thousand people!

Who would choose sleepy little Bartlesville over the hustle and bustle of Tulsa?

Bessie might.

No one sits next to me, and the bus departs the station. As the bus winds its way north to Bartlesville, I lay out my plans. The family doesn't know I was in Tulsa for a job interview today. If I tell them about the job offer tonight, it will be clear I was keeping it from them on Monday. However, if I wait to tell them about the job offer, say, until Saturday, it might seem like the folks in Tulsa offered me a job after meeting me. I want to break the news to Bessie and Eddie first. If I tell them Saturday during our trip to Claremore, Johnny won't be there. He'll be working his first day at the golf club. I like the idea of getting Bessie and Eddie on board before I tell Johnny. Poor Johnny! He's so excited about his job at the country club. He will not want to leave Bartlesville this summer, but Aaron Linn wants me to start by the end of June. We'll need to move in a few weeks.

As I hoped, my new position as a manager includes vacation time. I've never had a day off with pay in my entire life. I know the first place we'll go on holiday—the beach. I look out the bus window and let myself daydream.

I can picture the whole family driving down to the Texas coast and having a holiday in Galveston—walking on the sugar-colored sand, dipping our toes in the cool salty water, lounging in striped beach chairs, and eating seafood in one of those outdoor cafés with red umbrellas. Aunt Emma, my mama's youngest sister, sent us a postcard from Galveston a few years ago. It's an illustration of Galveston at night. People stroll along the seawall, and the moon reflects in the rippling water. None of us has ever seen the Gulf of Mexico or any large body of water, for that matter. I keep Aunt Emma's postcard in my bureau drawer. It reminds me of the postcards John and I used to collect from the Fuller's Hotel. Having been in the hospitality business for many years, John's parents knew people from all over, and folks would send them postcards from their travels. When we were first married, John and I loved to dream about taking trips. We always kept a stack of postcards on the little table in our apartment to inspire us.

I lean my head against the bus window and close my eyes again. As soon as I do, I see John's face as clear as day. It's his youthful face. It's his face before the war. It's the face I fell in love with . . .

"Come on, Flossie, let's take a walk." Tall and lanky, John Fuller reaches his hand out toward mine.

I'm still getting used to his facial hair. It makes him look older than nineteen, which he says is an advantage working at the hotel. The early stubble isn't as dark as the thick brown hair on his head. His mustache is growing in with a reddish tint and looks dashing against his handsome pale complexion. John's face isn't tanned and leathery—one of the many benefits of non-farm work. His hands are soft, too, not rough and calloused. I held hands with Rufus McAvoy once, and they were like burlap. John's hands are like silk.

"What if someone sees us, John?" I roll my eyes but take his hand anyway.

My small hand fits so completely in his, I'm sure we're made for each other. We've been going steady for almost two years, but we've had to keep it quiet because my father doesn't approve.

"We can sit on our bench by the library. No one is going to see us. I've got something I want to talk to you about." He swings my hand and leads me down the path toward our favorite bench under a large sycamore tree.

Once we take a seat, John turns to face me.

"Flossie, things are going very well for me at the hotel. My folks are letting me fix up the apartment out back—for us. We've always talked about how someday, when you and I get married, you'll come and work at the hotel with me. Well, with your birthday coming up and all, I've been wondering if maybe someday might be just around the corner." He stares at me with his big brown eyes.

"What do you mean?" I ask.

"I think I'm asking if you're ready to marry me—that is, once you turn eighteen."

"Oh, John! Are you really proposing?" I ask.

"I suppose so, yes," he answers.

"Then I think you need to ask me properly."

"Oh, right." He clears his throat. "Florence Lucille Blackwell, I love you. Will you marry me?"

"I will!" I say, throwing my arms around his neck.

The safe warmth of our embrace fades into the green of the leaves and the blue of the sky and then dissolves into a pair of blue checkered curtains as a new scene comes into focus.

Now, I am sitting at the kitchen table in the back room of the Pack and Run. The entire family is gathered—Mama, Rachel, little Mae, Eddie, and Bessie. We are having supper, but Daddy is screaming. He's screaming at me, and I'm not letting the words get in. Instead, I'm thinking about what my new life will be like as John's wife. Working at a hotel will be much more interesting than helping at the Pack and Run. I'll meet new people from all over the country, maybe even the world. At a hotel, you never know who might walk in. At the Pack and Run, I am stuck with the same people day after day, including my daddy.

The biggest problem with Daddy's outbursts is that they are unpredictable. Sometimes he can go weeks without attacking one of us. Other weeks he can be drunk and angry about something every night. Not knowing when he might explode is the hardest part—the fear is enough to spoil even a good day. It always starts the same way. He begins by questioning one of us at the supper table. At some point, his tone changes, and he builds up to screaming. Once he is screaming, like he is screaming at me now, we never know if he will wind up pulling one of us into the corner. Anytime he drags me to the corner, odds are pretty good I'll end up getting smacked.

He picks on me and Bessie the most. I figure it's because we're older than the other children—we're more satisfying to torment. Bessie thinks it's because we're a disappointment to him and we need to try harder to be "good."

She takes everything he says to heart—as if trying to be good would make a difference to a drunk man. When Daddy fires questions at Bessie across the supper table, she tenses up and stutters. Then he makes fun of her halting speech. He's constantly telling her she'll end up an old maid because no man wants to marry a woman who's too scared to answer a simple question.

I figured out early on that it's easier not to listen to his spiteful words. On the nights when he screams at me, I see his red face and his angry mouth moving, but I never hear a word he says. Like right now, I'm thinking about Mrs. Fuller's collection of store-bought dresses she wears to work at the hotel. There's an emerald-green one I'm fond of. I wonder if we're the same size.

When I started dating John Fuller, Daddy was furious with me. He yanked me from the dinner table, pushed me into the corner, and yelled at me when a neighbor told him we'd been sitting together at church. He cornered and slapped me when the farmer down the road reported they had seen us holding hands in town. Those darn gossiping men at Cowboy Coffee Hour have no idea what their idle chitchat costs me come suppertime.

Now, Daddy stands and pulls me up out of my chair by my shoulders. He pushes me into the corner. My arms ache where he grabbed me. He holds on to my chin so I can't break eye contact with him. He's really mad about something. Like rain working its way through a hole in the roof, his words drip into my ears.

"I drove into Claremore today, and I told those uppity city folks no daughter of mine is going to marry their lazy, good-for-nothing son. I know all about your plans to get married after your birthday, Flossie, and I'm telling you it's over. It's all settled."

He's so enraged, he is spitting on me as he screams. His breath reeks. He's been drinking more than usual. How did he find out? Those snitches at Cowboy Coffee Hour, no doubt. My chest feels tight and hot.

"No, it's not all settled," I say, talking back to him. "John and I have plans to marry."

He slaps me hard across the face. My nose breaks open and starts bleeding. I instinctively cup my hands over my face to keep the blood from staining my favorite blue and white pinafore. For all his storytelling fame and his faithful audience around the cookstove, he's nothing but a drunk and a bully. In a single movement, I place both of my bloody hands on my daddy's chest, and I push him away as hard as I can. He stumbles back in surprise, and his boot catches on the edge of a kitchen chair. He falls backward and lands on his rump.

Free from the corner, I race out the kitchen door, dart around the back of the shed, and run down the overgrown footpath to Mrs. Redbird's farmhouse on the allotment next to ours. Minnie Redbird is friendly with John's mother and goes to church with us in Claremore. I must be quite a sight when I arrive on her side porch—no bobby pins left in my hair, my face swollen and dripping with perspiration, my hands covered in blood.

Mrs. Redbird walks out her kitchen door onto the porch, wiping her hands on her apron. I try to speak, but I can't. All I can do is sob. She puts her arms around me and ushers me inside. She sits me down at her kitchen table and begins gently washing my face and hands with warm water. It takes several wash basins of clean water and I don't know how many rags to rid me of all the blood. Mrs. Redbird tells me to put a little petroleum jelly up my nose to stop the bleeding and gives me some lavender-scented lotion to use on my hands. We sell this lotion at the Pack and Run. It smells divine. She gives me one of her daughter's old dresses to put on and starts soaking the stains out of my blue and white pinafore.

Floating around her kitchen like a spirit from another world, Mrs. Redbird mutters to herself in Cherokee as she makes me a pot of tea. She has a single long braid of silver and black hair running down her back and a wrinkled yet kind face.

Her husband died several years ago, and her son and his wife live on her homestead and help her run the farm. She lives in this house by herself with three large dogs for company. The dogs are very interested in licking the lotion off my hands.

After pouring both of us a cup of tea, she joins me at the table. "You have a birthday coming up in a few days, don't you?" she asks.

"Yes, ma'am, I do." These are the first words I've spoken.

"And you'll be eighteen, I reckon." She nods.

"Yes, ma'am, I will."

"Well, my dear, you have a decision to make. You can walk home and apologize to your father, or you can stay here and use my telephone to call John Fuller at the hotel," she offers.

I'm shocked, not only by her unexpected understanding of my situation, but also because she has a telephone in her house. There's no way I'm apologizing to my daddy.

"I'd like to use your telephone, if I may," I say.

"Be my guest." She smiles and points toward her front parlor.

"I'm not sure how to place a call," I stammer as I stand up and hang on to the back of my chair, a little lightheaded.

"No worries, my dear. I can help you," she says as she rises and gently guides me forward.

The floorboards of the kitchen dissolve into a mix of grass and gravel as the scene changes once again.

I see Bessie walking up Mrs. Redbird's driveway with my mama's big old suitcase in her hand. It's the Saturday of my eighteenth birthday—my wedding day.

"You look wonderful!" Bessie exclaims as she puts down the suitcase, and we embrace. She squeezes me tighter than she ever has.

"Mrs. Redbird put warm wet pieces of fabric soaked in some sort of sassafras root mixture on my nose every day this week."

"It worked. You look beautiful, Florence. I've missed you."

"I've missed you, too," I say. "I stayed in Mrs. Redbird's daughter's old room all by myself this week. It was way too quiet without you and Eddie and Rachel and Mae. I had to invite the dogs to sleep with me, or I never would have gotten any rest."

"Has John arranged everything?"

"Yes, I've spoken with him on the telephone several times this week." I smile.

"Talking on the telephone with your fiancé—how glamourous!" Bessie smiles.

"He has the license, and the minister is all set to marry us at three o'clock."

"Mama convinced Daddy to drive her over to Collinsville today to look at a new line of dried meats, jams, and jellies," Bessie says. "Cousin Wahya is minding the store, and Rachel and Eddie are looking after Mae. I packed all of your books and clothes. You are in the clear."

"Thank you, Bessie."

"Mama's heartbroken she can't attend the ceremony, but she said the best gift she can give you is peace of mind. She promises Daddy will be nowhere near Claremore this afternoon." Bessie reaches out for my hand and gives it a squeeze. "I will be there with bells on, and we have gifts for you—gifts for your birthday and your wedding day." She pats the suitcase.

"Let's head inside," I say.

Bessie carries the enormous bag into Mrs. Redbird's kitchen.

"As a birthday gift, Mama would like you to have her suitcase, and she hopes you and John will have the opportunity to travel. She knows how much you want to see the world. Maybe you'll even take it to Florence, Italy, someday and finally see the city that shares your name."

"Oh, you know I love this old suitcase. Please thank her for me."

"You'll be able to thank her yourself. Mama's planning on bringing us down to Claremore for church as usual tomorrow. I doubt Daddy's going to find religion at this late date and decide to join us. She's hoping we can all have lunch together with you and your new husband after the service, if you can fit us into your busy married-lady schedule." She grins.

"That sounds perfect," I say, blinking away a few tears.

I've felt so isolated from my family this week, but once I'm married, Daddy won't be able to do anything about it, and I can have my family back.

"Now, for your wedding present." Bessie sets the suitcase flat on the floor, turns the knobs, and presses them to unlock it. She lifts the top of the suitcase and pulls out my peach-colored dress. They've altered it. "Mama and I added layers of lace to make it a proper wedding dress."

I can't stop the tears now. "I love it, Bessie. It's beautiful." I hold the dress up to myself as Mrs. Redbird enters the kitchen.

"Hello, Bessie. What a lovely wedding dress!" Mrs. Redbird turns to me. "Everything is ready for your special day. Florence, it's time for you to make a fresh start."

The bus sways, and my head bumps up against the window. I open my eyes and take in my surroundings. I am on the bus from Tulsa to Bartlesville, but I still hear Mrs. Redbird speaking to me.

Florence, it's time for you to make a fresh start.

CHAPTER ELEVEN

Bessie

PUTTING MR. DAVIS in his proper compartment hasn't been as easy as I'd hoped. I remind myself every hour on the hour that he's just another lodger at Henderson House, but the message doesn't seem to be sinking in. Keeping my distance helps, which is why I went up to my room last night after supper. But I can't avoid Mr. Davis completely—we live in the same house. He walked out of the kitchen a moment ago and, when we were close enough to touch, I felt the warmth of his body seeping into mine. My knees turned to jelly again.

Mrs. Henderson smiles at me from across the table as if she can hear my thoughts. Once again, I'm an open book. Proverbs says, "He who walks with the wise will become wise," and I'm looking at two of the wisest women I know.

"I need your help," I say.

Edna rushes over to the table and takes the seat on the other side of me

"Oh, Bessie," Mrs. Henderson says, "we're here for you."

"I think I'm attracted to Mr. Davis."

"Well, it's clear he's smitten with you," Mrs. H replies.

"What?" I croak.

"He practically lit up like a Christmas tree when you came into the kitchen," Edna says. "We were sharing a little with him about Florence and how things didn't quite work out for her and her husband, and Mr. Davis said something about knowing how hard it is when you hope something will work out and it doesn't. And then he asked us if we thought it was ever too late for new dreams!"

"And you think those new dreams have something to do with me?"

"Yes," they say in perfect unison, beaming at me.

"I'm not the young starlet in some romantic matinee double feature." I throw my hands up in the air, and they land on the table with a thud.

"True, you're no Rita Hayworth," Edna responds. "You're more like Olivia de Havilland. What was that movie we saw where Jimmy Cagney ended up with Olivia's character, the less glamorous friend, and then he realized she was the one for him all along?"

"*The Strawberry Blonde*," Mrs. Henderson answers.

"Olivia de Havilland is twenty-five years old," I point out.

"But only five foot three," Edna counters.

"I'm a mess when it comes to men. Plus, there are . . ." I hesitate, unsure how to start down this path. "Obstacles," I say, finally.

"You're not a mess, Bessie, at least not where Mr. Davis is concerned. You were completely charming a few minutes ago, chatting with all of us," Mrs. Henderson says. "Are you hesitating because he's divorced?"

"His divorce is one concern."

Mrs. Henderson closes her eyes for a moment and then opens them slightly as she speaks. "We don't know the details surrounding Mr. Davis's first marriage," she says. "My intuition tells me he didn't have a choice in the matter."

"I think you should relax and give yourself permission to get to know him better," Edna encourages. "If it turns out the divorce wasn't his fault, would that ease your mind?"

"Partially," I say.

"What else is holding you back, honey?" Mrs. Henderson asks. "You know you can tell us anything." She leans across the table and takes both my hands in hers.

"You know how you're always looking for signs? Well, I think I saw one Monday night telling me not to get involved with Mr. Davis," I say.

"Really?" Mrs. Henderson releases my hands and sits back in her chair, a look of surprise on her face. "Tell me about it."

"So, I was at the top of the stairs saying good night to Mr. Davis, and I got all tingly."

Edna can't control a giggle of excitement. Mrs. H shoots her a "be quiet" look.

"Continue, please," Mrs. H says.

"When I was all tingly, a memory popped into my head. A memory I normally keep tucked away."

"Was it a bad memory?" Mrs. Henderson asks, her voice soft and gentle.

"No. It was the memory of a very special night. But it's a memory from a romance that ended terribly for me."

Silence fills the kitchen as Edna and Mrs. Henderson wait for me to continue. Other than a few conversations with Florence, I've never talked to anyone about my relationship with Doc Jenkins.

"I once loved a man, and I thought he loved me," I say quietly, "but he was leading me on. He talked about marrying me—even described the ring he was going to buy me. But that ring was already on another woman's finger."

My words hang in the air surrounding the kitchen table. Mrs. Henderson looks like she's rereading them, as if my heartbreak is printed in invisible ink over my head. When she finishes, she looks back down at me.

"Honey, I'm so sorry." She reaches over to pat my hand. "And you think this specific memory appeared to warn you away from Mr. Davis?"

"What else could it mean?" I ask.

"Well, in my experience, a sign is usually an angel pointing you in the right direction, not steering you away from trouble."

"The right direction," I repeat to myself.

"You said you were tingling when the memory appeared, correct?"

I nod silently.

"And was there . . ." she pauses and gives me a delicate smile, ". . . tingling happening in the memory?"

I nod again, and Mrs. Henderson squeezes my hands while she stares at me—not directly into my eyes, but at the space around my face.

"I think your feelings for Mr. Davis opened a door, Bessie. A door to a part of you you've kept locked for a long time. I don't think the memory was a warning sign. It was an invitation to walk back through that open door and give love another chance."

A look of concern slowly replaces the sweet smile on Mrs. Henderson's face. "There's something else keeping you from moving forward," she says.

After all these years, I know I shouldn't be surprised by Mrs. Henderson's powers of perception, but I'm still amazed. How can she know?

"I have secrets I can't share with Mr. Davis," I say, looking down at the table. "Secrets I can't even share with you."

"Oh, I wouldn't worry about that now," Edna says, rising from her chair to stand behind me. She pats and rubs my shoulders like a coach getting ready to send me into the game. "You'll have plenty of time to figure out if Mr. Davis needs to know your secrets once you get to know each other. Take it one step at a time. Getting to know each other is the first order of business."

Johnny interrupts our heart-to-heart as he strolls into the kitchen, followed by Mr. Davis. In a pale blue shirt and a navy-and-maroon-striped tie, Mr. Davis is sure to be the handsomest man at the church supper. He smiles at me from across the kitchen, and when I return his smile, every nerve in my body springs to life. Is Mrs. Henderson right? Has Mr. Davis opened the door for me to love again?

Dear Lord, thank you for the love and wisdom of loyal friends. I would like to walk through this open door, get to know Mr. Davis better, and if it's your will, be completely honest with him someday. Guide me, Lord, on this unfamiliar path. Amen.

"My, what a fine driver we have for this evening," Mrs. Henderson says, making a small curtsy.

"At your service, m'lady," Mr. Davis says in a terrible English accent as he tips his hat. Laughter rolls around the kitchen.

"I was thinking," Mrs. H starts, "Bessie and Johnny should sit up front, and Edna and I should sit in the back with the food."

"Sounds good to me," Johnny says as he heads over to the back door.

"I'll scoot out first," Mr. Davis says, "and help everyone get in."

Johnny holds the screen door open for Mrs. Henderson and Edna as they walk out with the casserole and deviled eggs. I carry the cookies. Mr. Davis holds the back passenger door open. Mrs. Henderson hands him her towel-wrapped casserole as she slides into the back seat, and he hands the casserole back to her. Then he repeats the process with Edna and the deviled eggs. Next, he opens the right-side passenger door. Johnny slides over to the middle, and I scooch in next to him. Mr. Davis makes sure I'm all the way in with the cookies before closing the door.

The interior of the automobile is incredible. The deep bench seat has a high back and is upholstered in a soft gray fabric. It's as comfortable as Mrs. Henderson's sofa. The dashboard is green and tan with plenty of dials and knobs. For once, my nephew appears to be speechless. Mr. Davis starts the engine. The car rumbles to life, and we're off.

"What a smooth ride," Edna says from the back seat.

"She's a real beauty, Mr. Davis," Johnny adds.

"Thanks, Johnny. I agree. So, I've been wondering about something—do you have a special dish you cook for the Wednesday Night Supper, Miss Blackwell?" he asks.

I hear Edna gasp and Mrs. Henderson nudging her to be quiet in the back seat. It's an honest question. All part of getting to know each other.

"Mr. Davis, I think it's fair to say I do very little cooking," I reply.

"Very little?" Johnny giggles. "I'm not sure I've ever seen Aunt Bessie boil an egg."

Edna swats at Johnny's head from the back seat.

"Ouch," he cries.

"Now, Johnny," Edna says, coming to my defense. "You've enjoyed Aunt Bessie's famous chipped beef gravy on toast many times."

"I suppose that is one of my best dishes," I agree.

"*Only dish* is more like it," Johnny snickers.

"Do you make real gravy with your chipped beef?" Mr. Davis asks, never taking his eyes off the road.

"Oh, no. I cheat and use evaporated milk," I confess. "Most people prefer me to stay out of the kitchen altogether," I explain. "There are plenty of family stories about how my mere presence ruined a chicken dinner, apple pie, or pan of cornbread."

"So, you don't cook at all?" he asks.

"Not really. No," I respond. "However, I'm not a believer in the saying, 'You can't teach an old dog new tricks.' If the right situation presented itself, I might enjoy learning my way around a kitchen someday," I say.

Edna coughs in the backseat, probably more from fear than surprise.

"You're not an old dog," Johnny says to me.

"Thank you, Johnny."

"And I'm sorry if I let the cat out of the bag about you not being able to cook." My nephew smiles sheepishly at me, and then turns to Mr. Davis. "Aunt Bessie may not be able to cook, but she sure can sing," he says. I do love this boy.

"Good to know. No cooking. Excellent singing," Mr. Davis says as if making mental notes. "Johnny, do you have many friends at church?"

I'm thankful for the subject change, though I think I handled the first round of getting-to-know-you questions rather well. It was almost fun.

"Mom and I are members at First Presbyterian Church," Johnny says. "So is Uncle Eddie. We come to the Wednesday Night Suppers with Aunt Bessie, but mostly I have friends at First Presbyterian, like my friend Tommy who helped me get the job at the golf course."

"Yes, we were all raised Presbyterian," I say. "Our mama, Jennie Belle Blackwell, was Scots-Irish and about as Presbyterian as they come. I joined the Baptist church when I moved to Bartlesville."

"And what a fine member of the church you are," Mrs. Henderson pipes up from the back seat for the first time during the ride. "Bessie completely reorganized our adult Sunday School over the past few years. I don't know what we would do without her."

"I had a lot of help," I say.

"Still, your background as a schoolteacher helped you take charge and get everyone moving in the right direction," she states.

"You were a schoolteacher," Mr. Davis says, not as a question but rather as another item to add to his notes.

"Yes, it was my first job, after Eddie—" I stop myself. "After I left the Pack and Run. When I finished eighth grade, several of my teachers encouraged me to continue my schooling. After high school, I sat for the teacher's examination and passed. I didn't start work as a teacher right away, but when the time was right, I secured a position in Claremore."

Oh dear, I'm rambling on and on. I need to ask Mr. Davis a getting-to-know-you question in return.

"How are you enjoying your new job, Mr. Davis?" It's a boring question, but at least it's a question.

"So far, so good," he says. "Everyone has been very welcoming, and there are some smart people working in the research department. I'm optimistic about what we can accomplish."

"I've never been inside the research facility. Is it a well-designed building?" I ask. Still boring.

"Oh, yes. It's fine. It's good for us engineers to have our labs and our privacy. Though it would be nice to work at headquarters. Then maybe you and I could have lunch together sometime."

An awkward silence fills the car, and I feel all tingly inside, but my legs are holding strong. I'm making significant progress on the whole weak-in-the-knees challenge since we got in the car.

"Here we are, Mr. Davis. If you pull over in front of the sidewalk, Johnny can help us unload and carry everything inside," Mrs. Henderson directs from the back seat. "Bessie, you ride along with Mr. Davis and show him where to park. We wouldn't want him to be uncomfortable finding the fellowship hall downstairs all by himself."

Mr. Davis pulls up to the curb and hops out to help the ladies in back. Johnny slides over behind Mr. Davis, gets out on the driver's side, comes around to open my door, takes the plate of cookies from me, and closes the door again. It feels strange to stay put in the car while everyone else is bustling and passing plates. Before I know it, Mr. Davis is back at the wheel.

"The parking area is down there to the right," I say.

We're alone in the car. My heart beats a little faster.

"This sure is nice," Mr. Davis says. "I enjoy driving folks around. Guess your brother and I have something in common in addition to storytelling." He pauses. "So, I was thinking, I don't have much to do this weekend, and I'd be honored to drive you and your family out to Claremore on Saturday for your early Decoration Day visit." His voice waivers. Is he nervous, too?

"Oh, Mr. Davis, it's such a long trip, and I can't imagine it would interest anyone but us," I say.

He pulls into a parking space and turns off the car. He turns to face me.

"Based on the Blackwell stories I've heard so far, I'm already interested. I'm curious to see Claremore, too. Please, Bessie, I'd like to take you."

I'm alone in a car with a divorced man who just called me by my first name. I grip the straps on my handbag tighter. "Well, if you're sure you have nothing better to do," I say, trying to determine if he's genuinely interested.

"There's nothing I'd rather do."

He grins, gets out of the car, and comes around to open my door. He offers me his hand, and I'm almost afraid to take it, given the effect touching Mr. Davis seems to have on me. Perhaps my gloves will protect my knees from giving out this time. I slip my gloved hand in his and rise to stand next to him.

"Thank you, Frank," I say, deliberately using his name in return.

He breaks into a smile that shines all the way through me to the back buttons on my blouse. We stand quietly for a moment. I lean against the car, and Frank puts his right hand on the roof next to me. In this early evening light, I can see his hazel eyes clearly through his round wire glasses. His eyes are equal parts green and brown with orange specks.

"May I ask what made you decide to become a Baptist?" he asks.

"Of course." I've told my conversion story many times. I always start with my friend Anna Porter and how I came to church with her to meet Mrs. Henderson. But if Frank and I are getting to know each other, there's more to the story.

"When we were little, Mama drove us to Claremore in the wagon to attend First Presbyterian Church," I begin. "I loved the beautiful stone building. Back then, the Presbyterians shared the church with the Methodists. We had the church on the first and third Sundays and Wednesday nights. The Methodists used the church on the second and fourth Sundays and Thursday nights. Mama called it the 'House of God,' and I used to imagine God and Jesus living in it like a father and son. Cooking and eating and reading and sleeping—sometimes having Presbyterian friends over and sometimes having Methodist friends over." Frank smiles and I continue. "I used to lie in bed and wonder if God and Jesus had a dog. We had a wonderful dog when I was little. Actually, he was my Cousin Wahya's dog. Anyway, I remember being pretty sure God and Jesus had a dog. Growing up, I thought Jesus only existed in the church and the pages of the Bible," I say.

"And then something changed?" Frank asks.

"My mama always said there are stories to share and stories to keep. This isn't a story I usually share," I say to the stones in the parking lot.

Frank puts two fingers under my chin and lifts my head back up so our eyes meet again.

"I'd like to think maybe you and I could tell each other anything," he says, and I nod in agreement.

"Well, I never understood how Jesus is everywhere until the night my mama asked me to leave home and take Eddie with me."

"Oh." Frank's eyes widen.

"My daddy was very strict and quick to anger. He had—" I search for the right word, "—outbursts, especially when he had been drinking. After Florence ran off and married John Fuller against his wishes, Daddy was angrier than I'd ever seen him, and for some reason, he took it out on Eddie." I pause.

"I'm so sorry, Bessie," Frank says.

"To the world, Billy Blackwell was an entertaining character who had a story about everything, but to his family, he was unpredictable and downright frightening." I sigh. I can't believe I'm telling Frank the truth about my daddy. "Eddie was only ten at the time, and I was about to turn twenty," I continue. My words flow like well water through a hole in a bucket. I can't stop them.

"One night after Daddy beat Eddie and then passed out on the sofa, Mama came to me and told me she had spoken to Pastor Gardner in Claremore, and he and his wife were expecting me and Eddie to show up on their doorstep any day. I packed a bag, gave my mama a hug, and snuck Eddie out of the house. It was a beautiful summer night. The moon was so bright, we had no trouble seeing as we walked the eight or nine miles to the minister's house. Eddie and I started singing as we often did while out walking together. We were alone, and then we weren't. Jesus was with us. It was as if he had caught up with us on the road and was walking right beside us, singing along."

"You raised Eddie from the time he was ten?" Frank asks.

"Yes. That's why I became a teacher, so I could provide for us. I took care of Eddie right up until he left to pursue his cowboy dreams."

"And in all that time, you never learned to cook?" he asks in a playful tone of amazement.

"Never," I say with a little laugh. "We lived in a boarding house with two meals a day. It was nothing like Henderson House, but it kept me safely out of the kitchen." I push off from the car and begin moving toward the church. "The day I visited this church for the first time, I was shocked they knew all about Jesus being with me." Frank walks beside me as I keep talking. "This church knows Jesus is everywhere, not just inside a certain building or a special book, but with me every minute of every day. During my first service here with Anna, I knew I had found a new church home and a new life in Christ." I sigh.

We take a few steps in silence. I thought I would feel anxious having shared something so deeply personal with Frank, but I don't. I feel lighter somehow. And hopeful. Maybe I could tell him my secrets someday.

Frank stops, and I turn to look at him.

"Bessie, thank you," he says.

"For what?"

"For sharing a story you normally keep." He offers me his right arm.

"You're welcome," I say. I accept his arm, and we walk together to the supper.

CHAPTER TWELVE

Mrs. Henderson

EDNA, JOHNNY, AND I wave to a few early birds as we scoot past the neat rows of tables and chairs in the fellowship hall. My ears tune to the banter streaming out of the doorway in the back corner—the church kitchen, my home away from home. As soon as we enter, Johnny says good evening to the Kitchen Ladies, puts the cookies down on the center table, and zips off in search of friends.

"Mildred, thank goodness you're here!" Bertie Crane bellows from the range.

The back wall of the church kitchen has a row of ivory cabinets and metal countertops punctuated by two high windows, a commercial-sized range, and an exhaust hood.

Bertie's white hair rests in a spiral bun suspended above the nape of her neck by an antique hairpin. She's stirring what I'm sure is another fabulous batch of homemade soup. The steam rising from the pot creates frizzy tendrils of loose curls around her long, narrow face.

"Put those things down and help me find the onion powder. It's in this kitchen somewhere, but no one can find it," she howls.

Originally from Wyoming, Bertie is a pioneer woman at heart. You always know where you stand with Bertie Crane. She was one of my first friends when I moved to Bartlesville. Our boys played ball together, and we spent many an afternoon happily chitchatting in the stands. Bertie, like the rest of the women in this kitchen, kept me moving forward when Charles died. She was one of my biggest supporters when I started the boardinghouse.

"Oh, Bertie, let Mildred get settled before you start bossing her around," Kitty Rogers instructs from the sink, where she's rinsing out pitchers to fill with sweet tea. A double enameled cast iron sink dominates the right side of the kitchen while the icebox and pantry command the left.

Kitty's closing in on eighty, but you'd never know it. Oklahomans hesitate to pick sides in the whole unsweetened iced tea versus sweet tea debate, but Kitty feels strongly that, being a member of the Southern Baptist Convention, our church should fall firmly in the sweet tea camp. And there is not a soul in this congregation who would question Kitty Rogers, especially when it comes to important religious matters, like sweet tea.

"We have news," Edna announces.

She puts down her deviled eggs and takes both of our pocketbooks to the vault. The Kitchen Ladies store their purses in the pantry during the Wednesday Night Supper and Coffee Hour on Sunday. As a result, we jokingly refer to the pantry as "the vault."

"Do tell," Kay Owens pipes up as she unwraps plates and platters and begins organizing them on the long metal worktable in the center of the kitchen. Kay groups similar items so some will go out to the buffet now, and some will replenish the tables as dishes become empty. Salads. Entrees. Sides. Desserts. Kay's got the Wednesday Night Supper staging process down to a science. She is by far the most fashionable Kitchen Lady. Her husband, Richard, is a successful commercial banker and loves to keep Kay decked out in the latest glitz and glamour. She looks dynamite in everything she wears. One of my favorite things about Kay, though, is that she couldn't care less about all the jewelry and fancy clothes. She's probably wearing a fifteen-dollar dress right now and hasn't even bothered to put on an apron.

"We have a new lodger at Henderson House," I say, moving over to the electric percolator. I'm still getting used to this machine. "His name is Frank Davis, and it seems as if . . ." I say, pausing long enough to make sure I have everyone's attention, ". . . as if he and Bessie have taken a shine to one another."

"What?" Dolly Tinker squeaks as she looks up from the cake she's frosting. "Our Bessie? She's never taken a shine to any of the men we've introduced her to. Never!"

Dolly turned eighty last month, and unlike Kitty, her age shows. She shrinks a little every week and for some unknown reason, as she gets smaller, her voice gets higher.

"Remember Bob Wilkins?" Bertie taps her wooden spoon on the side of the pot for emphasis.

"I sure do," Dolly chirps. "Poor man followed her around like a lost puppy dog. Sat next to her every chance he could. Remember the first time he asked her out to dinner? She practically had a nervous breakdown—stuttering while she turned him down. It was painful to witness," Dolly warbles, spinning the cake stand to make sure she hasn't missed any spots.

"Well, this is completely different! We've entered unfamiliar territory." Edna smiles as she picks up two salads and shuttles them out of the kitchen to the buffet tables in the hall.

"Give us the scoop on Mr. Davis," Kay demands. "Single? Widowed? Divorced?"

"Divorced," Edna says, returning to pick up two casseroles before heading into the fellowship hall again.

"We don't have many details, but it doesn't seem like he was the one who wanted the marriage to end," I explain.

I open the cupboard above the percolator to retrieve the coffee and spot the missing jar of onion powder hiding on the second shelf. It should be in the vault with the other spices. I pass the onion powder to Bertie, who sighs with relief.

"Divorced? Too bad. Too bad," Kitty tuts.

"And Mildred's right. He's still torn up about it." Edna somehow manages not to miss a beat in the conversation while shuttling food back and forth. It's funny how she only calls me Mildred when we are in the church kitchen; otherwise, I'm Mrs. H.

I pour a pitcher of water into the base of the percolator. "That's all we have to go on at the moment."

"Do you think his wife was unfaithful? If she was unfaithful, then he would be free to remarry in the church under Matthew 5:32," Bertie asserts.

"I suppose it's possible she was unfaithful, but he certainly hasn't let on as much to us. He only moved in on Monday, Bertie," I say.

"Of course, the state would marry them, but our Bessie would never marry outside the church's blessing," Dotty tweets.

Leave it to the Kitchen Ladies to get her all the way to the altar in less than five minutes.

"I bet she cheated on him. He must have been heartbroken," Kay moans.

"Well, there's no one sweeter than our Bessie to mend a broken heart." Kitty puts a wrinkled hand on Kay's shoulder.

Bertie scoffs at Kay's dramatic response and asks, "What do we know about him? Why did he move here? What does he do for a living?" She pours onion powder into her hand, adds a dash more, and then sprinkles it into the soup.

"He's originally from Missouri, had been living in San Francisco, and started a job as a research engineer in the aviation fuel division at Phillips this week," I say.

I double check the amount of water in the percolator, insert the rod and basket, and count the scoops of coffee carefully. I'm sure the coffee was too strong last week. Eddie said it was "strong enough to float a colt." These modern devices will be the death of me.

"A smart fellow, huh? Is he good looking?" Dolly gathers up the utensils from her frosting station.

"Oh, Dolly, looks aren't everything." Kay rolls her eyes.

"Easy for the prettiest girl in the room to say." Dolly shakes the cake knife in Kay's direction before putting it in the sink.

"We walk by faith, not by sight," Bertie says over her shoulder.

"The most important thing is that he and Bessie look comfortable together, and she is interested in getting to know him better." I secure the lid and plug in the percolator.

Every time I plug this contraption in, I say a brief prayer. I'm so used to making coffee on the stove, where you can see the flame and know the water is going to boil. The little red light comes on in front. I guess it's working.

"Does he know she can't cook?" Kitty asks.

"Yes. Johnny brought it up in the car on the way over," Edna says with a shrug.

"Better to get it out in the open early on," Bertie says.

Our conversation lulls, and the kitchen falls into the familiar clinking, sloshing, and swooshing sounds of women working to get dinner on the table—for more than a hundred people.

Edna reaches for two baskets of bread and heads back to the hall. I bend down to pull the soup tureen off the low shelf and place it next to the range. Bertie turns off the burner and carefully pours her creation into the tureen. The steam from the stew fogs up her glasses and somehow knits together the curls around her face until her hairstyle is perfect. It is indeed her vegetable beef stew, and it looks as beautiful as it smells. Cubes of tender beef, carrots, potatoes, onions, and green beans—all in Bertie's rich beef stock. Heaven.

"Well, the good news is, you will all get to form your own opinions of Mr. Davis and our Bessie soon enough," I say. "She's helping him park the car. I'm sure they're in the hall by now." I shift the angle of the soup tureen, and Bertie finishes pouring.

"He's here with her? Tonight?" Kitty stops in her tracks, a pitcher of tea in each hand.

"Yes, he drove us all over in his Chrysler Imperial," Edna adds, looking at Kay, who raises her eyebrows in approval.

"Well, that is good news, Mildred. Very good news," Kitty declares as she marches out the double doors.

I carry the soup tureen to the buffet and return to help organize. But as usual, Kay's strategic plan for replenishing the tables is already complete. Kay works the kitchen until we serve everyone. She removes empty casseroles and replaces them with new ones, keeps the buffet tidy and the pitchers filled with sweet tea and ice water. Kay's on duty during serving, so the rest of us can eat with our families. Her husband, Richard, doesn't come on Wednesday nights.

The second phase kicks in when people begin to clear their dinner plates. That's when Edna and I excuse ourselves from the supper and take over the kitchen duties for coffee and dessert. We wash the empty platters and casserole dishes and return them to the buffet tables so the folks who brought food can pick up their plates and platters when they leave. When all is said and done, Bertie, Dolly, and Kitty bat cleanup, which involves washing the remaining dishes and wiping everything down. We've been following this plan for over a decade. Sometimes we talk about switching things up, but as Bertie likes to say, "Don't interfere with something that ain't bothering you none."

Even though our pastor says grace for everyone gathered in the hall, Kitty Rogers leads the Kitchen Ladies in our own prayer each week before the supper starts. She motions to us to gather around the center table. Once in assembly, we bow our heads.

"Dear Heavenly Father, thank you for this opportunity to minister to our congregation. Help us, oh Lord, to feed the hungry, both in body and soul. Dear Lord, we ask your special blessing today for our beloved sister in Christ, Bessie Blackwell. If it is your will that Bessie and Mr. Davis should find love at this late stage in life, we place their budding relationship in your capable hands. As they draw closer together, may they draw ever closer to You. In Jesus's name we pray, Amen," Kitty finishes, and we all say, "Amen."

Edna nods knowingly at me from across the counter, and I nod back. Over the years, it's astonishing what we've accomplished in this kitchen—not by chopping, boiling, and baking, but by praying together.

"Away with you." Kay shoos us out to find our families. "Except for you, Mildred. May I have a word?" She stares at Edna. "Alone."

"I'll go see if I can find the two lovebirds," Edna says and exits the kitchen.

"What's on your mind, Kay?" I ask. Kay is one of the few people I've known who carries a pure red color around her. Like Edna's purple, Kay's shade is very consistent, so I'm surprised to see that it's darker than usual.

"You know how sometimes I go to Tulsa with Richard when he has business there?" she starts.

"Yes."

"Well, last week I rode down with him, and I had the loveliest lunch with the wife of one of his banking associates. Her daughter works at the University of Tulsa."

"How nice," I say, wondering where on earth this is going. You never know with Kay.

"Well, as we were talking, something came up about our husbands and how many dress shirts they go through in a week, and then Linn Brothers came up, because you know they have an even larger store in Tulsa."

"Yes, they do," I respond. My mind turns to Florence. I hope she's had a wonderful day. She could use a dose of happiness.

"And so," Kay says, then stops mid-sentence and frets with a piece of loose tin foil sitting on the counter.

"What is it, Kay?" I ask.

"It's about Mr. Linn's son. The one they call Sonny."

"Yes, the good-looking one who manages the store," I confirm.

"Well, Lorena, the woman I had lunch with, said her daughter shared some unsettling stories about him—scary stories."

"What kind of scary stories?" I ask.

"Stories about him making unwanted advances, you know, physical advances toward women when he was in college. She said he didn't always go after young women. He often targeted older women," Kay whispers even though the noise of the crowd in the hall makes it impossible for anyone to hear us.

"Oh, my," I murmur.

"I mentioned to Lorena that I know a woman who works for Sonny—an attractive widow in her forties. Lorena looked me right in the eye and said, 'He's a predator. If I were you, I'd warn her.'" Kay's face fills with worry, and a wave of protectiveness rolls over me.

"Florence hasn't mentioned anything to me," I say, mostly to myself.

"Lorena didn't come right out and say it, Mildred, but I think her daughter had a personal encounter with Sonny, and it frightened her. This isn't idle gossip, or I wouldn't be sharing it with you."

"Thank you, Kay." I put a hand on her shoulder.

"I know you're not as close to Florence as you are to Bessie," she says, "but you need to warn Florence about Sonny, Mildred."

"Yes. I do. I will," I promise. I knew Florence was hiding something from us the other night. Now, I wonder if it had to do with Sonny Linn.

Kay nods with relief, and her color shifts back to its usual vibrant red. "I better get out there and check on the buffet."

"And I better get out there and check on Bessie." I smile.

Kay and I walk out of the kitchen into the dazzling light and deafening buzz of a full fellowship hall. Since the hall is in the basement, natural light only comes in through a few high small windows, like the ones in the kitchen. With all the evening activities hosted in this room, the church installed fluorescent ceiling lights during the renovation. Bertie jokes we could perform surgery in here if need be.

I scan the food line. It winds all the way around the perimeter of the hall and flows in and out of the first few rows of tables. I see Johnny with the Jenkins family and his friend Martin. Johnny waves. Then I spot Bessie and Mr. Davis. They are talking with her good friend Anna Porter and a woman

I don't recognize. In fact, I practically don't recognize Bessie. I've never seen her look so relaxed. She's usually all business at the Wednesday Night Suppers, talking about Sunday School matters or checking up on someone's health. This evening, she's simply enjoying herself. Her rosy glow extends out to encompass the entire group—Edna, Mr. Davis, Anna, and the stranger. The stranger appears to be in the middle of a very amusing story.

As I observe them from across the room, I'm struck by the notion that Bessie and Mr. Davis are standing like a couple. They are a smidge closer than acquaintances of the opposite sex normally stand at church. Their bodies angle toward one another as if to say, "we're together." It's a subtle difference, but it's not lost on me.

"So, there was Bessie, covered from head to toe in dirt, burrs, and prickers," the stranger says as I join them. "She had holes in the knees of her britches and two of the cutest little fox kits you've ever seen peeking over the rim of her berry-picking basket."

"Well, I couldn't just leave the poor things there after finding their mama in pieces," Bessie replies, putting her hands on her hips. I've never seen her so animated.

"Were you able to nurse them?" Frank asks.

"Yes, we had a goat in those days and luckily the kits loved goat's milk. The hard part was finding the time to feed them four or five times a day. Once they were big enough to fend for themselves, I took them back into the woods and set them free. One time, I imagined I saw the two of them, all grown up, hiding in the tall brush behind our house, watching me work in the garden." Bessie smiles at Mr. Davis and then notices I've joined their cluster. "Oh, Mrs. Henderson!" she exclaims. "I'd like you to meet my wonderful friend Joyce Simmons. Oops, I mean Joyce Moore. Joyce and I grew up together in Oologah."

"How wonderful to meet you," I say to Joyce. She must be a true friend to draw Bessie's color out around the whole group like a pink fog.

"The pleasure is mine," Joyce replies. "I've known the Blackwell family my entire life."

"And I thought twelve years was something to write home about," Anna Porter says.

I try to focus on Joyce's pale blue color and how it matches the blue of her wide sparkling eyes, but I can't stop thinking about Florence and her situation at work. Some nights, Florence closes the store with Sonny, all by herself. *He's a predator.* I hear Kay's voice in my head, and a chill runs up my spine. I've never sat down for a heart-to-heart talk with Florence, but I won't let myself sleep tonight until I talk to her. I promised Kay.

"Yes. I've been getting quite an education about Bessie's childhood adventures," Mr. Davis says. "Growing an enormous prize-winning squash, rescuing fox kits—"

"Even playing matchmaker," Anna adds.

"Matchmaker? I'm intrigued." I turn to Joyce, forcing my attention on this conversation.

"Yes, I have Bessie to thank for over twenty-five years of wedded bliss." Joyce nudges Bessie, who grins.

"Oh, don't be ridiculous," Bessie says to Joyce. Then to us, she explains: "I turned down a date with her husband Carter in eighth grade because another boy had already asked me to the picnic. Then I encouraged Carter to ask Joyce because I knew she was sweet on him. I was just being a good friend—not a matchmaker."

"Well, you sure made a match for me!" Joyce exclaims, and we all laugh.

"I'd say it worked out well for Carter, too. You have such a lovely family, and Carter's been so successful. I heard he's moved into home building," Bessie adds.

"That's why I'm here in Bartlesville. We're building a new neighborhood just off Baker Hollow Road. I'm staying with Carter's sister, Gertie, this week while I get some of the homes ready for open inspection this weekend. We're calling the development Hidden Hollow."

"How charming," I say.

"We have three original floor plans ready to show. Anyone who is interested can come by and take a tour. Oh, come this weekend, Bessie. It's such fun to see the latest and greatest appliances and home designs. You're all welcome to have a tour!" she offers.

"It sounds like fun, but we're heading to Claremore to do our Decoration Day remembrance this Saturday," Bessie replies.

"I won't say this too loudly in church, but the houses will be open for inspection on Sunday afternoon as well," Joyce pretends to whisper into her hand. "A perfect stop for you two on a Sunday drive." She directs her comment to Bessie and Mr. Davis with a smile.

"What do you say, Bessie? A drive and some house inspecting after church on Sunday?" Mr. Davis asks.

"Why not, Frank?" Bessie smiles, and her rosy color pulsates.

"It's a date," Mr. Davis announces. His neck flushes slightly.

"Wonderful!" Joyce says. "I'll see you two again on Sunday. I'm off to find my sister-in-law in this crowd. Enjoy your supper." Joyce blows a kiss to Bessie and disappears.

"I should find Wyatt. So nice to meet you, Mr. Davis. And I'll see you at lunch tomorrow, Bessie. Oh, and don't forget your change purse—you owe me two bits." Anna winks at Bessie before heading back into the crowd.

Bessie and Frank take a step closer to the serving tables. Edna grabs my arm and whispers, "Did you hear her call him

Frank? And she agreed to go for a Sunday drive with him. This is progress!"

"You're clearly taking all the credit for these miraculous developments as the result of your parking lot plan," I say under my breath.

"It might be my parking lot plan." We move up with the line, standing a few paces behind Bessie and Mr. Davis. "It might be you helping her interpret her memory from last night. Then again," Edna continues speaking softly, "you and I both know there's no denying the power of a Kitchen Ladies' prayer."

"Amen to that," I agree, but as I remember Kay's warning, I wonder if we needed to pray for both Blackwell sisters tonight.

CHAPTER THIRTEEN

Florence

THE DINNER PLATE slips out of my fingers, and I catch it in the nick of time. The fork clangs and clatters as it bounces off the kitchen counter and the cabinet before settling on the floor. Louie snaps to attention and trots over to sniff and investigate. This is what happens when I want something—I turn into a nervous wreck! Why are they so late? Are they driving home from the church supper by way of Johnstone Park? I finished my leftover chicken and green beans at least ten minutes ago.

I bend down to pick up the fork and pat Louie on the head. He returns to his spot under the dinette. I stand in front of the sink, clutching the plate in one hand and the fork in the other. I hoped to be at the sink cleaning up when they arrived home. I suppose I could wait in position until they pull into the driveway and start washing my plate as soon as I hear the car. That way, when they walk through the door, I'll be at the sink just the way I envisioned it. They will ask me to tell them about my day, and everything will go according to my plan. I let out an audible sigh.

There's no reason to be anxious, Florence.

Right. I'm not going to tell them about the job offer tonight. It makes more sense to wait and talk to Bessie and Eddie when we're alone on our drive to Claremore. Saturday is the right time to bring it up, not tonight. Not in front of Johnny. I need to stick to the plan I worked out on the bus. I will tell them the job offer came in on Friday—that the folks in the Tulsa store fell in love with me during my visit and offered me a job later in the week. If I stick to my plan, there's no reason to be nervous tonight. The fork slips out of my hand again and clangs against the porcelain sink. I practically leap out of my skin. Louie raises his head to check on me one more time.

"I'm as jumpy as John was after the war," I say to the pup, who appears to nod in agreement.

After my husband returned from Europe, we went back to working together at his parent's hotel in Claremore. But our life didn't return to normal. John was on edge all the time—the sound of a dropped suitcase in the lobby or a chair sliding across the café floor was all it took to send him ducking for cover. He struggled to keep regular hours. Sometimes I would find him in our apartment out back, staring into the alley when he should have been manning the front desk. Then there were the nightmares. He would thrash about and wake up in a cold sweat almost every night. He didn't want to talk about any of it.

John's mother told me I needed to give him a child—as if I could order one from the mercantile down the street. She was sure a baby would bring John to his senses. She didn't know I was already doing everything I could to get John back into our bed. He slept in an old armchair most nights, hoping it would curb the bad dreams. On the evenings he sought comfort with me, there was a tenderness bordering on despair, but no passion. After he'd been home for a few months, he started disappearing. First for days at a time, then for weeks. No warning.

No discussion. Some mornings I would wake up to find his chair empty. His extended absences strained my relationship with his parents even further. His mother was sure my empty womb was to blame.

When the need arose for me and my sisters to go to Wichita and stay with our aunt Maude for a while, I was more than happy to hop on a train with them. John had been missing for almost a week. I hated living alone in our apartment, working under the accusatory stares and clucking tongue of my mother-in-law. I needed a new chapter then, like I need one now. Of course, I didn't know little Johnny was about to come into my life.

At last, I hear gravel spitting out from under a car's tires in the driveway. As I turn on the water at the sink, the sound of Johnny's voice wafts through the open kitchen window.

"So, I put the frog in the bathtub upstairs. You know, because the little fellow needed a pond." Boy, does he sound like his uncle. "I filled the tub with a couple of inches of water," Johnny continues, "put a rock in there for him to rest on, closed the curtain, and went to bed. Unfortunately, the first person to find him was Edna when she went in to clean the next morning!"

"Yes, and as I recall, I screamed so loudly the neighbors called the police!" Edna laughs and I see her poke Johnny in the arm as they open the screen door and find me at the sink.

"Hiya, Mom!" Johnny says.

"Hi yourself," I reply. "From all that racket, I wasn't sure if you were back from the church supper, or if the circus was in town."

"Well, I need to scoot straight home," Edna says. "I've got some leftovers for Douglas, and he's had a long day working all the way out in Nowata. Give me the short version—how was your trip?"

"It was very nice," I say, trying to sound casual. I set my clean plate and fork on the drainboard.

"Happy to hear it. Good night, all," Edna says as she departs.

She walks to and from Henderson House every day, rain or shine. She cuts through a hole in the Thompkins' fence and then it's only a few blocks to where she and Douglas live. Why she's stayed with this job and weird Mrs. Henderson for all these years is beyond me.

"Really, Mom, it was a good day?" Johnny asks, walking over to me. "I want to hear everything!"

"Yes, please, Florence," Bessie encourages. "We've all been wondering about your trip. Why don't we move into the living room so you can hold court?"

Bessie's certainly in a good mood. Last night, she disappeared after supper. I figured her normal discomfort around a new lodger had finally kicked in, but the twinkle in her eye this evening is unexpected. We make our way into the living room as Eddie walks through the front door. He's had a long day, too, but appears to be as chipper as Bessie.

"Howdy! Looks like the gang's all here," he says. "Did I miss the play-by-play on your big day?"

"No," Bessie responds, "we were about to settle in and hear all about it."

Since when is my sister the social director?

"Let me grab my plate from the icebox, Flossie, and I can sit at the dining table and listen in while you regale us with your tales of Tulsa." Eddie heads for the kitchen. Eddie rarely calls me by my childhood nickname, but he seems to be using it all the time this week.

The rest of the party gathers round in the living room. I take the chair with its back to the foyer. Johnny sits in the chair next to mine. Mrs. Henderson takes her usual place in the floral chair near the window. After an awkward glance at each other, Bessie and Mr. Davis decide to share the sofa.

"Oh, Florence," Bessie says while we're waiting for Eddie, "Frank has offered to drive us to Claremore on Saturday."

Hmm, so it's Frank now, is it?

"Mom, Mr. Davis's car is so plush. You'll feel like you're riding on a cloud," Johnny adds.

"Oh, Mr. Davis," I say, "surely you have something better to do on your first Saturday in Bartlesville?"

Other than ruining my plan to talk to my brother and sister.

"I can't think of anything else I'd rather do." He smiles at Bessie.

Heat builds in my chest. I shift my position in the chair and count to ten silently before responding. "Well then, thank you, Mr. Davis. I can't wait to ride to Claremore on a cloud!"

I force a laugh, and everyone joins in, except for Mrs. Henderson. She stares at me with one of her all-knowing looks. Ignoring her gaze, I continue to laugh.

"Who's riding on a cloud?" Eddie asks as he returns to the dining room.

"Frank has offered to drive the three of us to Claremore on Saturday," Bessie says over her shoulder.

"Excellent. That'll be a real treat for me. I never get to relax in the back seat!" Eddie jokes. "Now, give me a minute to arrange my supper so I feel like I'm part of the audience, even if I am in the cheap seats." He angles himself at the end of the dining table so he can see me. "You may begin," he says with a wave of his napkin.

"Mr. Linn warned me the ride down Route 75 was like following the trail of a drunken man," I start, "and it was true! The road twists and turns like you wouldn't believe. The bus drove through plenty of little towns that all looked like they'd sprung up just because of the highway. There were a few general stores as well." I pause. "We'll have to explore them on our next trip down to Tulsa."

Don't give anything away, I remind myself.

"When you grow up over a general store, you notice them wherever you go, and you feel compelled to stop and go in," Bessie says to Mr. Davis.

"Yup, and then they feel compelled to talk to everyone in them for hours and hours," Johnny groans.

"Ahem." I clear my throat to get everyone's eyes back on me. "Downtown Tulsa did not disappoint. It is just as impressive as Peggy described it—"

"Florence works with Peggy at the store," Bessie interrupts to explain to Mr. Davis.

"Yes, I do," I say. "Peggy was in Tulsa last month for a friend's wedding, and she gave me a lengthy review of the architectural highlights of the city during our lunch break yesterday. She did an excellent job describing the tall buildings but seeing them for myself was really something. Most of the buildings downtown are over ten stories high, built in the twenties and thirties in the art deco style. Waite Phillips built the Philtower in the late twenties and it stands twenty-four stories. Seeing it dominate the skyline was a highlight. He finished his Philcade building in '31, and it's thirteen stories high."

"Wow, real skyscrapers," Johnny says, his eyes wide.

"Today, I learned that Mr. Phillips built a tunnel connecting his two buildings. He can walk from his apartment to his office without having to cross the street. It made me think of the Medici family in Italy. They built a passageway from their palace across the Arno directly to their offices in the Palazzo Vecchio—"

"Ever since we covered world geography in middle school," Bessie says, interrupting me yet again to speak to Mr. Davis, "and Florence discovered there was a city with her name in

Italy—and not just any city, a beautiful and famous city—she's read anything she can find about it."

I don't like the way Bessie and Mr. Davis are sitting together on the sofa, or how she keeps leaning into him with her explanations each time she cuts into my story. The searing heat in my chest intensifies. Maybe my dinner isn't sitting well.

"It's true," I say, working to take control of the conversation again. "I drove Mrs. Masterson, the librarian in Claremore, crazy by constantly asking her if anything new had come in relating to Florence. Most of the books she gave me were boring histories, but I read them anyway. Then one day, when I was about fourteen, I walked into the library, and she was smiling from ear to ear. As I approached the desk, she handed me a copy of *A Room with a View* by E. M. Forster. It was the first grown-up novel I ever read, and it had quite an effect on me. You could even say it changed my life."

"How so?" Mr. Davis asks.

"Learning how the upper class felt about the lower class, not to mention the working class, well, it was the first time I realized we were poor. I never knew we were on the bottom rung of the social ladder until I read that book. Our family had as much, or as little, as any other family in Indian Territory. I had no idea people could go on holiday for months just to study art and architecture—and talk about each other," I say with a laugh.

"I suppose by British standards, your family might have been able to climb up from peasant to merchant class, since your father owned a store," Mr. Davis adds.

"Possibly, but as I walked alongside Miss Lucy Honeychurch in those pages, it became painfully clear to fourteen-year-old me that if I was going to break out of my lower-class circumstances, I needed to get busy," I say.

"Look at us now," Eddie chimes in from the dining room, "living in the lap of luxury!" Everyone laughs a little, and Mrs. Henderson smiles at the compliment.

"Back to Tulsa," I say. "As I exited the bus station, which is located smack dab in the middle of downtown, I noticed that the men and women dress a touch nicer there than the folks in Bartlesville—broader cut suits on the men, shorter length skirts on the women, lots of bright patterned blouses, and tons of accessories. I was glad I memorized the directions from the bus station to the store. I didn't want to seem like a tourist, looking at a piece of paper as I made my way around town."

"That was smart, Mom," Johnny says.

"I walked confidently out of the bus terminal and knew exactly which streets would take me to Linn Brothers."

"What's the Tulsa store like?" Bessie asks.

"It has more street frontage, but it's not on a corner like the Bartlesville store. The building is taller—six stories high. The men's store occupies the first three floors. They rent the top floors to other businesses. I saw a lawyer's office and an advertising agency on the directory board in the elevator. The elevator has a uniformed attendant. You sure would look sharp in a blue uniform and matching cap like that, Johnny," I say.

"Thanks, Mom. What about their window displays?" Johnny asks. "That's why they brought you down there, right, to work on their window displays?"

"Yes, of course," I respond.

Mrs. Henderson studies me closely as I speak.

"Their display space is stunning. The windows are tall and wide, and the display area is extra deep. A lighting system I've never seen before illuminates the windows in the evenings. Overhead panels hold bulbs you can angle to highlight certain aspects of the display."

"Fascinating," Mr. Davis says as he shifts his seat on the sofa and moves slightly closer to my sister.

"Were you able to teach them the strategies you've been using to boost sales?" Bessie asks.

"Yes, yes, all of my meetings went very well," I say.

Mrs. Henderson squints at me. What does she expect to see? She can't know I'm not telling the entire story by looking at me. Though her intuition is strong. Once she insisted I keep Johnny home from church because she said he was coming down with something. Sure enough, he spiked a fever not two hours later. What does it matter? My meetings did go well. I'm not lying. I'm sharing true excerpts from my day.

"Did they put you to work designing some displays for them?" Eddie asks from the dining table.

"No, not really. Mostly we talked."

"Wow, a business trip with no work, that's not something you hear about every day!" Eddie takes another bite of chicken.

"Continuing on," I say, rolling my eyes, "it felt like a trip to the big city. There are more than a hundred and forty thousand people in Tulsa. I know it's not San Francisco, Mr. Davis, but compared to Bartlesville, Tulsa is quite energizing!"

I take stock of Bessie and Mr. Davis on the couch. Something has changed. Last night, she was pulling away, running scared as usual. I didn't think I had anything to worry about. Now, she looks a little too comfortable with him for my liking.

"What is the population in San Francisco, Frank?" Bessie asks.

Does she have to use his name every time she speaks?

"Gosh, the last count I heard was well over six hundred thousand, including all of San Francisco County. I agree with you, Mrs. Fuller. Once a city gets over a hundred thousand people, there is a different level of hustle and bustle on the streets," he adds.

"Oh, please, call me Florence—we all seem to be getting to know each other so quickly," I say, grinning at my sister. She's glowing this evening. Her smile lights up her rosy cheeks.

"Of course, and please call me Frank," he says and then smiles—not at me, but at Bessie.

Well, isn't this fabulous? Fabulous Frank and Blushing Bessie smiling tenderly at each other on the sofa. My chest flutters, and a wave of nausea bubbles up from my stomach. All my plans for Tulsa include having Bessie by my side.

"Did you go out for lunch, Mom? To a restaurant?" Johnny asks.

"Yes, two of the women from the office took me to a wonderful place on Second Street and Boston Avenue called Ike's Chili Parlor. They've been serving chili there since 1910. Well, it had to be the best chili I've eaten in my whole life. Will Rogers used to go there, and he called their chili a 'bowl of blessedness.' They have it on a sign in the restaurant with his picture."

"Oh, Will Rogers," Bessie says wistfully.

"I loved Will Rogers! What a tragedy to lose him so early," Mr. Davis says, again more to Bessie than the rest of us. "They called him 'Oklahoma's Favorite Son,' right?"

"They sure did," Eddie says, joining us in the living room. "Will Rogers came from Oologah Indian Territory, just like the three of us. He was born on a big ole ranch on the Verdigris River near where our daddy grew up." Eddie takes a seat next to Mrs. Henderson. "Daddy was a couple of years older than Will. He used to say he was sure he had a positive influence on him because he used to tell little Will funny stories when they went fishing. Then he'd catch Will retelling the stories to his friends. Even Daddy had to admit, the stories were funnier when Will told them!"

"He was part Cherokee like we are," Bessie adds. "One of his early nicknames in vaudeville was 'The Cherokee Kid.' His dad was a leader in the Cherokee Nation—used to come into the Pack and Run all the time when I was a girl. I'm not sure his father lived to see his son become a household name."

"Tell Mr. Davis about the picnic, Aunt Bessie," Johnny interjects. Everyone's attention turns to my sister, and the fire in my chest spreads into my throat. I'm so frustrated with all these interruptions, I want to scream.

"Well, I met Will Rogers at a company picnic out at Woolaroc a few years before he died in that horrible plane crash. Will was friendly with Frank Phillips. Anyway, someone told him I was from Oologah. When he found out I was Billy Blackwell's daughter, he came right on over and introduced himself," Bessie says without faltering.

"How exciting," Fabulous Frank says with a big grin.

"I suppose it was. We ended up talking for the longest time. It was strange to hear someone talk about my daddy when he was a little boy." She pauses. "I must admit, Will Rogers was as funny and insightful in person as he was on the movie screen or in the newspaper."

"Were you nervous, talking to a big celebrity?" Frank asks.

"Maybe at first. I usually get very nervous around strangers, but he put me at ease right off the bat. He was a very likable man." Bessie looks directly into Frank's eyes and smiles again. I haven't seen this smile on my sister's face in a long time.

"There's a Will Rogers museum in Claremore. It opened a few years ago. We could go on Saturday after we visit the cemetery if we have time," Eddie offers.

Gee, isn't this swell? Here we are, talking about good old dead Will Rogers instead of my first ever business trip to Tulsa. I don't know why I was nervous about what I was going to say to everyone this evening, as I can't get a word in edgewise. I might as well not be in the room at this point. And now they are talking about Joyce Moore?

"Joyce Moore was at the Wednesday Night Supper?" I ask.

"Yes, she's in town, working on a new home development. Carter's sister is in my Sunday School class. Joyce is staying with her this week while she gets the houses ready for open inspection this weekend," Bessie says.

"How odd." I sink back into my chair and cross my arms. "I was thinking about Joyce the other evening, and now here she is in Bartlesville."

"Really? What were you thinking about?" Bessie asks.

"Oh, just about the time you blew your chance to go to the Farmer's Picnic with Carter because you'd already promised what's-his-name you'd go with him, and 'a promise is a promise,'" I say, realizing too late that I'm mocking Bessie's high-pitched voice.

My imitation isn't funny like Johnny's the other night—it's cruel. Bessie looks down at her hands folded in her lap. Frank immediately comes to her defense.

"Well, to hear Joyce tell the story, Bessie's a hero! She's the best matchmaker on the planet," Frank says to me and then turns to Bessie.

It seems my sister's little romance may not be as one-sided as I thought. This is quite a development. So much for having the best day I've had in a long time. I've got a big problem here. A big problem. She can't fall in love. Not now. Not when the family has such an incredible opportunity in front of us. A heaviness settles into the burning in my chest. I look at Bessie, Johnny, and Eddie. We are a family—a family with a chance for a fresh start in a new city. We are closer to buying a house now than we've ever been. I must keep us together.

"Well, I'm exhausted. What a day. I think I'll head upstairs," I say. "Johnny, didn't you promise your uncle a game of chess this evening?"

"I sure did. You up for it, Uncle Eddie?" Johnny asks.

"Up for it? I've been planning my opening moves all day!" Eddie rises from his chair and heads back toward the dining table. "Give me a minute to tidy up my dishes."

Thank goodness. I need some time to think. Thanks to Fabulous Frank butting into our family time on Saturday, I need a new plan to tell Bessie and Eddie, alone. Plus, now I have to think of a way to discourage Bessie's schoolgirl crush before it goes any further.

"Florence," Mrs. Henderson speaks for the first time this evening. "Could I have a word with you before you head to bed?" She motions to her suite.

My chest is so tight, I can hardly breathe. I need to get upstairs. I need to be alone so I can plan.

"Is there any way it could wait until tomorrow, Mrs. Henderson? I'm wiped out after my big day," I say.

"I'm sorry, Florence, but it can't wait. I need to speak to you tonight."

She opens the door to her room and waits for me to comply. I drag myself across the foyer and into her sitting room. She waits for Louie to follow and then closes the door. In nine years, Mrs. Henderson has never asked to speak to me alone. I plop down on her settee and much to my surprise, she sits next to me, not in the chair across from me.

"Florence, we haven't confided in each other much over the years," she begins, "however, something has come to my attention, and I promised I would share it with you."

This isn't about my trip to Tulsa. It's about something else. I remain silent. I see no reason to make things easier for her—she's keeping me from getting my time alone while Johnny plays chess.

"Someone I trust," she says haltingly, "told me Sonny Linn might be dangerous."

A lump forms in my throat, and it takes a dedicated effort to swallow.

"She told me there were multiple complaints about him making unwanted physical advances on women while he was at the University of Tulsa, and not just young women." She pauses, waiting for my reaction, but I don't have one to give. I'm in shock.

"Florence, I don't know if you've had any bad experiences with Sonny, if he's done anything to make you feel uncomfortable," she continues, "but I want you to know you can always come to me, and I will do whatever I can to keep you safe. You, Johnny, Bessie, and Eddie, well, I think of you as family."

It's strangely comforting to know Sonny is a bad guy. The situation at work is not my fault. He's done this before. Other women have complained about him. Tears well up in my eyes, but I learned to control my tears years ago. I stop them in their tracks, and yet, for a moment, I consider letting my guard down. Would it be a relief to bury my head on Mrs. Henderson's shoulder and sob? I can visualize her arms comforting me while I tell her everything—about Bessie and Johnny, about Sonny's advances and the job interview, about how much I want to move to Tulsa and have a fresh start and how Bessie can't fall in love.

I depend on my sister's emotional support, but I also depend on her financially. I need her portion to stay in the savings account. She makes more than Eddie and I combined. If she decides not to move to Tulsa, she might want to pull her money out. I'm not sure I'd ever be able to afford a house without Bessie's contribution. Plus, I've spent more on myself and

Johnny than Bessie knows. If she takes a good look at the bank statements, she might want me to pay some of it back.

But Bessie is the one who owes you, Florence, the voice in my head whispers. *She told John the truth about Johnny. She's the reason John's nightmares returned. She's the reason he jumped off that bridge.*

Blood pounds in my temples, and I feel as if there's a weight sitting on my chest. Mrs. Henderson places a hand on my knee. Would the heaviness in my chest disappear if I poured all my secrets out to this strange woman and her little dog?

Don't be ridiculous, Florence. You don't need to tell her your secrets to feel better. You need a new plan. That's all.

Right. I need a new plan to tell Eddie and Bessie about the job and a strategy to dump cold water on my sister's budding romance. That said, this revelation about Sonny might be an opportunity to get crazy Mrs. Henderson on my side. If she is concerned for my safety at Linn Brothers, she might be very supportive if a job offer from the Tulsa store came in later this week.

I turn to face Mrs. Henderson and allow a few tears to fall down my cheek.

"There was an incident last Saturday," I begin.

THURSDAY
MAY 22, 1941

CHAPTER FOURTEEN

Bessie

EVERY MORNING, MRS. Henderson's dining room enchants me as much as it did the first time I laid eyes on it. Dark wood furnishings, light tan wallpaper smothered with images of cream-colored palm fronds, and floor-length, rose-colored silk curtains set a scene that is elegant without being stuffy. I pour myself a cup of coffee at the sideboard and take my usual seat, looking out the tall windows into the side yard. Sunlight casts a pattern diagonally across the mahogany table. I stretch my hands into the light and watch the tiny leaf shadows dance on my skin. I can remember doing the exact same thing as a child. The morning sun made designs on our kitchen table, too. Ours was a sturdy beast constructed of long planks of ash and, although Mama scrubbed it clean twice a day and oiled it once a month, it was scratched and scarred. A hard-working table—nothing like the shiny, smooth perfection stretched out in front of me today.

I open the Daily Enterprise to its full length, and the headline "Nazis Seize Strategic Crete Bases" jumps out in large, bold ink below the masthead. Seems like I do more praying than reading when I pick up the paper these days. A map of Crete on the front page outlines which bases are critical to the British fleet. The sidebar says Britain is losing the battle in the Atlantic. Frank thinks we will enter the war by the end of the year, and the local draft board announced plans to increase calls in June and July. Eddie's number could come up any day. He's only thirty-three, and they're drafting men from eighteen to forty-five. Frank turned forty-six in March.

Dear Lord, help this world know peace. Give your strength and mercy to all the men and boys fighting over there. Surround those worried about their loved ones with your comfort and grace. And guide the leaders of our nation during this uncertain time with your wisdom and understanding. In Jesus's name, Amen.

"Good morning," Florence says as she enters the room and makes her way over to the coffee service.

"You're up early. Did you get a good night's rest after your busy day?" I ask.

"Oh, yes. Slept like a baby. Hmm. What a funny expression. As if babies know anything about sleeping. Remember how many times Johnny used to wake up during the night?" She pulls out one of the intricately carved dining chairs and sits across from me.

"It was a good thing we could take turns caring for him during those early months," I say.

"It's been a good thing all along, Bessie, for us to raise him together." She pauses. "I know it hasn't always been easy, but I think we made a good decision. The right decision."

I don't know how to respond since I'm not sure we made the right decision. In all her talk about us raising Johnny together, Florence conveniently forgets that she sent me away from Wichita. She banished me from Johnny's life for three years. If her husband, John, hadn't died, would they ever have come back into my life?

"You've been a good mother, Florence," I say, and I mean it.

"And you've been a wonderful aunt. Since Eddie's come back to us, we've been able to give Johnny a proper family." She runs her fingers up and down the handle of her cup. Something's bothering her.

"What did Mrs. Henderson want to talk to you about last night?" I ask.

"Oh, it was nothing. She's thinking about new curtains for room number five," Florence says. "So, you and Frank Davis?"

"Yes." I smile. "We do seem to be getting along nicely."

"Hmm, yes," she says. "And so quickly. It's really something. And now he's driving us all to Claremore on Saturday." She clicks her tongue and sways her head from side to side in amazement.

"That's not the half of it." I put my coffee down and lean on the table. "We're also going for a drive after church on Sunday to see the new houses Joyce and Carter are building. Oh, honey, I've never felt so at ease with a man in my life. After I found out he was divorced, I tried to treat him like any other new lodger. Tuesday, I did my best to stay away from him, to see if my feelings went away, but they didn't. Mrs. Henderson thinks he's opened a door for me to reconsider falling in love. It feels like we're supposed to be together. I can't explain it any other way. I can talk to him about anything. No stuttering, no second guessing myself. It's like a miracle."

"A miracle?" Florence scoffs. "Don't you think that's a little over the top?"

"Maybe so, but it feels miraculous to me. I'm thinking about wearing my smart afternoon dress on Sunday. You know, the jade-colored one I usually wear for Easter and weddings. Do you think it's appropriate for a Sunday drive?" I smile at her tentatively.

From the sour look on her face, I can tell my sister's not pleased. There was nothing in our decision about Johnny to keep me from pursuing a romantic relationship. Of course, it's never been an issue because I haven't been interested in a romantic relationship until now. I wait for her answer about the dress.

"Bessie, I need you to listen to me," she says, raising both of her hands as if she's calming a startled filly. "You need to proceed with caution. We know so little about Frank Davis. We don't know why his first marriage ended or why he left San Francisco to move to Bartlesville. Doesn't it seem a little suspicious to you? Who would ever leave San Francisco to come here?"

"But he told us why," I respond. "He said he'd always wanted to work for Phillips Petroleum, and he was ready to get back to the Midwest. Don't you believe him?"

"Not everyone values the truth as much as you do, sweetheart. Some people find lying as easy as breathing, especially when there's something they want." She sighs. "All I'm saying is that you need to be careful. I don't want to see you get hurt again. Remember last time?"

I don't want to remember what happened the last time I fell in love. Edna and Mrs. Henderson encouraged me to step through the open door. I'm ready to look forward, not behind. But Florence is right when she says we don't know much about Frank or his first marriage.

"You need to ask Mr. Davis more questions," Florence instructs. "Ask him about his family, his love life in San Francisco, and his ex-wife."

We sit for a moment, sipping coffee, then she starts again.

"Have you noticed how interested he is in all of our Blackwell family stories, yet how little he shares about his own past? It makes me uncomfortable. I must say, I'm worried about you being alone with him on Sunday." She frowns.

"We were alone for a little bit last night," I say. Florence raises her eyebrows, so I elaborate. "It was nothing. We dropped everyone else off at the entrance to the church and then I helped Frank park the car. We talked for a minute and walked in together—just the two of us," I explain. "He was a perfect gentleman."

My sister shakes her head from side to side and purses her lips as if I can't possibly know what I'm talking about. I think back to the parking lot last night. I remember the butterflies I felt when he leaned against the car next to me. And when he lifted my chin with his fingers, we were close enough to kiss.

"Florence, I know my last romance—well, my only romance—ended badly, but I've gained a world of life experience since then, and I'm a good judge of character," I say.

"Of course you are, sweetie." She drums her fingers on the table. "I'm just asking you to proceed with caution. That's all." She looks off into the living room for a moment and then returns her gaze to mine. "I've read so many sad stories about men who move from town to town and prey on unsuspecting single women," she tuts.

"Florence, you don't think Frank could be dangerous?"

"Well, it seems a little too good to be true. Don't you think?" She looks at me sideways as she purses her lips again.

"What do you mean?"

"Bessie, I love you, but even with all the widowers those Kitchen Ladies have thrown at you over the years, you haven't had one official date since moving to Bartlesville—not one! And of those potential suitors, how many of them were ever really interested in you?"

"Bob Wilkins," I say.

"Okay, there was Bob Wilkins," she concedes.

"Of course, I wasn't interested in him—at all." I exhale.

"And now, out of the blue, a divorced man shows up from the big city, in his fancy car, with his important job, and his well-cut suits, and he is suddenly, overnight, in just three days, smitten with you, Bessie Blackwell, the old maid who can't even scramble an egg." She pats the table for emphasis. "It's ringing far too many alarm bells for me."

My eyes sting. I open them as wide as I can and focus on the coffee pot sitting on the sideboard to keep from crying. Daddy made fun of us if we cried. Florence and I have a million and one tricks to keep our tears from falling.

"Maybe it doesn't make sense," I whisper.

Could it all be a lie? Could Frank be lying to me to take advantage of me? I did fall for that once before. But everything with Frank feels mutual, natural. We're pursuing each other. With Frank, I'm on equal footing. My sister and I sit in silence for a minute. She seems satisfied that she has sufficiently warned me. It's what families do. We look out for each other.

"Thank you for your concern," I say. "I will proceed with caution, as you recommended. I will ask him lots of questions, and I promise not to get into any trouble. So, what do you think about the dress?"

"What dress?" Florence sounds annoyed with the subject change.

"My smart afternoon dress. The jade one? For my date on Sunday after church?" I grin.

"Oh, my dear sister. If you could see the look on your face." Florence shakes her head. "You're in trouble already."

"Mornin', Mom, Aunt Bessie!" Johnny saves the day as he bounds into the dining room and gives me a peck on the cheek.

"Good morning." I pick up the paper, relieved to put the conversation with Florence behind me. "I think you're growing again, Johnny. Do you feel taller today than yesterday?"

Johnny takes stock of his limbs. "You know, I think I might," he says, "and I certainly have been hungry lately." He wiggles his fingers, selects a biscuit from the basket at the center of the table, and sits down in one of the dining chairs next to Florence.

"I heard you." Mrs. Henderson's voice rings from the kitchen, and she appears in the doorway, Louie at her heels. "Would you like scrambled eggs this morning, Johnny?"

"Oh, yes, ma'am, I sure would."

"Coming right up." With a wave of her dish towel, Mrs. Henderson turns and heads back into the kitchen. Louie follows in perfect rhythm, tail wagging. I love the back and forth of breakfast at Henderson House. People entering the dining room one-by-one, Mrs. Henderson and Louie shuttling in and out. The danger of tears from a moment ago passes as the occupants of Henderson House settle into our familiar morning routine.

"Hi-de-ho." Eddie's baritone voice fills the room as he makes a beeline for the coffee service.

"Good morning, everyone," Frank says with a smile directed mostly at me. When he looks at me, I feel as if I'm the most important person in the world.

"Good morning." I smile in return.

Frank looks casual this morning in a pair of slacks and a dress shirt. He hasn't bothered to put on his suit coat or tie for breakfast. Seeing him relaxed like this makes me think about what it would be like for the two of us to eat breakfast together—alone. My face feels warm. If I'm blushing now, it's my own fault.

Suddenly, an idea hits me. It's such a powerful sensation, I wonder if one of those illustrated cartoon character lightbulbs might be glowing over my head. The idea won't let me sit still. I need to ask Mrs. Henderson something right away, but I can't walk directly into the kitchen—everyone would worry the eggs would stick to the pan and the next batch of biscuits would burn.

"Excuse me for a moment," I say, rising from the table.

I hurry out of the dining room, through the living room, and into the foyer. My heart races. I glance backward. No one can see me. I open the door to Mrs. Henderson's suite and close it behind me. The room smells of citrus and lavender with a hint of eucalyptus. I've been in Mrs. Henderson's suite hundreds of times over the past twelve years, but I've never entered the kitchen from here. I walk to the back door of the suite, push it open slowly, and quietly slip into the kitchen.

"Mrs. Henderson," I whisper.

"Scare me to death!" Mrs. Henderson jumps. "What on earth are you doing coming into the kitchen through my secret door?" she asks.

"I have a question for you, and I didn't want anyone to see me come in. Mrs. Henderson, may I watch you make the scrambled eggs this morning?" I ask. "Unless you're worried about the stove catching on fire."

"I'm not worried. Not one bit. You're welcome to watch," Mrs. Henderson says as she gestures to the stools at the peninsula.

I take a seat. "How did you learn to cook, Mrs. Henderson?"

"Oh, it wasn't easy. My mother, a champion of political reform and a woman's right to vote, could not abide the thought of her only daughter stooping below our social status and doing her own cooking."

"So, did you teach yourself after you got married?"

"When I married Charles, Mother personally selected a middle-aged Jamaican woman named Liliana Johnson to run my kitchen—just to make sure I didn't try to take things into my own hands. Lucky for me, Miss Lily was the kindest, most approachable woman I'd ever met. I went to her about a week after she started and begged her to teach me how to cook."

"She agreed?"

"She laughed. Miss Lily had a marvelous laugh—bubbling with a joy that seemed to come from a place deep inside her. She said, 'We better hope your mother never finds out.' Then she handed me my first apron. I was eighteen."

"Did she teach you from cookbooks?" I ask.

"Oh, no. Miss Lily never opened a cookbook. 'What I don't know how to make by heart, I make by feel,' she used to say." Mrs. Henderson clasps her hands over her chest and sighs. "I bought a wooden recipe box and meticulously wrote out cards for everything dear Miss Lily taught me. When my parents dined with us, Mother would go on and on about the perfect consistency of Miss Lily's corn pudding or the tenderness of Miss Lily's pork roast. She never knew I had prepared the dishes myself! Miss Lily and I would laugh about it over a glass of iced tea the next day."

"So, you learned in secret," I say.

"Yes, I did."

"Do you still have those recipe cards?"

"See the wooden box on the shelf above the stove?" She points. "That's my old recipe file, stuffed with hundreds of cards. I haven't opened it in years. Now, what I can't make by heart, I make by feel." Mrs. Henderson smiles.

The breakfast conversation floats into the kitchen. Florence is telling the story about Cousin Wahya and his dog, Inola, winning the blue ribbon for obedience at the county fair. During the awards ceremony, the second-place dog jumped up and snatched the ribbon out of Wahya's hand and ran off with it. Laughter seeps under the dining room door.

"Family stories sure are powerful, aren't they? We tell the same ones over and over again. They're not always funny," I say.

"No, they are not always funny," Mrs. Henderson replies.

"We laughed about the fact that I can't cook in the car last night, and I didn't think it bothered me, but Florence made a comment this morning about me not knowing how to scramble an egg and it hurt. To be honest, I can only recall one incident when Florence and I were baking cookies, and I lost track of time. The cookies burned. But I don't remember causing any other kitchen disasters. I think my mama sent me out to work in the garden because that's where she needed help, not because she was worried dough wouldn't rise if I was nearby."

"Bessie, dear, it's probably not my place to say this, but sometimes I think your sister is a little jealous of you, and she likes to repeat family stories that don't paint you in a very flattering light."

I consider Mrs. Henderson's observation. "My sister's life has not turned out the way she hoped it would. I suppose I can understand why she shares the stories she does."

"You are the kindest person I know, Bessie Blackwell. But what about your life?" she asks.

"What do you mean?"

"Has your life turned out the way you hoped it would?"

"I never had any grand plans for myself like Florence did. The Lord has been good to me. I don't have many regrets," I trail off, thinking back to the idea that brought me to the kitchen in the first place. "Mrs. Henderson, will you teach me how to cook?"

"Well, I'll be." She shakes her head slightly.

"And can we keep my lessons a secret at first? Like yours were with Miss Lily? You know, just in case the stories are true, and I am hopeless?"

"Of course. Your lessons can be our little secret, but I want you to know that I have complete faith in you. Why don't you watch me make the scrambled eggs this morning? Then you can sneak back to the table before I serve. No one will be the wiser." She pauses, thinking for a moment. "It will probably be easier to keep this a secret if you come down early and work with me before everyone else comes down in the morning."

"No problem. I'm up with the sun."

"Tomorrow, you're making the biscuits." She points at me, and I shrink back. "The only way to learn how to cook, Bessie, is by doing. Look in the recipe box later. I'm sure there's a card or two for biscuits. But for today, I'll do a little show and tell."

Mrs. Henderson places a large mixing bowl, a carton of eggs, a bottle of milk, and a long-handled fork on the counter in front of me.

"One secret to delicious scrambled eggs is to add the right amount of milk to the mixture. It's important not to add too much," she instructs. "You want the eggs to come out fluffy, not watery."

I watch Mrs. Henderson beat the milk and eggs, pour the batter into the pan, then stir and scrape until the eggs are perfect. I didn't know eggs cooked so quickly. I sneak back through her suite and take my seat at the table—my first secret cooking lesson in the books.

"Are you feeling all right, honey?" Florence asks once I'm back in my chair.

"Better than ever," I reply.

SATURDAY
MAY 24, 1941

CHAPTER FIFTEEN

Mrs. Henderson

"HAVE A WONDERFUL day! We'll see you for supper!" I wave as Mr. Davis pulls out of the driveway with the Blackwells on board. "My, my," I mutter, "this may prove to be a very interesting day. Something big is on the horizon, Louie. I can feel it. Let's get inside and get our Saturday started, too."

I talk to Louie every day. But when the house is empty, I talk to him nonstop. We head through the kitchen and take the back entrance to my suite.

"Bessie's biscuits were darn good today. Only her second time making them, and she's already getting the knack of cutting in the cold butter and leaving the lumps just the right size to make them flaky. Did you hear Mr. Davis complimenting me on them? The smile on Bessie's face was priceless."

The dog nods in agreement, finds his bed next to the settee, circles several times, and paws out some lumps of his own before nestling in.

"Let's take roll call. Johnny left for the country club bright and early. The Blackwell gang is on the road to Claremore with

Mr. Davis. Edna has the day off and so does the professor. Knowing him, he'll stick to his usual schedule. Imagine sleeping in on a day like today?"

Louie shoots me an incredulous look as he is clearly considering a morning nap himself.

"Maybe the professor will wake up early, and we'll get more time with him today." The pup raises his little black eyebrows. "Oh, don't look at me like that. It's a harmless infatuation. There's nothing wrong with enjoying the company of a charming man." The beagle yawns. He's right. It's time to move on to the business of the day.

"I have a very important appointment at Linn Brothers today, Louie. Mr. Linn was quite cordial when I asked to meet with him." The dog stretches his paws over the edge of his bed, lays his head across them, and closes his eyes. "He's in for a bit of a surprise, I'm afraid. But as I told you yesterday, Louie, if there was a rumor going around about one of my sons, I'd want to know about it."

I change out of my housedress and into something more appropriate for a trip downtown.

"There's not a doubt in my mind, a face-to-face conversation with Mr. Linn is the proper course of action," I say to the sleeping pup. "But I'm nervous."

The best protection any woman can have is courage. I hear my mother repeating one of her favorite suffragette slogans as I look in the mirror.

"Yes, Louie, I must arm myself with courage today. It takes courage to have a difficult conversation. On the plus side, I can pick up a gift to send Robert for his birthday while I'm at the store—two birds with one stone, as they say. Two birds."

The dog wakes and cocks his head at the word "birds" but, not seeing any in the room, resumes his nap. I glance at the letter on the side table. Robert will be expecting my response any day. Perhaps I'm waiting for a sign that will never come.

I finish dressing and head out through the kitchen. My gaze lands on the empty windowsill behind the dinette. I had starter pots of parsley and thyme growing there and sent them home with Edna yesterday. The window looks bare and lonely this morning. I'll stop at the florist when I'm in town and pick up some African violets.

I put on my hat and gloves and walk outside. The brilliant sunlight blinds me for a moment. I close my eyes and have the strangest feeling I've stepped out onto the front porch of my son's summer house in Spring Lake. I hear my grandchildren's laughter in the front yard. I smell the salt of the ocean a block away. When I open my eyes, I am back on the path to my garage in Oklahoma. The Atlantic Ocean is more than a thousand miles east, but it's calling to me.

Parking in Bartlesville on a Saturday can be a daunting task, but I have a lucky spot. There is a small lot behind Cuinn-Taylor Market, and it almost always has a space. Today is no exception, and I am parked in minutes. I take a quick look at my watch. There's plenty of time to enjoy a stroll to Steinhauser's Florist before my appointment with Mr. Linn. I get out of the car and start walking between the buildings toward the main street.

My thoughts turn to my meeting with Mr. Linn. I'm not sure how to deliver disparaging news to a father about one of his children. There's no doubt Sonny is trouble—Florence confirmed everything Kay told me. I hang back for a moment in the cool shadow of the alley. Am I meddling in something that's none of my business? No. This is important. For all my mother's shortcomings, she did teach me that women need to stand up for each other.

I take a few long strides and pop out of the alley onto the sunlit sidewalk. My courage grows with each step on the way to the flower shop.

"Good morning, Mrs. Henderson." Leo Steinhauser greets me the moment I enter the shop.

I find his German accent charming, though his business suffered after the Great War—as if he had anything to do with it.

"Mr. Steinhauser, I don't know what's more delightful about your store this morning: how glorious everything looks or how fragrant everything smells."

"Thank you, Mrs. Henderson. It's always a pleasure to have you visit the shop. What can I help you with today?" he asks.

I tune in to the silver glow around his head and shoulders. It's very similar to the color I used to see around my grandmother.

"I'm in the market for some African violets for my kitchen windowsill."

"Right this way."

He leads me past an array of frilly ferns, graceful orchids, and stately lilies to a shelf with small decorative house plants next to his cash register. The cooler on the back wall is overflowing with an astounding array of cut flowers.

"How's business?" I ask.

"No complaints." He looks heavenward and smiles. "Mother's Day, graduations, weddings, Memorial Day—May is an excellent month to be a florist."

Mr. Steinhauser is a stocky gentleman with thinning gray hair and tiny rectangular spectacles that he keeps on a chain around his neck. "You'll be having a graduation party at Henderson House soon, won't you?" he asks.

"Not too soon. Johnny still has one more year of middle school."

"I can't believe it. He's so tall. I would have sworn he was already at College High."

"He's getting taller every day, it seems. Mr. Steinhauser, how many years has your shop been here?"

"Oh, my father and I opened the store in 1916, when we moved from New York to Bartlesville. I was much slimmer back then," he says, patting the belly under his vest.

"Weren't we all?" I say with a laugh. "May I ask you a somewhat personal question?" I inquire.

I am filled with courage today.

"Of course, Mrs. Henderson."

"Is it difficult to be a German-American with another war on the horizon?"

"That is a good question." He thinks for a moment. "You are originally from Missouri, correct?"

"Yes."

"If a group of people from Missouri banded together and killed innocent people in their desire to, oh, I don't know, take over Iowa, would it be difficult for you?"

"Yes," I nod. "I'd be outraged, scared, probably a little angry."

"But you'd know not everyone from Missouri is like that," he says.

"Yes, I would."

"And you'd certainly know you would never do any of those terrible things, even though you are originally from Missouri."

"Yes."

"You would probably also be very glad to be living here, not in Missouri, during those troubled times. In fact, it might make you even prouder to call Oklahoma your home."

"It might at that." I agree with a nod.

"But you would still cherish all of your wonderful memories of growing up in Missouri, wouldn't you?"

"Of course I would."

"Then you understand exactly how I feel right now." He turns his attention to the plant shelf and pulls a few more options for me to choose from.

"You and I have something in common," I say.

Mr. Steinhauser stops to look up at me.

"Neither one of us is native to these parts," I continue. "We both immigrated to Bartlesville."

He smiles and nods his head in agreement. "Now, which one of these little beauties would you like for your windowsill?" He gestures to the African violets on the counter.

"These two look perfect," I say, pulling two of them forward.

"Please, select a third one, Mrs. Henderson," Mr. Steinhauser says. "There's a special promotion today, for immigrants only—buy two, get one free." He winks.

Back on the sidewalk, with three African violets carefully packaged in white tissue paper and nestled in a brown shopping bag, I continue down Johnstone Avenue. My conversation with Mr. Steinhauser boosted my resolve and reminds me of something in addition to courage I need to take into my meeting with Mr. Linn—empathy.

When I stop to think about it, I realize that my sons never got into any serious trouble. Artie stole a library book once. He forgot his library card and needed a book on the civil war, as I recall, to write a speech in ninth grade. He snuck the book out of the building in his knapsack. When the librarian called me, we laughed about it. I made Artie march right back down to the library with his card, apologize, and check out the book properly. The librarian asked him to come in the next Saturday and shelve books as his penance. Oh, how I wish today's situation with Mr. Linn and Sonny was that easy to fix.

I walk into Linn Brothers, and Peggy hurries to the front of the store to welcome me. I hadn't thought about Peggy. She might be in danger from Sonny's advances as well.

Courage and empathy, I repeat in my head.

"Good morning, Mrs. Henderson." She smiles broadly. "How lovely to see you out shopping this morning."

"Good morning, Peggy. How is your mother feeling?" I ask. "I heard she was under the weather earlier this month."

"Oh, she's much better. Thank you for asking. What brings you in to see us today?"

"Two things. I have an appointment with Mr. Linn at eleven, and I'm in the market for a new boater to send to my son Robert for his birthday." I smile and look at my watch. "I think I should have my meeting with Mr. Linn first."

"Of course," she says.

"Peggy, would you mind storing my shopping bag behind the counter?" I ask. "I picked up some flowers earlier."

"I'd be happy to," she says, taking the bag from me. "I can sit the bag right here for safekeeping. Isn't it exciting about Florence and the Tulsa store?"

"Yes, it is." I agree. "Sounds like they gave her the royal treatment on Wednesday."

"They certainly did! Let me escort you upstairs, and I'll inform Mr. Linn you've arrived."

Peggy gestures toward the staircase in the back corner of the room. I look around. Sonny is nowhere in sight.

As we climb the stairs, the sweet smell of roses fills the air. I noticed Peggy's perfume earlier, and it was citrusy rather than sweet. I check her desk at the top of the landing, but I don't see a vase. The rose scent grows stronger for a moment and then begins to fade. It's the same fragrance as the bouquet Charles brought me all those years ago when he announced our move to Oklahoma. It's the smell of change. My heart beats faster, and a lump forms in my throat.

Courage and empathy, I repeat to myself.

Peggy knocks on Mr. Linn's door and sticks her head in to announce me. "Go right on in," she says. "I'll pull some hats for you to look at after your meeting."

Mr. Linn rises from behind his desk to greet me. His orange color is very stable. I don't think he has any idea why I am here. "Mrs. Henderson, what a pleasure to see you," he says, motioning for me to take a seat in the chair opposite his desk. "I wasn't at all surprised you wanted to come in and talk," he says with a smile.

"You weren't?" I ask, puzzled.

"Of course not. It's only natural for you to have Florence's best interests at heart."

"That is why I'm here," I respond. It sounds as if he already knows Sonny has been making Florence uncomfortable. He can't approve of his son's behavior, can he?

"Florence and her boy must feel like family, after living with you for so many years," he says, sitting back comfortably in his office chair.

"Yes, they do. I suppose that's why I felt justified in coming to speak with you today about the—" I pause, "—situation."

"Hmm, well this is a once-in-a-lifetime opportunity for Florence," he says. "I spoke with my uncle yesterday, and he said Florence is planning on giving him her answer on Monday. I'm sure she wants to talk it over with the whole family this weekend. I admire how they stick together—so nice for her son. But I suppose if the entire family decides to move to Tulsa, that would be a big change for you and Henderson House. What questions do you have for me?"

Once-in-a-lifetime opportunity? The entire family moving to Tulsa? My ears ring, and my throat feels scratchy.

"Questions?" I buy myself another moment to get my bearings. "Well, I was wondering if you could tell me a little more about the opportunity," I say, hoping Mr. Linn will say something, anything, that will help me understand.

"Certainly," he says. "It all started on Monday when my Uncle Aaron—he owns the Tulsa store—told me he was looking for a new store manager. Immediately, I thought of Florence and recommended her for the position. She's the best person for the job. As you know, she went down for an interview on Wednesday and, as I expected, my uncle was very impressed. Offered her the job on the spot." He pats the arms of his desk chair. "She'd be crazy to pass this up!"

"Crazy, indeed," I croak.

Florence lied to all of us. She went to Tulsa for a job interview, not to teach them about window displays. Not only did she lie at supper Monday night, but she also conveniently left the job offer out of her recap on Wednesday evening. Florence had the perfect opportunity to confide in me when we were alone in my suite, discussing her incident with Sonny. We even talked about options for her to change her situation at work, and she didn't say a word. Not one single word.

"When is your uncle hoping she can start?" I ask, wishing I had a glass of water.

"He'd take her tomorrow if she could get there, but he understands the effort required to move a family. Mrs. Henderson, I believe this job in Tulsa is a wonderful step up for Florence and the whole family."

"Thank you, Mr. Linn," I respond slowly. "I'm glad to hear you are in favor of this opportunity."

The whole family. My hands tremble. I wrap them around the pocketbook in my lap, attempting to keep them still. The ringing in my ears turns to a loud buzzing, and I feel dizzy. No wonder Florence hasn't been very supportive of her sister's interest in Mr. Davis. I'm sure her plans don't include Bessie falling in love, staying in Bartlesville, and not chipping in on a house in Tulsa. I knew their shared savings account was a bad idea from the beginning. I always imagined problems would occur if Eddie met someone, wanted to get married, and needed to withdraw his share. Who knows what Florence might do to make sure Bessie—and her money—moves to Tulsa. I squeeze my pocketbook tighter.

Mildred, you need to pivot the conversation, I remind myself. *Don't lose sight of your original mission.* Right. I must put this unexpected news out of my mind and tap into my courage again. I sit up a little straighter in my chair.

"Mr. Linn, discussing Florence's new position is not the only reason I wanted to see you this morning."

"What else is on your mind?" he asks.

"Let me begin by saying that I have great admiration for you and your family and the successful business you have built. I'm also very grateful for the career you've provided for Florence, even before this . . ." I pause again, searching for the right words: ". . . exciting development in Tulsa."

"Thank you for your kind words," Mr. Linn says as his eyes narrow.

"As a mother of four boys, I've always said I would rather have a friend tell me if one of them was in trouble than hear it from a stranger on the street," I begin.

Mr. Linn's Adam's apple bobs up and down as he swallows hard. His orange glow darkens slightly.

"Last Wednesday evening," I continue, "a good friend at church, a woman I would trust with my own life, told me she heard some troubling stories about Sonny and the way he treated women while he was at the University of Tulsa."

"Oh," he says, looking down at his hands on the desk.

"I spoke to Florence about it, and she told me Sonny's behavior has made her uncomfortable recently. I'm not the gossiping kind, Mr. Linn. I promise I won't share this information with anyone else."

"Thank you for your discretion," he says.

"However, in my experience, once one person hears of something like this, well, it's usually not long before it spreads."

"Yes, that is how these things often play out." He sighs.

"Did you know about his difficulties in Tulsa?" I ask.

"I heard from a school official. A woman complained about his . . ." he pauses, glancing down at his desk before meeting my gaze again, "advances. I figured it was inexperience mixed with youthful exuberance. A onetime mistake. I didn't know there were more incidents."

"I wish I could offer you some advice, but I'm afraid I don't have any."

"Sounds like I need to start by having a serious chat with him this evening," Mr. Linn says. "Mrs. Henderson, I don't know if this will make you feel better, and I would never want Florence to know because she is completely qualified for the job in Tulsa, but I noticed Sonny's interest in her, and it concerned me. The complaint in Tulsa was also from an older woman. It's one of the reasons I was so pleased to recommend Florence for this promotion."

"It's nice to hear that you care about Florence's welfare, Mr. Linn, but you cannot relocate every woman who strikes his fancy."

Mr. Linn closes his eyes for a second and presses his lips together into a tense smile. "Thank you for coming in to speak to me, Mrs. Henderson. I'm grateful."

"You're most welcome. Now, I think I'll head downstairs to find a hat for Robert's birthday." I rise from my seat and exit Mr. Linn's office.

I've completed my mission, but I feel hollow. I stand motionless in the empty reception area. As if to keep my heart from spilling out, I clutch my handbag closer to my chest. My head spins as I try to make sense of Florence's deception and the possibility that the whole family might leave Henderson House. Would I want to stay in the house without them? Rent their rooms to strangers?

Inching my way to the top of the staircase, I'm mesmerized by the glowing light of the showroom below. It's the same disorienting sensation I had earlier today, when I walked out into the sunshine and imagined I was at Robert's beach house. I release my panicked grip on my bag and place it in the crook of my arm. Grasping the railing with my other hand, I take the stairs one at a time. In the back of my mind, a seagull squawks and my grandchildren beckon me to play.

CHAPTER SIXTEEN

Florence

EVERYTHING ABOUT TODAY is wrong. I'm in a strange car with a stranger driving. Bessie's sitting up front, all dolled up for a trip to the cemetery. Eddie and I are floating around in the big back seat, and Johnny isn't here at all. I suppose this is the beginning of Johnny doing more on his own. This big machine feels lonely without my boy. Eddie scooches next to me so that he is sitting in the middle. He leans forward and puts his head between Frank and Bessie. He's probably waiting for the right moment to ask my sister to sing with him.

Usually when we go on car trips, Eddie drives Mrs. Henderson's car, and Bessie sits up front so they can sing together. Johnny and I sit in the back and listen. Johnny's getting more comfortable with his own voice and has started singing along recently, leaving me out in the cold. As my brother Eddie likes to say, I couldn't carry a tune in a bucket. Bessie, on the other hand, has the voice of an angel. Clear, strong, and perfectly in tune.

The most frustrating thing about my lack of musical talent is that I appreciate music. I marvel at the harmonies. I'm moved to tears by a beautiful ballad. I listen to the organ in church and feel confident I will begin singing a hymn on exactly the right note, yet when I open my mouth, somehow it's never quite right. I'm usually able to slide my voice into the right key by the end of the first verse, but the awkwardness is humiliating. At least hearing them sing in the car today will feel normal, even if it will be annoying.

"Hey, Bessie, how 'bout a little song? I was thinking maybe we could do 'You Are My Sunshine.' Whaddaya say?" Eddie asks, as expected.

"Oh, I like that song," Frank says, nodding.

"You start, Bessie, and then I'll come in," Eddie encourages.

"All right," Bessie responds with a quiver in her voice. Is she nervous about singing in front of her new boyfriend? I fold my arms across my chest and roll my eyes as she begins:

"You are my sunshine,
My only sunshine
You make me happy
When skies are gray"

Then Eddies joins in on a low harmony line and they sing together:

"You'll never know, dear
How much I love you
Please don't take
My sunshine away"

They begin the next verse and, much to my dismay, Frank comes in at tenor:

"The other night, dear
As I lay sleeping
I dreamed I held you
In my arms
When I awoke, dear
I was mistaken
So I hung my head, and I cried
You are my sunshine
My only sunshine
You make me happy
When skies are gray
You'll never know, dear
How much I love you"

They pause and slow down for the last line, savoring every note of their three-part harmony:

"Please don't take
My sunshine away"

They hold on to the final note. Their voices make an exceptional trio. As the last chord fades, the three of them break into giddy laughter.

"Hey! What do you know? Frank's a tenor!" Eddie exclaims. "We've been searching for a tenor all our lives!"

They laugh again.

"We sounded pretty good," Frank chimes in. "If this engineering gig doesn't work out, maybe we should go on the road."

"Eddie and I used to sing together all the time," Bessie says.

"Boy, did they!" I pipe up from the back. "And when she says, 'all the time,' she means it!"

"I can see why," Frank says. "Your voices blend incredibly well. Johnny wasn't kidding when he said you have a beautiful singing voice, Bessie."

My sister shrugs. "With my squeaky speaking voice, it always surprises folks when I sing," she says.

"Your speaking voice isn't squeaky," Frank responds. "Your speaking voice is charming. Your singing voice, however, is spectacular."

Wow, he's really laying it on thick with the compliments this morning.

"Thank you, Frank," she whispers.

"You know, sis," Eddie says, "one of the worst things about you switching over to being a Baptist is that I don't get to sing with you in church anymore. You're in for a treat tomorrow, Frank. There is nothing like singing next to Bessie Blackwell in church. People turn around to see if there's an angel in the congregation."

"I was already looking forward to sitting next to you in church tomorrow. Now I can hardly wait," Frank says, and he sounds completely genuine.

Really? I feel sick to my stomach.

My plan to sow concern in Bessie over Frank's potentially nefarious intentions doesn't seem to have taken root. He can't be as perfect as he appears. No one is. Time to move on to plan B. If Bessie won't ask him the tough questions, I will.

"Frank, you want to take this next right onto 169 South. It will bring us down through Oologah, and then we'll hop on Route 88," Eddie directs.

"Got it. Thanks, Eddie."

We'll be on this stretch of road for at least thirty minutes. Now is the perfect time to delve into Fabulous Frank's mysterious past. He's hiding something. I'm sure of it. We're going to learn more about Frank Davis today, whether he likes it or not.

"So, Frank, did you grow up with music in your house as a boy?" I ask.

"Oh, sure. My mother played the piano. My sister Helen and I both took lessons. I never stuck with it, but my sister did. My older brother, Pete, plays the fiddle." Frank pauses. "At least, he did the last time I saw him."

"Yes, you've been living away from your family for a long time, haven't you? When was the last time you saw them?" I continue.

"Gosh, let me see. I went home to Joplin for my father's funeral in '37, so four years ago. I saw my mother, my sister Helen and her husband, and their two boys. There were loads of cousins and aunts and uncles there—people I hadn't seen for ages." He pauses again. "Pete and his wife weren't able to make it."

"Oh, that's too bad. When was the last time you saw your brother?" I ask.

"Well, Florence, it's been a long time. I haven't seen him since before I left for San Francisco, I guess." Frank looks into the rearview mirror and makes brief eye contact with me before returning his gaze to the road.

I have the feeling I've pulled on a loose thread. Let's see if I can get something to unravel.

"Were you very close to your brother growing up?" I ask.

"Yup, we were thick as thieves. Born not quite two years apart, sort of like you and Bessie. We loved playing baseball together. Tossing the ball around with Johnny the other day brought back a load of fond memories. My brother, Pete, had an accident when he was fifteen and damaged his right leg. When he recovered, he could walk but with a limp. He couldn't play sports anymore. That's when he took up the fiddle." Frank's voice trails off.

"I'm sorry about his accident, Frank. What happened?" Bessie asks.

"We were out riding at my uncle's place. Pete's horse got spooked, threw him, and stepped on his upper leg. It was a bad break. The doctor set it as best he could, but it didn't heal quite right." Frank rubs the steering wheel with his hands. "His bum leg kept him out of the war, though."

"Was that difficult for him?" I ask. "Bessie and I knew several young men in Claremore who wanted to fight and weren't eligible. They were simply beside themselves when they couldn't serve. Remember Jimmy Jackson?"

"I do remember Jimmy," Bessie says. "He had dental issues, as I recall."

"Yes. Couldn't serve because of rotten teeth," I confirm. "When anyone from our county died, he took it personally, as if he could have saved them if he'd been over there. Did your brother feel like that?"

"I'm not sure," Frank says, slowing the pace of his speech. "When I shipped out, we wished we were going together." Frank rolls his window down for a little more air. "Things changed between us while I was away. Then he moved." He pauses again. "To Cincinnati. We don't . . . we aren't . . . we haven't seen each other in a long time."

"I'm so sorry, Frank," Bessie offers. "It's never easy when family members drift apart, especially if you were close when you were young."

"No, never easy," I agree and wait a moment before trying to pull the thread completely free. "Did something happen to push you apart?"

"Really, Florence," Bessie says, intervening. "Frank, you don't have to answer her."

"No, no, it's only natural for your sister to want to know more about me and my family." Frank shifts his grip on the wheel. "Gosh, I've learned enough about the Blackwells this week to write a book! It's my turn in the spotlight." He swallows. "To be honest, I don't talk about what happened between me and Pete very often, if ever."

"Frank, I agree with Bessie. Don't feel you have to satisfy my sister's unending curiosity," Eddie says from beside me in the back seat, giving me a little nudge.

"What was it your mother used to say, Bessie?" Frank asks.

"There are stories to share and stories to keep," my sister replies.

When did she find the opportunity to bestow such a personal piece of family wisdom on him?

"Right," he begins. "So, this is a story I normally keep, but it may answer several of the questions I'm sure are burning a hole in your big brain back there, Florence." Frank glances in the rearview mirror and catches my eye again.

Hmm. As if he knows what all my questions are. Just you wait, Mr. Davis. I've got plenty of questions on deck for you.

Frank lets out an audible sigh. "So, where to begin? I married my high school sweetheart. Her name was Annie. Her name is still Annie. She's still Annie." He's flustered. This is good. Frank continues: "Anyway, we'd been married just over a year when I left for active duty. In late August 1918, there was an error." He takes a deep breath in and blows it out, making a whoosh sound.

"Frank, really you don't have to tell us anything you don't want to," Bessie says. I see her left arm reach across the seat. Did she just put her hand on his knee?

"It's okay, Bessie. This is important for you and your family to know."

I try to peer over the seat to see if her hand is actually touching him, but there's no way to do it inconspicuously.

Frank resumes his story. "At the end of August, my family received a telegram from the War Department, regretting to inform them that I had been killed in action. My folks held a memorial service for me and everything. I heard it was real nice."

"I can't even imagine," Bessie whispers.

"Whoa, I've heard stories about those kinds of mistakes happening, but I never thought they were true." Eddie shakes his head.

"Yep, it's very rare, but it happened. No one knows how they made the mix-up. I still had my dog tags on. It's possible it was another Frank Davis. It's not like I have a unique name. Anyway, we never got an answer as to who really died. Clearly it wasn't me," Frank says with a tilt of his head.

I can tell I've put him on the spot.

"Where were you during the confusion?" Bessie asks.

"While my family was back in Joplin mourning, I was lying in a hospital bed in France," Frank replies.

"Is that when you got your scar?" Bessie asks.

"Yes," Frank says, running his right hand through his hair. "I worked in a small advance team of combat engineers. We'd finished a mission cutting barbed wired and repairing some bridges on the Meuse River in anticipation of the next Allied offensive."

"Oof," Eddie moans. "I didn't know you were a combat engineer, Frank. That's risky business working out front to clear the way."

"Yeah, well, the funny thing is, I was injured after I returned to the safety of my unit. We got shelled, and my forehead took a direct hit," Frank says. "It took over a week for me to regain consciousness and at least another before I was well enough to write a letter to Annie." He exhales.

"While I was still recovering, my letter arrived in Joplin and the postmark was weeks *after* the date on the telegram. My sister said it threw the entire family into a tizzy. I guess my mother got on the phone to Washington and didn't stop talking until she finally reached someone who could confirm I was indeed alive and in a hospital in France." He rests for a moment.

"What happened next?" Eddie asks, sitting on the edge of the back seat.

"I lay in a hospital bed, waiting for a reply from Annie. Only, I never got one. Instead, I got word I was being discharged—sent home. I was surprised 'cause I thought I was close to being fit enough to return to duty. I still didn't know about the mistake. I didn't know my family had spent six or seven weeks thinking I was dead. To this day, I wonder whether I got sent home because the war was almost over or because my mom made all those phone calls to the War Department." Frank shakes his head. "On the ship crossing the Atlantic, a chaplain finally told me the government had mistakenly reported me as killed in action."

"Oh, Frank," Bessie gasps as she brings both hands to her mouth. At least I know where her hands are now. "And when you got home to Joplin, what happened then?" she asks.

"When I got home . . . well, there was a hero's welcome for me at the train station—the whole 'soldier back from the dead' story got most of the town to turn out. I saw my mom in the crowd first. When I hugged her, she sobbed like I never knew any person could. It was like every inch of her body was crying. I wiped her tears and smiled at her and looked around. I couldn't see Annie anywhere. When I asked where Annie was, my mother said the rest of the family was waiting to greet me at home. I figured Annie didn't want to deal with all the commotion—it was quite a scene. Mom and I walked home from the station, hand in hand. It was the day before Halloween—bright blue sky, the last of the fall colors still on the trees, carved pumpkins smiling from every porch. I was so happy to be home. Everyone was calling out to us and waving as we walked.

"When we got to my parent's house, my dad was at the door. He gave me a great big bear hug and then said everyone was going to wait outside so I could greet Annie on my own. I stood in the doorway for a moment. Annie and Pete were sitting on the sofa together. Her face was white as a sheet. Pete encouraged her to get up, and when she stood, I ran to her and we embraced. I remember how good she smelled—like lavender." He rubs his hands on the steering wheel again. "Anyway, she broke our embrace, and I threw my arms around my brother next. That's when I knew something was wrong."

"How did you know?" Bessie asks, sounding as if she's on the verge of tears.

"His hug didn't feel right. When we were little, Pete would hug me as hard as he could—pick me up, clean off the ground, and practically squeeze the wind out of me. Even when I got too big for him to pick me up, he still hugged me with the same intensity. I loved those fierce hugs. But I didn't get one that day. When Pete stepped back, I asked what the heck was going on. Annie started crying, Pete started crying, then I started crying. Pete did most of the talking. Said how they thought I was dead and found comfort in each other's company. Everyone in my family loved Annie. It sort of made sense for Pete and Annie to be together if I was never coming back. Pete said that when they found out I was alive, he planned to move away to give me and Annie a chance to start over." Frank sighs. "And then Annie said there was a recent development that made it impossible for Pete to leave her."

"Oh," I gasp. "She was pregnant, wasn't she?"

"Yup," Frank says. "About six weeks, which meant she and Pete, well, they didn't exactly waste much time before comforting one another."

"So, you granted her the divorce," Bessie says.

"Yup," Frank says again.

"And they moved to Cincinnati," Eddie adds.

"Right again," Frank replies.

"And then you moved as far away from your family as you could—all the way to San Francisco," I whisper, almost as if talking to myself.

"Bingo," Frank says as he raises his right hand off the wheel for a moment before returning it with a thud.

"Geez louise, Frank." Eddie pats Frank's shoulder from the back seat.

"Oh, Frank." Bessie dabs at her eyes with a handkerchief. "I'm so, so, sorry. For you, for Annie, and for Pete. For your whole family."

I lean forward, and I see Frank take Bessie's hand.

"Thank you, Bessie. Now you know why I focused on my career and stayed away for so long. But it's time to put it all to rest. This summer, I am determined to make a trip home. I wrote my sister Helen and asked if I could visit for the Fourth of July. She's going to reach out to Pete and Annie to see if they might consider coming from Ohio to join us. It's time for us to be a family again," he says as he squeezes my sister's hand.

Bessie looks at him adoringly.

This car ride is not turning out at all the way I hoped it would. My questions have done nothing but turn Fabulous Frank into a wounded bird Bessie can rescue and nurse back to health. Plus, she won't see his divorce as a roadblock to a relationship now. Frank's wife was unfaithful. His divorce will be acceptable in her mind and probably with the church. My plan to discredit Fabulous Frank has hit a dead end. I need a new strategy. Maybe I've been approaching this from the wrong direction. I've been trying to push Bessie away from Frank. Perhaps I should be pulling her closer to me and Johnny, where she belongs.

"Good man, Frank," Eddie says. "I'll be wishing you the best of luck with your reunion this summer."

"Thanks, Eddie," Frank replies. "So, Florence," Frank says, looking up in the rearview mirror and catching my eye one more time, "what's your next question?"

And then I say something I've never said in my entire life: "How 'bout another song?"

CHAPTER SEVENTEEN

Bessie

"THERE'S THE ENTRANCE, Frank." Florence points to the brick columns marking the main gate of Woodlawn Cemetery. Frank pulls onto the dirt road that encircles the cemetery.

Florence continues to direct from the back seat: "Stay on the big road until we get to the third little intersection on the right. There it is. Turn here. Do you see the series of gravestones in front of the elm tree? That's our family plot. If you drive past it a bit, there's a spot to park. Park in the shade over there, where the drive widens."

Frank does as he's told. "I have to say, this is new to me." He puts the car in park.

"Taking directions from my sister?" Eddie asks from the backseat with a laugh. "You'll get used to it."

"We all have," I say.

Florence huffs.

"No, not that. I've never tended to a gravesite before," Frank says. "I've visited them but never tended to one."

"Never?" I ask.

"What do we do?" Frank opens his door.

We all follow suit, then get out of the car and stretch. I take off my gloves and place them on the front seat as I pick up my new hat. Florence bought us each a broad-brimmed summer hat at Martin's this week. I guess they were on sale for only two dollars and, according to my sister, look exactly like the ones featured on the current cover of *LIFE* magazine.

"Don't worry; Bessie will tell you exactly what to do," Florence says. "If today is like every other cemetery visit, you're about to see her get very bossy."

"Frank already knows I take our Decoration Day flowers seriously," I respond.

"First, we clean up the gravesites," Eddie says to Frank across the trunk of the car. "Then we plant the flowers, and then we have a big picnic." He reaches his arms way up high and brings them down to pat his belly in anticipation of the lunch Mrs. Henderson packed for us this morning.

Of course, no one knows that I helped make the egg salad sandwiches.

The day is getting warmer, but it's still pleasant for late May. Eddie takes off his jacket and lays it on the back seat of the car. Frank rolls up his sleeves after he sheds his coat. He keeps his fedora on, and it reminds me of the first time I saw him playing catch with Johnny. Was that only five days ago?

"Don't get any ideas about opening that picnic basket yet." I wiggle a finger at Eddie. "Let's unload the car and get to work."

Frank opens the trunk. "How on earth did all this stuff get into my car?" he exclaims as he pushes his hat back on his head in disbelief, placing his hands on his hips.

With his hair caught up in his hat, the pink-and-white zipper pattern of his scar shines across the top of his forehead. My heart aches for Frank after the story he shared in the car.

Dear Heavenly Father, please bless Frank Davis as he works to reconcile with Pete and Annie this summer. Open their hearts to your healing power of forgiveness and love. Amen.

"Oh, you gotta keep an eye on these two!" Eddie laughs. "You never know what they're gonna decide we can't live without on a car trip!"

I give my brother a playful jab in the ribs. "Nonsense. I bet we will use every single item we packed today. You'll see," I say, nodding in Frank's direction. "Now, the first thing we need to do is get everything out of the trunk." Frank and Eddie start unloading.

"I'll put the picnic basket under the tree," I say, taking the basket from Frank.

"What do you want to do with the crates of flowers?" Eddie asks.

"Let's leave them here in the shade until we are ready to plant them," I answer.

Frank takes out two large pails and looks at me for direction.

"You can put those down right there. Thank you," I say.

"Sure thing." Frank puts the pails down, and I dig through them.

"Florence, here are your gardening gloves." I hand her a pair of gloves and take my own. "I packed work gloves for you two as well," I say, handing a pair of gloves to Frank and then a pair to Eddie. "We need to clear away any weeds and rake the entire plot. Then we'll focus on the planting beds in front of each headstone," I say. "Eddie and Frank, would you mind carrying the pails over?" I pick up the rake.

"No problem!" Eddie says, and we all begin walking back to the gravesites with our collection of tools.

"I've never seen her so commanding," Frank whispers to Eddie.

"Yup, when it comes to gardening, Bessie's the biggest toad in the puddle," Eddie replies.

"Once Mama figured out that our sister was a disaster in the kitchen, she set Bessie up outside with a kitchen garden," Florence adds. "Mama thought the least Bessie could do was learn to *grow* food."

For once, my sister's comment carries no sting. I smile, remembering working in the kitchen with Mrs. Henderson this morning. Frank went on and on about how light and fluffy the biscuits were. No one has a clue about my secret cooking lessons.

"Gardening came easy to Bessie," Eddie adds, "like licking butter off a spoon. She spent every moment she could outside with her plants."

"Cousin Wahya built a little bench for her garden so she could sit out there and read, too," Florence remembers.

"I loved my bench," I shout over my shoulder as I continue to walk in front. "Then I could be surrounded by my two favorite things at once, books and plants." I grin and swing the rake as I walk.

"Oh, is it any wonder you're an old maid?" Florence moans.

"Spinster," I correct. "I've decided I'm not an old maid. I'm a spinster. Has a nice ring to it, don't you think?"

"Spinster. Sure, I like it," Frank agrees. "But I wouldn't get too used to it if I were you," he adds playfully, and Eddie makes a *whoop-whoop* sound.

I'm blushing again, but this time, I couldn't care less if my sister sees.

"Really, Edward," Florence scolds, "we are at a cemetery. Try to be on your best behavior."

"Yes, ma'am. Sorry," Eddie says with mock remorse.

The four of us reach the plot and stand, looking at the headstones. There are four markers in total: one for Grandma and Grandpa Blackwell, a small one for the twins who were born before Eddie, a single stone for Mama and Mae, and one for Rachel.

"Frank, here's a garden hand fork," I say.

He takes the tool from me and gives it a once-over.

"Is that what you call this? A garden hand fork?" He stares at the implement in his hand.

"Oh, I don't know for sure. That's what I've always called it," I say.

"No, no, I think that is its official name, a garden hand fork," Florence confirms.

"You learn something new every day," Frank says.

"You can use it to remove the weeds and old roots from the little flower beds in front of each headstone and loosen the soil," I say. "You want to turn the soil over so it's ready for the new flowers. Here's a pail for the weeds and roots and leaves you dig up. Eddie, would you take this trowel and start edging the beds? Florence, why don't you take the other hand fork and start weeding the plot while I rake," I say.

"Cheers," Frank says as he lifts his garden fork up to Eddie's trowel.

"Long life to you," Eddie replies as they clink their garden tools like champagne glasses.

"Oh, really, you two." I roll my eyes and giggle. It's nice to see Frank and Eddie getting along so well.

The four of us work in silence. A warm breeze and plenty of birdsong keep us company. I rake up a final pile of dead grass and cedar needles and deposit it into the pail. Tilting my head back so the sun slips under the brim of my new hat, I soak up the warmth of the almost-summer sun on my face. Carolina jessamine blooms along the cemetery fence and fills the air with its sweet scent. An eastern kingbird sings a high-pitched chattering tune from a nearby tree. I close my eyes. Right now, in this moment, I am happy.

Lord, thank you for the warmth of the sun, the fragrance of flowers in bloom, and all the creatures who share this earth with us. Help me, dear Lord, to take time every day to be grateful for this beautiful world you have created. Amen.

"You'll wrinkle up like a prune if you keep your face in the sun," Florence says as she walks over to dump her last handful of weeds in the pail. I keep my eyes shut a moment longer, basking in the sun.

And Lord, please bless my sister Florence and help her know your peace. Amen, again.

"Let's see how the hired hands are coming along," I say as I open my eyes and drop my face back into the shade of my hat. "Oh, the beds look good," I observe. "I'd say we're ready to plant. Frank, can you help me get the flower crates?"

"Absolutely." We start back to the car together.

"Bessie?"

"Yes, Frank?"

"I hope I didn't overwhelm you with too much information in the car. Florence kept asking questions, and I had an all-powerful desire for you to know the truth about what happened with my first marriage," Frank says. "I planned on telling you in private, but it just sort of came tumbling out this morning. I hope it wasn't too much too soon."

"Not at all," I respond. "I'm glad you told us."

Frank stops walking. He removes his hat, runs his fingers through his hair, and replaces the fedora over his scar. I understand this habit now. When he runs his fingers through his curls and touches his scar, does it remind him of his sorrow or of his good fortune? He survived. He didn't die in France, and I'm so thankful he's here with me today.

"There's something I'd like to tell you as well," I say.

"What is it?" Frank asks.

Frank's been completely honest with me about his past relationship. Should I return the favor and tell him about Doc Jenkins? Edna said getting to know Frank was the first order of business and that I have plenty of time to figure out when and how to share my secrets. I know where to start my story, but I'm not sure where to stop. I don't have permission from Florence to tell Frank about Johnny. Edna's right. I have plenty of time to share my secrets with him. Today is about honoring Frank's story, not muddying the waters with mine.

"I'm sorry for your heartbreak," I say.

"My heart's been feeling a little better lately," Frank replies. "Thank you for letting me tag along today."

He bumps his shoulder into me lightly as if we are two school friends joking around on the playground, and we continue walking.

"Oh, my goodness, we are the ones who should thank you for driving."

"No. Really, I'm so grateful. It's been way too long since I've taken part in a family event like this. When I lived in California, I had work friends, but outside of the office, well, I mostly kept to myself. It's nice to be . . ." he pauses, "part of something."

"We're delighted to welcome you as an honorary member of the Blackwell clan today," I say with a little bow.

"I'm not sure Florence is so happy about it," Frank says as we reach the car and the flowers.

"Don't pay Florence any mind. She's having a fit of the blues because Johnny isn't with us today. His job at the country club is only the beginning. Johnny's going to have more and more activities that don't include her. I know a young woman at work whose new mother-in-law is making things difficult for her. I worry Florence won't be the easiest mother-in-law herself."

"From what I can see, she's not the easiest sister," Frank says.

"No, I suppose not. But she's the only one I've got left." I pause. "How different life would be if there were four Blackwell sisters still alive."

"Four Blackwell sisters? I'm not sure I could follow that many directions," he says.

I laugh lightly. Frank holds my gaze without blinking, and my heart races. I look away first.

"Things are going well at work, and it's going to be a busy week," he says, changing the subject. "I want to make sure you and I set aside some time for each other." Frank takes my garden-gloved hand in his own work-gloved hand. It's sweet and comical at the same time. "I was thinking," he continues, "we already have one date set for tomorrow—we're going to church and then out for a drive to look at houses."

"Yes," I say.

"I would like to drive you to the Wednesday Night Supper, again, but I'd like it to be just the two of us this Wednesday, if that's all right with you."

"So that it's more like another date?" I ask quietly. He swings our clumsily gloved hands back and forth and looks up at me.

"Exactly, so it's another date," he says, smiling.

"Agreed," I nod.

"And then, if it's not too much to ask, I'd like to take you out to dinner and a picture show next Saturday night."

Our hands continue to swing back and forth.

"Three dates in one week? Mr. Davis, I don't know what to say!"

"Please say yes. I've been waiting a long time to meet someone like you. Bessie Blackwell, will you go on three dates with me this week?" He raises our clasped hands and adds his other hand around them, pulling me into him. A tremor runs through my body.

"On one condition," I say.

"You name it."

"I get to hold the popcorn bucket at the movies." I smile.

"Agreed," he says with a sigh of relief.

Once again, we're close enough to kiss, but the cemetery is certainly not the time or place. I pull my hand out of his grasp and say, "Let's get these flowers planted." When I bend down to pick up one of the flower crates, I'm so lightheaded, I almost fall over.

CHAPTER EIGHTEEN

Florence

BESSIE AND FRANK return with the flower crates. She's blushing again. I wonder what they've been up to. I don't like her spending time alone with Fabulous Frank. After his confession in the car today, I bet she's dying to bare her soul to him. I need to find a way to make sure my sister keeps our secret. She swears she never said a word to my husband, John, but I don't buy it. If she's broken our promise once, she could break it again.

"I've been trying to piece together the Blackwell family story here," Frank says, "but I'm not sure I can do it from these four headstones."

"Allow me to take you on a brief tour. Our ancestors came to Oklahoma on the Cherokee Trail of Tears," Eddie begins. He tells Frank about the Indian Removal Act, sharing the details of how our grandfather and his family were forced out of North Carolina, while our grandmother's family was rounded up in Georgia one night when they were at the dinner table. Grandma's family owned a large farm and lived in a proper house, yet the soldiers didn't even allow them to bring a change of clothes or a blanket.

For the first time today, I'm glad Johnny isn't here. I hated listening to my grandparent's stories about the removal when I was younger. Grandma said we needed to hear and repeat the stories to honor the dead and celebrate the resilient spirit of the Cherokee people, but her stories only made me sad and angry. They still do.

Eddie continues the sorrowful tale of our grandparents' journey. They met as teenagers during the removal. Their families survived several months in an internment camp in Tennessee, then left in the same detachment of over a thousand Cherokee for the long walk to Indian Territory. The winter of 1838 to 1839 was brutal. When they reached the Ohio River, their detachment had to wait in Kentucky for the ice to melt before the flatboats could carry them across the river. They camped near the ferry crossing for several weeks under harsh winter conditions huddling together in canvas tents. Local farmers wouldn't allow them to cut wood to make fires and keep warm. Both of Grandma's younger siblings died—one during the wait for the ice to melt and the other a few days after they crossed into southern Illinois.

Fabulous Frank walks over and places a hand on my grandparents' headstone. Bet he wasn't expecting a depressing history lesson today. Bessie sets the bright orange and yellow blanket flowers next to my grandparents' grave.

Eddie moves on to the grave for the twins, William and Teddy.

"Mama gave birth to the twins just after Rachel turned two," Bessie says. "They only lived about six weeks. Mama started bringing us here to care for the gravesite and have picnics after they passed. We plant the forget-me-nots on their grave." She sets their blue flowers down.

"This grave holds our mama, Jennie Blackwell, and our sweet baby sister, Mae," Eddie says, taking his hat off as he looks down on them. "They died in the Spanish Flu epidemic. Mae wasn't quite seven."

"How tragic," Frank says.

Well, what did you expect, Frank? You volunteered for a trip to the cemetery.

"We buried them in one coffin. There was a shortage due to all the funerals at the time," Bessie explains. "They get the marigolds," she continues. "Our mama brought marigold seeds with her when she married our daddy and moved from Kansas. We grow them every year, plant them on her grave at Memorial Day, and collect the flower heads on Labor Day to harvest the seeds for next year."

Does she really think he'll be interested in the history of our marigold seeds?

"So, these plants can be traced all the way back to the seeds she originally brought to Oklahoma?" Frank asks. "That's amazing."

Oh, maybe these two really are meant for each other.

"And finally, we have our sister Rachel's grave," Eddie says, concluding his overview.

"Rachel is the sister who loved the color of lilacs. I remember from my tour of the flower project," Frank says.

"Correct. And this year we grew love-in-a-mist for her," Bessie says. "Though I'd hoped they'd be more purple than blue. It's always hard to find something the right color."

"Do you mind my asking how your sister Rachel passed?" Frank asks.

"She had an episode while she was sleeping." I jump in. "A seizure is what they called it. It was completely unexpected."

"I'm so sorry. Did she die in Wichita?" Frank asks.

"Yes, that's right. She died while we were in Wichita, living with my aunt. Bessie brought Rachel's body back to Claremore. We wanted her to be buried here with the family," I respond. "I stayed in Wichita with little Johnny. He was a newborn." I smile. I can almost hear his engineering brain working overtime as he tries to add everything up.

My apologies, Mr. Davis. This is one puzzle you won't be solving any time soon.

Over the years, I've mastered the ability to determine which details to include and which to leave out so that I'm not exactly lying but also not completely telling the truth. Bessie glares at me. I'm not sure whether it's fear or regret I see in her eyes.

"Um, where is your father buried?" Frank asks.

Silence. Even the birds seem to stop singing for a moment.

"Have you ever heard the expression 'some people are too mean to die'?" I ask.

Frank hesitates. "Yes."

"Our daddy is still alive," Bessie clarifies.

"What?" Frank asks.

"Yup. He lives here in Claremore with Cousin Wahya," Eddie says, scratching his chin.

"I guess I thought from the way you talk about him, he was no longer living." Frank hesitates. "Do you visit him much?"

"Rarely," I say. "And we certainly aren't paying the old goat a visit today," I add, staring back at my sister.

She looks away.

"Well, after what Bessie told me, I suppose I understand," Frank says.

"What did Bessie tell you?" I fire back at Frank.

Bessie steps forward and positions herself between me and Fabulous Frank. "I told Frank about leaving home and taking Eddie with me to keep him safe from Daddy's outbursts," she says.

I'm paralyzed. I can't move a muscle or blink an eye. My chest tightens. If she's already confided in him about Daddy, what else has she blathered on about?

"Well, the cat's out of the bag," Eddie says. "The King of Cowboy Coffee Hour has horns holding up his halo." Eddie's attempt to ease the tension falls flat. "Daddy used to have one heck of a temper, but he's pretty harmless now at seventy-eight and sober," he adds.

"Harmless for you!" I shout. "You didn't endure eighteen years of his bullying. Bessie got you out before he had the chance to inflict any permanent damage. You don't remember the tirades as clearly as I do. I still can't stand to be in the same room with him." The harshness of my voice reverberates off the headstones and rings in my ears.

"As our old friend Will Rogers used to say, 'Don't let yesterday use up too much of today,'" Eddie says in another attempt to lighten the mood. "I think we've taken Mr. Davis far enough down memory lane this morning."

"Eddie's right." Bessie claps her hands together. "Let's get these flowers in the ground and then tidy up so we can eat."

"Good with me, sis. I'm as hungry as a bear!" Eddie chimes in.

"What about this crate of flowers?" Frank asks.

"These bachelor buttons are for John's grave, Florence's husband. He's buried in the Fuller family plot," Bessie says, turning to me.

Since lashing out at Eddie, I've been standing perfectly still, focusing on a broken section of fence in the back corner of the cemetery. A stabbing pain shoots through the center of my chest. I can't believe Bessie told Frank about Daddy and taking Eddie out of the house. I must find a way to make sure she doesn't tell him our secret—and fast. I'm not ready for Johnny to know the truth—not even close to ready. I bend over and put my hands on my thighs. For a moment, I think I might be ill.

"Florence, are you all right?" Bessie whispers.

"Just a little short of breath," I say, straightening up. "Better now."

Bessie passes me the crate of marigolds for Mama and Mae, and I kneel to plant, though it feels like it takes me a long time to reach the ground. Frank takes care of the bed in front of Grandma and Grandpa, and Eddie handles the twins' plot. Bessie tends to Rachel's grave.

We work in silence, thank goodness.

"Looks like we've got everything in apple-pie order," Eddie exclaims as he steps back to survey our work.

"I'm always amazed at how long it takes to prepare the beds and how quickly the new flowers go in," Bessie says. "Now, if you and Frank don't mind, please dump the pails over in the debris pile next to the pump house and fill them up at the well. Then we can get these watered and dive into the lunch hamper."

Frank and Eddie each take a pail and head to the pump house near the cemetery entrance.

"We still have flowers to plant on John's grave," Bessie says to me. "Shall we walk over together? I'm happy to help."

I nod but struggle to get up from my knees. Bessie offers me her arm and helps me stand. "Are you sure you're feeling okay?" she asks.

"Just a lot on my mind," I say. Like whether she's already betrayed me. If she hasn't yet, it's only a matter of time. I must pull her back to her promise—away from Frank and back to me and Johnny. If Bessie renews her promise to me, she won't be free to fall for Fabulous Frank. She's told me before she could never love someone unless she could be completely honest with them. I need to make sure she knows she can't tell him the truth.

Bessie picks up the crate with the bachelor buttons and hands me a trowel.

"Bessie, dear?" I say as we're walking.

"Yes, Florence?"

"I owe you an apology."

"About what?" I ask.

"Frank Davis," I say. "He seems like a decent fellow, one who has had hard times of his own. I'm sorry for being suspicious of him and his intentions."

Bessie knows it's a big deal for me to say I'm sorry. It should soften her to my plea.

"Thank you, Florence," she says as we arrive at John's grave. "I'm happy you're not worried about Frank anymore."

I turn away from her. "Well, I'm worried about something else." As someone who rarely cries, I'm surprised my tears come so easily this morning.

"Oh, sweetheart." Bessie puts her hands on my back. "What's the matter?"

"Now, I'm worried he's going to take you away from me. Away from me and Johnny," I cry.

"No one is taking me anywhere, honey. You know how important you both are to me," she says, trying to assure me.

"Really?" I sniffle and turn back to her. "Sometimes I think we made the wrong decision. Sometimes I think Johnny should have stayed with you—you would have been a better mother than I've been." I weep. "Oh, I need you, Bessie. Johnny needs you. Please stay with us. Don't leave us."

"Of course. Of course I will stay with you. I promised you would never have to raise Johnny by yourself. Nothing is going to change that."

"But what if Frank really is the one? What if you two are falling in love? What if he wants to marry you?" I ask through my tears.

"Whoa, don't put the cart in front of the horse. We're going for a Sunday drive, not picking out wedding bands. And even if Frank is the one, we would all still be in Bartlesville. His new job is in Bartlesville, where our family lives. No one is going anywhere."

Should I mention my job offer in Tulsa? This is the perfect opening. But I remain quiet, and the moment passes. Bessie reaches out and gives my hand a little squeeze.

"We're a family. Nothing can ever change that," she says.

I stare into her eyes. "Promise me you won't tell him our secret, Bessie. Promise me." Panic replaces the sadness in my voice. "It's been a big morning of people sharing stories they usually keep. I don't want you to tell him about Johnny. Ever. It's for your own good, Bessie." I pause. "Promise me you won't tell Frank. Promise. On the bones." I search her eyes for an answer.

She takes her hand from mine and steps back.

"I do want to tell him the truth," she admits. "I've been thinking about it all day."

"You can't, Bessie. You just can't. Johnny's not ready to know the truth. He's my everything," I wail.

"I know he is, honey, but I can't promise I will never tell Frank. If we end up getting serious about each other, I will want to tell him the whole story."

"Then promise me you will wait, that you won't tell him unless—" I pause, wracking my brain for a condition that will keep her tied to me and Johnny. My eyes dart this way and that before resettling on hers. "Unless he proposes marriage to you. If he asks you to marry him, you have my blessing to tell him everything."

Bessie takes another step back and wrings her hands. "I feel like I should tell him sooner rather than later," she says. "I believe if I tell him the truth, he will understand our situation. I trust him to keep our secret safe until you are ready to tell Johnny."

"And what if he doesn't understand? What then, Bessie?" I swallow. "He might not be interested in you after he learns what really happened in Wichita. Have you considered that possibility? Then there will be an ex-boyfriend roaming around Bartlesville who knows our deepest, darkest secret." Tears roll down my face again. "He might even tell Eddie or Mrs. Henderson. Johnny might find out from someone else. Can you imagine how hurt and confused our baby boy would be?" My upper body shakes with each sob. "How would you feel then?"

"I don't know." Bessie takes a deep breath. I've never seen her so calm and determined.

"Promise me, Bessie," I beg through my tears. "Not unless he asks you to marry him."

"I promise," she says. "And I have faith in our Lord above that everything will work out exactly the way it should." Bessie moves back toward me and puts a hand on my shoulder.

"You always do," I mutter.

"Have a little faith, Florence. 'And the prayer of faith shall save the sick, and the Lord shall raise him up; and if he have committed sins, they shall be forgiven him,'" she quotes.

I swear, my sister has more than ninety percent of the Bible memorized.

"Now, let's get these beautiful flowers planted and spruce up your husband's grave," Bessie says.

"He isn't really here," I whisper. The authorities buried John's remains in Topeka after his accident. His parents held a service in Claremore and put up a headstone. But he's not here.

"No, he's not," she says. "But it's a wonderful opportunity to remember when you ran off to get married and how crazy you were about him."

"I was crazy about him, wasn't I?"

I wipe away my few remaining tears. They've accomplished their purpose. I've reminded her that her ultimate loyalty is to me and Johnny. She promised not to tell Fabulous Frank unless he proposes to her. That was a stroke a brilliance if I do say so myself.

"Here come Frank and Eddie. And someone else is with them," Bessie says.

I squint at the figures in the distance. I see a man walking next to them—a tall, slender man in a well-worn cowboy hat. It's Cousin Wahya.

CHAPTER NINETEEN

Mrs. Henderson

A RIPPLE OF happiness skips through the house as the professor and Louie return from their walk, but it does little to settle the apprehension building inside me. I've been feeling uneasy ever since I left Mr. Linn's office this morning. From my spot at the kitchen table, I can't make out what Professor Rutledge is saying to the dog, but his tone indicates that he's praising him for exemplary behavior. I can picture the professor stooping to take off Louie's leash, patting the dog sweetly on the head, and then hanging the leash on the correct hook on the coat tree in the foyer. Most Saturdays, the professor and I walk Louie together, but I sent the two of them out on their own today. I hear heavy footsteps and quick little paws making their way back to me in the kitchen. The door swings open, and Louie trots over for a rub.

"How was the walk?" I ask as I scratch Louie's ears.

"Splendid," says the professor.

"Thank you again for taking him. I don't know why I'm so tired this evening." Of course, I know exactly why I'm so tired—the thought of selling Henderson House and moving away forever is exhausting.

"It was my pleasure, though I missed your company on such a perfect late spring day," he says and then recites poetry:

"Fair Daffodils, we weep to see
You haste away so soon;
As yet the early-rising sun
Has not attain'd his noon.
Stay, stay,
Until the hasting day
Has run
But to the even-song;
And, having pray'd together, we
Will go with you along."

"That's lovely," I respond. "I'm not sure I've ever heard it."

"It's the first stanza of the poem 'To Daffodils' by Robert Herrick, a mostly uncelebrated poet of the seventeenth century. Written circa 1650, I believe."

"Do you know any more of it?" I ask.

The professor clears his throat and continues:

"We have short time to stay, as you,
We have as short a spring;
As quick a growth to meet decay,
As you, or anything.
We die
As your hours do, and dry
Away,
Like to the summer's rain;
Or as the pearls of morning's dew,
Ne'er to be found again."

My eyes mist over as he finishes. We regard each other in silence.

"Are you all right?" he asks.

"I'm fine. It just struck a chord," I reply.

"Good poetry can do that," he says.

"Do you have a copy of that poem in one of your books? As much as I enjoy hearing poems recited, you know how I like to read them. Seeing the form always adds meaning to the piece, don't you think?"

"I couldn't agree with you more," he says. "I don't know if I have it in my library upstairs, however, I would be happy to write out the stanzas so you can have your own copy."

"Thank you. I'd like that."

"Something smells 'very-good-delicious' in here." He turns his head toward the stove.

Hearing him use Eddie's expression makes me happy for a moment and then a little melancholy. My years with the Blackwell family are ending.

We have short time to stay, as you, I recall from the poem.

"It's meat loaf, Professor Rutledge," I respond.

"Excellent. I do enjoy your meat loaf." He takes a seat at the dinette with me.

Whenever the professor sits at the dinette, it reminds me of an adult sitting at a children's tea party. He dwarfs the little metal chairs and the red-and-white enamel table. There is something very dear about him sitting here with me. I don't want my years with him to end either.

"Have the troops returned from their sortie?" he asks.

"Not yet. I expect them any minute." I glance up at the wall clock. It's almost five. I serve supper an hour earlier on Saturday evenings, so people have time to go to the cinema.

As if he's reading my mind, the professor asks, "Do you feel like taking in a show tonight? There's a new Joan Crawford film playing at the Osage and a western at the Odeon."

"Thank you for asking, but I've got a feeling I need to be right here this evening," I say, taking another sip of tea.

"Really? Is it just a feeling, or is something going on?"

"Oh, there are quite a few things going on at the moment. I'm not sure how they are going to play out." I change the subject. "Tell me, have you given any more thought to the conversation we had last Saturday?"

"About my returning to university life?"

"Uh-huh." I take a sip of tea.

"A little," he replies, pursing his lips and stroking his chin as if contemplating something.

"You know, when Charles died, all I wanted to do was hide," I say. "I didn't want to bump into anyone I knew. I didn't want anyone asking me if they could bring me a casserole. I barely left the house for six months."

"Do you think I'm hiding?" he asks, looking at me sideways across the little table.

"I know you are," I say with a wry smile.

Do I have the courage for one more brave conversation today?

"What would it take for you to go back to teaching this fall?" I ask.

"This fall? I don't know, the right opportunity at the right institution perhaps. It's serendipitous that you should bring this up. I got a letter from a colleague yesterday about a position that might be worth pursuing." He furrows his brow and studies me for a moment. "Is there a reason I should start looking?" he asks.

I'm unsure how to answer.

"Mildred, is something wrong?" He rarely calls me by my first name. It sounds comforting in his rich, deep voice.

"Oh, Albert," I say, exhaling. "I've had the most unusual day." I raise my hands in surrender.

"I'm all ears." He leans back in the tiny chair, ready to listen.

I look at the three African violets on the windowsill and tell Albert everything, beginning with Kay confiding in me about Sonny at the Wednesday Night Supper and my promise to warn Florence. I go into the details of my heart-to-heart with Florence and her frightening description of Sonny's improper advances at work. I tell him how I made the appointment with Mr. Linn and about the courage and empathy I knew I'd need to carry it through. I even tell him about the fascinating conversation I had with Mr. Steinhauser. Then I stop cold.

"What happened when you met with Mr. Linn?" he asks.

"Well, he thought I was coming in to discuss something else." I move the salt and pepper shakers to the center of the table and fidget with them as I continue. "He thought I wanted to talk about Florence's job offer in Tulsa," I say.

"What job offer?"

"Exactly. It seems Florence's trip to Tulsa on Wednesday wasn't to teach them about designing window displays—it was to interview for a job. They want her to be the new manager of the Tulsa store, and I'll bet you dollars to dumplings she wants the entire family to move with her." I finish arranging the salt and pepper and return my hands to either side of my teacup.

"The entire family," he repeats.

"Yes. The Tulsa store wants her to start as soon as possible."

"That must have thrown you for a loop." Albert leans forward. "Were you able to regroup and talk to Mr. Linn about Sonny?" he asks.

"I was, though I was a little distracted by then."

"It couldn't have been easy to follow his good news with bad news. How did Mr. Linn respond?"

"He was concerned and uncomfortable. Though, it wasn't the first time someone had come to talk to him about Sonny's behavior."

"There's something else on your mind. What is it?" he asks.

"I got an interesting letter last week, too," I say, "from my son Robert."

"The one in Princeton?" he asks, raising an eyebrow.

"Yes. He and his wife are renovating the carriage house on their property, and they would like me to come and live there permanently. Ever since Robert's letter arrived, I've been waiting for a sign, something to tell me it's time to go."

"And you think the possibility of a Blackwell family exodus is the sign?" he asks.

"Maybe. Maybe it's finally time for me to sell Henderson House and move on."

It's the first time I've said it out loud. It didn't sound as scary as I thought it would. I listen for the house to respond, but I don't sense an immediate reaction.

"That's a nice offer from your son. You'd be with them, but you'd have your own place. Sounds ideal," he says.

"Yes, it does, doesn't it? I feel like I need to see how everything plays out with Florence before I give Robert my answer."

"Is there anything I can do to help?" he asks as he stretches across the table, placing one of his large hands over mine.

"You've already helped by listening. I feel much better having gotten this out in the open. I'm a little nervous about supper ending in fireworks this evening." I put my other hand on top of his. It looks so delicate resting there.

"Dinner and a show! I love hiding out at Henderson House." The professor smiles and pulls his hand away. I miss the warmth of his touch immediately. "Why don't I leave you in peace before the cast and crew arrives?" He rises from his dinette chair. Louie lifts his head in response. As the professor passes by, he gives my shoulder a tender squeeze. "Everything is going to work out exactly the way it should, Mildred. I'm sure of it."

"I can't believe you met Cousin Wahya," I say to Mr. Davis as I pass the carrots and potatoes to Professor Rutledge on my right. "He's like a character in a book to me. Larger than life."

Mr. Davis and Bessie sit next to each other on my left. Eddie is at the opposite end of the table, and Florence is between Eddie and the professor. I can't remember the last time we changed up the seating order.

"Yup, I met him. What a friendly fellow," Mr. Davis says. "I'll tell you one thing, Florence, the family resemblance between Cousin Wahya and Johnny is mighty strong. Guess they both take after your father's side of the family."

"Oh, but Frank," Eddie responds, "Cousin Wahya isn't actually our cousin. He's not related to us by blood. You're just seeing the Cherokee in Johnny shining through. Same way it shows in Wahya."

"What?" Mr. Davis drops his fork. "Cousin Wahya's not really your cousin?"

"Nope. Daddy sort of . . . found him," Eddie says as he takes another bite.

"What do you mean, *he sort of found him?*" Mr. Davis asks.

Everyone waits for Eddie to chew and swallow.

"Well, the way Daddy tells it, he was out hunting one crisp autumn day, back in the early 1890s, before he brought Mama to Oklahoma. He'd traveled north and then west, up into Osage Territory, and he came upon a little boy and a puppy cowering in a ditch. The little boy couldn't have been more than three or four years old, and he was terrified. He couldn't even speak. Daddy told him everything was gonna be all right and asked him to stay put while he did some investigating. Sadly, he found the boy's parents not too far away, dragged off the road and lying under some brush. They had been robbed, then shot. Daddy was pretty sure he had met the family at one of the Cherokee tribal gatherings. He remembered that the little boy's nickname was Wahya because it means 'wolf' in Cherokee," Eddie says.

Mr. Davis shakes his head in disbelief.

"Yup, it was still the Wild West back in those days, with plenty of bandits hiding out in the Osage Hills. I've heard some stories that'd put hair on your chest! Anyways, Daddy rode his horse back to where Wahya and his puppy were huddled in the ditch. He got off his horse and got down in the ditch with the little boy and his pup. When Daddy tells the story, he always crouches down low to illustrate how he kneeled to talk to Wahya." Eddie gets down low over his plate as he tells the tale. "Daddy called Wahya by his nickname and introduced himself. He told him he knew his parents. Daddy said Wahya looked up at him with his dark eyes and said, 'They're not coming back, are they?' Daddy nodded at the little boy and said, 'Let's get you and your pup back to my house for some supper. Are you hungry?' Wahya nodded. Daddy made a sling out of a blanket to hold the puppy close to his chest, then he got Wahya up behind him on his horse, and they rode home to my grandparents' house. Wahya has been a member of the family ever since." Eddie takes a sip of ice water. "He was the little brother Daddy never had. Daddy adored him. Still does."

"I don't think Mama knew she was going to start married life with an orphan under foot," Florence says, groaning.

"Oh, Mama loved Wahya. Plus, he moved next door into his own cabin when he was fourteen. That's not exactly under foot," Bessie adds. "The Pack and Run wouldn't have been the same without Wahya and Inola."

"Was Inola Wahya's puppy?" Professor Rutledge asks.

"The dog who won the blue ribbon at the fair?" Mr. Davis asks.

"Yes. He grew into a fine dog. Inola means 'black fox' in Cherokee. The name suited him well, with his sleek and shiny black coat and charcoal eyes. Inola was the smartest, sweetest dog I've ever known. Oh, Louie, you didn't hear that, did you?" Bessie grimaces as she peeks under the table, and I chuckle.

Bessie continues: "Every day, when Wahya and Inola would arrive to help at the store, Inola would run up to Daddy, tail wagging. He would spin around and around, then lie down and roll over to offer his tummy for a belly rub. Day after day, that morning ritual brought them both so much joy. The only time I ever saw my daddy cry was when Inola died. That dog lived a good long life, and one afternoon he curled up in the sun on the front porch of the store and never woke up. Everyone was heartbroken, but I always thought it seemed like a peaceful way to die—dreaming in the afternoon sun," Bessie says.

"I'm pretty sure Daddy loved that darn dog more than he ever loved any of us," Florence says, as if it's supposed to be funny. A long silence follows.

"I still can't get over the resemblance between Wahya and Johnny," Mr. Davis muses, rubbing his chin.

"Actually, Johnny's the spitting image of our sister Rachel," Eddie says.

"Once again, it's just the Cherokee showing up. Both Mae and Rachel had beautiful dark hair like Johnny, not the mousy brown curls Bessie and I ended up with!" Florence forces a laugh.

She is nervous about this topic of conversation. I can tell. Her green color is dark and muddy. I don't think she told anyone about the job on their outing today.

"Mrs. Henderson, what did you do on this fine day, other than prepare a delicious supper?" Mr. Davis asks, and I sense Florence's relief with the subject change.

"Well, Mr. Davis, since you were kind enough to drive the family to Claremore, I realized I had my car today, so I ran some errands downtown," I say. "I picked up a few flowers, and I stopped in at Linn Brothers. The window displays really are wonderful, Florence. You've outdone yourself. I thought a new boater would be a perfect gift for my son Robert's birthday. The pretty woman with the big smile, Peggy, waited on me." I look directly at Florence.

"Oh, she did? How nice," Florence says as she rubs the knuckles on her left hand. She definitely hasn't said anything to them. Johnny's staying over at Tommy's house tonight. It's the perfect time for her to tell Bessie and Eddie about the job offer. I could help move things along.

"Yes, and I saw Mr. Linn. He shared some exciting news with me," I say.

"Exciting news about what?" asks Eddie.

"Well, it's not my story to tell. Florence, would you like to do the honors?"

"Spill the tea, sis," Eddie prods.

Florence shifts in her chair and shoots a surprised glance back at me. I respond with a smile. She takes a deep breath and turns her gaze across the table to her siblings.

"Of course. I was originally planning to talk to you and Bessie about this on our trip to Claremore, but with Frank offering to drive and all, it didn't seem appropriate. So, I was waiting until after the cemetery trip. In fact, I was planning on calling a family meeting after supper this evening," she says.

"A family meeting?" Bessie asks. "This must be big news."

"Now, you need to understand I haven't given anyone a definitive answer yet," Florence says, clearly hedging on the issue.

"An answer about what?" Eddie asks.

"The situation is this: Linn Brothers offered me a management position." She slows down as she continues. "At the flagship store in Tulsa. My business trip down there on Wednesday was an interview for the new position. I'm sorry I didn't tell everyone up front, but I wasn't sure they were going to offer me the job, and I figured why get everyone all wound up if they might not even offer it to me?" Florence says.

Well, I'll be. Her green color turns bright and clear right in front of my eyes. For once in her life, Florence Blackwell Fuller is telling the truth.

CHAPTER TWENTY

Florence

MRS. HENDERSON TILTS her head at me in approval. I'm not used to having her on my side. I can't believe she brought up the subject of my job offer. Normally, I'd be infuriated by her interference, but this might be the perfect way to get the ball rolling.

"Don't keep us in suspense, Florence. Did they offer you the job?" Eddie asks.

"Yes. They did," I say.

"A management position? Wow, good for you, sis!" he says, reaching over and giving my arm a little squeeze. "How long do you have to consider the offer?"

"I told Aaron Linn, the owner of the Tulsa store, that I would give him my answer on Monday. I would like to accept the job. However, I was hoping, and of course it would be a decision for all of us to make, but . . ." I hesitate, looking around the table. ". . . I was hoping we would all move to Tulsa together, as a family."

"Why does everybody need to move?" Fabulous Frank butts in.

"Because we've been saving up to buy a house together," I say. "We had dreams and plans for the future before you moved in last Monday, Mr. Davis."

"Right. Eddie mentioned buying a house the other night." Frank pushes a piece of meat loaf around on his plate.

"If we move together, we can finally become homeowners and kiss our boarding house days goodbye—forever." I pause. "No offense, Mrs. Henderson."

"None taken," she replies.

"Eddie, doesn't your cab company have an operation down there?" I ask, knowing full well they do because I already checked. "I bet all you would have to do is ask for a transfer."

"I suppose that's a possibility," Eddie says.

"And Bessie, with your references, I'm sure you could get an even higher paying job at one of the oil companies in Tulsa."

"Hold yer horses, Flossie. I'll pack up and move with you in a heartbeat," Eddie says, pushing his chair back from the table a bit. "But house or no house, I can't see asking Bessie to leave Phillips." He turns to face my sister. "I've always envisioned you passing away, right there in the office machine room while you were changing toner fluid or reloading paper." He grins at Bessie, who responds with a half-hearted smile.

I wish I had told her about the job offer when we were alone at the cemetery today. I don't want Bessie questioning her renewed promise to me.

"You know, Tulsa Central High School has the best athletic program in the state. Johnny's chances of being offered a scholarship to college will improve greatly if he goes to Central High." I look at my sister, and she holds my gaze for an uncomfortably long moment before speaking.

"This is certainly good news, Florence," Bessie says, taking a deep breath. "You don't need my approval to accept this job. I'm so proud your hard work is paying off. If you and Eddie want to take Johnny to Tulsa, you have my blessing."

"But we can't go without you, Bessie. You know that. We stick together. Johnny needs you. I need you. We're a family, remember? Nothing can ever change that," I say, harkening to her words at the cemetery earlier today.

"If you accept the position, when would they want you to start?" Eddie asks.

"Monday, June thirtieth," I reply.

"That's so soon!" Fabulous Frank interjects.

"Not really. It gives us an entire month to work everything out and for Bessie to find a wonderful new job," I state, as if it is a foregone conclusion.

"Johnny isn't a child anymore," Bessie says. "He's a young man, Florence. I don't think he needs all three of us to care for him."

"That's right," Frank agrees. "Besides, he'll be off to college and on his own before you know it."

"Well, not everyone is as comfortable living far away from their family as you are," I respond with an unfortunate edge to my voice.

"Easy there, Miss Florence," Professor Rutledge rumbles like distant thunder. He doesn't usually interfere in Blackwell family business.

Silence descends over the dining room. The weight of it settles on my chest. I want to say something to clear the awkwardness away, but I'm not sure what would do the trick.

"There's something I think you should know, Frank," Professor Rutledge says.

My mind races. What does the professor know? Is it something about Johnny? Has he overheard me talking with Bessie?

What on earth is he going to tell Frank? My heart pounds in my chest as I wait for him to speak.

"On Saturday evenings at Henderson House," he continues, "the menfolk take care of the dishes so the ladies can relax a bit. I doubt anyone is going eat much more after Florence's big announcement. What do you say, lads? Shall we get started on clean-up duty?"

I let out a sigh of relief.

"Absolutely," Eddie says. "I could stand to move around a bit and clear my head."

"Me too," Frank says. He stands and puts a hand on Bessie's shoulder for a moment before he starts helping the other men collect plates and serving dishes.

"Ladies, shall we head out to the porch?" Mrs. Henderson offers.

Bessie hasn't moved a muscle since she spoke earlier. She's staring off into space with her lips pursed as if she's working on a long division problem in her head.

"Thank you, Mrs. H," I say, "but I think I'll pop upstairs and take a bath. It's been a long day, and I need to think about how I'm going to break the news to Johnny tomorrow after church."

"Oh, there's plenty of time for your bath. It's early," Mrs. Henderson says. "Please join me and Bessie on the porch."

"Yes. I'd like to continue our conversation about the move, Florence," Bessie says, clearing her throat.

"What are you three still doing in here?" Eddie asks as he and Frank return to take another load of dishes into the kitchen. "Get out on the porch and start relaxing. That's an order."

"Are you okay?" I hear Frank ask Bessie as he puts his hand on her shoulder again.

"I'm fine," she says looking up at him. "It's just unexpected."

"Come on. Let's leave the men to their work," Mrs. Henderson says. She takes Bessie's arm as they head to the foyer.

I suppose now that I've got Mrs. Henderson backing me up, it might make sense to keep the discussion going.

"There is such a sense of satisfaction when a glorious spring day gives way to an even more beautiful evening. Don't you agree, Florence?"

"Yes. Certainly," I say as we walk out onto the porch and each of us claims one of the white rocking chairs.

Streaks of pink and purple radiate across the sky. Mrs. Henderson's right—it's still early. The sun sets around eight thirty these days. I've got plenty of time to talk about Tulsa and still relax in the bath. I have to take advantage of these rare evenings when Johnny spends the night at the Westfeldts. Oh, but I'll have my own room in my own house by the end of next month.

"What will you do if the four of us leave Henderson House?" Bessie asks Mrs. H once we are settled.

"Oh, sweetie, I've been thinking about that all afternoon," Mrs. Henderson says. "As it turns out, my son Robert and his family have invited me to come and live with them in New Jersey."

"Is that why you've been reading his letter over and over?" she asks.

"Yes. Robert thinks Louie and I should head east for our regular August visit with them at the shore and then return to Princeton—for good. By the time September rolls around, the guest house they are renovating for me will be ready."

"Are you going to accept their offer?" Bessie asks.

"I'm leaning in that direction. Maybe it's time for me to start the next chapter of my life. I've been a wife and mother. I've been a landlady. Now, I might be ready to tackle my next career as a full-time grandmother." Mrs. Henderson smiles.

"You've been a wonderful part-time grandma for Johnny," Bessie says.

"Thank you," Mrs. H replies.

The three of us sit and rock for a moment. The sky fades to pink. So far, the conversation is going very well. If Mrs. Henderson wants to move to New Jersey, Bessie won't have any guilt about leaving her.

"Bessie," Mrs. Henderson says, "I want to encourage you to consider all your options before you commit to moving to Tulsa with Florence."

"Really, Mrs. Henderson, this is family business," I interject.

"Mrs. Henderson is family," Bessie challenges, "in every way that matters."

I look out into the yard and feel uneasy. Twilight bathes the trees and shrubs in a peaceful glow, but I sense something's not right. Out of the corner of my eye, I could swear I see a figure lurking behind the neighbor's hedge.

It's just the wind. I look at the spot again and see nothing out of the ordinary. Still, my stomach churns and my chest tightens again. Breathing has become such a chore lately.

"You've built a wonderful life here in Bartlesville, Bessie," Mrs. Henderson continues. "You have your job and your friends, not to mention the church. I don't think you should feel you need to uproot everything you've built just because Florence has a job offer in Tulsa." She pauses. "No offense, Florence."

"None taken," I reply. So much for having Mrs. H on my side. "Mrs. Henderson, this is about more than a job. We're a family. We keep our promises to each other," I say, looking directly at Bessie.

Mrs. Henderson tuts. "A promise is only as good as the intention behind it," she says, squinting at me in her strange way. Her penetrating gaze tonight is more than creepy—it's infuriating!

"What on earth is that supposed to mean?" I ask, worried I'm not concealing my exasperation very well.

"I know Bessie promised to help you raise Johnny, and I think we can all agree she has kept her promise. You need to let her go, Florence."

"Let her go? You make it sound like I'm holding her prisoner!" I throw my hands up in the air.

"I have a feeling this is about more than Bessie being there for you and Johnny. You need her for another reason." She points one of her long bony fingers at me.

"That's ridiculous. What reason do I need other than wanting her being part of Johnny's life?" I turn to my sister. "And as I recall, before Fabulous Frank showed up, being part of Johnny's life was important to you, too."

"Florence, you know I love Johnny as if—" Bessie pauses abruptly, "as if he were my own son. But Mrs. Henderson is right. You already told us the other reason."

"What are you talking about?"

"When Frank asked you why we all needed to move together, you said we'd been saving to buy a house." She sits up straight on the edge of her chair. "You need me to move with you because you need my money to stay in the savings account."

My heart sinks. I responded to Frank out of annoyance, and I showed my cards. How could I be so careless?

"Florence, I'd be happy to sit down with you and look at the bank statements. Maybe there's a way for me to stay in Bartlesville and still contribute to your housing fund," Bessie offers.

The last thing I need is my sister reviewing those bank statements and calling my spending into question. Mrs. Henderson nods at me as if everything is all settled. Her satisfied smile sets my blood boiling.

"You know what, Mrs. H, I'm getting a little tired of—" I begin, just as the men walk onto the porch and interrupt me before I can unleash the full force of my frustration.

"The kitchen is in shipshape, Mrs. H," Eddie announces. "And Mr. Davis and I have been having a rather serious discussion," he says, looking at Bessie and patting Frank on the shoulder.

I glance over at my sister to see her face soften the moment Fabulous Frank appears. "Oh, really? What were you two talking about now?" Bessie asks.

"Well, not to put too fine a point on it, sis, but we've been discussing your courtship and how Florence's job offer in Tulsa is sort of a rotten tree fallen across the highway to happiness." He gestures across the horizon with his hand.

"I didn't realize I had a courtship to be discussed," Bessie responds, a rosy glow spreading across her cheeks.

"I told him about our three dates," Frank admits. "Bessie and I have three dates planned this week," he says to me and Mrs. Henderson.

"Three dates in one week certainly constitutes a courtship in my book," Mrs. Henderson says with a grin.

I try not to roll my eyes.

"Here, here," says Professor Rutledge from the doorway. He appears to be enjoying the fraternal banter this evening.

"The ayes have it!" Eddie says. "This is officially a courtship." He beckons to Bessie, and she gets out of her rocker to move next to him. "Mr. Davis asked me, as the apparent head of the Blackwell household, if you could wait another week before you give Florence your answer about moving to Tulsa, and I, in my infinite wisdom, agreed."

He nods first to Bessie on his right and then to Frank on his left. Professor Rutledge and Mrs. Henderson clap lightly, and everyone laughs. Everyone except me.

"Eddie, I have to give my answer to Aaron Linn on Monday. I can't wait a week!" I exclaim.

"That's correct," Eddie says. "You have to give *your* answer on Monday—not Bessie's. I've already said I'll come with you, sis. You won't be raising Johnny in Tulsa alone. If you want to accept the job, you should, knowing I'll be by your side."

"I don't see how one more week is going to make any difference," I mumble.

"Maybe it won't, but maybe it will," Frank says, crossing in front of Eddie and taking Bessie's hand.

"And what if it does make a difference? What then?" Bessie asks, glancing sideways at him. When did she learn how to flirt?

Movement in the hedge catches my attention again. I scan the shadows. Either something is there, or I'm losing my marbles. Could it be the Thompkins's cat?

"Ladies, Professor Rutledge, let us adjourn to the house and leave these two lovebirds to enjoy some porch time. They need to make the most of the coming week." Eddie moves toward the front door. Mrs. Henderson and I get up. I feel a little shaky.

"Are you all right, Florence?" Mrs. Henderson asks.

"I'm not sure," I respond.

"Should I put on some coffee?" Professor Rutledge asks.

When the professor and Mrs. Henderson don't go to the movies, he likes to make coffee and play board games. The professor has gotten pretty good at brewing coffee in Mrs. Henderson's old stove-top percolator.

"I should take Louie on one last lap around the block before bed," Mrs. Henderson says. "I might enjoy a cup when

I get back. Why don't you join me, Florence? I'd like to tell you more about my conversation with Mr. Linn today."

Taking the stupid dog for a walk with Mrs. Henderson has to be the last thing I'd like to do right now. I want to be alone, soaking in a hot tub, figuring out how to tell Johnny about the move. Plus, thanks to Fabulous Frank and my sophomoric brother, I've got to come up with a plan to make sure Frank and Bessie's relationship goes nowhere this week—and fast. I tried getting Bessie to doubt Frank's intentions. I tried convincing Bessie that her obligations lie with me and Johnny. Now it may be time to work the problem from the other side. Maybe Frank needs to learn that my sister isn't as sweet and innocent as she appears. Yes, I think that's exactly the strategy I should try next.

"It's getting a little chilly," Mrs. Henderson says as she drapes one of her elaborately embroidered shawls around my shoulders and gives me yet another peculiar smile. "Come on, Louie," she calls and puts the leash on him. "Let's go out through the kitchen so we don't disturb the happy couple," she says.

The expression makes my skin crawl. I follow her through the house like someone under a spell. We walk out the kitchen door. The shawl feels heavy and unfamiliar. It smells like Mrs. Henderson, like oranges and lavender. We walk down the side of the driveway farthest from where Bessie and Frank are sitting on the porch. My eyes scan the privet hedge as we draw near. No sign of the Thompkins's cat.

"I made an appointment to speak with Mr. Linn about Sonny, today," Mrs. Henderson says.

"You did what?" I ask.

"I spoke to Mr. Linn about Sonny today," she repeats. "He thought I was coming in to talk about your job offer. That's how I found out. Then I talked to him about the Sonny situation."

This night just keeps getting worse.

"What on earth did you tell him?"

"That someone confided in me about Sonny's inappropriate behavior in college," she says. We turn onto the sidewalk.

"Did you mention anything about me?"

"Just that Sonny was making you uncomfortable," she says. "That's all."

We continue down the street and around the corner. So much has been revealed since we sat down to supper. I feel a little numb. There's a vacant lot where Louie loves to stop and sniff. While we wait for Louie to explore a patch of dandelions next to the sidewalk, I hear footsteps behind us.

"Good evening, ladies." A familiar voice sends a chill up my spine. I turn around.

"Good evening, Sonny," I say. "What brings you to our neck of the woods?"

Sonny stands in the middle of the sidewalk at the edge of the vacant lot. I've never seen him in casual clothes. He's always in a suit and tie at work. Dressed in a pair of loose-fitting khakis with an old navy sweater vest over a striped T-shirt, he barely looks older than Johnny. It's hard to tell in the twilight, but I could swear there are fresh grass stains on the knees of his trousers.

"I needed to see you, Florence." Sonny slurs his words and takes a wavering step toward us.

"Well, here I am. What's on your mind?" I ask.

"I always thought my dad would end up sending me away, but I guess he's sending you away instead." He points at me as he stumbles a little closer.

"What do you mean, Sonny?" I ask.

"He knows I'm sweet on you, so he's sending you to Tulsa," he says, sputtering and teetering his way even closer. "To make matters worse, your landlady here has been sticking her nose into matters that are none of her business." He waves an unsteady hand back and forth at Mrs. H as he moves toward her.

I step between Sonny and Mrs. Henderson. Louie instinctively takes a position at my side. The fur stands up on his back.

"Oh, I assure you, the safety of the women in our community is most certainly my business," Mrs. Henderson says, stepping forward. I put my arm out to keep her slightly behind me. Sonny awkwardly closes the gap between us, and we now stand face-to-face.

"Sonny, why don't you walk back to Henderson House with us, and my brother Eddie can give you a ride home?" I say.

"I think I've got a much better idea," he says, leaning in to whisper to me. The stench of whiskey on his breath triggers a hundred horrible memories of growing up. "Why don't you and I go for a little walk of our own? If you're a good girl, maybe we can kiss and make up." He reaches out to touch my hair but catches his toe on the sidewalk, and his hand lands on my shoulder instead. He leans on me to keep from falling.

"Get your hands off of her!" Mrs. Henderson commands. Louie, sensing her concern, growls.

Sonny turns to face Mrs. Henderson. "Well, hello there! I almost forgot you were here." He takes a few unstable steps as he looks Mrs. Henderson up and down.

"Florence, you and I are heading back to the house right now. I suggest you head home as well, Mr. Linn," she says, walking forward. Sonny blocks her path. "Step aside, Mr. Linn, or I shall scream at the top of my lungs," Mrs. Henderson announces.

"Hah, a fancy lady like you? Scream? I doubt it."

"Step aside and you won't have to find out," she says. Louie growls a little louder.

"You gonna make me?" Sonny slurs in a drunken version of his flirty voice.

He takes another wobbly step in Mrs. Henderson's direction, and she lets out a shrill, bloodcurdling scream. Mrs. H sustains the scream with the force of a train whistle blaring to clear livestock off the tracks. Sonny puts his hands over his ears and stumbles backward. Finally, the deafening blast emanating from Mrs. Henderson's mouth ceases.

"Why would you wanna go and do that?" Sonny asks. "Right when Florence and I were about to have a little romantic stroll?" He reaches out, grabs my arm, and yanks me toward him. The shawl falls to the ground.

"What's going on here?" Professor Rutledge's voice booms as he comes sprinting around the corner, Eddie and Frank at his heels.

"We heard someone scream," Eddie says, out of breath.

"Oh, Albert, thank goodness, you're here!" Mrs. Henderson exclaims.

"We ended up with some unexpected company on our walk around the block," I say as I pull away from Sonny's grasp.

"Howdy, gents!" Sonny tips his cap to the new arrivals and almost falls into a juniper bush. "Everything's just fine. You can head on home. I've got it all under control."

"I find that highly unlikely," the professor says. "Eddie, Frank, please escort the ladies back to Henderson House."

Eddie and Frank each extend a hand to us.

"No, no, noooooo," Sonny protests. "Everything's just fine," he repeats.

"Sonny, you need to let the ladies leave so you and I can have a little chat," the professor says in a calm yet commanding tone.

"Why would I wanna chat with you?" Sonny pushes the professor in the chest. "If you want the ladies, why don't you fight for them?" He pushes the professor a second time—this time, hard enough for the professor to take a small step back.

"Sonny, you don't want to fight m—" the professor begins, but before he can finish, Sonny winds up his arm and tries to land a punch on the professor's jaw.

Professor Rutledge dodges the blow easily, but Sonny tries to land another jab. The professor blocks it with his left hand, and Sonny stumbles back. He regains his footing and tries to take a swing at the professor's face again. In a single powerful move, the professor lands his fist perfectly in the center of Sonny's stomach. Sonny doubles over, and the professor immediately sends another blow down on the top of his back with both hands. Sonny crumbles into a heap on the sidewalk.

"Albert," Mrs. Henderson marvels. "I didn't know you were a boxer."

"I was on the rugby team at Princeton. There was an occasional brawl," he replies. "Are you two all right?"

"We're fine. Just shaken up a bit," I say as I pick up Mrs. Henderson's shawl off the sidewalk.

My arm aches where Sonny grabbed me. I'll have a bruise. Years of experience has taught me that this deep, throbbing pain is the kind that leaves a visible reminder. I won't be able to wear any summer dresses for at least a week. Wonderful. Long sleeves at the end of May. Thank you, Sonny.

"I'm so glad no one's injured. That was one heck of an alarm bell you rang, Mildred." The professor shakes his head. "Eddie, please escort Louie and the ladies home. Frank, can you help me get Sonny to his feet? If it's all right with everyone, I'd like to take Sonny back to the kitchen and get some coffee in him before we drive him home."

"Of course," Mrs. Henderson responds.

"I think he was hiding behind the privet hedge earlier, spying on us while we were out on the porch," I say. "Maybe you knocked some sense into him, professor."

"Well, I'm certainly going to try to *talk* some sense into him once we can get him to sober up a bit."

Sonny moans, sits up, and looks around as if he has no idea who we are or what he's doing on the ground.

"What do you think is going to happen to Sonny?" I ask as we walk home.

"I think he's going to be mighty embarrassed when his head clears. I also think his father needs to put him on a shorter leash until he can get his behavior under control," Mrs. Henderson says.

"Do you think Mr. Linn made up this job offer to get me away from Sonny?" I ask.

"Of course not. I think his uncle needs a new store manager in Tulsa, and you're the best person for the job." She takes my arm. "I bet you're ready for your bath now."

"More than ready," I reply.

"Thank you for stepping between me and Sonny back there," Mrs. H says, tapping my arm gently. "It's nice to know you care about me—even if I don't think Bessie should move to Tulsa with you."

"I've gotta say, I'm with Mrs. Henderson on this one, sis," Eddie adds. "Bessie's future may be here in Bartlesville with Frank."

Bessie's future? Isn't that typical! Everyone's focused on Bessie's future when you're the one bringing new opportunities to the family.

I drop Mrs. H's arm and quicken my pace as I feel the heat building inside me. This is no time to explode.

"Let's give Bessie and Mr. Davis this week to get to know each other better," Mrs. Henderson says, catching up to me and placing a hand on my back.

"Of course," I respond through gritted teeth.

One week is plenty of time for me to figure out how to help Mr. Davis see Bessie's faults. She can't be trusted. I know that firsthand. I imagine trust is important to Mr. Davis. Afterall, his first wife took him for dead and fell in love with his brother—rather quickly from the sound of it. After his wife got his letter, she never wrote back to him in the hospital. She waited to tell him. She let him come home elated and full of hope, and only then did she tell him the truth. I bet he wouldn't like it if he found out Bessie was waiting to tell him the truth about something important. I bet he wouldn't like that at all.

SUNDAY
MAY 25, 1941

CHAPTER TWENTY-ONE

Bessie

I'M AWAKE, BUT I'm clinging to a dream—a dream about Frank and Henderson House. Afraid the fantasy will fade in the morning light, I squeeze my eyes to keep them from opening. The details linger in my mind, filling me with contentment and longing at the same time. I pull the quilt over my head and replay the scene in my mind. I'm in the Henderson House kitchen with Frank, and I hear Daddy and Cousin Wahya making conversation in the dining room, which is odd because in all the years I've lived here, they've never visited Henderson House. Daddy is telling a story about a lovesick chihuahua devoted to Wahya's current dog, Yona. I look down at the kitchen floor and see big, brown Yona curled up under the dinette. He's in the spot where Louie usually sleeps. Dream Frank is helping me do the dishes.

"Thank you for another incredible breakfast, Bessie," Dream Frank says, handing me a plate to dry. "And to think, I almost didn't marry you because Johnny said you couldn't cook!"

"He was telling the truth at the time." I smile. "I'm eternally grateful to Mrs. Henderson for my secret cooking lessons."

"As am I. Everything about you just continues to get more and more delicious, Mrs. Davis," Dream Frank says as he slips his hands around my waist and pulls me in for a kiss.

Mrs. Davis, I repeat to myself. I sink deeper under my quilt as I remember this part of the dream. I can almost feel his soft, warm lips on mine.

"It's Saturday," Dream Frank says, pulling back but keeping his arms around me.

"Yes, it is," I say.

"Which means Edna isn't coming into work this morning."

"Correct," I respond.

"And your father and Wahya are keeping our guests entertained."

"Yes, they are."

"So, theoretically, we could finish cleaning the kitchen later this morning."

Dream Frank reaches up and strokes my hair gently before pulling me in for a longer kiss. He unties my apron and places it on the kitchen counter. Then he takes my hand and leads me through the back door into Mrs. Henderson's bedroom suite, only it isn't Mrs. Henderson's bedroom—it's our bedroom. A few pieces of Mrs. H's furniture remain, but my dressing table and bench are between the windows where her desk used to be, and Frank's books are on the bookshelf flanked by photographs of our families, not Mrs. Henderson's grandchildren.

Dream Frank unbuttons my dress. It falls to the floor, and I stand before him in my slip and stockings. He kisses my neck and shoulders and runs his hands down my back. He places one hand on my leg and gently slides it up under my slip and past the band at the top of my stockings onto my upper thigh. Both in my dream and now as I remember it, the sensation of his fingers on my bare skin leaves me breathless. And that's it. The dream ends.

I kick the covers off my bed and sit up. Pulling a shawl over my shoulders, I walk to the dressing table and take a seat. I moan audibly when I see the mess staring back at me. My hair might as well be a nesting box for tree swallows. I search the center compartment for my brush, but it's not in its usual spot. I open the left-hand drawer and find it on top of my prayer book. I suppose I was off my routine last night as a result of Sonny Linn's impromptu visit and the unexpected news of my sister's job offer. I pick up my brush and the corner of faded blue stationery at the bottom of the drawer catches my eye. Odd. I'm diligent about keeping this letter hidden. I would never want Johnny to find it. And I've never been able to get Florence to read it. I lift the books and stacks of letters out of the drawer, set them to the side, and pick up the old letter with care. The paper is flat from years of living under the weight of my Bible, but it still bears the pattern of having been crumpled up and pressed smooth again. I unfold the letter and trace my late sister Rachel's delicate script with my finger. I don't need to read it—I know it by heart. A tear falls down my cheek, and I move the paper just in time to keep it safe from harm.

If only Florence would read Rachel's letter. Maybe then she would believe me. I never said a word to her husband about Johnny. John pieced things together for himself. But Florence thinks I broke our promise. That's why she kicked me out of Wichita—sent me away from Johnny. The memory of my last conversation with my brother-in-law rushes over me, taking me back to a summer evening in Kansas and a path toward the Arkansas River. I pull my shawl tighter as I surrender to the scene playing in my head.

I pick up a rumpled piece of blue paper. Thinking it's rubbish, I squeeze the paper tight and stick the tiny ball into my skirt pocket as I continue down the dirt path. Florence asked me to find her husband and let him know supper was ready. She saw John come home from work and head straight to the river to check on his catfish traps. Bright beams of sunlight slice through the trees, casting long end-of-day shadows across the forest floor. My brother-in-law comes into view. He's crouching by the river, rinsing his hands. He scrubs and rubs and dunks them back in the water again and again. I wonder what he's working so hard to wash off.

"Hello, John," I say. "Anything in the traps today?"

He wipes his hands on his shirt and moves away from the river. John sits on a nearby boulder. "Haven't checked 'em yet," he says without making eye contact.

John keeps his head down and rolls it from side to side. Then his eyes meet mine. "The Americans weren't ready, you know. We didn't have the training we needed to fight in the trenches."

John doesn't talk about the war much, and when he does, it's often out of the blue like this. Florence says the best thing to do is listen. Listen with love—one of Mama's favorite pieces of advice.

I take a seat on a fallen log as John continues. "The Army gave us something called a trench knife. It had a blade a little longer than this one." He picks up his fishing knife and turns it over in his hand. "A rifle wasn't any good on the night raids, unless you used it as a club. And you didn't want to accidentally fire a weapon and alert the enemy. Even bayonets were too cumbersome for fighting in close quarters. The trench knife became my favorite tool. It had metal knuckle protectors and a second, stubby blade on the bottom." He taps the bottom of his fist. "Just right for smashing someone's skull. My friend Jacques called it the 'walnut cracker.'"

My stomach lurches at the expression. Florence says it helps John sleep when he lets the memories out. "You've never mentioned Jacques before. Where was he from?" I ask.

"Jacques was from Laval, a city north of Montreal. Yeah, the Canadians were the best in the trenches. Some soldiers darkened their faces with grease paint before a raid, but Jacques showed me how to burn the end of a cork and use that instead. He taught me how to survive. At first, I tried to subdue the enemy with my hands, but Jacques taught me to use my feet, my legs, my head, and my elbows far more effectively. He also taught me how to use my knife. How to make it part of my body." John rotates the blade, and it catches a few rays of the setting sun. "I met a man on the road home this evening," he says, his eyes returning to mine. "Something in the way he walked reminded me of Jacques. He was looking for the three Blackwell sisters. And a baby."

I place Rachel's letter back in the bottom of the drawer, then stack my letters, Bible, and prayer book on top, making sure it's completely covered. Then I pick up my brush. I'll have to tackle the tangled sections one by one.

Since learning the details of Frank's divorce, nothing stands in the way of our relationship—nothing except my secrets and my sister's announcement that we're moving to Tulsa. I thought Frank and I had all the time in the world to get to know each other. Now, everything feels sped up and urgent.

In the office machine room, when someone drops an unexpected project on my desk, I've learned to stay calm and continue to work at my normal pace. In my experience, rushing only leads to mistakes. And correcting mistakes takes far longer than doing things right the first time. I don't want to feel like I'm hurrying to get to know Frank or cutting corners to make decisions. At least Eddie negotiated for the extra week. I've got a little breathing room before I have to give Florence my answer about moving to Tulsa.

Oh, but I made another stupid promise in the cemetery. How could I agree not to say anything to Frank about Johnny unless he asks me to marry him? Florence and her ridiculous stipulations. Then again, my sister had the perfect opportunity to tell me about her job offer in Tulsa, and she didn't. Is a promise binding if the person asking you to make it isn't being honest with you?

Dear Lord, I feel as if I am standing at a fork in the road, and I'm not sure which direction you want me to go. Am I obligated to move with Florence and Johnny, or am I free to choose another path? Am I bound to keep my promise to Florence, or can I trust Frank to keep our secret? Fill me, oh God, with your peace so I might have the strength and courage to follow wherever you lead. Amen.

Tangles removed, I sweep my hair back and secure it with a simple clip at the base of my neck. That'll do for now. I'll have time to pin it up when I dress for church after breakfast. My smart afternoon dress hangs on the closet door—ready for my Sunday drive with Frank. I change into my blue housedress and walk over to the window to grab my cardigan off the back of the chair. The weather shifted overnight. Thick clouds moved in. Yesterday's bright blue sky is flat gray today. It's not raining, but it looks like rain. Professor Rutledge quotes a French writer on days like this. He looks up at the cloudy sky and says, "Gray is the color of truth." I asked him once what that means, and he said most people want simple black and white answers to life's questions. They want to know that one answer is right, and the other is wrong. The truth, however, often lies in the middle. Gray is the color between black and white.

Last night, Mrs. Henderson said that a promise is only as good as the intention behind it. What was Florence's intention in the cemetery yesterday? Why did she make me promise without telling me about her job offer? She said she is worried Frank will take me away from her and Johnny, when she is the one planning on going away. She said Frank won't understand our secret, and he'll no longer be interested in me if I tell him the truth. And she's worried Frank might accidentally tell someone, and Johnny will find out. But I don't think any of those are the real reasons she begged me to promise. Florence knows I won't fall in love with a man if I don't think I can tell him the truth. I think she made me promise to keep me from falling in love with Frank. That's not a good intention, is it?

"The color of truth is gray," I say out loud as I look at the heavy morning sky. I wrap my arms across my chest and squeeze them tight. Soaking up the warmth of my sweater, I stare at the pale sky. I watch the long, pearly clouds spread themselves so thin, they almost disappear. And then I decide. One moment I don't know what I'm going to do, and the next, I'm sure. I don't believe the promise I made to Florence yesterday is binding, yet I respect her concerns. I have one week to get to know Frank. Come Saturday evening, if I trust Frank to keep our secret, I am going to tell him the whole messy story. God willing, Frank will know all my secrets before I dream again next Saturday night.

Encouraged by my resolve, I slip on my shoes and head down to the kitchen. The hallway still smells of Lux soap from Florence's long bath last night. I hope she got some sleep. The encounter with Sonny Linn left her wound tighter than a drum. I emerge from our little hallway onto the upstairs landing. The view of the marble foyer below is lovely. It's no surprise I continue to live in Henderson House in my dreams. It's hard for me to imagine living anywhere else. I make my way downstairs and into the dining room. Light streams out from underneath the kitchen door. Mrs. Henderson's already hard at work. There's no reason to sneak through her room into the kitchen this early. The rest of the house is fast asleep.

"Good morning," I say as I walk in. "Coffee sure smells good."

"We're going to need a boatload of it this morning. I doubt anyone got a full night's sleep," Mrs. Henderson says as she lights the oven. "I thought we might make sausage gravy and biscuits this morning. Your biscuits are improving, Bessie." She checks the percolator on the stove and then turns to me. "I've never seen you wear your hair pulled back in that style. It's very becoming." She looks at me the way only Mrs. Henderson can—as if she sees something no one else does. She smiles. "You look a little like Barbara Stanwyck in *The Lady Eve.*"

"Does Pastor Harper know you go to those movies?" I tease. "I tossed and turned all night and ended up wrestling with my hair this morning as a result."

"Oh, I like your curls loose on your shoulders. It's chic and confident. Keep it that way through breakfast, and see if anyone else notices," she says with a wink.

"Did you wait up to talk to Eddie and Professor Rutledge?" I ask.

"Yes. They didn't get home until after eleven," she answers. "Albert said Sonny seemed genuinely sorry for his behavior, and Mr. Linn practically died of shame when they rang the doorbell and delivered his inebriated son."

"What a night! Thank goodness the professor heard you scream."

"And you should have seen him knock out Sonny," she marvels.

"Looks like the professor is your knight in shining armor."

"Well, he was certainly my hero last night," Mrs. H says, straightening her apron.

"I had no idea Sonny was bothering Florence at work. She never mentioned a thing." I lean back against the counter. "Sometimes I don't know what to make of my sister."

"That makes two of us."

"I'm worried about her." I take a deep breath. "Florence can only hide so many things before she erupts. She didn't tell me about her trouble at work, she lied about the job interview, and she was crying at the cemetery. Florence never cries."

I don't tell Mrs. Henderson that to top it off, when I offered to look over the bank statements, Florence almost jumped out of her skin. I don't think my sister knows that Eddie and I are aware of her extra spending.

"I've sensed something building up inside her," Mrs. Henderson says. "Now, when you're making coffee on the stove in a percolator," she instructs, "you'll notice it bubble up into the little globe at the top. The hotter the water gets, the faster it will perk. As it gets darker, you know the coffee is close to being done. See how fast it's sputtering now and notice the color?"

"Yes," I say, looking over her shoulder.

"It's ready."

Mrs. Henderson takes a mug down from the shelf above the stove and pours me a cup. I love watching her glide around the kitchen. She navigates the various appliances and cabinets like a yellow perch swimming around the rocks and sticks in the Verdigris River. Effortless.

"No major decisions before coffee," Mrs. Henderson says. "That was a rule Dr. Henderson lived by, and it served him well."

"What if I've already made a major decision this morning?" I ask.

"Oh," Mrs. Henderson says, looking at me in surprise. "Then I suppose you should enjoy a good cup of coffee and revisit your decision to see if it still rings true." She holds up a large black skillet. "For today's lesson, I'd like to talk about this."

"It's a skillet," I say.

"Ah, but it's not just any skillet. This is a cast-iron skillet. It is the most important piece of cookware you'll ever own. This one is over thirty years old. It's been seasoned and reseasoned dozens of times. It's the seasoning that makes it special."

"Seasoning? Like salt and pepper?" I ask.

"No, no, my dear. Here, take the skillet and have a look at it." She hands it to me. "See the dark black coating on the pan?"

"Yes."

"That's the seasoning. Once you get a cast-iron skillet seasoned, it makes cooking so much easier: food doesn't stick, everything browns up just right, and it's quick to clean. When you first buy a skillet, you need to heat up the oven nice and hot, to about three hundred and seventy-five degrees. Then you rub the whole skillet, inside and out, with vegetable oil. You place it in the oven, upside down, and bake it for an hour. It's a good idea to put a sheet pan on the shelf underneath the skillet, or some tinfoil, to catch any of the oil that might drip off," she instructs, and I nod.

"It's very important to only wash the skillet with warm water, no soap, and dry it immediately. Don't scrub it too hard, because you'll wear off the seasoning," she says. "However, the wonderful thing about a cast-iron skillet is that even if you do burn something terribly in it, and you have to scrub it until the seasoning comes off, you can always reseason it! No matter how big a mess you make, you can always set things right again," she says, looking deep into my eyes. I stare back at her.

"No matter how big the mess?" I ask.

"No matter how big," Mrs. Henderson says, putting a gentle hand on my shoulder. She turns to open the refrigerator and takes out the milk, butter, and sausage.

"I had a dream last night," I say.

"What was it about?" she asks.

"I was here, in the kitchen at Henderson House. Frank was helping me dry the breakfast dishes."

"That sounds like a wonderful dream," she says.

"It was."

"Who else was in the dream?"

"Well, it's funny you should ask because Cousin Wahya and my daddy were in the dream, and Wahya's dog, Yona," I say.

"That's very interesting," Mrs. H says, unwrapping the bulk sausage and shaking her head.

"What makes you say that?"

"Well, whenever I have a dream that takes place in Henderson House, it comes true."

CHAPTER TWENTY-TWO

Mrs. Henderson

A DIZZYING ARRAY of blooms swirls around the church kitchen. As chance would have it, all the Kitchen Ladies are wearing floral dresses this morning.

"Well, what I don't understand is how Joyce Carter and her husband can be allowed to have open home inspections on a Sunday. Isn't it against the Sunday closing laws?" Kitty asks while she arranges deviled eggs on a plate. Her dress is pale blue with white daisies. "These eggs aren't half as pretty as yours, Edna."

"I don't think it's against the law for folks to tour the houses because they are only looking. They aren't buying anything on a Sunday. There is no transaction taking place," Bertie replies. She's sporting a yellow shirtwaist dress dotted with red poppies. She looks rather feminine this morning.

"Still, it seems like it should be an activity for a Saturday, not a Sunday. Are you sure it's legal, Mildred?" Kitty asks.

"Yes, Kitty, I'm sure it's legal. Bessie and Mr. Davis are not breaking any laws by going to inspect these new houses today after church. I assure you."

I take two cans of apple juice down from the shelf. My pastel floral dress flutters with my movement. The ruffled collar ties in front and gives it a capelet effect. Wearing this dress always invigorates me and, like the other members of Henderson House, I'm a little tired this morning.

"Now that we've settled the legal implications of Bessie's Sunday drive, can you please go over the details of Florence's job offer and the porch conversation?" Bertie asks as she uncovers a platter of tea sandwiches.

Our church holds Sunday school at 9:30 a.m. and has worship at 10:45 a.m., followed by coffee hour. Depending on how long Pastor Harper preaches, the congregation might not gather in the fellowship hall until after noon, and by then, folks are looking for a bite. The Kitchen Ladies sneak out of the sanctuary quietly during the invitation for new members at the end of the service. Leaving early gives us the time we need to set up coffee hour. We put out a nice spread. Some churches only serve Ritz Crackers and Nilla Wafers, but the Kitchen Ladies make sure we offer a wide selection of finger sandwiches, deviled eggs, and home-baked goods.

I pulled Edna aside between Sunday school and worship to give her a synopsis of the evening's events. I didn't want her to hear it for the first time in the church kitchen with everyone else. Edna agreed with my decision to keep the Sonny incident under wraps. Kay is the only other Kitchen Lady who knows about Sonny, and I'd like to keep it that way if possible. I certainly don't want to be the one to start the rumor mill churning.

"Mildred?" Bertie prompts me again.

"Yes, yes, the porch conversation. Frank asked Eddie if Bessie could wait a week before she gives Florence her answer about moving to Tulsa," I say as I open the juice cans, putting two holes on opposite sides of the top so the juice will pour more easily.

"I know why he needs another week," Dolly titters as she opens a fresh bag of sugar and tops off the sugar bowls.

Dolly's wearing her favorite light green dress with dark green and white blossoms and a white lace collar. I bet I've seen her wear that dress a hundred times. "People would think he was crazy if he proposed to a woman he'd only known for a week, but after two weeks . . ." she trails off, her voice trembling like a whip-poor-will.

"Oh, Dolly," Kay exclaims, "don't be ridiculous. Who gets engaged after only knowing someone for two weeks?"

As usual, Kay's dress is the most elegant—a rich green silk print with navy flowers and navy embroidery around the neck.

"At their age, why wait?" Bertie exclaims.

"All I know is a week is plenty of time for Florence to figure out some reason Bessie has to go with her," Edna chimes in. "I don't trust Florence. Never have. Not since the first day she set foot in Henderson House."

Edna's in a simple cream-colored cotton dress with a tiny rose pattern. The color of the flowers brings out the red in her hair.

"Do you really think Florence would conspire against her own sister?" Kay asks.

"Yes," Edna and I reply at the same time. I pour the juice into two pitchers.

"Bessie has been holding their family together for a long, long time," Bertie says as she loads cups onto a tray. "Family ties are hard to break, even if you are falling in love. I imagine our Bessie is wrestling with her decision. She's such a good girl. I bet this week will be hard on her. Florence and Frank are pulling her heart in two different directions. Only God knows which path she should take. We should pray for her."

A murmur of agreement floats around the kitchen.

"Oh, she's already wrestling with it—said she tossed and turned all night. She was down in the kitchen with me mighty early."

"In the kitchen with you? Did anything burn?" Edna asks.

"Oh, Edna. Nothing burned. In fact—" I stop short. Bessie asked me to keep her cooking lessons a secret.

"In fact, what?" Edna asks.

"In fact, it was rather nice having her company this morning," I reply.

"Really? You always say you like to spend time by yourself in the kitchen while you're cooking breakfast," Edna says.

"Well, I suppose I'm getting lonely in my old age."

I toss the empty juice cans into the garbage.

"How are you feeling about all this, Mildred?" Kitty asks and then continues before I can answer: "It seems no matter which path Bessie chooses, the Blackwell family is leaving Henderson House."

"True," Bertie chimes in. "Now might be the right time to accept your son's offer to move to New Jersey."

Leave it to Bertie to cut to the chase.

"I am seriously considering his offer," I say.

"Are you really thinking about leaving us, Mildred?" Dolly asks.

"I can't imagine this church without you." Kitty wipes her hands on a dish towel.

"Maybe it's time. I'm going to wait and see what happens this week before I respond to Robert. I'll know when it's time to put pen to paper. If I do decide to move to New Jersey, I suppose I'll put the house up for sale this summer."

The room goes silent. I can hear the growing murmur in the fellowship hall.

"Who could afford such a fine home?" Kay asks.

"*Pfft.* The top executives at Phillips are all making a bundle these days. I bet one of them would snap up Henderson House in a heartbeat," Bertie responds.

My stomach flip-flops at the thought of a stranger living in Henderson House. What if the new owners don't realize that the house is special? What if they can't hear it?

"I always knew you'd wake up and want to be with your boys again someday," Kitty says as she wipes down the back counter. "And all those grandchildren."

"What on earth will *you* do, Edna?" Dolly asks.

"I don't have a plan yet, Dolly. When I do, you'll be the first to know," Edna says. Her purple color flickers slightly. "It's strange to think our lives might change—and so quickly," she says to me as we walk out to the serving table.

Edna puts the sandwiches down on one end, and I put the juice pitchers on the other.

"Change always feels sudden." I turn to look at her. "Unexpected events happen and take us by surprise. Even the changes we try to anticipate and plan for always seem to pick up speed at the end. What am I going to do without you, Edna?"

"Oh, stop it. If you move on, you'll be fine, and so will I. Let's not talk about it until it's decided. I'm not ready to cry—not yet." Edna turns away and walks back to the kitchen. "We better bring the rest of the goodies out. The natives are getting restless. You coming, Mildred?" she asks.

"I'm right behind you."

Edna and I return to the kitchen and the ladies stand for a moment like an arrangement of flowers—taller stems in the back, smaller blooms in front. I wish I had a camera, but I capture the moment in my heart and tuck the image away for a rainy day.

CHAPTER TWENTY-THREE

Florence

EDDIE AND I wait in line to greet Reverend Morrison after the service. Johnny's already outside, catching up with his friends. The weekly ritual of saying something flattering to the minister as you exit church always seems ridiculous to me. Everyone tells the reverend how marvelous his sermon was, how meaningful, how moving. He's a fine preacher, but it takes forever to get out the door when each individual parishioner sees this moment as their personal opportunity to get in good with God. Finally, Eddie and I arrive at the front of the line.

"Thanks, Reverend. We sure enjoyed your sermon," Eddie says as he shakes the minister's hand. I smile and incline my head before walking out into the heavy, gray day outside.

At least it's not raining. Rain would spoil my plan to tell Johnny about the move. I went over my strategy a hundred times while I was in the bath last night. First, I'll suggest we drive to the park and go for a walk. We often take an after-church walk in the park. My request won't seem out of the ordinary. I'll tell Johnny about the move to Tulsa while we're driving.

He's bound to have a million questions, and I can start answering them while we're on our way to the park. It's always easier to discuss difficult subjects when we're in the car. Something about the confined space keeps me calm and focused.

You can do this, Florence. Keep your tone light and happy.

"Reverend Morrison is a fine speaker," Eddie says, offering me his arm as we walk to the far end of the parking lot. "Did you read the summary of his speech to the College High graduating class? They reprinted it in the paper last week. It was all about moving from living in the singular to living in the plural. He encouraged the graduates to tear up their selfish desires. He said that, instead of living life looking in a mirror, we ought to live life looking out the window. That we should work harder to understand the needs of others, and then rise to meet those needs."

"Mm-hmm. Well, I need you to rise and meet the needs of our family this week, Eddie," I say. "You and I both know Bessie's place is with us. She'll come around with our guidance. We need to keep this family together. Bessie listens to you. I know you can help her see that family is more important than a temporary case of puppy love."

"Did you even hear what I was saying?"

"Something about Reverend Morrison and a graduation speech."

"Be careful, sis. I've seen you get downright mean when you think one of your perfect plans is in jeopardy."

"What are you talking about?"

"I understand because I have a mean streak, too." Eddie stops walking. "Something else to thank Daddy for, I guess."

"Mean streak? You don't have a mean bone in your body. You drive around in a taxi all day telling people funny stories. You make people happy."

My brother sure is in a strange mood today. Then again, we're all tired after last night. Eddie and the professor probably didn't get to sleep until midnight, after taking Sonny home.

"I didn't leave Montana just to help you and little Johnny," Eddie says. He looks around the parking lot as if he's making sure we're far enough away from the other church families to continue. "The week before I got your letter, I almost killed a man." He pauses, waiting for my response. I examine his face to see if he's joking. His furrowed brow makes it clear—this is no joke.

"What happened?" I ask.

"There was a kid working with the cook on my last cattle drive. Kid's name was Wendell, but everyone called him 'the kid.' Anyway, one of the cowboys, a big bellowing oaf who went by Hoss, was always giving the kid a hard time. One night, Hoss called the kid over to complain about his cornbread being burnt. By this point, the kid was terrified of Hoss—who could blame him? And the kid started stuttering, trying to apologize. Hoss made fun of the kid's stuttering, mocking and imitating him. A few of the other ranch hands laughed. When the kid started crying, Hoss began slapping him upside the head, telling him to toughen up. Well, that triggered one too many memories of the good old days for me. Daddy making fun of Bessie's stuttering. Daddy slapping you so hard, he broke your nose. Daddy hollering at me to toughen up while he was beating me."

"Oh, Eddie." I reach out and put a hand on his shoulder. "I'm so sorry. What did you do?"

"I stood up and told Hoss to lay off the kid. He spun around and charged me like a bull, knocked me flat to the ground next to the campfire. As we rolled around in the dirt, I punched and kicked him as hard as I could. Then I grabbed a log from the woodpile and started beating him with it. If one of my buddies hadn't pulled me off, I swear, I would have beaten him to death."

"Standing up to a bully doesn't make you mean," I say.

"Maybe not, but my fight with Hoss shook me to the core. I enjoyed it. Anyway, I left and came to Bartlesville to see if living with my sisters and my little nephew might help me keep my anger in check."

"Has it worked?"

"The role of brother and uncle seems to keep the angry bear in hibernation. But I know he's only sleeping. The mean streak is still in here." He points to his chest and then to me. "I think it's in you, too."

"Me? I've never picked a fight in my life!" I exclaim.

"No, but I've seen you boil over and lash out plenty of times. Like Wednesday night, when you made fun of Bessie for keeping her promise to that boy in eighth grade. It was a mean thing to say. Why did you do it, Flossie? Did it feel good to put her down?"

"Don't be ridiculous!" I squawk, wincing at the shrillness of my own voice. "We were reminiscing, that's all."

"Words can hurt people as much as punches, sis. Maybe more," he says.

"I don't see what any of this has to do with keeping our family together." I start walking again. "That's the matter at hand."

"You're so focused on your own selfish desires, you're completely overlooking your sister's happiness." Eddie catches up with me and takes hold of my sore arm. Even though my brother's touch is gentle, my arm aches where Sonny grabbed me last night, and I pull away. "Frank's genuinely sweet on Bessie. They're falling in love," he says.

I walk away. My frustration with my brother grows with each step. First, he tells me he thinks I enjoy being mean, and now he's lobbying for Bessie's happiness over what's best for the family. A burning sensation builds in my chest and rises into my throat. I want to scream at Eddie and tell him Bessie is the one who stole my happiness. If anyone's happiness is being overlooked here, it's mine! Bessie ruined everything the day she told John our secret. She brought his nightmares back. She might as well have pushed him off that bridge in Topeka with her own two hands. I'll be damned if suddenly Bessie's happiness is more important than mine.

What's more, I *am* considering my sister's happiness. Bessie won't be truly happy unless she honors her promise to me and Johnny. Her infatuation with Frank Davis is clouding her judgment. I realized yesterday, I need to work this from the Frank side of the equation. Bessie is, in fact, keeping a very important secret from him. Considering his big confession in the car, my guess is that Frank would be very disappointed if he found out Bessie's not being honest with him in return. I'll give the two love birds all the space they need this week. I'll be the most supportive sister in recorded history. Next Saturday afternoon, before their big night out, I'll have a little heart-to-heart with Frank.

This plan is a slippery slope, Florence, the voice in my head warns.

True. I'll need to play my cards right.

And you're sure this isn't about keeping the money in the savings account?

Don't be ridiculous. Someone has to make sure our family stays together. Clearly, Eddie's not going to be any help. It's up to me now.

What if it backfires? What if Bessie tells Frank the truth?

Nonsense. She reaffirmed her promise to me yesterday. She won't betray me a second time. This time, the voice doesn't respond. I take a deep breath and square my shoulders. It's decided then. I have a plan. I'll back off this week and plan on having a chat with Frank next Saturday afternoon.

"Let's see where their romance stands at the end of the week," I say to my brother in the most soothing tone I can manage.

"Where whose romance stands?" Johnny appears at my elbow.

"Mr. Davis and Aunt Bessie's," Eddie says, ruffling Johnny's hair.

"I skip one trip to the cemetery and miss out on all the juicy stuff! Give me the scoop and don't skimp on the details," Johnny demands.

"There's nothing to tell, sweetheart," I say.

"Oh, I'm sure there is, Mom. They took a liking to each other right off the bat. Didn't they, Uncle Eddie? They just seem to sort of go together."

"They sure do—like ham and eggs." Eddie winks at Johnny.

"Toast and jam," Johnny replies, and they begin their familiar snip-snap game of topping one another with things that go together.

"Laurel and Hardy," says Eddie.

"Rogers and Astaire," Johnny replies.

"Rogers and Trigger." Eddie grins.

"Oh, would you two please stop kidding around?" I say, trying to conceal my exasperation. Eddie's strange confession and his accusations about my behavior have put me in a foul mood.

Keep things happy today, Florence. Remember, light and happy.

"Frank wasn't kidding around last night when he called this a courtship," Eddie says.

"Like an old-fashioned courtship, leading to marriage?" Johnny asks.

"Could be. Cornbread and honey," Eddie slips in while giving Johnny a little poke in the ribs.

"Woo-hoo!" Johnny cheers. "Isn't this exciting, Mom?" Johnny sways back and forth chanting, "Aunt Bessie's got a boyfriend."

"Yes, it's quite . . . unexpected," I offer.

"Biscuits and gravy," Johnny says under his breath. "Are we heading over to pick up Mrs. H?" he asks. "Are Aunt Bessie and Mr. Davis still going for their Sunday drive?"

Time to shift the focus away from Blushing Bessie and Fabulous Frank and back to my plan to tell Johnny about the move. I wish the weather wasn't so dreary. Blue skies and sunshine would make all of this easier.

"Mrs. Henderson is getting a ride home with Edna and Douglas," I say, doing my best to sound cheerful. "We've got her car. I thought we might head up to Johnstone Park for a walk. Plus, I've got something I'd like to talk about."

I'm back on plan. The tightness in my chest subsides.

"Sounds good to me." Johnny smiles.

"Looks like we better get a wiggle on if we're going to get in a walk before the rain," Eddie says as we climb into Mrs. Henderson's car and head north on South Dewey Avenue toward the park.

"Johnny, I'm not sure how to start this conversation, but you're a young man now, so I'm going to tell you straight out," I begin.

"Sure, Mom. Shoot." Johnny scooches into the middle of the back seat. I turn my head to look at him over the seat rest.

"Well, sweetheart, I've gotten a wonderful promotion at work. It's more responsibility and more money, but it's not at the store in Bartlesville. It's at the store in Tulsa. If I take the job, we will move to Tulsa this summer. I never thought about leaving Bartlesville, but this offer is too good for us to pass up, honey."

Step two of my plan is complete. The silence from the backseat feels like it goes on forever.

"Gosh, Mom. I'm, uh, well, I don't know what to say." He pauses. "I'm real proud of you." More silence.

I exercise restraint and let the silence simmer. I don't want to overload him with details about Tulsa. In sales, we use the "Rule of Three." You focus on three benefits of the product that meet the customer's needs. If you highlight more than three, you can overwhelm the client, and they might not make a purchase at all.

Identify three benefits of the move and don't oversell.

"What questions do you have for me, sweetheart?" I ask.

"Will it be the two of us? Will we move by ourselves?" Johnny asks.

"I'm not gonna let you have all the fun in the big city without me!" Eddie chimes in. "My company has an outfit down in Tulsa. Should be easy as pie to start driving a cab down there."

That's benefit number one. *Thank you, Eddie, for the first helpful thing you've said all day.*

"What about my friends and my job at the club this summer?" Johnny asks. Then he adds, "And what about Aunt Bessie?"

"I've invited Aunt Bessie to move with us, too," I answer. Eddie makes a coughing sound.

"But she's so happy here," Johnny says. "She belongs here, Mom. She loves her job and her church, and now maybe she even loves Mr. Davis. We can't ask her to leave Bartlesville. We just can't."

"That's exactly what I said," Eddie agrees. The searing sensation returns to my chest. After everything my brother said to me this morning, I must not prove him right and boil over. I wait until the fiery feeling dies down, then I respond.

"Your aunt Bessie is free to make her own choice, but I think she will choose to come to Tulsa with us. Family is more important to her than anything," I say.

"Do you really, really want the job?" he asks.

"Yes, Johnny, I do. It's a big step up for me to become a manager, and there will be lots of new opportunities for all of us in Tulsa."

"When would we have to leave Bartlesville?" he whispers.

"They would like me to start at the end of June," I say.

"Whoa," he says, looking down at the floor of the car. "That's so soon, Mom. I don't want to miss the entire summer. I've been looking forward to it for months—working at the club and playing golf, goofing around with Tommy. Why can't I stay here in Bartlesville for the summer? I could stay at Henderson House or maybe at the Westfeldts."

"We'll buy our own house in Tulsa," I say.

"Really?"

"Yes. And you'll have your own room and your own yard to play catch in when you have friends over."

Benefit number two: our own house and his own room.

"That would be swell. But what about Mrs. Henderson? What will she do if we all leave her at once?" Johnny asks.

I hear the concern in his voice. Why on earth is he thinking about Mrs. Henderson? He should be worried about leaving his friends and his baseball team, not the eccentric landlady at our boarding house.

"Mrs. Henderson will be fine," I say. "As luck would have it, her son invited her to live with him in New Jersey. She'll be closer to her grandchildren and—"

"She's leaving Oklahoma? We'll never see her again," Johnny mumbles. "Or Louie."

I think of a third benefit.

"But when we get our own house, we can have our own dog, sweetheart. You'd like that, wouldn't you?"

"You bet I would," Johnny says. "Maybe we can get a beagle like Louie." His voice perks up a bit but not as much as I'd like.

Three benefits are on the table: Uncle Eddie is coming with us, Johnny will have a room of his own in our own house, and he can get a dog. Time to stop selling.

"What should I tell the caddy master at the club? If I'm going to leave at the end of June, I think I should tell him right away so he can fill my spot on the roster."

"Good man, Johnny. You always want to be up front with your employer," Eddie says.

"Don't be too hasty," I jump in. "You said there were a lot of boys interested in caddying at the club. Mr. Harrington will have no trouble filling your spot. I think you should enjoy your job until the last possible minute."

Eddie chews on his bottom lip and glances at me sideways.

"Don't look at me like that, Eddie. Why shouldn't Johnny enjoy the club for as long as he can? It won't take them long to train someone else to carry a bag of sticks. Johnny stands to make good money between now and the end of June. What other job will pay him as well during his final weeks in Bartlesville and give him access to playing golf?"

"Some boys from the baseball team are going to be pickers this summer. There's no commitment. You show up at a designated spot in the morning, and they load you on a truck and take you out to whatever field needs harvesting. Jimmy Leach said they feed you sandwiches all day. Then they drop you off again in the evening."

"Absolutely not!" The harshness of my voice slices through the interior of the car. Johnny flinches.

"What's wrong with doing an honest day's work for honest pay?" Eddie asks.

Why is my brother challenging me at every turn today? The fire in my chest returns. I can't control the heat, and it shoots up my neck and into my face.

"Johnny Fuller, you will not work as a field hand!" I shout. "I won't have your skin burned and your hands calloused. Do you know the sacrifices I've made to pull us up out of the dust and dirt? You're not going back to it!"

I close my eyes tightly, trying my best to stop the tears from coming, but I can't. Johnny leans over from the back seat and puts a hand on my shoulder. My heart feels as if it might pound its way out of my chest.

"It's all right, Mom. It was just one idea. I'm sure we'll figure something out. Won't we, Uncle Eddie?"

"Of course we will. We always do, don't we, sis?" I reach my left hand out to touch my brother on the knee and cross my right hand over my shoulder to place it on Johnny's hand.

"Yes, we always do," I say through the tears.

Eddie pulls into the parking lot at Johnstone Park. He gives me an all-knowing glance and hands me his handkerchief before hopping out of the car. I proved him right when I boiled over and lashed out, but I didn't say anything mean. All I did was tell the truth. And that's all I'm going to tell Frank Davis next Saturday afternoon—the truth. Well, part of it.

CHAPTER TWENTY-FOUR

Bessie

FRANK AND I walk up the stairs from the basement of the church. I pull my gloves on over my sweaty palms. Every muscle in my body thrums in anticipation of spending time alone with Frank this afternoon.

"It sure was nice of Kay and her husband to invite us to go fishing on Friday." Frank smiles. "Is it too much for you? That puts us up to four dates this week."

"In for a penny, in for a pound," I say as I take his arm.

I look down at my white-gloved hand resting on the sleeve of his linen suit jacket, and I can't help but smile. This time last week, I'd never heard of Frank Davis and now, here we are, walking arm in arm.

"Eddie wasn't joking. People do turn around in church when you sing," Frank says.

"They do not." I shake my head.

"Oh, yes, they do! And no wonder, you have a beautiful voice, Bessie."

"Thank you." My cheeks warm with the compliment. "Smells like rain."

"Sure does. San Francisco never smelled this good before the rain, trust me." He takes a deep breath.

"Do you miss it at all, living in the big city?" I ask.

"Not—one—bit," he says, emphasizing each word. "Bartlesville is everything I hoped for and then some." He pulls me into him slightly, and I giggle.

"Mr. Davis, I swear, you make me feel like a teenager—heading out on one of my adventures."

"I'm glad. You and I have plenty of adventures ahead of us."

"Do you really think so?"

"Absolutely. The first one starts right now with our exciting Sunday drive and house inspection!" We arrive at his car, and he ushers me around to the passenger door.

I turn to say something just as he is reaching for the door handle, and we wind up nose to nose—maybe the closest we've ever been. Our first kiss is coming soon, but it's certainly not going to happen in the church parking lot. I should slide over and put some room between us, but he holds my eyes with his, and I'm entranced.

"When I taught school in Claremore, after Eddie and I left home," I say in a voice just above a whisper, "I was strictly forbidden to go riding with any man other than a family member. No buggy rides, no wagon rides, and certainly no automobile rides." I put my index finger between our faces and shake it back and forth, imitating the head of the school board.

"Really?" Frank whispers back.

"Oh, yes, there were very strict rules for unmarried schoolteachers."

"You didn't even go riding with Doc Jenkins?" he asks, raising an eyebrow.

"What makes you ask that?" The words catch in my throat.

"Your brother has a few theories about you and the good doctor. He says you were pretty friendly before you moved to Wichita with your sisters."

"Well, I never went riding with Doc Jenkins," I say quickly and turn toward the passenger door.

My stomach tightens. I may not be able to tell Frank everything until Saturday night, but I need to tell him what I can about Doc Jenkins—today.

Dear Lord Jesus, help me this afternoon as I share with Frank. Help me know what to say and when to stop. I put my trust in you, Lord, knowing that with you all things are possible, for you are the God who can move mountains. Amen.

"I suppose this is an adventure, and a scandalous one at that. Going for a drive with a man who's not a family member." Frank leans in to open the door and our bodies graze each other, sending a now familiar tingle up and down my spine.

"Your buggy awaits." Frank helps me into the passenger side of the car.

I adjust my dress as he walks around and gets in behind the wheel.

"Do you know where we are going?" Frank asks, turning over the engine.

"I think so. Joyce said it was just off Baker Hollow Road. Head south on Cherokee and look for Baker Hollow on your right once we get out of town."

We drive in silence as we start our journey, but it's not an awkward silence.

"There's Mr. Phillips's house," I say as we pass Frank Phillips's mansion on our right.

"I think that might be too big for just little ol' me," Frank jokes as we continue down South Cherokee Avenue. "I suppose Henderson House would be too big for one person, as well."

"Oh, and that would never do. Henderson House is a house that needs people," I say in my best impersonation of Mildred Henderson. Frank laughs.

"In San Francisco, people often turned large homes like Henderson House into bed-and-breakfasts," he says.

"What's a bed-and-breakfast?" I ask.

"It's like a boarding house, only it's run more like a hotel. The owners offer lodging and breakfast. As opposed to having long-term borders, they welcome travelers for shorter stays. We have a couple of engineers working in my department right now who wish there was a nice bed-and-breakfast in town. They're here for another few weeks and are sick and tired of living in a hotel."

"A bed-and-breakfast. Hmm," I mutter.

"What?"

"Oh, I was just thinking about my daddy and Cowboy Coffee Hour. He loved entertaining folks in the morning over coffee. He would have been a good bed-and-breakfast host. He was really quite charming early in the day—" I stop before finishing my thought.

"Before he started drinking?" Frank asks.

"Yes."

"Eddie said he's as sober as a judge now. Has been for years."

"True."

"I don't mean to pry, Bessie, but if your father has changed his ways, why don't you see him more often?"

"Florence has a hard time with forgiveness. And to be honest, we've never taken the time to mend our fences. Listening to you talk about patching things up with your brother, well, it makes me want to redouble our efforts to spend more time with him."

I remember the beginning of my dream—Daddy and Wahya telling stories over breakfast at Henderson House. "Ha," I mutter aloud. Mrs. H said dreams that take place in Henderson House come true. She also said my feelings for Frank opened the door for me to love again. It's time to take another step through that door.

"Frank, I'd like to talk to you about Doc Jenkins."

"Bessie, you know you don't have to tell me about all of your past relationships. I was only teasing you earlier about going riding with another fella."

"I know, but this is important. It's my only past relationship. If we're trying to get to know each other this week, you need to know what happened." I adjust my skirt and put my gloved hands in my lap. "When Doc Jenkins arrived in Claremore, he began attending the Presbyterian church. He was a dashing man—reminded me of Douglas Fairbanks. I was surprised and flattered when he asked if he could take me out for a Sunday drive. Everyone in town already considered me an old maid. I was almost thirty. I declined his invitation and told him about the rigid code of conduct for unmarried schoolteachers. Doc suggested we make a game of it. Keep our dates a secret. So, we snuck around."

"Snuck around?" Frank asks, sounding almost amused.

"Yes. I couldn't afford to lose my job, and Doc made sneaking around so exciting. It was the first time in my life I'd ever broken the rules—and the first time I'd ever been in love. Doc and I kept our romance hidden from everyone in Claremore. Florence was the only person I told, and it sounds like Eddie picked up on it. Doc and I would meet for secret picnics in faraway fields and meadows where no one would see us, never arriving or departing at the same time. Doc told me he wanted to marry me. He even described the ring he was going to buy me in great detail. I believed him, and we were . . ." I struggle to say the word out loud. "Intimate."

"What went wrong?" Frank asks.

"One day—it was a Tuesday, as I recall—his fiancée, a young woman named Ruby Sinclair, arrived on the afternoon train from Kansas City."

"How did you find out?" Frank asks.

"She checked into the Fuller Hotel, and Florence was on duty at the front desk. Miss Sinclair told Florence all about her upcoming marriage to the good doctor," I say. "Florence gave me the news that evening, and Doc introduced me to Ruby the following Sunday at church. Wouldn't you know, she was wearing the exact diamond ring he had described to me."

"Did he try to explain himself?"

"Never. Doc acted as if nothing had ever happened between us. When I look back on it, I realize that he convinced me to sneak around because that's the way he needed it to be. Maybe he even picked me because I was the pathetic old maid school-teacher, and I had plenty of reasons to go along with his plan. All Doc wanted was a secret diversion while he was waiting for Ruby to arrive. I was never his girl. I was nothing but a game to him."

"Is Doc Jenkins the reason you left Claremore and went to Wichita with your sisters?" Frank asks.

"He was one of the reasons," I say.

My story needs to end here. The other reason for moving to Wichita will have to wait until Saturday night. By then, I'll be ready to trust Frank with the whole story. But for now, I can skip ahead.

"It's also why I moved to Bartlesville when I left Aunt Maude's. I couldn't go back to Claremore and live in the same town with Mrs. Ruby Jenkins."

"Bessie, I'm so sorry," Frank says.

"Me too." I answer. "One of my mama's favorite pieces of advice was 'don't dwell.' I think maybe I've been dwelling on the past. Afraid every man would be the same as Doc Jenkins—a liar and a cheat. Then I met you, and I realized it was time to put my fears behind me."

Frank reaches across the seat, and I slip my hand in his.

"This is not a game to me, Bessie," he says, giving my hand a squeeze before he returns it to the wheel.

"I know," I reply, and I realize that I did it. I told Frank about Doc Jenkins, and the world didn't stop spinning. There are still secrets to share, but I've made a good start. I look out the car window, and everything seems brighter, even on this dreary day.

"Have you ever thought about buying a house?" I ask.

"I thought about it when I took the job here. The personnel department tried to set me up with a real estate agent, but I wanted to get the lay of the land first. Finding a room at Henderson House seemed like the perfect way to settle in and start looking around. Guess I better get busy. From what you said, Mrs. Henderson's seriously considering moving and selling the house."

"Yes, she is," I say with a sigh. "I'm not very experienced when it comes to house hunting. Today will be good for me, too. I don't seem to be able to visualize myself living anywhere but Henderson House."

"Really? Not even with Florence pushing for you all to buy your own place?"

"Nope. In fact, I dreamed about Henderson House last night."

A pulsating warmth stirs in my belly as I remember the sensation of my dress falling to the floor, and Frank touching my bare skin.

Frank takes his eyes of the road for a moment to look at me. "That's funny. So did I," he says.

Another tingle runs up my spine. The thought of Frank dreaming about me in the same way I was dreaming about him makes me giddy.

"Maybe we can do some dreaming together this week," he says. "After everything that happened with Pete and Annie, well, I sort of stopped."

"Stopped dreaming?"

"Pretty much. I mean . . . I had goals for my education and career, but none for my heart. I swore I'd never trust anyone with my heart again, Bessie. But now—"

"I guess we're both learning to trust again," I say.

A wave of urgency rushes over me as I utter the word "trust." I'm aching to tell Frank the whole complicated story right now, but I stop myself. For once, "the glue" is going to take a page out of Florence's book and stick to my plan. Saturday night. If all goes well this week, I will tell Frank everything on Saturday night.

"I've been asking around about you at work," I say, lightening the tone of the conversation.

"And what did you find out?"

"You have a master's degree in engineering from Berkeley, hold several patents on various refining techniques, and were hired as the Senior Vice President of Special Projects—a new position Boots Adams created just for you."

"Guilty on all counts." Frank grins. "What was it like when Boots Adams took over for Frank Phillips?"

"Oh, it was probably one of the easiest transitions in corporate history," I respond. "Everyone already knew and loved Mr. Adams. The board voted him in unanimously."

"I'm not surprised. He's much younger than I thought he would be, but I like him so far."

"You already met him?" I ask.

"Yes, he spent time with my team on Thursday. He's a man who believes in science and engineering, that's for sure. Now, I have a confession to make," Frank says. "I've been asking around about you, too."

"Oh, really? And what did you find out?"

"Mostly that you're a duplication machine legend. You've been with the company for more than a dozen years; you always have at least one assistant, sometimes two; your work is impeccable; and . . ." he says, pausing as a broad smile crosses his face, revealing those adorable wrinkles around his eyes, "you're the Dorothy Dix of Phillips Petroleum. Seems all the young women at headquarters rely on you for romantic advice." He turns and raises his eyebrows at me.

"You have been asking around." I smile back at him. I smile so much when I'm with Frank, sometimes the muscles in my cheeks start to ache.

"I was hoping, maybe you could give me a little advice," Frank teases. "See, I've met this girl and I really like her, but I only have one week to get to know her before an evil dragon swoops in and carries her away to Tulsa."

We both start laughing.

"In the end, the only thing we have to give those we love is our time. So, my advice is to spend as much time with this girl as you possibly can this week."

"Whoa, where'd you learn to dish out advice like that?" Frank asks.

"Listening to my mama counsel the ladies who came into the Pack and Run. I asked her once how she got so good at giving advice and she said that people don't really want you to tell them what to do—they just want someone to hold their stories and keep 'em safe. That's what I do for the young women at Phillips."

"Other than helping the lovelorn, what's your favorite thing about your job?"

"Well, I get projects from all the different departments. I know a little bit about everything going on at the company, and I learn something new every day."

"You like learning new things, don't you?"

"Yes, I do." I glance out the window. "There's Baker Hollow Road," I say, pointing.

Frank turns onto the street. A sign with an arrow marks the entrance to Hidden Hollow.

"This isn't far from town," Frank says, turning into the development. "It's a good location."

"What a lovely little street this is," I say, noticing the abundance of mature trees. "Should we start there? I point to a banner in front of one of the finished homes. Half a dozen cars are parked along the street.

"Do you want me to drop you off in front?" Frank offers. "There aren't any sidewalks."

"Oh, no. The walk will do me good after a morning of sitting in church," I say. "Besides, it's an adventure. Who needs sidewalks on an adventure?"

Frank parks the car down at the end of the street. He comes around to open my door and helps me out. We walk hand in hand down the center of the unpaved road and up a newly laid set of pavers to the house with the welcome sign. It seems to be the largest of the three finished homes. Joyce opens the door to bid farewell to a couple who walks past us. She sees me and Frank, and her eyes light up.

"Oh, I'm so happy you're here!" She hurries out and squeezes my arm. "Cute dress," she mouths to me silently.

"Hello, Joyce, it's nice to see you again," Frank says.

"How's the rest of your week been?" I ask.

"Busy, busy! But it's been wonderful to stay with Gertie and spend some time with my nieces and nephews."

"Looks like you've got this new neighborhood up and running," Frank says.

"Yes, we have three models ready for inspection. I'm pleased with the progress."

"How many houses will be in the neighborhood when all is said and done?" I ask.

"Twelve," Joyce answers. "Come in, come in. Let me show you the lot plans."

She heads through an open archway into a dining room, which is partially furnished with a large wooden table, chandelier, and six matching chairs. The table holds a myriad of plans, handouts, and folders. Joyce shows us the master plan for the street and points out the model homes, purchased lots, and parcels still available.

"That's a nice pie-shaped lot at the end of the cul-de-sac," Frank says, pointing to the plan.

"Yes, and it has wonderful sun exposure for a garden out back," Joyce agrees. "Here's an information packet." She hands Frank a blue folder with "Moore Construction" printed on the front in raised white lettering.

"Are you sure you want to waste a fancy packet on us? We're just here for fun," I say.

"I want you to have the complete experience," she says, pressing the folder into Frank's hands. "There's a floor plan for each model and a list of additional options. There's also a list of kitchen appliances and upgrades in the back. You can start by touring the house we're in now."

"Wow, I'm impressed," I say.

"Thank you, Bessie. Selling homes is more satisfying than I ever imagined. I love it, and I love working with Carter." She winks at me.

"I'm so happy for you."

"I'm thrilled you and Frank came by. If you have any questions, please stop in on your way out."

"Will do," I say.

"Thanks for the information, Joyce," Frank chimes in. "Shall we start in the kitchen, Bessie?"

"Let's go." I link my arm through his and wave to Joyce as we exit the dining room.

"Have a good time, you two!" Joyce calls after us and then turns to greet another couple as they enter through the front door.

CHAPTER TWENTY-FIVE

Bessie

FRANK AND I hold hands as we walk across the street to the third and final model home. We stand at the end of the walkway and survey the little white house in front of us.

"I feel like Goldilocks," I say.

"How so?"

"Well, the first house was way too big, and the second house was still a little too big, but this house seems just right, doesn't it?"

"And you thought you didn't know anything about house hunting."

"True. And now, after touring two houses, I'm a pro."

"Tell me what you like about this one?" Frank asks.

"Well, I guess one thing I've learned today is that I like symmetry," I say.

"Symmetry! We're moving into expert territory," Frank teases.

"Remember, I was a schoolteacher for many years, and I even attended college for a while."

"College?"

"Oh, yes. I attended the Municipal University of Wichita part-time before I moved to Bartlesville."

"I bet you loved being in college," he says.

"I sure did." I return my attention to the home in front of us. "I like how this porch runs across the entire front of the house. And the door is in the center with matching windows on either side. Why, it's almost a teeny-tiny version of Henderson House. What's this model called?" I ask.

"This is The Adams," Frank says, referencing the packet Joyce gave us.

"The Adams," I repeat.

"Carter and Joyce have a bit of a founding father's theme here in Hidden Hollow—The Washington, The Jefferson, and now The Adams," he says.

"True. But, in these parts, it could also be in honor of Boots Adams," I say.

"I like your thinking. I could live in a home named in honor of the president of our company." Frank reads from the packet, "'The Adams is the smallest of the models. It's a simple four-room house with an oversized bath, an expanded dining area off the kitchen, and ample windows to bring in hours of cheery light. A cellar is standard in this model and a second-story bedroom can be added at your request.'"

"Shall we look inside?"

We walk up the path and onto the little porch. The front door opens directly into the living room.

"This room is cozy," Frank says.

I look around the room with its fireplace, wood floors, and large windows. "Yes, it is. I also learned today that I like it when I walk into a house and know instinctively where I should go next," I say, gesturing to the archway in front of us.

We walk into the heart of the home. A long hallway runs through it. The kitchen is on the left, and two bedrooms are on the right. There are two doors on the wall directly in front of us. Frank opens the door to the left.

"Aha! The stairs to the cellar," he says.

I open the door to the right

"Aha! The bathroom," I say.

We walk past the bathroom and into the larger bedroom at the front of the house.

"This bedroom has two closets. It must be the master," I say, walking over to look out the side window. I back up from the window, trying to get a sense for where you might put a bed in this room to take advantage of the natural light, but I back myself right over Frank's foot and lose my balance. He slips his arms around my waist and catches me.

"Oh, dear!" I exclaim.

"This is the second time I've had to stop you from falling." Frank smiles down at me, displaying the little wrinkles around his eyes again, and my heart melts.

His hat sits precariously on his wavy hair much as it did the first time I saw him. Slowly, he lifts me back onto my feet. I feel my body dissolving into his arms. Frank's eyes never waver from mine as he draws me in close. This is it. This is the perfect moment for our first—

"Hurry up. Hurry up," a man's voice echoes in the front hallway.

"We're coming, George," a woman's voice grumbles.

The indistinct chatter of several children fills the air. Frank and I stare wide-eyed at each other and giggle. We release our embrace.

"Phew, that was a close call," I say, standing upright and straightening my dress.

"Oh, Bessie, if you only knew how much I—"

"This must be the bigger bedroom here," the woman says, interrupting Frank as she walks into the bedroom we're standing in. "Afternoon," she says.

"Good afternoon," Frank replies. "Are you enjoying touring the houses?"

"Well, it would have been easier if my sister had been willing to watch the kids."

The children's voices in the other room escalate from chattering to screeching and squawking. Their hard-sole Sunday dress shoes sound like galloping horses. They must be chasing each other around and around the empty living room.

"Do you know how many bedrooms this model has?" the woman shouts over the noise.

"Two," Frank shouts back, checking the packet. "But I believe there is an option to add a third bedroom on the second story."

"Thank you." She turns and yells. "George, this one isn't big enough! Enjoy your day." She leaves us alone in the bedroom again.

We listen as they corral their herd and depart. The front door slams shut. Frank looks at me and reaches for my hand.

"How many children do you think were running around out there?" I ask.

"More than her sister wanted to watch," he replies.

"Sisters are a complicated business," I say.

"Yes, I'm figuring that out." He takes a step toward me and pulls me closer.

"Mr. Davis, now that I'm aware anyone might join us on our tour, at any moment, my desire is on temporary hold," I say.

"*Temporary* hold?" Frank asks with a raised eyebrow.

I smile but slip out of his embrace and exit the bedroom. We inspect the rest of the house. I particularly like the dining nook in the kitchen—it reminds me of the one at Henderson House. We leave through the kitchen door so Frank can look at the garage. Then we start the walk back to Frank's car. We've walked to the end of the development opposite from where we parked.

"The Adams is definitely my favorite," Frank says.

"Mine, too," I agree.

"But judging from the number of times you compared these three houses to Henderson House, I'd say Henderson House is your true love."

"And always will be. Frank, it's getting dark all of a sudden." I look up just as the skies open. The rain falls in sheets, drenching us in a matter of seconds.

"Let's make a run for the car!" Frank shouts as we take off down the street.

The dirt from the newly cleared lots instantly turns to mud, and the street becomes a rushing river of brown water.

"Here, slide in on my side," Frank says, opening the driver's side door.

My soaked dress clings to me. I climb in behind the steering wheel and start to scooch over to the passenger side. Frank hustles in after me. I try to move over farther and rebound back into him like a rubber band. Frank's sitting on my skirt. I slosh into him, and we both start laughing. I can't even see him because my glasses are completely fogged. Frank reaches up and removes my glasses, placing them on the dashboard. Then he removes his own glasses and sets them next to mine. The sound of the rain on the car is louder than those children tearing around the model of The Adams. My hair has fallen completely out of the clasp and sticks to my face and neck. Frank takes both of his hands and pushes my sopping hair behind my neck.

When his fingers touch my wet skin, my pulse quickens. I feel it beating in my temples, in my neck, and in some other places where I haven't felt my pulse beat in a long time. I reach up and push his wet curls off his forehead. I trace his scar with the tips of my fingers. It's smoother than it looks—years of healing working their magic. Frank pulls me to him, and our lips meet. His mouth is soft and warm—just like in my dream. My lips match his perfectly. When Frank pulls away, I'm not ready for the kiss to end. I slip my arms around his neck and pull him back toward me in an even closer embrace. I glimpse the delight in his eyes as I draw him tight against me. Our wet clothes meld together like damp laundry waiting to go out on the line. We kiss again, this time for longer. The car windows fog up as the rain pounds on the hood. This is the private moment I've been waiting for—it feels as if we are the only two people in the world. When our second kiss ends, I keep my arms wrapped around Frank's neck and lean back.

"Excuse me, sir. I believe you're sitting on my dress," I say.

Frank laughs his lovely melodic laugh.

"I'd given up, Bessie. I'd given up on love, and now, here you are, dripping all over my car," he says, and we chuckle again.

"If someone had told me a week ago that I would be soaking wet in a car, necking with a handsome man, and looking at houses, I would have laughed hard enough to cry!"

"Yet here we are. I'm so happy, Bessie. Are you happy?"

"Very happy."

"I could stay here and smooch all day, but I don't want my girl to catch a chill. Let's head home and get into some dry clothes."

He shifts his weight toward his door to release my dress. I pull the soaked fabric out from underneath him.

"I've never been somebody's girl," I say.

Frank reaches over and touches my cheek. "You are now."

SATURDAY
MAY 31, 1941

CHAPTER TWENTY-SIX

Mrs. Henderson

I PULL ROBERT'S letter out of the envelope. The paper feels thin and silky after handling it over and over these past few weeks. I take a seat, and Louie curls up at my feet. This settee suits my sitting area perfectly. I wonder if it will fit in a carriage house in Princeton. I read the letter one more time, and for some reason, the second paragraph jumps out at me in a way in hasn't before. I've been so focused on the latter portion of my son's letter with the details of his offer, the proposed timetable, the plans for the carriage house, et cetera, that I failed to see a deeper meaning in this earlier mention of my granddaughter.

Alice can read people like you do. She always knows exactly how we are feeling. There's no sneaking anything past her! She reminds me so much of you. I know you would enjoy getting to know her better. She's grown into quite the little lady this past year. She'll be nine this September and was already asking if you and Louie could come to her birthday party, and if you could bake her an angel food cake like the one you made at the beach house last summer. We're all inviting you to come and live with us, not just me. Please come, Mother.

"Oh, Louie! How could I be so blind?" I reach down and put a hand on the dog's head. "The sign I was waiting for—it's been here all along." I wave the letter in front of my face. "Sweet Alice is turning nine, and she always knows exactly how everyone is feeling. Could it be that one of my granddaughters sees the colors the way I do? If I only needed one reason to move, this would be enough. I can only imagine what a blessing it would have been if someone had been there to help me understand my gift. It's time to put pen to paper! I'm ready to leave Henderson House."

The dog raises his head in apparent agreement. I stand and walk over to my writing desk.

My beloved mahogany front slant writing desk was a gift from Charles on our first Christmas in Henderson House. Charles said the dealer estimated it had been built in the 1790s. I often daydream about who wrote crucial documents and love letters on it over the years. I pull out the two supports for the writing surface, open the slant top, and place it gently on top of them. Inside the desk is a row of small drawers with mail and stationery slots above them. There are three full-size drawers under the desk that are large enough to hold important papers, photographs, and whatever else I want to keep safe. I saw this desk in the window of Duggins' Antiques on West Second Street one afternoon when Charles and I were out for a stroll. I commented on it, and then he went back and bought it for me as a Christmas surprise. I run my hand across the writing surface, remembering how touched I was by the gift, and how Charles was even more pleased by my reaction.

"The desk is definitely coming to New Jersey," I say to Louie as I sit and take out a piece of stationery.

Saturday, May 31, 1941

Dearest Robert,

I am pleased to accept your invitation to come and live with you. It is time for me to leave Oklahoma and rejoin my family. Your proposed schedule of coming east for my usual stay in Spring Lake and then moving into the renovated carriage house this fall sounds perfect. I will inquire about selling Henderson House this week.

Thank you, darling, for encouraging me to move east and for providing me with a cottage on your property. Your warmth and generosity remind me of your father's. He would be so proud of you and so happy we are all going to be together again.

Tell Alice that Louie and I will be happy to bake an angel food cake for her birthday in September. I will send updates as my preparations proceed. Thank you again for inviting me.

All my love to you and Lucy and the children,
Mother

I reach for an envelope to address when I hear a knock at the door.

"Come in," I respond.

Johnny steps into the room. He looks classy in a brand-new pair of pleated lightweight slacks and a summer-weight oxford. Thanks to Florence, I bet he's the best dressed caddy at Hillcrest.

"Hello, Mrs. Henderson. Is my mom home?"

"I think she's upstairs enjoying her second day of vacation." I smile. "What are you doing home so early?" His light green color is much cloudier than usual. It's as if he has been injured in some manner. "Did something happen at the golf club?"

"Oh, Mrs. H, I don't know if I did the right thing or the wrong thing," he says as he shuffles his way into my sitting area.

"Have a seat, dear, and tell me what happened." I rise from the desk chair to sit with Johnny on the settee.

"Well, Mom encouraged me not to say anything to the caddy master about moving. She thought I should be able to enjoy my job right until the end."

"Okay."

"But Uncle Eddie mentioned something about how it's always good to be honest with your employer. And when I asked Aunt Bessie about it, she agreed with Uncle Eddie and added that the Westfeldts helped me get the job, and I wouldn't want to do anything that might reflect poorly on them."

"That also makes sense," I say.

"Ever since I told Tommy about the move, it's just sort of been eating at me to tell my boss, Mr. Harrington, sooner rather than later. This morning, I went right out on the course with a foursome. I caddied for Mr. Hibner."

"Mr. Hibner? He's quite a bigwig."

"I suppose so. He's a fine golfer and a good tipper. Anyway, after my first round, I was standing outside the caddy hut, waiting for my next loop, when Mr. Harrington and I started chatting. I told him about Mom's new job and how we were moving to Tulsa at the end of June. It felt like the right thing to do."

"Was he upset?" I ask.

"Not at all. He couldn't have been nicer. He said how much he was going to miss me and what a fine caddy I was, how I had a natural sense about reading the greens, and the members really liked me. He said there were several boys already on a waiting list to caddy at the club this summer, and he wouldn't have any trouble replacing me. At the time, it felt like he was going to let me stick around and caddy right up until we moved." Johnny reaches down to pet Louie, who is hanging on every word.

"Did something else happen?" I ask.

"Yeah. As Mr. Harrington and I were finishing up our conversation, the Spencer twins walked by on their way to the putting green."

"Oh," I respond, remembering that those boys have taunted Johnny before.

"They looked me up and down and asked Mr. Harrington what 'Geronimo Johnny' was doing on the club grounds, and if there was going to be a powwow later. It's the dumbest nickname—Geronimo wasn't even Cherokee; he was Apache—anyway, Mr. Harrington told the boys to move along. Then he turned to me and said that, on second thought, it might make sense to fill my spot on the roster right away so another boy could get up to speed before the big tournament next weekend. He said he'd be happy to give me a good reference if I ever needed one. He paid me for my morning round, we shook hands, and I left."

"Do you think Mr. Harrington was telling the truth about wanting to get another caddy up to speed?" I ask.

"No, I don't." Johnny scratches at a patch of dirt on his pants for a moment. "I don't think Mr. Harrington ever thought of me as an Indian until those rotten twins said something. Last weekend, I overheard one of the caddies saying Mr. Harrington was more likely to hire a black man than he was an Indian."

I'm shocked to hear such a racist remark attributed to Mr. Harrington. How can someone sit in church, Sunday after Sunday, and still not understand that we are all equal in the eyes of God? Johnny's upbringing has shielded him from any bigotry up until now. But with his dark hair and facial features, something like this was bound to come up sooner or later.

"Do you think of yourself as an Indian?" I ask him.

"Gosh, I don't know. I mean . . . I know I'm part Cherokee, but nobody ever talks about it. We don't have any Cherokee traditions. Cousin Wahya seems to be the only one in the family who's still involved with the tribe and all."

I watch Johnny's color pulsate. His light green swirls with a yellow green I haven't seen before. I sense the need in him to find something—a missing piece, perhaps.

"Someday, you might want to learn more about being Cherokee," I say, patting his hand.

We sit together in silence for a moment, then Johnny turns to me and manages a half-hearted smile. "I'm still glad I told Mr. Harrington about the move. I didn't want him to hear about it from someone else. That wouldn't have been right. And I sure wouldn't have wanted anything negative to get back to Mr. Westfeldt when he's been so kind to me."

"I'm proud of you for telling Mr. Harrington, Johnny."

"Thanks. I don't know if my mom is going to be very happy about it. She wanted me to keep making money. What job can I find now? Who needs help for only three or four weeks?"

He shakes his head, and an idea pops into mine.

"Johnny, I was talking to Mr. Mogel at the Wednesday Night Supper. He's one of the owners at Lonnie's Ice Cream Parlor down on West Third. He mentioned that his cousin usually comes to help for the summer months but can't start this year until after Independence Day. I bet he'd love to have your help for a few weeks."

"That would be great, Mrs. H. I'd get to wear the Lonnie's uniform with the little white hat. Mom always likes a job that comes with a uniform."

"Yes, she does," I agree with a chuckle.

"I'm going to hop back on my bike and buzz downtown to talk to Mr. Mogel right now." Johnny springs up from the couch and heads toward the door of my room.

"I like your initiative, Johnny. I hope it works out," I say.

"Thanks, Mrs. H." He stops in the doorway and turns around to look at me. "I don't think I'm going to tell my mom about the whole 'Geronimo Johnny' thing with the Spencers. It would only upset her."

"I won't tell a soul." I cross my heart.

"Thanks for everything, Mrs. H." He smiles and disappears across the foyer.

"Knock, knock," Mr. Davis says, looking into the room.

"Come in. I seem to be holding court this afternoon." I smile. "What's on your mind?"

"Actually, I'm stopping by to see what's on your mind. Have you made a decision about your son's offer?"

"You must be developing my intuition, Mr. Davis. I just finished writing my acceptance letter to Robert."

"How do you feel about leaving?"

"I'm confident it's the next place I'm supposed to go. I only wish I felt better about selling the house."

"So, about that . . ." Frank begins as he checks his watch. "I need to drive into town and pick something up this afternoon, but if you've got a few minutes, there's an idea I'd like to run by you."

"Mr. Davis, I'm all ears."

CHAPTER TWENTY-SEVEN

Florence

WHAT AN EXHAUSTING week. I was worried my situation at work might be awkward after Sonny's impromptu visit last weekend, but the young man couldn't have been more polite or apologetic. No, the most draining part of the week wasn't working alongside Sonny—it was keeping my mouth shut while Bessie ran around like a lovesick teenager. I've never seen her fuss so much over her hair or clothes. I doubt another living creature has ever giggled or blushed as much as she did this week. But I stuck to my plan. I stood back and let them have their three dates, which turned into four dates when they went fishing yesterday. Of course, Bessie caught a million perfect fish, and Mrs. Henderson and Edna swung into action to cook up a Memorial Day fish fry last night. Listening to Fabulous Frank sing my sister's praises at the supper table was enough to kill anyone's appetite. But Saturday afternoon has arrived, and it's time for me to have my little chat with Frank.

Are you sure about this plan, Florence? my inner voice asks. *Frank has money. He's a top executive at Phillips. He was talking to Joyce Moore about buying one of those new houses. Having a rich brother-in-law might not be such a bad thing. Especially once he finds out the truth about Johnny. If Bessie was taken care of, she might let you keep the whole savings account.*

"This is not about money," I announce to my empty bedroom.

Is it revenge? Are you trying to get back at Bessie for telling John the truth? She swears he figured things out on his own. You never even let her explain what happened down by the river in Wichita. You've never even read the letter she found.

"Nonsense! This is about keeping the family together. That's all!" I wave the voice away with my hands and look at the clock.

Professor Rutledge won't be awake for another hour or so. Eddie's working a shift at the cab company. Johnny's still lugging golf bags. Bessie is off on a mission of mercy to visit some old biddy from her Sunday School class, and Fabulous Frank is out running errands. It's the perfect time to head downstairs. I want to position myself in the right spot before Frank returns. The timing of our conversation is critical.

I gather up the pieces of my sewing project and make my way down to the living room. Judging from Mrs. Henderson's closed door, she is probably reading a book or napping with Louie. I settle into the elaborate tufted chair facing the dining room and the kitchen beyond. Frank always enters the house through the kitchen door. He'll have to walk right past me when he gets home. I thread a needle and survey the fabric in my lap. There's nothing like a good piece of sewing to calm my nerves. I have always thought this skirt was a tad long and, after seeing higher hemlines in Tulsa last week, it's time to shorten it. Besides, I don't want to look like I'm waiting to pounce. Engaging in a little handiwork sets the scene perfectly.

The weight of the skirt in my lap is comforting. It's a durable navy twill A-line skirt—a staple in my limited wardrobe. I've already removed the old hem stitches, pressed the new hem line into the skirt, trimmed the excess material to two inches, turned under a quarter inch at the bottom of the fabric, and pressed it. With the skirt turned inside-out on my lap, the band of fabric at the bottom is bright and a little shiny against the wrong side of the fabric. I enjoy working with a fabric when it's easy to tell the right side from the wrong. The blind hem stitch is one of the first stitches Mama taught me, and it's still one of my favorites. With the correct thread color and a deft hand, hem stitches are nearly invisible.

Slide the needle inside along the fold and out, then make a tiny stitch in the fabric. Back into the dark and out into the light, then take a stitch. Through the tunnel and into the sunshine, then into the fabric. One stitch at a time.

I hear my mama's voice coaching me as I learned to make perfectly spaced stitches, time after time. When we were little, everyone we knew had homemade dresses. Truth be told, between my mama's talent and our access to fabrics and notions through the Pack and Run, I grew up thinking we were the best dressed family in Indian Territory. Our clothes weren't fancy, but they had style. Mama could always work magic with a little trim, pleats, or a ruffle.

Back in those days, it was common to save flour, sugar, and feed sacks to make everyday clothes, dish towels, and even curtains. Mama made the most adorable sack cloth aprons for us. We wore them when we worked at the Pack and Run. She had a knack for combining the various logos and prints from the sacks into playful designs. We got so many compliments on our aprons, she decided we should make more to sell. I learned to sew by making sack cloth aprons as a child.

I never set foot inside a dress shop until after I married John. Ah, but Bessie and I loved window-shopping. We could spend hours strolling about, looking at window displays and imagining what we might buy and what we would do with our treasures. But not just clothing. Oh no, we could window-shop for just about anything and then create a detailed story around our pretend purchases.

One of my most vivid memories is of a garden party we created when we were teenagers. It all started when we saw a lovely tea set in the window at the Rogers County Mercantile. Bessie got the ball rolling by suggesting we should invite our Grandma Blackwell, Mama, and Mrs. Redbird over for afternoon tea in the garden. After we pretended to buy the tea set, the next stop was the bakery. I could see macaroons in the case inside, and I wanted those. Bessie wanted shortbread, as usual. Then we walked arm in arm until we were standing in front of Haas, the finest women's clothing store in Claremore at the time.

We stood out front, evaluating everything in the windows and looking deep into the store for other options. First, we picked something elegant for Grandma Blackwell. Every time I saw her, she was in the same faded calico skirt with the same tired blouse and yellowed apron. We selected a striking blue day suit for her to wear. Of course, this must have been around the turn of the century when the skirt of a woman's day suit was full to ankle length. Bessie spied a pastel-colored full-length taffeta dress with intricate smocking for Mama and an emerald-green gown for Mrs. Redbird. I set my sights on a cream-colored walking suit with a wide, full skirt and a belted jacket with fur trim. Usually, it was next to impossible to get Bessie to choose something for herself. "I'm so grateful for what I already have," she would say. It was annoying. But that afternoon, we spotted a deep pink high-waisted dress with myriad pleats and a white lace top in the window, and it caught her fancy. Without hesitation, Bessie pointed and said, "I'll wear the lacey one."

Mrs. Mood, the mayor's wife, appeared behind us and asked what we were doing. To my horror, Bessie told her we were window-shopping for a pretend garden party. I turned hot with anger and embarrassment. Mrs. Mood smiled, touched Bessie on the arm, and said, "How sweet," as she walked into the store to shop.

I exploded on my sister. "Why don't you just broadcast to the world how poor and pathetic we are!"

I was so angry at Bessie for embarrassing us that I didn't talk to her for the rest of the day. Why did my sister always have to ruin everything by telling the truth? Why couldn't she have said we were out running errands for our daddy or on our way to McClure's Drug Store to pick up something for our mama? Well, today I'm going to beat her at her own game. As expected, my tearful plea at the cemetery last weekend seems to have kept her from telling Frank about Johnny.

Be careful, Florence. Make sure you don't get carried away and say too much to Frank this afternoon.

Not to worry. I've practiced my lines over and over this week. All I'm going to do is plant a kernel of distrust. A confused Frank will confront Bessie this evening. She won't be able to tell him the truth, because "a promise is a promise." Frank will realize Bessie can't be trusted. And this will all be over before you can say Jack Robinson.

I'm making excellent progress hemming my skirt. The perfectly spaced stitches are barely visible. I better slow down. No telling when Frank will be back from town. *Wait.* I hear a car on the gravel driveway. I take a deep breath and focus on the stitching. It will take Frank a moment to make his way inside.

Through the tunnel and into the sunshine, then into the fabric.

The screen door squeaks open and closes with a thud. Frank hums as he makes his way through the kitchen and into the dining room. I look up from my sewing and catch his eye as he enters the living room.

"Hello, Frank," I say. He's not carrying any packages. I wonder what errands he was running.

"Good afternoon, Florence. Lovely day, isn't it?"

"Yes, this makes two perfect Saturdays in a row. May has always been my favorite month in Oklahoma."

"It's starting to be mine as well." He smiles. His cheeks are rosy from being out and about this afternoon.

I deliver my opening line: "Frank, there's something I'd like to discuss."

"Um, of course. Anything, Florence. What's on your mind?"

"Why don't we go sit on the front porch for a little privacy?" I offer as I stand up and place my sewing neatly on the coffee table.

"Sure," he says, though he sounds unsure. I have him guessing already.

The two of us head toward the front of the house. Mrs. Henderson's bedroom door is still closed. Frank holds the front door open for me, and we walk out onto the porch. The air is heavy with the scent of May flowers, and the breeze is warm but not hot. I take a deep breath and let it out.

Don't stray from your script, Florence.

"Let's sit over here, shall we?" I gesture to the rocking chairs on our right.

When I rehearsed the conversation with Frank in my mind, we were sitting at the far end of the porch, safe from any listening ears.

"Whatever you say." Frank follows my lead.

We sit.

"Well, it's been quite a couple of weeks, hasn't it?" I begin.

"It certainly has."

"Frank, I just want to thank you for your open-mindedness and for agreeing to protect our secret," I say.

"I'm not sure I understand, Florence," he replies.

"Well, it couldn't have been easy when Bessie told you, and I'm pleased it hasn't changed your opinion of her—or me—for that matter."

"I don't think I'm following you." Frank begins tapping his foot.

"Oh, dear." I pause and fold my hands in my lap. "I was certain she had told you by now."

"Told me what?" Frank leans forward.

"With all the time you've spent alone this week, and the fishing trip yesterday, she's had plenty of opportunities to speak with you privately, but . . ." I pause. "She hasn't had the courage to say anything, has she?"

"Say anything about what? What are you getting at, Florence?"

He's annoyed. I can hear it in the crispness of his voice. The conversation is going exactly the way I rehearsed it.

"Frank, this is not my story to tell. I'm so sorry I brought it up. Just forget I said anything." I rise out of my rocking chair, ready to make my exit and leave Frank with his thoughts.

"Hold on there. Not so fast. What would change my opinion of Bessie?"

I sit back down. "Frank, I really shouldn't—" I break off my sentence abruptly. He stares at me, wide-eyed and waiting.

"So, this is what Eddie was talking about," he says mostly to himself.

"Eddie? What does my brother have to do with this?"

"He warned me, Florence. He said you might say something to try to break us up. Is that what you're up to? Because—"

"That is not what's happening here," I say, raising my voice.

My stomach churns. In all the scenarios I played out in my mind this week, Frank never challenged me. I can't believe Eddie said something to him—warned him! A blaze of anger ignites in my chest. "I'm the one trying to warn you about Bessie." I snap. I'm off script now. "She's not as innocent as she seems, Frank."

"Florence, I know my timing has been terrible," Frank says. "I showed up here, fell head over heels for your sister, and started messing up all your plans, but—"

"We've been lying to you," I interrupt.

Careful, Florence, the voice warns, but I can barely hear it over the thumping of my heart.

"Lying to me?"

"Yes." I look away. "We didn't go to Wichita to visit Aunt Maude."

"I don't understand," Frank says.

"We moved to Wichita because my sister was pregnant—pregnant and unmarried!" I'm close to shouting. I must lower my voice.

"Excuse me?"

"I'm not Johnny's mother," I say, regaining my composure. "I didn't give birth to him."

The porch grows silent. I listen, but I can't hear a dog barking or a bird singing. No children playing or even a car running. The only sound is the pounding of my pulse in my temples. I've crossed the line, and yet, I can't stop myself from continuing.

"After the baby was born, Bessie and I decided it made sense for me to raise him as my own, my being married and all."

Frank tilts his head to one side and puts a hand to his chin.

"I shouldn't be the one telling you this, Frank." I pause. "I was certain Bessie had already confided in you. Now do you understand why her place is with me and Johnny in Tulsa?"

Frank takes off his hat and runs his hands through his hair. "Bessie is Johnny's mother," he states as a fact.

I dig my nails into the palm of my hand and stay silent.

"I can't believe she didn't tell me. I thought we trusted each other." Frank stands up and begins walking around the line of rocking chairs at the end of the porch, bumping into them and knocking the chairs askew. His voice grows quiet as he walks and mumbles to himself. Frank stops and looks back at me. "Does Eddie know?"

"No. Aunt Maude knew, but since she passed away, only Bessie and I know the truth." For the first time, I realize what I've done. Tears spill down my cheeks. Why did Eddie have to go sticking his nose into my business? He derailed my plan, and I let my anger get the best of me, again. "I'm sure you can understand how important it is for us to keep this secret safe," I murmur through the tears. "It would devastate Johnny if he learned the truth from . . ." I pause to gather myself. "From someone who's practically a stranger. Promise me you will protect our secret. Please, Frank."

Frank's expression darkens, the rosy glow from his errands long gone. He puts a hand on my shoulder and gives a weak nod of agreement. Then he slumps down in one of the cock-eyed rocking chairs.

"Thank you for keeping our secret and our family safe. I knew we could trust you. I told Bessie we could."

"Well, I guess she didn't agree with you," he says, eyes downcast. "I guess she thought I could only handle part of the story."

Hearing the pain in Frank's voice, I know I'm in trouble. Now when he confronts Bessie, she has every right to tell him everything. Our promise is broken, and I'm the one who broke it. Frank puts his hands over his face for a moment and then runs his fingers back through his hair. I see his scar and hear my brother's voice: *Words can hurt people as much as punches, sis. Maybe more.*

"I should tidy up my sewing project," I say, wiping my tears. "Mrs. Henderson doesn't like it when I leave my mending all over the living room."

"I think I'll sit out here for a while," Frank says with an audible sigh.

"Of course," I reply. As I turn toward the front door, something catches my eye. White lace curtains billow in and out of Mrs. Henderson's wide-open windows.

CHAPTER TWENTY-EIGHT

Bessie

MOST SATURDAY AFTERNOONS, I visit people from my Sunday School class who've been absent. When Agnes Whitlock missed last week due to illness, I phoned her, and we made plans to catch up today. We spent the last hour chatting in her beautifully manicured backyard, sitting under a pergola wrapped in morning glories. Mrs. Whitlock is an inspiration, living on her own and tending a large vegetable garden at the ripe old age of eighty-six. Eighty-six. I'm half-way there. Could I really have as many years ahead of me as I have behind? Forty-three more years on this earth suddenly feels like a precious gift, especially if those years might be spent with Frank Davis.

"Thank you so much for coming by, Bessie, dear," Mrs. Whitlock says as she sees me out.

I start down her front walkway. "My pleasure, Mrs. Whitlock. I'm glad you're feeling better. Maybe we'll see you in church tomorrow."

I turn to wave and trip over a loose paving stone. I don't know why I'm such a clodhopper today. I've been dropping things and stumbling about since breakfast. I'm excited about tonight, I suspect. Saturday is finally here, and I'm ready to tell Frank the rest of my story. I'm not worried or afraid; I'm simply ready. Mama once said, "Ready is not a feeling; it's a decision." I didn't understand her at the time, but I do now. I've decided I'm telling Frank about Johnny. I've decided I'm staying in Bartlesville.

I regain my footing by holding my purse out to the side for balance like a circus prop. Mrs. Whitlock continues chattering in her birdsong voice.

"Oh, I hope I feel well enough to attend tomorrow. I can't wait to meet this Mr. Davis everyone is talking about. Thank you again for stopping by, Bessie. You're an angel."

Mrs. Whitlock reaches to close her screen door. As she moves, the afternoon sunlight catches her white hair. Her thinning curls glow for a moment before gliding into the dimness of her house.

Dear Lord, thank you for the gift of health and healing. I pray you will continue to lay your healing power upon your faithful servant, Agnes Whitlock, and grant her comfort and strength as she returns to her normal activities. Amen.

I've only known Agnes Whitlock personally since she joined my Sunday School class two years ago, but I've known about her for some time. Her youngest daughter, Susan, worked for me at Phillips back in the early thirties before she got married and moved to Arkansas. Susan was a bold, chatty young thing with large green eyes and pencil-straight dark hair. Her constant banter disrupted the workflow of the office machine room at times, but I always enjoyed her stories about her mother.

Susan described her mother as the "sweetest tough guy you'd ever meet." One day, when we were standing around stuffing envelopes, Susan told a story about her mother banishing her father from the bedroom because he came home smelling like whiskey. Susan came downstairs on a Saturday morning to find her father folded up on the couch. I guess Mrs. Whitlock had very clear house rules, especially where her husband's drinking was concerned. I remember Susan's vivid description of her father waking early in his wrinkled clothes, making a pot of coffee, and taking a steaming cup into her mother to smooth things over. She said that in no time, she could hear her parents laughing and giggling in the bedroom. I still recall the pang of jealousy that shot through me when Susan told this story. To be close with a spouse—to disagree and then forgive and laugh together—was something I feared I would never experience. But all that is changing now.

Frank and I have gone for a walk after supper every evening this week. We've strolled, hand in hand, to the little park on Eighth Street between Cherokee and Delaware. There's a bench under an elm tree, near the swing sets. Sitting on that bench, we've laughed and dreamed and planned while listening to the children play. We've already started to create a life together. After tonight, there will be no more secrets between us. We'll be free to move forward with our dreams.

The rhythm of my sensible brown pumps tapping against the concrete pulls my attention back to the sidewalk. I look down just in time to avoid tripping on a branch. Eyes cast downward, I begin carefully avoiding the cracks.

Step on a crack, break your mother's back. Step on a line, break your father's spine.

The old rhyme rings in my head as I strategically place my footfalls. I hesitate and then, *bam!* My left foot lands smack-dab in the middle of a huge crevice, and I stumble.

Dear Lord, please help me through the rest of this day. I need to talk to Florence when I get home. I want to share my decision to tell Frank with her first. Maybe that's why I'm tangled up in knots and tripping over everything. I've never been good at standing up to my sister. You know my heart, Lord. I ask for Your continued guidance and strength. Help me find the way forward. Amen.

And Lord, help me get home without twisting an ankle or falling flat on my face. Amen, again.

As I turn onto our block, the aroma of the fading peonies is powerful. I inhale deeply, taking in the complicated bouquet around me. The smell is at first pleasing but sours as an element of decay slips in. It's as if the blossoms are clinging to their former glory with all their might. Gone is the beautiful, easy-going scent of last week—now the air hangs heavy as the blooms make their final push.

Looking down our street, I see a figure on the front porch. As I draw closer to Henderson House, I realize it's Frank. My heart pounds a little faster at the sight of him. It's a new kind of excitement, deep in my belly. I didn't expect to see him until I had freshened up for our evening out, but there he is, in one of the rocking chairs. I'm sure my hair is a mess, and I'm a little overheated from my walk home. I must look a sight, but I don't care. I can't wait to tell him about my visit with Mrs. Whitlock. I quicken my pace. Deep in thought, he doesn't notice me approaching. I could share everything with him right now, but no. I want to speak with Florence first and tell Frank tonight.

"Good afternoon," I say as I start up the brick walk to the porch.

"Oh, Bessie," Frank looks up and then stands.

He's such a gentleman. I've clearly startled him, as he looks somewhat uncomfortable with my unexpected arrival on the porch. I take a step toward him, and he flinches slightly.

"Frank, is everything okay?"

He shifts his weight from one foot to the other and puts his hands in his jacket pockets. His eyes refuse to meet mine. A knot forms in my stomach.

"Um, Bessie, I didn't expect you home so soon," he says with a tinge of what sounds like disappointment, or maybe dread, in his voice.

The knot tightens another notch—something terrible has happened.

"Frank, what's wrong?" I ask.

"Nothing. Everything. I really don't know, Bessie." He finally looks at me and shakes his head.

"Well, something's not right, I can tell. Is there anything I can do to help?" I move a step closer.

Frank instinctively takes a step back and knocks the rocking chair to the side. He pulls his hands out of his pockets and puts them out in front of his chest, as if he's asking me to keep my distance.

"Bessie, I'm not sure I'm ready to talk to you yet. I'm not sure I want to see you right now," he says firmly.

"Frank, what's going on?" My voice trembles. I can barely breathe.

"You know, Bessie, I should probably ask you the same question." There's a sharpness to his voice I've never heard before. "I had an interesting conversation with Florence earlier this afternoon. If you two didn't look so much alike, I'd never guess you were sisters. She's a genuine piece of work. On second thought, maybe you two are cut from the same cloth, after all." He scoffs.

"Frank, what are you talking about?" I shake my head. "I don't understand."

"No, Bessie, I'm the one who doesn't understand. We've spent hours this week getting to know each other and planning our future together. Sharing intimate details about our hopes and dreams. How could you . . ." he pauses, "I don't know . . . conveniently forget to tell me the truth about Johnny?"

I'm stunned. "What?" It's the only response I can manage.

"Florence told me, Bessie. She told me she's not Johnny's mother. She told me the real reason you moved to Wichita!" Frank snaps.

I can't move a muscle. He looks around as if he feels trapped between me and the rocking chair behind him. In a single move, he slides out of the seating area and begins walking toward the front door.

"I wanted to tell you, but—" I stop.

"But what, Bessie? But what?" he says as he turns to face me again.

"She made me promise not to tell you, unless . . ." I swallow. "Unless you asked me to marry you."

"How on earth could you make a promise like that? And then, how could you keep it? Florence was sure you had already told me." He walks back and forth nervously. Two steps one way, then two steps back in the other direction. "After I confided in you about my brother and my first wife, how could you tell me about Doc Jenkins and then not tell me about Johnny? It goes against everything I thought I knew about you. I thought we trusted each other. This calls all our plans into question."

"I was planning to tell you everything this evening," I say, but the words sound too little, too late. "Can we talk this out, Frank? Please?" I plead.

He stops pacing and strides over to where I am standing. "I can't do this right now, Bessie," he says. I hear controlled anger in his voice. "I'm too upset to talk to you." His eyes are darker than I've ever seen them. "I might say something I'd regret, and I don't want to hurt you." Frank turns and walks away. Without looking back at me, he says, "I'm going up to my room. I won't be down for supper. I have to sort this out by myself first. I'm sorry." Then he leaves me alone on the porch, drowning in the acrid smell of spent flowers.

I wander over to the rocking chair Frank knocked out of alignment. I take a seat, set my purse next to the rocker, and place my hands in my lap. I'm wearing a pair of white gloves Mrs. Henderson crocheted for me last year as a birthday gift. I stare at the openings in the pattern where my bare skin shows through the yarn. I can't take a full breath. It feels as if a rope is tied around my chest, and someone keeps pulling it tighter and tighter. Florence told him. She made me promise not to tell him, and then she told him. It doesn't make any sense. Tears roll down my cheeks. I'm sure I have a handkerchief in my purse, but I refuse to search for it. Let it sit in there unused. Let the tears come. Let them fall on my blouse and into my lap. My collar is damp with them already.

What's the matter, kid? Can't you take it?

My daddy's taunting rings in my ears. I cried easily when I was younger. I learned to hold back the tears, to not give Daddy the satisfaction of seeing me cry. But not today, not now. Maybe I will sit here and find out how long it takes to cry all the tears I've held inside over the years. All the tears I sucked back when Daddy was drunk and bullying me to toughen up, when I was learning how to take it. Maybe I can't take it, Daddy. Maybe I never could. Maybe I don't want to take it anymore. I'm tired of being the glue. Maybe I don't want to be the good girl who keeps the family safe anymore. Maybe I wanted something for myself this time, and now I've lost my chance. I held on to secrets and promises for too long, and now I've lost everything. My shoulders shake as crying turns to sobbing.

CHAPTER TWENTY-NINE

Florence

I PLACE THE needle and thread neatly in my sewing box and hang my freshly hemmed skirt in the wardrobe. Not exactly a relaxing vacation day. I spent most of it practicing for my conversation with Frank, only to completely lose control of the situation in the heat of the moment. My head is killing me. I have no idea what might happen next, and I'm all out of plans.

A sharp pain pierces my chest. I make my way over to the chair next to the window. Late-afternoon sun bathes the cushions in a golden glow. I sink down into the seat and close my eyes as a ray of sunshine falls across my face. Who knew trying to keep this family together would be so difficult? The warmth of the sun eases my headache, and I begin to nod off when Johnny bursts into the room.

"Hiya, Mom!"

"Hi yourself," I say, half awake. The crushing pain in my chest continues. What did I eat for lunch?

"I've got good news," Johnny says.

"I can't wait to hear it." I adjust my position to see if I can lessen the pain.

"I've got a new job, and it will carry me right up until we move to Tulsa," he announces as he walks over to me.

"A new job? What happened to your old job at the country club?"

"Yeah, so, about my old job . . ." He looks down and shuffles his feet. "I told Mr. Harrington the truth about us moving by the end of June."

"I thought you were going to wait to tell him. What made you change your mind?"

"I talked it over with Uncle Eddie again and then with Aunt Bessie. They both urged me to tell him the truth right away. Once I was standing there, looking at Mr. Harrington, well, I just had to give it to him straight."

"Did he fire you?"

"It wasn't like being fired at all. Mr. Harrington pointed out that there were other boys interested in caddying, and those boys could make a commitment for the entire summer. It only seemed fair to give my spot to someone else. He was very impressed I was up front with him, and he said if I ever needed a recommendation, he would be happy to give me one."

"Well, I suppose that's something." I roll my eyes and they ache, too.

"Uncle Eddie says it's a lot! You always want to leave a job knowing your boss will give you a positive recommendation in the future," he says, imitating his uncle's slow drawl.

"And now you miraculously have a new job lined up?"

"Yup, that's the best part about the whole thing. I came home early from the golf course and told Mrs. Henderson about losing my job. She mentioned that Mr. Mogel, who owns Lonnie's Ice Cream Shop, was looking for extra help between now and July. His cousin is planning on coming up from Muskogee after Independence Day to help him for the rest of the summer." He takes a quick breath and continues, "So, I hopped on my bike and rode straight down there to talk to him. I start Monday as an official soda jerker. Here's my uniform." He removes a crisp white shirt, red bow tie, white cap, and small white waist apron from the bag and lays them out on the desk in front of me.

"Well, I'll be." It takes some effort to push myself out of the chair and walk over to marvel at his display. "Well done, Johnny, honey. Congratulations!" I put my arms around him, and he hugs me nice and tight. I wince.

"Are you okay, Mom?"

"I'm fine, just a little heartburn, I think."

"I need to thank Mrs. Henderson, but I wanted you to be the first to know. I'll be back in a jiffy." He dashes out of the room, closing the door behind him.

I return to the chair in the sun. Sinking deep into the warm cushions, I close my eyes once more, hoping to ease the pain in my chest. Sleep envelops me so quickly, I wonder if my conversation with Johnny was real or part of an earlier dream. A cool, white mist fills my mind and carries me away.

I can't tell where I'm going. I walk through layers of dense fog. Tendrils of gray and white vapor swirl around me. A bright light draws me forward. I step out of the fog and into the kitchen at the Pack and Run. Or is it Henderson House? Mama's long wooden table occupies the center of the room, but Mrs. Henderson's curtains and African violets are in the window. Louie and Inola snuggle together by the stove. Dots of sunlight reflect off one of Mama's prisms hanging in the sunshine. The dots dance around the room to the tune of a wind chime swaying on the back porch.

"Come and sit with me," Mama says from the table. I pull out the rickety wooden chair across from her and sit. Jennie Blackwell looks exactly the way she did the last time I saw her alive—the Sunday before she came down with the Spanish flu. My mama's wearing one of her flour sack aprons over a church dress. Her reddish hair is swept up on top of her head. Seeing her now, I realize she is younger than I am. Mama was thirty-nine when she passed.

"Why am I here?" I ask.

"There are a few things I'd like to discuss with you, Flossie," she says. My heart aches when Eddie calls me Flossie, but hearing the nickname in my mama's voice stirs up an unbearable sadness deep inside.

"You're gone. You died. We buried you with Mae. You've never come to me in a dream before. Why are you here now?" I study her face, the tiny freckles on her cheeks, the small scar above her right eye. She runs her finger around the top of her teacup, the way she did whenever she was worried about me.

"You've been twisting the truth again. Not exactly lying, but not exactly being honest," she says.

"What do you mean?" I ask.

"Flossie, you can't get anything past me. You never could. Did you really think your plan to break up Frank and Bessie would work?" she asks.

"I didn't have a plan to break them up," I protest. "I had a plan to keep this family together."

"No," Mama says, shaking her head. "You convinced yourself you were working to keep the family together, but you and I both know you were doing everything you could to derail your sister's chance at happiness."

"That's not true!" I shout.

"Oh, Flossie. Sometimes I think the biggest lies you tell are the ones you tell yourself."

"But Bessie promised me we would raise Johnny together. I will not let a—"

Mama holds up her hand to stop my excuse making. "This is not a schoolgirl crush, Flossie. Frank Davis and your sister are in love. People who love each other will talk things through. They will get to the heart of the matter even if hashing out the details is hard work. Bessie will uncover your deception, and then she will tell Frank everything."

"Everything?" I ask.

"Everything," Mama repeats. "She'll do whatever is necessary to set things right with Frank. You've behaved horribly."

I weigh her words.

"What should I do now, Mama?" I ask.

"Sweetheart, it's time for you to start living an honest life. Tell Bessie the truth. Tell her how difficult things have been at work with Sonny. Tell her this promotion is the chance you've been waiting for to break free from him and keep your career on track. Tell her you've been spending more money on yourself and Johnny than you've been saving."

"But what if Bessie asks for her portion of the savings back? I want Johnny to live in a proper home in Tulsa, not a rented room," I plead.

"That will come to pass, honey," she says. "But you cannot get your dream by tricking your sister out of hers. No how. No way."

"Mom? Mom?" A voice penetrates the fog surrounding the kitchen.

"Johnny is back," she says. "It's time to set the record straight with him, too, Florence. He's a young man now. You need to tell him about his birth as soon as possible. He will have questions, and you need to listen to him with love."

The fog rolls into the kitchen. First it covers the floor and the legs of the table.

"Stop dwelling in the past, honey. Learn to forgive and, most importantly, learn to forgive yourself. Your heart will feel better once you do . . ." Mama's voice fades as the mist rises, filling the entire space.

"Mama," I call out. I can't see her anymore. I've lost her.

"Mom?" Johnny's voice calls to me from the churning vapor. I hear him, but I can't find him in the mist. I wander deeper into the thick fog, waving my arms in front of me, hoping to touch him by chance, but all I feel is cool, damp air. Have I lost Johnny, too?

"Mom?" Johnny gently rocks my shoulder. I open my eyes, and there he is, standing over me. "Wake up, sleepyhead," he says.

"I must have dozed off. What did Mrs. Henderson say?"

"She wasn't in her room, and I heard voices on the porch. I didn't want to interrupt. But I saw Professor Rutledge and gave him the news. I can tell Mrs. H at supper. I'm getting excited about moving to Tulsa. I think Uncle Eddie is, too."

"Hmm," I reply, but my mind is still in my dream.

Bessie will uncover your deception, and then she will tell Frank everything.

"We'll be fine on our own," Johnny says. "It will be fun for us to have a new adventure." He puts his hands on my shoulders. The tone of his voice sounds exactly like my sister Rachel's did—passionate and confident. "We don't need anybody else, Ma. We go together like biscuits and gravy . . ." he says, waiting for me to play along.

"Sugar and spice," I say.

"Ice cream and sprinkles." He winks.

"Thank you, Johnny," I say.

"For what?" he asks.

"For just being you. For being my son."

"I'll always be your son, Mom. I love you. Nothing's ever gonna change that."

I hope he's right.

CHAPTER THIRTY

Mrs. Henderson

"BESSIE, DEAR?"

I pick up her purse, take her arm, and help her out of the rocking chair. She's trembling from head to toe.

"We need to get you inside," I say.

Like someone half asleep, she follows my lead. I guide her through the front door and straight to my room. Bessie sits obediently on the settee. Louie hops up next to her.

"Would you like a hanky?" I extend a fresh white handkerchief to her. She glares at it. "Dry your tears, and then we'll talk."

I push the handkerchief closer. After a moment, she takes it.

A dull purplish-brown haze churns around her head and shoulders. There's barely a strand of her usual rosy pink running through it. I close my bedroom door and the windows on either side of my desk before taking a seat across from her. Bessie looks smaller than usual. Secrets have a way of diminishing people. They prevent us from living the life God intended. It unnerves me to see Bessie so miserable, yet I'm angry with her at the same time. How could she stay silent all these years, watching Florence raise that precious boy? How could she give up her only child to someone else? Even if it was her sister? Once again, my gifts have failed me. In the past twelve years, I never once sensed Bessie Blackwell held such a dark secret in her heart.

Her shoulders shudder as she takes a few deep breaths. Finally, she dries her tears. The house feels heavy, weighed down by heartache and hopelessness. The ceiling hangs lower, and the walls move in closer now that Bessie is in the room. The rawness of her grief overwhelms my senses. If there is one thing I've learned when trying to help someone in deep despair, it's that I must stay on the outside looking in. It's the only way to be of help. If I let my empathy venture too far inside, I will get lost in the misery, and then I'm no good to anybody. Oh, but my own broken heart adds to the sorrow in the room—my dear friend is not who I thought she was. She is a stranger to me now.

Bessie exhales with a sound louder than a whimper, softer than a wail.

"That's better," I say.

I wait another moment—no need to rush. Louie curls up into a ball and presses against her side. Good dog. Part of me wants to fire questions at her. How did this happen? Who is Johnny's father, and where is he now? How could she live under my roof for all these years and never tell me Johnny was her son? Why didn't she tell Frank sooner? But with one look at the fomenting colors around her, I know it's not my role to cross-examine. I'm here to help Bessie pull herself together. As angry and disappointed as I am, she is still my friend. Bessie's breathing sounds almost even. It's time to talk.

"While I was writing letters this afternoon," I say, "I opened the windows in honor of this beautiful day. I overheard

Florence speaking with Frank on the porch. I did not intend to eavesdrop, Bessie, but, well, your sister has one of those voices that's hard to ignore."

"She certainly does," Bessie whispers. A vacant stare resides behind her glasses where her sparkling green eyes should be.

"I heard everything she said to Frank, plain as day. I know she's not Johnny's mother."

Bessie's shoulders slump. She drops the handkerchief into her lap.

"Oh, Mrs. Henderson." Bessie puts her head in her hands. She's still wearing her gloves. They are the ones I crocheted for her last year. The gloves look strangely prim and proper against her mussed hair and splotchy neck. "How could I let Florence convince me not to tell Frank the truth right away? I wanted to tell him so many times this week. He's been completely honest with me, and I wasn't—I wasn't completely honest with him." She shakes her head from side to side, her gloved fingers digging deeper into her tousled hair.

"What do you mean Florence convinced you not to tell him right away?" I ask.

Bessie takes her head out of her hands and starts removing the gloves as she speaks.

"Florence made me promise not to tell Frank the truth unless he proposed to me," she says.

There is a resignation in her voice I've never heard before. She places one glove on the end table and then starts removing the other.

"She was afraid that if I told Frank and he changed his mind about me, he could expose our secret. She's terrified Johnny will find out before she's ready to tell him." Bessie puts the second glove on top of the first one, lining them up perfectly in prayer position, palms touching.

"Curious," I say. "The way their conversation started, it sounded as if Florence thought you had already told Frank about Johnny."

"Why would she think I already told him when she made me promise not to?"

"I don't know. Unless—" I stop short.

I have a clear picture in my mind about what's going on, but it won't be easy for Bessie to hear. She's already a mess. Perhaps my job today isn't to make her feel better, but to make sure we get all the cards on the table, even if it causes more pain.

"Unless what?" she asks.

"Unless she set you up, Bessie."

"What do you mean?"

"Well, it's no secret Florence wants you to choose her and Johnny over a new relationship with Frank Davis. I thought it had to do with the savings account and her wanting to buy a house. Now I know there's more to it than that. My guess is that she was looking for a way to make sure you and Frank broke up for good."

"I don't understand." Bessie sniffles.

"Florence made you promise not to tell Frank the truth, and then she made sure he found out before you had the chance to confide in him. I heard everything she said. She told Frank you were free to tell him, but you didn't because you don't trust him."

"Don't trust him? That's ridiculous!" Bessie says, her voice growing stronger. "I'm the one who told Florence we could trust him with our secret."

"Funny. She said she was the one who told you to trust him."

"She did?"

"Yes. Bessie, I believe she orchestrated this little drama to put an end to your romance."

"Well, looks like it worked. Frank could barely make eye contact when he saw me on the porch. He flinched when I came near him."

A single tear falls down her cheek. I'm amazed she has any left.

"Can you blame him, honey? This had to come as a tremendous shock. It certainly has me in a tailspin. To think you've been living a lie under my roof for all these years. I always sensed Florence was hiding something, but not you, Bessie."

"If only I had told him sooner. I'd been planning to tell him the whole story tonight, but Florence beat me to it." Bessie puts her head back in her hands.

"I've always wondered why you let Florence have so much control over you. She picks out your clothes, your eyeglasses. She makes all the family plans and manages your money. I guess now I know why."

"What do you mean?" Bessie asks, looking up at me.

"Florence knows your deepest, darkest secret. Some people wield secrets like a weapon. I think she's been using the truth about Johnny to manipulate you ever since she arrived at Henderson House."

"Florence and I are equally guilty in this lie, Mrs. Henderson."

Bessie's shoulders rise and fall. She sits up a little taller. The house adjusts with her. The temporary contraction of the ceiling and walls relaxes.

"I let Florence push me around because I'm trying to make something up to her. She thinks I betrayed her."

"What do you mean?"

"Florence thinks I told her husband he wasn't Johnny's father. She thinks I broke our promise, and she blames me for John falling back into his despair."

"Did you break your promise?" I ask.

"No. John figured everything out for himself. It's complicated, but Florence is convinced I told him. Sometimes I think she even holds me responsible for his accident."

The darker colors around her soften as she continues her confession. Her rosy glow isn't back yet, but I can see it fighting to break through.

"When Florence realized John knew the truth, she was furious with me," Bessie continues. "She demanded I leave Wichita, and that's when I moved to Bartlesville."

"You left Johnny," I say in disbelief.

She nods. "It was the hardest thing I ever did, leaving him with Florence and John. Almost as hard as running away with Eddie."

"You told me that you and Eddie moved to Claremore so you could teach, and Eddie could have a part-time job in town after school."

"Another lie," Bessie says with a sigh. "After Florence ran off to marry John, Daddy's outbursts were uncontrollable. For some reason, he targeted all his anger on Eddie. One night, my mama asked me to sneak my brother out of the house and keep him safe. So, I did."

"You have been taking care of this family for a long time, Bessie," I say.

"Well, I'm not doing a very good job, am I? If I'd stood up to my daddy and stayed home where I belonged, I would have been there to care properly for Mama and Mae when they got sick." She turns her eyes down to her hands in her lap.

"Sweetheart, you can't take responsibility for you mother and little sister succumbing to that terrible illness. As my mother used to say, 'You can't change just one thing.' If you'd still been living at home, you might have died from the Spanish flu, too."

"But I would have been there to help Rachel. After Mama and Mae died, she ended up alone with Daddy and Wahya, managing the Pack and Run. It's no wonder she went looking for companionship. If I hadn't run away, maybe Rachel wouldn't have gotten pregnant." Bessie pauses for a moment, and I watch a weak smile cross her face. "But then we wouldn't have Johnny, would we? I wouldn't have a job and a church I love. I wouldn't know you and Edna, and I never would have met Frank Davis and fallen in love. Maybe your mother was right. You can't change just one thing."

"We moved to Wichita because my sister was pregnant," I say under my breath, remembering Florence's words. "Pregnant and unmarried."

"What is it, Mrs. Henderson?" Bessie asks.

"Rachel was Johnny's mother," I say.

"Yes."

"Oh, Bessie, that's not how Florence made it sound to Frank."

"What do you mean?"

"Your sister did everything she could to make Frank believe *you* were the one who was pregnant and unmarried. I'm pretty sure Frank thinks you are Johnny's—"

"Frank thinks the secret I kept from him is that I'm Johnny's mother?" Bessie interrupts me with a gasp.

"Yes, dear."

"Are you sure, Mrs. Henderson? Absolutely sure?" she asks.

"I'm positive because it's what I thought, too, after listening to their conversation. I'm sorry, Bessie. I should have known you would never—"

Before I can finish my sentence, Bessie jumps up from the sofa. Louie wakes with a start.

"I have to talk to Frank. I have to talk to him right now!" she says. "May I have your permission to visit him in his room? I know it's not normally allowed, but—"

"Permission granted. Go to him, Bessie. Just go!" I rise from my chair and motion her away with my hands.

Bessie races to the door, throws it open, and runs up the staircase to Frank's room. A bright pink glow trails in her wake.

CHAPTER THIRTY-ONE

Bessie

I BUMP INTO Professor Rutledge at the top of the stairs. No time to apologize. I make a beeline for Frank's door and knock twice. No response. I knock three times.

"Frank, it's me, Bessie," I say, out of breath. "There's been a terrible misunderstanding. Please, let me in so I can explain." I knock again. Harder.

Oh, Lord, please let Frank answer me.

Still nothing. "Frank, are you there?" I press my ear to the door and listen.

"No. He's not," the professor answers instead.

"What do you mean?" I swing around to face him.

"He went out for a walk. Said he needed some fresh air. What's going on?"

"I have to find him, Professor. There's been a terrible mistake. I have to find Frank!" I cry.

The professor puts a comforting arm around my shoulder.

"What's all the commotion?" Eddie's voice echoes in the foyer below. He dashes up the stairs, taking them two at a time.

"Aunt Bessie, are you okay?" Johnny hurries to join us in front of Frank's door.

I see my sister. She's standing on the other side of the landing, arms folded across her chest. She looks disoriented, like she just woke up.

"I'm fine," I say to the group, "but there's been a horrible mistake, and I have to find Frank and clear things up."

"What kind of mistake?" Eddie asks. "Is Frank all right?"

"I'm not sure," I respond.

"Tell us what happened, Aunt Bessie," Johnny says.

"Oh, sweetheart. I hope you can understand, but I can't tell you. I can't tell anyone. This is a private matter between me and Mr. Davis." I look at Eddie and the professor. "I'm sorry I can't go into any of the details right now, but I need you to believe me when I say how important it is for me to talk to him as soon as possible." My upper lip trembles as I speak.

"How long ago did he leave, Professor?" Eddie asks.

"About ten minutes," he replies.

"Ten minutes!" I cry.

"I'm sure he'll be home soon," Florence says from the other side of the hallway. "He's probably walking around the block. That's all. Why don't you wait for him here? There's no need to create such a fuss."

I glare at her. "This can't wait. I need to find him."

"We could help you," the professor offers. "If we split up and head out in all four directions, one of us will catch up with him in no time."

"Do you really think so?" I ask.

"Sure," Eddie says. "Frank's out for a leisurely stroll. We'll be moving out like we're on a mission."

"Let's organize a search party," the professor says. "Do you have any idea where he might have gone, Bessie?"

"Maybe," I say. "We've been walking up to the park in the evenings. He might have gone there."

Florence huffs. "Do you honestly think he'd walk that far?"

"Yes, I do," I snap. It's taking every ounce of my patience not to call her out, here and now, but I can't. Not in front of Johnny.

"Get on board, Flossie," Eddie says to my sister. "We're all gonna pitch in to help find Frank. If it's important to Bessie, it's important to all of us. You head north to the park, Bessie."

"I'll walk south," the professor says. "Johnny, why don't you go east? Eddie, you can search to the west. Someone should stay here in case he returns on his own."

Florence raises her hand. "I volunteer to stay home."

"Mrs. Henderson will be here," Johnny points out. "If Mr. Davis comes home before us, she can make sure he stays put."

"Good thinking, Johnny," the professor says. "I will fill her in on our search plans and let her know to hang on to him if he shows up."

"Fine, then I'll go with you, Johnny." Florence ambles over to join the group.

I point to her. "No, you're coming with me."

"Operation 'Find Frank' commences right now," Eddie says, giving me an encouraging wink.

We march single file down the stairs, Florence bringing up the rear. The professor heads to the kitchen, while Eddie, Johnny, and I hurry out the front door. Florence takes her own sweet time leaving the house and closing the door behind her.

"Come on, Mom!" Johnny shouts over his shoulder.

"Your mom needs to get more exercise. She's slower than dirt," Eddie says, elbowing Johnny while we walk.

We head to South Osage Avenue and turn north. When we reach the corner of Thirteenth Street, Eddie and Johnny stop. We wait for Florence to catch up.

"This is where we leave you, ladies," Eddie says. "Don't worry, sis. We'll find him."

"You bet we will, Aunt Bessie," Johnny says.

They turn in opposite directions and take off at a pace just below a jog. Florence and I continue north.

"I need you to keep up," I say to my sister.

I feel my blood pumping through my veins. My legs are strong and sure as I stride. A thick canopy of leaves shimmers bright green against the deep blue sky of early evening. Picket fences gleam as if freshly painted against overstuffed window boxes glowing yellow, red, and orange with new blooms. The world is awake, and so am I.

"I don't have much experience with being angry," I say. "But I'm pretty sure I'm angry with you."

"Whatever for?" Florence asks.

"Don't even think about playing dumb. Mrs. Henderson heard your conversation with Frank. She told me everything—some of it word for word."

"I can't imagine what you're talking about," she says, lagging a few paces behind me.

"Why did you do it, Florence? Why did you lie to Frank?"

"I didn't lie to Frank," she says.

"This isn't one of your convenient misunderstandings, Florence. You deliberately deceived him. You convinced him I am Johnny's mother. You told him I was free to confide in him but didn't because I didn't trust him enough! Your actions were intentional. Don't deny it."

I wait for Florence to launch into one of her elaborate excuses, but all I hear is the hurried click-clack of our shoes on the sidewalk and her labored breathing. We walk a moment longer before she answers.

"I wanted to keep the family together—for Johnny's sake," she says, winded by our brisk pace.

"I don't believe you. I think you wanted to sabotage my romance for your own sake. Maybe it was about keeping the money in the savings account or maybe it was just to be mean to me."

"How can you say such a thing?" Her voice quivers as she continues. "I like our family exactly the way it is right now. This is the happiest we've ever been, and I don't want it to change. Besides, you promised me I would never have to raise Johnny alone."

"Well, you know what, Florence? After what you did today, I don't feel any responsibility to keep my promises to you. You intentionally hurt me and the man I love. You schemed and plotted to steal my one chance at happiness." I realize I'm shouting and lower my voice. "And somehow, you made me out to be the bad guy!"

"But you promised, Bessie," she pleads.

"Like I said, I'm all done with you and your promises. As of this moment, I don't owe you a darned thing."

Florence and I catch up to an elderly gentleman strolling with a miniature poodle down the center of the sidewalk. We split and go around either side of him to keep up our speed.

"Bread and butter," Florence says. "Sorry, old habit. Remember when we used to go out walking hand in hand?"

"Don't do that, Florence."

"Do what?" she asks.

"Talk about the old days as if we were best buddies. I know you always wished I was more interested in boys and clothes than climbing trees and digging in the dirt."

"That's not true!" She takes a few extra steps to keep pace with me.

"You know it is. You hated having such a plain and ordinary sister who always played by the rules and never got into trouble. The only stories you ever tell about me are disparaging.

You're constantly disappointed in me. Well, now I'm the one who gets to be disappointed in you."

"Can you forgive me for"—she swallows—"for misleading Frank?"

"Let's be perfectly clear. You did not mislead Frank. You lied to him. And no. I'm not ready to forgive you yet."

Florence stops walking. Her face is beet red, and her chest heaves up and down.

"There are a few things that need to happen first," I tell her.

"What do you mean a few things need to happen first?" she asks. Her eyes widen and her brow shines with perspiration. "That's not how forgiveness works!"

"As if you would know! Well, this is how forgiveness is working this time around," I say.

"What needs to happen?" she asks. I hear the fear in her voice as it cracks.

"The first thing you need to do is keep walking. We have to get to the park." I pick up the pace again. "Next, we need to find Frank. I have to set the record straight. I don't know if he will take me back or not, but he needs to know the truth."

"I suppose you want me to apologize to him," Florence whines.

"At some point, you should apologize," I say. "After I tell him the truth, he may not want to talk to you right away. He may never want to talk to either one of us again."

We wait for traffic at the next intersection. I look in both directions. No sign of Frank. We're only a few blocks from the park now. The cars pass, and Florence and I hurry across the street.

"Next, I want us to tell Johnny the whole story."

"But—" Florence starts, and I cut her off.

"No, buts. It's time. We are going to tell him tomorrow."

"Tomorrow?" Florence wails.

"Yes. After Sunday dinner, we will meet as a family and tell Johnny and Eddie at the same time," I say. "I'd be fine having Frank, Mrs. Henderson, and the professor there as well. I want Johnny to know this doesn't change a thing for the people who love him."

"This is a lot to take in at once." Florence stops walking again.

I stop and turn to face her. "Well, you've got until tomorrow to prepare yourself." I do my best to keep my voice firm, though I'm not used to making demands. "We're telling Johnny tomorrow, no matter what. And lastly, I want you to read Rachel's letter," I say.

"What letter?" Florence sputters.

"The letter she wrote to Johnny's father. The one I found in Wichita. Every time I've offered for you to read it, you've refused. No more. You're going to read it tonight, and you are going to listen to what John told me down by the river."

Dear Lord in heaven, help me stay strong and see this through with Florence. Hold my family in your loving embrace this weekend as we tell Johnny the truth about his birth. Amen.

And, Lord, please let Frank be at the park. Amen, again.

"Bessie, my head is spinning. Can we take a break? Stop for a minute? Please?"

"Come on, Florence. We're almost there. We've got to keep moving," I say, walking even faster.

Florence groans but follows me. As we round the corner on Eighth Street, the sound of children playing fills the air.

"If Frank is at the park, I want you to head home and let the others know I found him. This is between me and Frank. I want to speak to him alone."

"What if he's not here?" she asks between gulps for air.

"He has to be, Florence. He just has to be."

My sister and I walk together through the entrance to the park, and I stop. Even from this distance, there's no mistaking Frank's fedora and the slight tilt of his head.

"He's sitting on our bench," I whisper.

"How can you be sure from this far away?" she asks.

"I'm sure."

Florence bends over to catch her breath. Out of the corner of my eye, I see her body sway awkwardly.

"Florence, are you all right?"

"I'm a little dizzy," she replies. "Everything is blurry."

"Eddie's right. You need to get out and move around more."

"Is that," she says, wheezing, "another condition for your forgiveness?"

Florence's knees buckle first. She gives me one terrified look before her eyes close, and then she drops to the ground. I thrust an arm behind her shoulders and barely keep her head from hitting the pavement as I tumble down with her.

"Florence? Florence? Can you hear me?"

No response.

A small crowd gathers around us.

"Is she all right?" a young mother asks. Her daughter peeks out from behind her skirt. From my position on the ground, I'm eye level with the little girl. She's frightened. So am I.

"I don't know," I say. "I think she fainted."

Oh, dear Lord, please let her be okay. Let her be okay.

"Do you live around here?" the woman asks.

"No, not close." I pat Florence's cheeks, hoping to revive her.

"Is she breathing?" I hear Frank's voice. He makes his way through the people encircling us, kneels beside Florence, and puts his head on her chest. "Does someone live nearby who can call for an ambulance?" he shouts.

"I do, mister," a boy about Johnny's age answers. "I'll run home and call now."

Frank takes off his jacket and rolls it up. "Help me get this under her feet," he says. "We want to elevate her legs to keep blood flowing to her brain." I help him prop up her feet. "Keep talking to her, Bessie."

I take Florence's hand and mutter reassurances to her. "Everything's going to be fine, sweetheart. Someone's calling for an ambulance. It will be here any minute."

"Bessie," Florence croaks. "Is that you?"

"Yes, I'm right here, honey."

"Mama told me," she says, gasping. "Wrong to lie. You and Frank love each other." Her eyes close and then open again. "Time to tell Johnny."

"When did you see her?" I ask.

"Napping," she says before drifting out of consciousness again.

I continue speaking softly to her until I hear the ambulance in the distance. The siren gets louder every second.

"Wrong to lie?" Frank asks.

I turn to see his tired face and puffy eyes.

"Oh, Frank, there's so much to tell you," I say as the ambulance arrives. "But I need you to get back to Henderson House and let everyone know what's happened. Send Eddie to meet us at Memorial Hospital." The ambulance team pushes Frank back into the crowd while they swoop in and lift Florence onto a stretcher.

"Are you related to the patient?" a young medic with curly hair asks.

"Yes, I'm her sister."

"You can ride with her in the back, ma'am. Do you know what caused her to pass out? Does she have a history of heart trouble or high blood pressure?"

"Not that I know of."

"What was she doing before she collapsed?"

"We were walking—briskly," I say. "And arguing."

I follow the curly-haired medic to the back of the ambulance. He helps me climb aboard. Another medic has my sister's arms lifted, while a third presses down on her chest. I look for Frank in the crowd, but he's already gone. The ambulance driver slams the heavy metal doors shut. A moment later, the siren wails, and we speed through the city streets toward the hospital.

"We should tend to your knees as well," the curly-haired medic says. I look down. My stockings are torn, and both my knees are skinned and bleeding.

CHAPTER THIRTY-TWO

Mrs. Henderson

PROFESSOR RUTLEDGE AND I sip iced tea in the kitchen. Louie's asleep under the dinette, twitching as he dreams. We're waiting for the remaining members of the search party to return from operation "Find Frank." Albert looks handsome this evening in a blue summer suit with a maroon and white polka-dotted tie. He needed a complete change of clothes after the search mission, and his fresh ensemble is more dashing than usual. All we've done since he dressed for dinner is sit and wait. The house feels stagnant, like an algae-covered lake begging for a good, hard rain.

I study Albert for a moment. He doesn't know it, but the suit complements the seaside-blue halo emanating from him. It comforts me when people dress in harmony with their color. Of course, they don't know they are doing it, but I wonder if they have an intuitive feeling of "just right" when they look in the mirror. One of the strangest things about having lived a life seeing colors around others is that I do not know what my own color is. Perhaps my granddaughter will put my curiosity to rest.

Albert's finger follows a bead of condensation as it drips down the side of his glass. He seems preoccupied. It's no wonder with all the excitement this afternoon, but I sense something deeper.

"Penny for your thoughts," I say.

His head snaps up and his deep brown eyes meet mine.

"I followed up with my old colleague on the teaching opportunity he mentioned to me," he says. "Seems there is an opening for a poetry professor at his current institution."

"Oh, Albert, what wonderful news!"

"It's not a tenured position, but it would keep me occupied for the next few years." His eyes twinkle.

"Is it somewhere you might want to teach?" I ask.

"Yes, it is."

"Don't keep me in suspense, Albert. Where?"

"The opening is at my alma mater." He grins.

"Princeton! Oh, my goodness. Is it possible we might both be living in Princeton next fall?" My heart beats a little faster at the thought of continuing to spend Saturday afternoons together. Is Albert's job offer another sign?

"I had a telephone call with the head of the English department yesterday. I might have an offer by the end of next week."

"Well, this is wonderful news," I say.

Albert continues running his finger up and down the side of his glass.

"Is that all you've got on your mind?" I ask.

"You are remarkable, Mildred. There is something else. I have been thinking about it for some time. Frank and Bessie's misunderstanding this afternoon lit a fire under me to speak up. If we don't tell people the truth, we have only ourselves to blame." He shifts in his chair, slides his iced tea out of the way, and leans in closer as if he is about to share a secret.

I'm not sure I can handle any more secrets today. The buttery smell of browning Ritz crackers coming from the oven distracts me. I don't want the top of the casserole to get too brown. I'm about to excuse myself to check on it when Albert begins quoting Shelley:

"The fountains mingle with the river
And the rivers with the ocean,
The winds of heaven mix forever
With a sweet emotion;
Nothing in the world is single;
All things by a law divine
In one spirit meet and mingle.
Why not I with—"

"Albert, I'm so sorry. Please hold that thought. I have to pull the casserole out of the oven."

I pop up from my chair and hurry to the oven to retrieve the large baking pan. It's perfect—bubbling around the edges and evenly golden brown on top. Miss Lily's Million Dollar Chicken Casserole never disappoints. I added the crushed Ritz cracker topping to the recipe last year. It adds a nice salty, crisp crust to the creamy chicken dish.

"I'm sorry. What were you saying, Albert?"

I turn to walk back to the table and slam right into him. I didn't notice him move with me to the stove. My hands look small, resting on his broad chest. His large hands land on either side of my waist. I feel delicate and feminine in his grasp.

"'Why not I with thine.'" Albert completes the stanza and moves his hands to the small of my back.

I prepare for him to draw me in closer when—

"Ahem." Edna clears her throat.

I pull away from the professor and turn toward the sound. Sure enough, Edna stands in the kitchen doorway, one hand on her hip, the other clutching a brown paper bag. Her husband, Douglas, peers over her shoulder. The smirk on his face makes it clear he's tickled by the situation. Given the buzzing over my head, the house is amused as well.

"Oh, what a lovely surprise," I say, tucking a stray hair behind my ear and walking over to the sink. "What brings you two by the house this evening?"

Edna moves to the counter directly across from me and places the bag on it. She eyes Albert up one side and down the other. Douglas enters the kitchen and closes the screen door. He's a jolly fellow; strong, too. Working construction all these years has kept him fit as a farmer.

"Douglas and I went blueberry picking today," Edna says. "And I was thinking you might like to make that overnight blueberry French toast casserole. You know, the one Johnny enjoys so much."

"Mmm, blueberry French toast casserole, that sounds delicious," Albert says.

"Humph," Edna grunts.

"Hi, Edna. Hi, Mr. Anderson." Johnny's voice erases the awkwardness in the kitchen. "Are you here to join the search party?" he asks as he holds the door open for Eddie.

"What search party?" Edna asks.

"We've all been searching for Frank," Eddie says, walking to the table, pouring himself a glass of iced tea, then downing it.

"Is Frank missing?" Edna asks with a twinge of alarm in her voice.

"Has anyone found him yet?" Eddie asks.

"Not that we know of," Albert answers. "I was the first one home. Now you two and still no word on Frank."

"I hope he's all right," Eddie shakes his head.

"Will someone please tell me what's going on? What's wrong with Frank?" Edna cries.

"Nothing's wrong with him," I say. "There was a misunderstanding this afternoon."

"Yeah, and Aunt Bessie was beside herself because Mr. Davis went out for a walk before she could clear things up. I've never seen her so flustered," Johnny says.

"What was the misunderstanding about?" Edna asks.

"That's the strange part. Bessie said she couldn't tell us." Eddie pours himself another glass of iced tea. "She was desperate to find him, so we split up and went out to look for him."

The sound of the front door slamming startles everyone in the room.

"Now do you see why I don't work on Saturdays?" Edna says to her husband.

"Eddie? Mrs. Henderson? Where is everyone?" Frank's voice carries from the foyer all the way into the kitchen.

The dining room door flies open. Frank rushes into the kitchen. He's drenched in perspiration, his jacket clenched in one fist and his hat in the other.

"Thank goodness you're all here." He walks over to Johnny and puts his hands on the boy's shoulders.

I'm concerned. Frank's color is all wrong—pale and flat. The air in the house falls flat, too. Now I'm doubly apprehensive.

"Your mom had a medical emergency," Frank says. "She fainted at the park, and an ambulance came and took her to the hospital."

Edna gasps.

"Is she okay? What happened?" Johnny asks.

Eddie moves closer to Johnny.

"I don't know what happened," Frank says. "I wasn't with her when she collapsed. I saw a crowd gathering at the entrance to the park and ran over to see if something was wrong. As I got closer, I saw your Aunt Bessie on the ground with your mom. Your mom regained consciousness for a moment. That's a good sign. She was breathing fine, just out cold. The ambulance got there in record time. She's in excellent hands."

"Where's Aunt Bessie?" Johnny asks.

"She rode in the ambulance with your mom to the hospital," Frank answers. "She asked me to hurry home and give everyone the news. Eddie, she's hoping you'll drive over and meet her at Memorial."

"Of course," Eddie says.

"I'm coming, too," Johnny announces.

"I don't know if a hospital is the right place for—" Eddie starts.

"I'm coming, Uncle Eddie," Johnny says. "If my mom is in the hospital, I'm going with you."

"You got it," Eddie replies.

"Frank, did you and Bessie have time to talk?" I ask.

"No," he replies. "Why were Florence and Bessie at the park in the first place?"

"They were out looking for you. In fact, we all were," the professor says.

"Why?"

"Bessie said you had some kind of misunderstanding. She was frantic to find you and set the record straight," Eddie says.

"Hmm," Frank mumbles.

"Frank, why don't you take Eddie and Johnny to the hospital," I recommend. "You and Bessie need to talk—the sooner the better."

"There's a clean shirt for you in the ironing basket," Edna says. She walks over to the back corner of the kitchen and pulls a fresh blue shirt out for Frank. "Here you go."

"Thanks, Edna. You're a lifesaver." Edna lays the shirt over Frank's arm. "I can change in the car."

"We'll be praying for your mom, Johnny," I say.

"You bet we will, honey." Edna gives him a hug.

"Let's go," Eddie says, and they hurry out the back.

Edna, Douglas, Albert, and I stand staring out the screen door, not saying a word. Louie gets up from his spot under the dinette, sits down next to me, and stares out back in the same direction. I'm not sure whether one minute passes or ten.

"Well, we've got a whole casserole here," I say. "Edna, do you and Douglas want to stay for supper?"

"How can you think about food at a time like this?" she asks. "Miss Florence may be lying in a hospital, dying at this very—"

"Now, Edna," I cut her off, "you know how I like to putter in the kitchen when I'm worried about something."

"So, you are worried. Do you have any sense about Florence?" she asks.

"I've sensed that something has been building up inside her, but I had no idea she might collapse."

"How long do you think they will be at the hospital?" Albert asks.

"Who knows? We could be in for a long night," Douglas says.

"Might as well keep our strength up," Albert replies. He places a hand on my shoulder.

Edna glances at Albert's hand and then at her husband. "Douglas and I would love to stay for supper," she says. "We wouldn't want you and the professor to wait all alone." She raises her eyebrows at me. "Shall I set the dining room table?"

"Why bother? Let's eat in the kitchen," I say.

Edna walks around to the other side of the counter, shoos Albert away, and opens the top drawer. She counts out four napkins and four place settings of silverware. I take lettuce, carrots, and a tomato out of the refrigerator to make a simple salad.

"It feels strange, having a nice dinner when we don't know if Florence is okay," Edna says, moving around the table, arranging each place. "I wonder what caused her to faint. Did Florence have anything to do with Bessie and Frank's disagreement, Mrs. H?"

Douglas, Edna, and Albert turn to me at the same time. They lean in, hungry for details.

"It's not my story to tell," I reply.

A collective sigh of disappointment fills the air.

"Let's eat," I say.

I put on hot mitts and carry the casserole to the table, setting it down on a metal trivet. Edna brings over the salad bowl and the oil and vinegar.

"Are you getting any feelings from the house?" Edna asks.

"Henderson House is waiting for something to happen," I say, sitting at the table.

"Something good or something bad?" Albert asks.

I close my eyes and tune in to the stillness. "Something good, I think." I open my eyes. "Edna, why don't you say grace?"

CHAPTER THIRTY-THREE

Florence

"FLORENCE, CAN YOU hear me?"

I roll my head toward the sound of my sister's voice. The pillowcase crinkles, stiff and cool against my cheek. Her face appears close to mine.

"Bessie?" I croak.

"Welcome back. You gave me quite a scare," she says.

"What happened?"

The room comes into focus. I'm propped up in a white metal bed surrounded by a tall blue-and-white checkered curtain. The curtain hangs on silver rings that ride high above me on an oval rod suspended from the ceiling.

"Why am I lying in a large shower?" I ask.

"You're at Memorial Hospital," Bessie responds. "You passed out when we arrived at the park. I rode with you in the ambulance. Don't worry. You're gonna be fine." She pats my hand several times, rubs it, then pats it again.

"I don't remember an ambulance ride," I say.

The curtain rings jangle as someone enters my shower room. "Well, look who's awake," an unfamiliar male voice says. "I'm Dr. Wilson. Let's take a quick look at you, Mrs. Fuller."

The doctor's unbuttoned white lab coat flows like a cape over a dark three-piece suit. The suit fabric is of moderate quality, perhaps a wool blend, not nice enough to be one of ours. He looks in my eyes with a flashlight, then has me stick out my tongue and say "ah." He feels my neck, listens to me breathe with a stethoscope, and takes my pulse.

"You're doing much better, Mrs. Fuller, but we have a few things to discuss."

"What happened? Why did I pass out?" I ask.

"I believe hypertension caused your episode today."

I give the doctor a blank stare.

"Hypertension means you have high blood pressure. When the medics arrived at the scene, your blood pressure was 190 over 120. That's high enough to cause a stroke. When we took your blood pressure here at the hospital, it was down to 145 over 95—still too high. A normal reading would be less than 120 over less than 80."

"Did I have a stroke?"

I wiggle my toes under the covers to make sure I can still feel them. Our neighbor, Mr. Holmes, had a stroke and ended up in a wheelchair for the rest of his life. He struggles to put sentences together, and when he can't remember a word, he fills it in with "tee-tee-ta-ta." How did Johnny pitch in the game last tee-tee-ta-ta? or It's nice to see you again, Mrs. tee-tee-ta-ta. Drives me crazy. Bessie visits with him at least once a week. She's got more patience in her little finger than I've got in my whole body.

"I don't think you had a stroke, Mrs. Fuller," the doctor says. "This time." He shakes his finger at me twice, emphasizing each word. "Your sister tells me that prior to your collapse, you were out for a brisk walk." He picks up my chart and flips through the pages. "Did you feel discomfort during the walk? Shortness of breath, chest pain, or light-headedness?"

"All of the above," I answer.

"Have you felt unusually tired lately?"

"Yes." I pause. "I've had a headache all day, and I fell asleep this afternoon sitting in a chair."

"It's not like her to nap," Bessie adds.

"Mm-hmm." Dr. Wilson makes some notes. "Mrs. Fuller, have you been under any extra pressure at home or work recently?"

"Yes. I suppose I have. My sister and I were arguing on our walk." I look at Bessie and roll my eyes.

A smile tugs at her lips.

"I think a sharp increase in blood pressure due to exercise and anxiety caused your episode today."

"Is there a cure for it?" I ask.

"No. There is no cure for hypertension. It's something you'll need to learn to manage."

"Are there medications I can take?"

"There are some, but personally I don't think the potential side effects are worth the risk. Given this was your first episode, and you are only in your early forties, I'd like to manage your condition through rest, changes to your diet, and a regular exercise regimen. We can talk more about the specifics later. For now, get some rest."

"How long will I be in the hospital?"

"At least overnight. I'll evaluate your condition when I'm on morning rounds. If everything looks stable, you can go home tomorrow afternoon, but you'll need to rest for an entire week and follow up with your personal physician before returning to your normal routine."

I nod to the doctor. I need to find a place to live in Tulsa and organize a move. How can I rest for an entire week?

"May I sit here with her a little longer, Dr. Wilson?" Bessie asks.

"Of course. Visiting hours end at seven. But no more arguments, you two," the doctor says with a cautionary wave of his hand before placing my chart back at the foot of the bed and exiting through the curtains.

"What happened, Bessie?" I ask.

"Do you remember walking from Henderson House to the park to find Frank?" Bessie asks.

I think back to everyone gathered in the upstairs hallway at Henderson House, my sister frantic about finding Frank so she could set the record straight. I recall the pain in my chest when I realized she knew I had misled him. After all the trouble I've gotten into in my life, you'd think I'd be used to getting caught by now. The dull headache continues to pulse behind my temples.

"Yes, I remember," I say. "And I remember our fight and the long list of things I have to do before you'll forgive me."

"Oh, Florence," Bessie sighs, "if I'd known you might collapse, I never would have—" she says, breaking off mid-sentence.

I examine my sister's haggard face, her furrowed brow, the dirt on her chin, bobby pins sticking out in every direction from her untamed hair. It would be easy to play up my condition. I could let her blame herself for my collapse. She might even forgive my horrible behavior with Frank to keep my poor heart from giving out again. The old Florence would have milked this for all it was worth, but the old Florence isn't lying in this hospital bed. Something stirred inside me when Mama spoke to me this afternoon. A different gnawing began in my stomach—not the anxious knot I'm used to but a churning of encouragement, maybe even hope. I know it was just a dream, but I still hear my mama's voice.

Sweetheart, it's time for you to start living an honest life.

She's with me now, in the hospital, repeating those words over and over in my head.

Mama, I hear you, I respond to her voice in my head. I want to live an honest life, but I'm not sure I know how.

I've already told you, the voice sings. *Through the tunnel and into the sunshine, then into the fabric. One stitch at a time.*

"Bessie, you had every right to say the things you did this afternoon. I behaved terribly with Frank. If there is anyone to blame for my collapse, it's me. I'm the one who dragged you into my web of lies, and I'm the one who tried to sabotage your romance. This," I say, gesturing to the hospital room, "is not your fault. It's mine. Bessie, I need to tell you something." I pause and swallow. "I've been spending money from the savings account on myself and Johnny without asking you and Eddie for permission."

Bessie squeezes my hand. "We know you have."

"You do?" I stare at my sister in disbelief.

"Eddie and I are happy we've been able to chip in and help you and Johnny. If we weren't, we never would have agreed to put you in charge of the savings account," she says. "We knew what we were signing up for."

"You did?" I'm dumbfounded. I got myself all twisted up in knots over something my brother and sister already knew.

"We can talk about that later," Bessie says with a tired smile. "Right now, you need to rest. I'll phone Mr. Linn this evening, let him know what happened, tell him you'll be recovering at home this week."

"Guess I'm finally gonna get more than three days off in a row," I say.

"I'm just glad you're okay, honey. The medics said Frank was a big help, elevating your legs."

"Frank was there?"

"Yes. He was at the park when you fainted. A crowd gathered around us, and he came to see what was going on. He asked someone to call the ambulance and knew it was important to raise your legs to keep blood flowing to your brain."

"A crowd? Did I fall all the way to the ground in front of a crowd?"

"I caught you, sort of, but you ended up on the sidewalk."

"How embarrassing." I squeeze my eyes shut and try to push away the image of my body crumpled on the pavement for all to see.

"You came to for a moment and said you'd talked to Mama. Do you remember telling me that?"

"No. I don't remember, but it's true. When I fell asleep this afternoon, Mama spoke to me in a dream. Her voice was as clear to me as yours is now. She knew about Rachel and Johnny. She knew I lied to Frank this afternoon."

"Don't wind yourself up. We don't need to talk about any of that right now."

"We do need to talk about it now. I could have died this afternoon. Mama told me it's time to tell Johnny the truth. We have to tell him as soon as possible. I can't die before he knows the truth." I attempt to pick my head up, but it's too heavy and falls back into the pillow.

"Sweetheart, you are not dying. We have plenty of time to talk to Johnny." She pats my hand again.

"I want him to know as soon as possible, but—" I look around the shower room. I can't tell if there are patients on the other side of the curtain. "There's something I need to tell you," I whisper.

"What is it?" Bessie leans in closer.

"I'm terrified to tell Johnny the truth. I'm afraid of what he might say when he finds out he was Rachel's baby, not mine. I'm so frightened that he'll hate me, Bessie. That he'll leave me. I don't know what I'd do if I lost my boy."

"Shhh, Johnny would never leave you. You shouldn't worry about telling him right now. It can wait," she says.

"No, it can't. Mama told me it's time, but I need your help."

"What do you mean?" Bessie drops my hand and sits back in her chair.

"I don't think I can be the one to tell Johnny. In fact, I'd rather not even be there when he finds out."

Bessie gasps. "How can you not be there when he finds out?"

"I'm too afraid. Will you tell him for me, Bessie?" I stretch my hand back out to her. She cocks her head to one side and rubs her lips together a few times before taking it.

"You want me to tell Johnny, without you," she says, lingering over each word.

"Yes. Please, Bessie. You'll know how to tell the story. Neither one of us has all the answers, but I'm too afraid to even get started. I need your help. Will you tell him?" I give her hand a squeeze. She pulls it away.

"I can't let you make a decision like this right now. You might feel differently tomorrow. You might not even remember asking me." Bessie tosses her hands in the air.

"I won't feel differently. I swear. I'd tell him tonight if I thought my heart could stand it." My eyes sting.

"You've had a very upsetting day, sweetheart. Let's put this on the back burner for now."

"But I want you to understand why I'm asking for your help."

"Okay. Why are you asking me?"

"You know how I always plan ahead? How I love to visualize a situation and practice it in my mind? I spend hours rehearsing an important conversation, running through possible outcomes, over and over, until I see things working out perfectly."

"Yes," Bessie says, drawing the word out into three syllables.

"I've tried to visualize myself telling Johnny a million times, and I can't see it. My brain can't imagine any of it—where we would sit, what I would say, how he would react, what questions he might ask. When I think about telling him, all I see is darkness. All I feel is fear." My heart pounds in my chest.

Take it easy. Being honest is new to you. One stitch at a time.

"Oh, Florence." She stares down at her lap and runs her right index finger over the knuckles of her left hand.

"Bessie, I can imagine you telling Rachel's story. I can see you sitting with Johnny, listening to him. I can hear you answering his questions, helping him understand how much we all love him. Telling him how I've been in love with him since the minute he was born. Please help me, Bessie. Please tell Johnny the truth for me. For us."

The small chair next to my bed creaks as Bessie shifts her position. She grimaces as if she's in pain. She licks her lips and shakes her head. "I'm honored that you think I would do a good job, but I told you this afternoon, I'm through making promises to you." She takes a deep breath. "This is your responsibility, Florence. You wanted to raise Johnny as your own. You wanted your husband to think the baby was his. You convinced me to lie to everyone I care about. And now, those lies may have cost me the man I love."

I don't know how to respond.

"I'm happy to be with you when you tell Johnny, but I will not tell him for you. My answer is no." Bessie rubs her hands on her knees. "Ugh," she utters a sound of pain or relief—I'm not sure which.

We sit in silence for a moment. The sounds of the hospital creep into my room—indistinct male and female voices, footsteps getting closer and then farther away, wheels spinning and squeaking. My mind wanders off toward the noises of the hallway.

Johnny is your responsibility. A voice pulls me back into the room. Maybe it's my voice. Maybe it's my mama's. I'm not sure it matters anymore. I turn to my sister.

"You are right to say 'no' to me, honey."

"I am," Bessie states as if reassuring herself.

"Yes, you are. Mama didn't appear to me in my dream and say it was time for you to tell Johnny. She said it was time for me to tell the truth, and that's exactly what I'm going to do."

CHAPTER THIRTY-FOUR

Bessie

A YOUNG NURSE in a light blue blouse, starched white pin-afore, and white cap strides through the curtains without warning. "Excuse me," she says, "you have some more visitors, Mrs. Fuller. Your brother and son are waiting outside."

"Eddie and Johnny are here?" Florence's face lights up. She's been so pale since her collapse. I'm glad to see some color in her cheeks.

"We only allow two visitors in the room at a time, and visiting hours are almost over." The nurse wrinkles her nose at me and pats her wristwatch.

"I'll step out immediately," I respond. It takes all my strength to push myself out of the little chair and stand. "Florence, there's no rush to tell Johnny. Please rest. You've got plenty of time."

"When you find Frank, how much of Rachel's story are you going to tell him?" she asks.

"I'm going to tell him everything I know." I lock eyes with her. "Everything."

The muscles in my sister's face contract for a moment and then relax. "Of course, and you should," she says. "After all, that's what people who love each other do. Thank you, Bessie, for all the kindness you've shown me and Johnny over the years."

"You're welcome. Promise me you'll try to sleep after you visit with Eddie and Johnny."

"I promise—on the bones," she says with a wink.

"I love you," I say.

Florence manages a weak smile. "I love you, too."

I turn to the nurse who's holding the curtain open for me, tapping the toe of one of her white shoes. "If Dr. Wilson decides my sister can go home tomorrow, what time should I be here?" I ask.

"Patients are discharged between eleven and one," the nurse recites, barely masking her impatience.

"It must be difficult having to answer the same question a million times a day," I say.

"Oh." She drops the curtain and stops tapping her foot. "It's no trouble. I'm just eager to finish my shift. My fiancé leaves for basic training tomorrow."

"Where's he headed?" I ask.

"Fort Sill," she says, avoiding my eyes by adjusting the ruffles on her pinafore.

"What's his name?"

"Robert. Well, Robbie." She looks up at me, and a slight smile crosses her lips when she says her fiancé's name.

"May I add Robbie to my prayer list?" I ask.

"Yes, thank you." She touches my arm. "If your sister needs a few extra minutes with the rest of your family, it's no bother."

"That's very kind of you." I nod. "I'll see you after church tomorrow," I say to my sister, then make my way through the curtains.

As soon as I enter the hallway, Johnny rushes to greet me, Eddie close behind.

"How is she?" Johnny asks, his eyes searching my face for information.

"She's awake and resting." I smile. "She's going to be fine." I give Johnny a little squeeze on the arm. "Visiting hours end at seven, so get in there and see for yourself. We can talk about what the doctor said later. I'll meet you in the waiting room."

Eddie and Johnny hurry to Florence's room. I walk gingerly down the long hallway to the waiting area. My whole body aches. The curly-headed medic warned me I might have some sore muscles after catching my sister and falling to the ground with her. I didn't think it would be all of them.

Dear Lord, thank you for watching over my sister today, for the skill of the doctors and nurses caring for her, and for the healing power of love. Amen.

Oh, and please watch over Robbie as he begins basic training at Fort Sill. Amen, again.

"Bessie?" a man murmurs at the end of the hallway.

I stare at the entrance to the waiting room. Frank stands with his hands in his pockets, rocking back and forth on his heels, smiling at me. It's not a big smile, but it is a smile. His warm greeting fills me with relief. And yet, I'm still not sure how to make him understand why I didn't tell him sooner.

"I've been looking for you," I say, pain pulsing through my stiff legs with each step toward him.

"So I heard." He continues shifting his weight back and forth. "How's Florence?"

"She's fine. It's a high blood pressure condition. That's all I know right now."

"I'm so glad it wasn't a heart attack. I was frightened when I found the two of you on the ground. Would you like to sit?" Frank steps out of the doorway and gestures to the back corner.

I take a few tentative steps.

"Are you okay?" he asks, putting a hand on my shoulder, then removing it quickly as if he's not sure he should touch me.

"I'm fine. Skinned both my knees while breaking my sister's fall. Nothing that would have slowed me down in my barefoot days, but I'm not as young as I used to be."

The waiting room feels cluttered after spending time in my sister's sparse white hospital room. An abundance of chunky wooden chairs and matching low side tables line the beige walls. A row of chairs placed back-to-back create an island of two-sided seating in the center. Small windows run along the back wall. Only a handful of people remain in the waiting area this close to seven o'clock. Three young ladies near the door prepare to leave, collecting their sweaters and purses. I touch the crook of my arm instinctively. I can't shake the feeling that I've put my pocketbook down somewhere in the building and forgotten it. I didn't bring a purse with me when I left Henderson House to find Frank this afternoon. In fact, my bag may still be resting next to Mrs. Henderson's settee.

The only additional occupants in the waiting room are an older couple sitting on the front side of the island. The husband is asleep, chin to chest, and the wife appears deeply engaged in an article in Women's Digest. Frank and I walk to the back right corner where I see his jacket draped over a chair, his fedora resting on the seat in front of it. We take the two chairs catty-cornered to each other. I lean past Frank to push open the small window behind him. My shoulder brushes his, and that familiar tremor runs through me. He smells manly—like earth and sun and sweat. Did he run all the way to Henderson House from the park? If he did, he must have grabbed a clean shirt. His spotless appearance makes me wonder about my own. I must look like something the cat dragged in.

"Sorry, I could use a little air," I say.

"I bet you could," Frank replies. He settles awkwardly into his chair, leaning forward, then sitting back, putting one of his arms on the armrest, then changing his mind and laying it over the back of the chair next to him. "Long day," he says.

"And it's not over yet. I'd like to clear things up between us before Eddie and Johnny are back. Visiting hours end at seven. We don't have much time."

"Are you sure you're up to it?" He leans forward. Our knees almost touch. I wish I could wrap my arms around him and kiss him. I wish I could tell him I love him, but there are other things I must tell him first.

"No, I'm not sure, but I've been working hard to find you, and now here you are." I gesture to him with my hands, and he smiles again, bigger this time, as the little wrinkles I adore sprout from his eyes. Even if Frank won't take me back, I have the chance to tell him the truth. All I've wanted to do since I woke up this morning was tell Frank about Johnny, and now that the moment is here, I don't know where to begin. My stomach flutters.

"I feel like I'm standing on the rock outcropping above our old swimming hole. I'm having a little trouble pushing off." I rub my sweaty palms on my aching thighs.

Dear Jesus, please help me find the right words and the courage I need to say them. Amen.

"Whatever it is, Bessie, you can tell me," Frank says. "The water's plenty deep. Jump. I'll catch you." His lips curl into a boyish grin.

It's all the encouragement I need to step off the ledge.

"My sister had a discussion with you on the porch this afternoon, correct?"

"Yes, she did," Frank replies, adopting a more businesslike posture. "Eddie said there was some sort of misunderstanding, but I'm pretty sure I understood what Florence was telling me."

"It wasn't a misunderstanding. Florence lied to you." I look at the other couple in the waiting room and lean closer to Frank. "I'm not Johnny's mother, and neither is Florence. Johnny is my sister Rachel's baby," I whisper.

"Your sister Rachel's baby?" Frank knits his eyebrows together.

"Do you remember when we were at the cemetery, and we told you about Mama and Mae dying of influenza?" I ask.

Frank nods.

"Well, after they died, Rachel and Wahya took over running the store. My sweet sister must have been terribly lonely with only Daddy and Wahya for company. Rachel was a tender, beautiful creature, inside and out. I'm not surprised she fell in love with someone."

"Who? Who did she fall in love with?" he asks.

"She never told us." I exhale. "And then . . ." I pause for another breath. "She died the night after she gave birth."

Frank tilts his head to one side. "Johnny is your sister Rachel's child," he repeats. His hazel eyes dart back and forth like the hummingbirds in our garden. Finally, his gaze settles back on me. "Well, that's a horse of a different color now, isn't it?" He rubs his chin and sighs loudly. "Why the heck would Florence lie to me about something like that?"

"I'm so sorry, Frank. I should have told you the truth earlier. Florence asked me to promise her I wouldn't tell you unless you proposed to me. I know, it was a ridiculous stipulation, but I promised her. When things started going so well for us this week, I decided I would break my promise and tell you everything tonight. But Florence got to you first. Mrs. Henderson thinks Florence set me up. Made me promise not to tell you, only to tell you a twisted version of the story herself so that you would lose confidence in me."

"She risked a lot lying to me. Imagine if Johnny had over-heard her? She could have hurt a lot of people in her attempt to break us up." He struggles to keep his voice low.

"Attempt to break us up?" I murmur. "Does that mean we're not broken up?"

"Did you think just because I didn't want to talk to you this afternoon, I was breaking up with you?"

"Maybe." I look away.

Frank cups my cheek in one of his hands and turns my face to him.

"Oh, Bessie, I went up to my room because my head was swimming with questions. I needed time to sort things out. I was afraid of what I might say in the heat of the moment."

"You were?" I press my face into the palm of his hand.

"Yes, darling." Frank brushes a strand of hair out of my eyes and takes both my hands in his. "I was terribly upset when I thought you had kept something so important from me. I assumed Johnny was the product of your relationship with Doc Jenkins. Florence made it sound like you didn't trust me enough to tell me the whole story. After everything I went through with my first wife, I have to know we're going to be completely honest with each other. After I saw you on the porch, I went upstairs and just paced in my room, but I wasn't getting any-where, so I went for a walk to clear my head. I was sitting on our bench at the park, working on all the ways we could fig-ure things out—even imagining telling Johnny the truth and adopting him so he could stay here with us in Bartlesville." He makes a sound between a snort and a chuckle. "Of course, that's when I thought you were his mother. I told you—I've waited a long time to find you, Bessie Blackwell. I'm not letting you go now." He leans forward. "I love you," he whispers in my ear, sending a tingle through my aching body.

"I love you, too," I answer.

"I was hoping to say those words to you this evening over a romantic dinner, not in the waiting room at the hospital." He pulls my hands to his lips and places one delicate kiss on them.

A young woman in a yellow dress enters the waiting room, and Frank and I lean back from each other. The woman in the yellow dress puts her hand on the shoulder of the wife, who sets the magazine down and wakes up her husband. The family resemblance is strong between the three of them. The young woman in the yellow dress has the wife's face and the husband's slight build. For the first time, I wonder if Johnny looks like his father. The family exits the waiting room together, and Frank and I are alone.

"So, Rachel is the other reason you dropped everything and moved to Wichita," Frank says as he rubs his forehead and then his eyes.

"Yes. She wanted to have the baby at my aunt's house. Aunt Maude and my mama were very close."

"And you wanted to get away from Doc Jenkins and his fiancé," he says.

"Oh, Frank. I don't know what I wanted. I grew up doing whatever I could on any given day to help my family. When Mama asked me to work in the garden, I worked in the garden. When she asked me to take Eddie away in the middle of the night, I left to keep my brother safe. I suppose it was the same with Rachel and her unexpected pregnancy. Yes, I wanted to get away from Doc, but mostly I went to Wichita to protect Rachel and the baby. All my life, I have done what my family needed me to do. No questions asked. I've never stopped to think about what I wanted—not until recently." I return the intensity of Frank's gaze. "I want this to work for us. I want to spend the rest of my life with you, if you'll have me."

Frank starts to say something, but I put my hand to his lips and stop him from speaking.

"You have to know everything before you can make that decision. Everything." He kisses my fingers lightly before I pull them away.

"What did Aunt Maude make of the three of you when you showed up?" His voice takes on a lighter tone.

"Oh, she adored having us there. She would have done anything for 'Jennie's girls,' as she called us."

"What did you tell Aunt Maude about Rachel being pregnant?"

"We told her Rachel's husband was working in Oklahoma and planned to join her as soon as he could. In those days, it was pretty common for the womenfolk to stick together while their men were off finding work."

"True enough," Frank says.

"I don't think anyone gave it a second thought. Florence took in piecework from a dressmaker in town, and I got an office job at Cessna, one of the airplane manufacturers. It was my first experience with business machines. Turned out I had a knack for them. Rachel baked muffins for a local café. We earned our keep," I say, almost smiling as I recall the warmth and laughter of Aunt Maude's kitchen and my delight at putting my hand on Rachel's growing belly and feeling the baby kick.

"In the cemetery, Florence said Rachel had a seizure. Is that true?" Frank asks.

"Florence didn't lie about that. Rachel had a seizure the evening after she gave birth," I say, clearing my throat. I lick my lips and swallow. "Aunt Maude found a wet nurse, and Florence and I took over caring for the baby. Florence began making her case to raise the infant as her own. She started calling the baby Johnny. Soon, we all were."

Frank frowns. "And you had to bring Rachel's body home for burying? All by yourself?"

"Yes. When the three of us left for Wichita on our adventure, we were so full of hope." A tear rolls down my cheek, and I wipe it away. "I could hardly take a breath without crying the day I traveled home with her body on the train. I watched the luggage handlers load my precious sister's casket into the baggage car with the same care and attention as any other trunk or suitcase. Knowing the engine was pulling Rachel behind me, dead, gnawed on my insides every minute of the journey. I arrived at the station in Claremore empty."

Several more tears fall. Frank fishes around in his jacket for a fresh hankie and hands it to me.

"That's when the lies started," I say. "I told Daddy and Wahya that Rachel had a seizure while she was sleeping, which was true. Still, it was a lie of omission. Florence gave me a letter addressed to John, and I left it at the hotel for him. I told his parents Florence had a beautiful baby boy waiting for John in Wichita. Again, partly true, but mostly a lie." I rub my neck with my hands and tilt my head back, trying to ease the tension.

"Didn't anyone know Rachel had a boyfriend?" Frank asks.

"No one was ever good enough in my daddy's eyes. I'm not surprised Rachel kept her romance a secret. I asked Wahya once if she was seeing anyone, and he said every boy who came into the Pack and Run was in love with her."

"It's hard to imagine you lying to everyone," Frank says.

I hear the disappointment in his voice and have no response.

"We've only known each other a few weeks, but it seems out of character for you, Bessie. Why did you do it? Why did you lie so Florence could pretend the baby was hers?"

I attempt to smooth my wrinkled skirt, noticing the dirt and grass stains for the first time. I search my heart for the right words. "Florence always wanted to be a mother. Aunt

Maude sent us dolls for Christmas one year when we were little. I wasn't very interested in playing with them."

"Too busy running around outside, collecting sticks and berries?" Frank asks.

"Exactly. Well, it only took Florence a matter of days to adopt my doll as her second child. She spent every minute she could mothering those two dolls—feeding them, reading to them, dressing them, asking me to be quiet when they were down for a nap. She adored helping Mama with Eddie, Rachel, and Mae when they were babies. Once she and John got married, getting pregnant was her first order of business, only it didn't happen. After the war, I know she kept trying, but it was difficult with him wandering off for weeks at a time. The days following Rachel's death, I couldn't eat. I hardly slept." I wipe another single tear. "I blamed myself. I thought if I'd gone back to living at the Pack and Run, Rachel would have had someone to confide in, someone to give her romantic advice."

"Hmm. No wonder you spend your time counselling all the young women at work," Frank muses.

"I've never thought about it like that before, but you're probably right. I couldn't be there for Rachel, so now I'm there for anyone who pops their head into the office machine room." I manage half a smile.

"I still can't figure out why you agreed to lie for Florence."

"Oh, Frank, I was a mess. I'd lost my mama, Mae, and then Rachel. At that point, I probably would have agreed to anything to support my only surviving sister. The only thing keeping me going was how happy Florence was taking care of the baby and how happy the baby was with her. Florence believed that little Johnny would bring her husband back to his senses, and she would finally have the family she'd always dreamed about. She begged me to let John think the baby was his. She said the timing worked, and he would have no trouble believing it." I put my head in my hands. "Please understand, I didn't know I was signing up for a lifetime of lying. I thought Florence would tell John the truth once he came to Wichita, and they would adopt Johnny as their own. I never imagined this would go on for thirteen years."

The ticking of a wall clock punctuates the silence of the waiting room in perfectly spaced intervals. It's seven o'clock. I'm out of time and not nearly finished.

"I understand," Frank says.

"You do?" I look up at him as more tears flood my eyes.

"I do. Given the situation, and knowing how much you care about your family, I can understand why you agreed to lie for Florence about the baby. I can even understand why you promised not to tell me unless we were serious about each other. Johnny is a great kid. I don't want to see him get hurt any more than you do."

"Thank you, Frank," I splutter. "Your understanding means the world to me." I wipe my face and nose, trying to find a dry spot on the hankie. "The good news is there's a way forward. Florence is committed to telling Johnny the truth as soon as possible."

"She is?"

"Yes. She wants to tell him tomorrow." I brush more hair out of my eyes and spot Eddie and Johnny entering the waiting room.

"She's a piece of work, that one," Eddie's voice bounces off the empty chairs.

"She certainly is," Frank says with a hint of sarcasm. "To be continued." He winks at me. Frank's understanding sends my head spinning. I'm not sure how I expected him to react, but I'm humbled, almost dazed by his kindness and compassion.

Eddie and Johnny join us in the back corner. Frank moves his hat and jacket so Eddie can sit next to him. Johnny plops down next to me.

"Mom said she has something really important to tell us when she comes home," Johnny announces.

"Oh, she did?" I respond, making eye contact with Frank.

"Yup, she's fired up about something," Eddie says. "What do you say we stop worrying, go home, and get something to eat?"

"Yeah, I'm starving. Can we head back to Henderson House, Aunt Bessie?" Johnny asks.

"We sure can. There's nothing to do here until after church tomorrow. If the doctor thinks your mom's ready to come home, she'll be at the table for Sunday dinner," I say.

Eddie and Johnny stand up at the same time.

"Any kind of dinner sounds good to me right now," Johnny says, rubbing his belly.

Eddie ruffles his hair as they head for the hallway.

I try to stand, but my aching legs refuse to cooperate. I moan, and Frank offers me both of his hands. It takes some effort on his part to extract me from the chair.

"How are you holding up?"

"I'm hanging in there," I say, leaning on him for support.

"If you want to finish our conversation tomorrow, I'm happy to wait," he says.

"No!" I surprise myself with the strength of my response. "I'm not going to sleep tonight until there are no more secrets between us, Frank. Not one."

CHAPTER THIRTY-FIVE

Bessie

FRANK GENTLY GUIDES my aching body into the back-seat next to Johnny. Eddie sits up front. He and Frank talk about the Boston Red Sox. Johnny knows Ted Williams's stats like the back of his hand, but he doesn't join in the conversation. Instead, he spends most of the ride looking out the window, fiddling with a piece of string he found in his pocket. Johnny wraps the string around one of his fingers until it turns purple, then he unwinds it and rubs the ridges he created in his skin before moving on to the next finger. I nearly ask him to stop but hold my tongue.

When Frank pulls into the driveway, I scan the front porch for Mrs. H and the professor. The rocking chairs have been returned to a straight line, but they sit empty. Frank parks around back on the far side of the garage.

"Home again, home again," Eddie says when Frank turns off the engine. "Let's round up some vittles. I think we're all a quart low."

Frank gets out and opens my door. My knees, stiff from the ride home, don't hurt as much as they did in the waiting room, but every inch of me is exhausted. I rotate my body so my legs dangle out of the car. Frank supports me as I slide off the seat, onto my feet, and into a standing position. He stays by my side, holding my hand, and we inch our way across the driveway toward the back door. Johnny and Eddie walk ahead. Eddie puts his arm around Johnny, and I see my nephew lean into his uncle.

Dear Lord, thank you for bringing my brother home to us and for the wonderful support he offers Johnny. Amen.

Frank pauses in front of the garden.

"Do you want to eat first and talk later?"

"Talk first," I say. My stomach rumbles so loudly Frank hears it.

"Are you sure?" he asks.

"Yes. I think the grumbling is more from unfinished business than from hunger." It growls again. "But I could be wrong."

"Eddie, we'll be along in a minute. You two go ahead," Frank calls as he opens the garden gate.

We walk under the vivid blue canopy of clematis and take a seat on the bench where the flower project sat one short week ago. Frank never lets go of my hand.

"Where were we?" he asks, bending toward me so our foreheads touch. For a moment, I consider closing my eyes and resting, but I can't risk falling asleep. I sit up straight.

"I told you about bringing Rachel's body home," I say. "And lying to Daddy, Wahya, and John's parents about Florence and her baby."

"Right, continue," Frank says.

"After Rachel's funeral, I returned to Wichita. I had a job to get back to and a sister and nephew who needed me. As much as Florence wanted little Johnny, she didn't want to raise him alone. She wasn't sure if her husband, John, would come to join her."

"But he came, didn't he?" Frank asks.

"Yes. He arrived at Aunt Maude's about a week after I got back from the funeral."

"Did he believe Johnny was his son?"

"He bought Florence's story hook, line, and sinker," I say. "And the baby did bring John back to life. He stopped drinking and got a job managing the front desk at the Broadview Hotel downtown. Aunt Maude let them fix up a little cabin on her property down by the river. The cabin wasn't much, but it gave them privacy. I think the last time my whole body ached like this was the day after Florence and I scrubbed that cabin from top to bottom. John put in a wood stove and rebuilt the front porch. Little Johnny was an easy baby. Florence and John were over the moon."

I watch the sun drop behind the tall ash trees, and the light in the garden shifts from yellow to almost blue. The wind picks up and plays a melancholy tune as it wanders among the deep green leaves. I strain to organize my thoughts as the rest of the story unfolds in my mind. My stomach churns again.

"I've kept these memories tucked away for so long. Sharing them is like opening up an old dusty box with a jumble of letters and photographs inside—nothing is in the right order," I say.

"It's okay, Bessie," Frank whispers, "take your time."

"Summer came," I begin. I tell Frank about Johnny as a five-month-old. How he'd learned to laugh and loved figuring out what he could do to make other people laugh. I tell him about walking down to Florence and John's cabin every night after supper to sit on the porch and let the baby entertain me. I begged Florence to tell John the truth. She kept putting it off, saying she was waiting for the right moment.

"One day, I came home late from the office and stopped at the cabin to say hello. My sister asked me to fetch John for supper," I say. "She'd seen him return from work, but he'd gone straight down to the river to check his catfish traps. Aunt Maude's property backed up to the Arkansas River. Anyway, on my way down to find John, I saw a piece of blue paper wadded up in the leaves to the side of the path. I thought it was trash. I picked it up and put it in my pocket. When I got to the riverbank, John was there, washing his hands in the water. He began talking to me about the war." Chills run up my spine as I remember John's description of his trench knife and his friend Jacques. "John told me he'd met a stranger on the road while he was walking home. A man who'd reminded him of one of his war buddies. The young man was looking for the three Blackwell sisters—and a baby."

"Was it Johnny's father?" Frank asks.

"I think so." I pause for a deep breath. "John said he told the young man that one of the sisters died last February. The man asked which sister, and John told him it was Rachel. Then the stranger asked him again if there was a baby—a baby around five or six months old."

"The same age as Johnny," Frank mutters.

"Yes. John's eyes flashed with hurt and anger as he spoke to me. I could tell he had figured out Florence's deception. John said he apologized to the stranger, told him there was no baby, and gave him directions back to the train station. Then he said we probably shouldn't mention the young man to Florence as it would only upset her."

"What was the stranger's name?"

"I asked John the same question, and his answer was, 'He didn't offer, and I didn't ask.'"

The sound of spring peepers fills the garden, and I rest for a moment, letting their song settle around me before continuing.

"Later that same evening, when I was getting ready for bed, I pulled the crumpled-up piece of paper out of my skirt pocket. For some reason, before throwing it away, I opened it and saw Rachel's elegant, slanted script on the page. She had written a letter to Johnny's father in early February, a week before Johnny was born. A week before she died."

Frank rubs his chin. "If she wrote to him in February, why didn't he show up until the summer?" Then his eyes open wide. "Wait, was his name in the letter?"

I shake my head. "No. Only pet names, like 'my darling' and 'my love.' Things were never the same between John and Florence after the young man's visit. The spell had been broken. And she blames me."

"For what?"

"Florence thinks I betrayed her and told John that the baby wasn't his. John refused to tell Florence about the young man on the road, so I did. And she got horribly angry with me, accused me of lying and making up the story about the stranger to cover up my betrayal. I tried to show her the letter, but she refused to read it. She stopped speaking to me, and she wouldn't let me see Johnny. She demanded I leave her family alone and move back to Oklahoma. She was acting like a crazy person."

"She kinda is a crazy person," Frank says with a wry laugh. It feels good to break the tension for a moment. "So, you left Wichita then and came to Bartlesville."

"I didn't want to leave Johnny, but I needed to get out of there. I couldn't live in Florence's make-believe world anymore. I left that beautiful baby boy behind with two unpredictable parents. I'm a terrible person." I drop my head into my hands.

The bench flexes as Frank scoots closer and wraps his arms around me.

"Bessie, sometimes it's okay if the person you need to keep safe is yourself."

He pulls me into him, and I lay my head on his chest. He strokes my hair, and I listen to the steady rhythm of his heart.

"When Annie and I were first married," he says, "I wanted to start a family right away. Then the war came, and, well, you know the rest of the story. Never having a child is one of my biggest regrets. I feel terribly sorry for that young man John met on the road. He has a wonderful son he doesn't even know exists. Once Johnny learns the truth about his situation, do you think he might want to try to find his father?"

"Yes, and I think it scares Florence to death. She's terrified of losing Johnny. My sister may be a little wacky," I begin, "but she has been a good mother to Johnny."

I adjust the position of my head on Frank's chest and close my eyes. There's nothing left to tell him. All my secrets are out in the open. I thought I'd feel lighter somehow, but mostly, I'm exhausted.

"Bessie," Frank says, playing with the loose hair around my neck. "Since we're getting all our secrets out tonight, there's something I need to tell you."

"Okay," I say.

"I talked to Mrs. Henderson earlier today. Was it only today?" he asks, more to himself, with his quiet musical laugh. "I spoke with her about buying Henderson House and our idea to run it as a bed-and-breakfast."

"You did?" I sit up and stare at him. His glasses, sitting slightly askew, reflect the light coming from the house.

"She thinks it's a wonderful idea," he says, "worth pursuing."

I swallow hard. "We've talked about a lot of plans for the future this past week, Frank, but I don't want you to feel any obligation to me. After everything I've told you today, I would understand if you don't want to be involved with someone like me."

"Someone like you?" Frank asks.

"I'm a liar and a coward. You deserve better." I turn away. My eyes land on the latch to the garden gate. It's sagging again. I'll ask Eddie to tighten it tomorrow.

"Sweetheart, look at me," Frank says.

I turn to him. In two short weeks, I have memorized every freckle, every wrinkle, every laugh line on his face.

"We all make mistakes." Frank takes my hands in his. "You got caught up in your sister's lies because you wanted her to be happy. And you left when she pushed you away. All that matters to me is that you trust me enough to tell me the truth. I still feel like the luckiest guy in the world to have found you."

Frank stands and pulls me up to meet him. He places his hands on either side of my face and leans down to me. Our lips meet, and what begins as a sweet, gentle kiss turns deeper as my weary body melts into his. It's a different kiss, more intense than any we've shared. The tingling of desire coursing through my body is a welcome change from my aches and pains. I run my hands down his back to his waist and pull him as close to me as I can. There is only one way we could be closer. When our kiss ends, I open my eyes. The garden spins in the twilight. I hold on to Frank tighter to keep from falling. He kisses my neck.

"You taste salty," he says, sampling my neck a few more times.

"I've done a lot of crying today." I pull back from him. "Frank, there is one more thing I have to tell you."

"Another secret between you and Florence?" He furrows his brow.

"Don't worry, this one is between me and Mrs. Henderson," I say with a smile. "And it's delicious."

SUNDAY
JUNE 1, 1941

CHAPTER THIRTY-SIX

Florence

DR. WILSON FLIPS the pages of my medical chart and scribbles a few notes. A nurse stands patiently by his side. It's not the same nurse as last night—this young woman clearly doesn't know how to iron ruffles. Her pinafore's a disaster. Natural light illuminates the back side of the curtains on my right, and the little blue squares glow.

Please let me go home, please let me go home, I chant silently.

"Miss Larkin," Dr. Wilson says to the nurse, "can you collect Mrs. Fuller's things and help her get dressed? I'm sending her home today."

The nurse exits on cue.

"Thank you, Doctor," I say.

"Here is a list of changes you need to make to your diet." He sets a pamphlet and a handwritten piece of paper on the table next to my bed. "I want you to make an appointment with your family physician for a checkup next week. You see Dr. Bennett, correct?"

"Yes," I reply, though I haven't been to the doctor in years.

"I'll send your file over to his office tomorrow. This week, you need to rest. No exertion. No arguing. You need to stay calm. Is that clear?" He turns to leave.

"Yes, sir," I promise to the back of his white lab coat.

I look around the room for something to do while I wait for Nurse Larkin to return. I take a sip of water, pick up the pamphlet and put it down again, arrange my covers neatly, and then return to counting the blue squares on the curtains. My record earlier this morning was 138.

"Here we are, Mrs. Fuller," Miss Larkin says.

She carries a large brown sack in one hand and a Linn Brothers shopping bag in the other. The brown sack is pre-printed with "Personal Possessions of" in black ink at the top, and "Florence Blackwell Fuller" is handwritten in blue ink on the line beneath. My name strikes me as rather elegant when I see it in the perfect strokes of Bessie's schoolteacher script. Miss Larkin puts the sack down next to the bed.

"Those are your clothes from yesterday," she says before turning her attention to the shopping bag. "And this is a fresh set of clothes and a hair brush your sister dropped off this morning on her way to church, in the hope you'd be coming home today."

"How wonderful," I say. "My sister told me I was out cold on the pavement yesterday. My other clothes may be ruined. It's strange not to remember what happened."

Miss Larkin turns her head slightly to one side, acknowledging my comment. I'm sure she's heard worse, but she looks sympathetic. "We want to go nice and slow," she says, pulling clean items out of the bag and laying them over the chair. "You may be a little light-headed when you move around today."

Bessie packed a white blouse and the navy skirt I finished hemming yesterday. I hope I like the shorter length.

Miss Larkin helps me into an upright position and then swings my legs around. I'm so short, my legs dangle over the edge of the bed.

"So far, so good," I say. She helps me into my blouse, and I button it with slow, sleepy fingers.

Thank goodness Miss Larkin's better at dressing other people than she is at ironing. When she is ready for me to stand, I hop off the mattress. A blur of tiny blue-and-white hopping squares makes me dizzy. I put a hand on Miss Larkin's shoulder to steady myself.

"Are you feeling all right, Mrs. Fuller?" she asks.

"Now I understand what you meant when you said I might be light-headed."

"Let's have you sit while we get your shoes on," she says, helping me turn around and back into the little chair Bessie sat in yesterday. I land in the chair with a thud.

"How does that feel?" she asks.

"Better. Getting dressed required more energy than I expected."

Miss Larkin tries to slip the first shoe on, but it doesn't fit. "Oh, dear," she says. "Looks like you have a little swelling. It's another sign you need to take what the doctor said seriously. Let me loosen these up a bit." She works to loosen the laces on both shoes.

I haven't had swollen feet a day in my life. I look down at my puffy ankles and think of my sister Rachel.

"Miss Larkin, can high blood pressure cause swelling during pregnancy?" I ask.

"Well, some women develop high blood pressure during pregnancy, and it can cause several problems. Swelling is one of them." She pushes my right foot into my shoe and ties it quickly, as if to contain it before it pops out again. "You're not pregnant, are you, Mrs. Fuller?" she asks.

"Oh, heavens, no!" I wave away her concern. "Just curious. I knew someone who had a great deal of swelling at the end of her pregnancy. She died from a seizure shortly after giving birth. I was wondering if high blood pressure might have had anything to do with it."

"It's possible," she says, working my left foot into place and tightening the laces. "Now, how do those feel?" She taps my overstuffed shoes with her hands.

"Like two Thanksgiving turkeys ready to go in the oven," I say.

Miss Larkin smiles. "Would you like me to help you pin up your hair?"

"Oh, no. I can do that with my eyes closed," I say, taking the brush from her.

Someone removed all the bobby pins from my hair yesterday and left them in a neat little pile on the table. I brush my hair and twist it up into a simple low bun and pin it in place.

"Are you comfortable sitting it the chair until your family arrives? I'll bring a wheelchair when it's time to take you down to the car."

"I'm fine waiting here for my sister."

"Would you like a magazine?"

"A fashion magazine would be nice—*Glamour*, *Vogue*, or *Charm*, if you have it."

"I'll be right back. No getting up and moving around without someone in the room to help you." She gives me a stern glance and shakes a finger for emphasis.

"I'll be good. Promise," I say, putting my hand over my heart. And I mean it: after those hopping squares, I'm not going anywhere until the wheelchair arrives.

❧

"Fair maiden, we've come to rescue you!" I hear my brother's voice before I see him. Eddie steps through the curtain, followed by my darling Johnny.

"What a surprise! I was expecting Bessie to spring me." I smile so hard at the sight of them, my face hurts.

"Oh, we decided Johnny and I are better suited for a jail-break," Eddie replies. "Bessie's too much of a rule follower, and Presbyterians get out of church earlier."

"How are you feeling, Mom?" Johnny walks forward and leans on the bed next to me.

"Just fine, honey. I sure missed you, though."

"I missed you, too," Johnny says. He kisses me on the top of my head in exactly the same way I usually kiss him. "You look much better than you did last night. Not that you didn't look okay, but, well, you were a little pale, and your color is much better now."

"What do we have to do to bust you out of this place?" Eddie asks, glancing around.

"Did you check in with the nurse when you arrived?"

"Yes," they say in unison.

"Then she should be here with a wheelchair any minute."

Johnny looks at me and then my legs. A shadow falls across his face.

"Oh, sweetheart, there is nothing wrong with my legs," I say. His shoulders relax. "It's standard hospital procedure to take me downstairs in a wheelchair. I can walk fine, but I am a little light-headed today."

"Here we go, Mrs. Fuller." The metal rings jingle a cheerful tune as Miss Larkin pushes the curtains wide open and wheels the chair in. Beams of sunlight cast bright stripes on the glass and metal cabinets outside my shower room.

"It looks like a lovely day. Can we stop at Johnstone Park on the way home?" I ask.

Johnny frowns. "The last time you wanted to go to the park, I found out we were moving." Then he smiles tentatively. "This time, are you going to tell us we're not moving? Are we staying in Bartlesville?" he asks through a guarded grin.

"Sorry. As far as I know, the move is still happening," I say. "But remember, I told you last night, there's something important I need to talk to you and Uncle Eddie about."

"Right," Johnny says, sounding a little disappointed.

"You boys make sure she doesn't do too much walking today," Miss Larkin says, placing the brush and the paperwork from the doctor into the bag with my old clothing. She hands the bag to Eddie. "Find a spot near the car for her to sit. She needs to rest, but the fresh air will also do her good."

Miss Larkin helps me into the wheelchair.

"So, what is this important news you have for us?" Eddie asks. He and Johnny walk beside me as Miss Larkin pushes the chair to the elevator.

"Take me to the park, and you'll find out," I say.

"How about that table over there?" Johnny says, pointing to a picnic table not far from the entrance to the park.

"Perfect," I say.

When I had trouble falling asleep last night, I rehearsed my conversation with them as if we were sitting on the front porch at Henderson House. I planned on Bessie arriving at the hospital and expected that Fabulous Frank would drive me home. When Eddie and Johnny showed up at the hospital unexpectedly, the park idea popped into my head. Thank goodness my sister brought me a nice, clean outfit. I wouldn't want to deliver this news looking like a hobo who'd been sleeping on the sidewalk. A change of plan usually throws me for a loop, but I'm excited to tell Johnny sooner rather than later. Once I make up my mind, look out. Mama used to compare me to a runaway train.

We take our time wandering down to a solitary wooden table with two built-in benches. Eddie keeps a protective arm around me, and Johnny holds my hand. It is a glorious day, warm with a steady breeze and hardly a cloud in the sky.

"Why don't I sit on this side?" I point to the first bench. "And you boys sit there. I want to be able to see both of you at the same time."

Eddie helps me get settled, then he and Johnny slide onto the bench across from me.

"I practiced having this conversation with you so many times last night. I don't know why I'm still nervous," I say.

"Johnny's coach says, 'Don't be scared. Be prepared,'" Eddie recites. "If you've been practicing, then you're prepared, and there's no reason to worry."

"That's right, and it's true, Ma," Johnny says, reaching across the table and taking my hand. "Whenever I'm nervous about pitching in a big game, I remind myself that I've been practicing and I'm ready to play. I don't need to be scared."

"That is excellent advice. Thank you, both," I say. "First, I want you to know, I'm not telling you this today because I'm afraid the clock is ticking, and I might expire. The doctor said I'm going to be fine. I only wish I'd told you sooner." I shake my head, and Johnny gives my hand a little squeeze.

"It's okay, sis. We're here now." Eddie smiles.

"I've been waiting for the perfect moment—or, at least, that's what I told myself."

I look down at Johnny's hand on mine. It's not the hand of a baby or even a little boy. In the blink of an eye, he's become a young man. I look back up at him.

"I had several ideas about where to start the story last night, but I never decided one way was better than the other," I say with a resigned laugh.

"It was a dark and stormy night?" Eddie proposes with a wink.

"Actually, it was an August afternoon." I smile at Eddie before turning to Johnny. "Your aunt Rachel came into Claremore to have lunch with me and your aunt Bessie. Rachel looked lovely, even though it was hotter than blazes."

"How long ago was it?" Johnny asks.

"Almost fourteen years ago," I say. "After lunch, the three of us went for a walk. Your aunt Rachel told us she was going to have a baby."

"But she wasn't married," Johnny says, wide-eyed.

"That's true. She wasn't married," I reply.

"Oh," Johnny says, his lips taking on the round shape of the vowel sound.

Eddie runs his hands through his hair. "Did you have any idea? Was she seeing someone?" he asks.

"We were completely shocked," I say.

"Were you mad at her?" Johnny asks.

"No, we weren't mad at her, honey. But we were worried."

"Did Rachel tell you who the father was?" Eddie asks.

I shake my head. "She said it was complicated, and she hadn't told the father about the baby yet, so she didn't think it was right to tell us who he was. She wanted to have the baby at Aunt Maude's house in Wichita. Aunt Maude was your grandmother's favorite sister," I clarify for Johnny. "And Rachel invited me and Bessie to come with her."

"I always wondered why you three packed up and moved to Wichita," Eddie says.

"So, what happened?" Johnny asks. "Aunt Rachel's dead, and I don't have any cousins, at least not that I know of."

Johnny's voice sounds slightly enthusiastic. He must think the punchline of this story is going to be . . . Surprise! You have a long, lost cousin!

"A few weeks before the baby was born, Rachel's hands and feet started to swell up something fierce. At first, we thought little of it, but Aunt Maude was concerned and called the midwife. She put Rachel on bedrest. When the time came, her delivery went well. The baby was beautiful—the most adorable baby boy I'd ever seen. Rachel seemed fine—tired, but fine." I swallow. "I took over caring for the infant so she could rest." Tears burn in the corners of my eyes. "A few hours later, she had a seizure and died." I look across the table and find two pairs of wet eyes staring back at me. Johnny gives my hand another squeeze.

"So, there Aunt Bessie and I were in Wichita with a new baby, no mother, and no idea who the father was." I clear my throat.

"What happened to the baby, Ma?" Johnny asks, leaning across the table.

My heartbeat remains steady in my chest. I listen to the birds chatter and feel the warmth of the sun on the back of my hair. This is the perfect moment I've been waiting for.

"He grew into the wonderful young man sitting across from me." I put my other hand on top of his.

Johnny looks down at our clasped hands and then up at me. "I'm the baby in the story," he whispers.

"Yes, Johnny."

"Whoa," Eddie lets out a low moan of surprise.

"Wait, wait, wait," Johnny says, pulling his hand back. "You're telling me I'm really Aunt Rachel's baby and . . ." Johnny squeezes his eyes shut for a moment and opens them slowly as he speaks: "You're my aunt Florence?"

"Aunt Rachel gave birth to you, but I've taken care of you from the minute you were born."

Johnny's leg starts jiggling. The table trembles.

"Did my dad—uh, I mean, your husband—did he know I wasn't his son?"

"Yes." I go for the simple answer.

"And he loved me anyway?"

"Very much."

"Why did you wait so long to tell me?" Johnny asks. The table vibrates as his leg bounces faster.

"I wanted you to be old enough to understand so we could talk through things, like we are now. It takes a certain level of maturity to understand people having babies even when they aren't married."

Johnny grimaces, but I can tell he understands. He only learned about the birds and the bees last year. Thank God Eddie was here to handle that discussion.

"My friend Walter just found out he's adopted. He seems pretty happy about it. Am I adopted?" Johnny asks.

"No, but that's a good idea. Would you like me to adopt you?"

"Well, I think it might help. It feels pretty weird to think I've been calling you 'Mom' all these years, and you're not really my mother."

His words sting, and I feel sparks of the familiar burning inside my chest.

Don't get defensive, Florence, I remind myself. *This is about how Johnny feels right now, not about you. Listen with love.*

"Johnny, I know this is a big surprise," Eddie says. "It's a shock for me, too. I had no idea about Rachel, but I've witnessed the relationship you have with that lady over there—" he points to me "—and I'm pretty sure she's your mom in every way that matters."

Johnny shrugs his shoulders and shakes his arms as if a bug just crawled up his sleeve.

"Oh, honey, we loved and wanted you so much. We never thought of you as anything except our son."

The picnic table can no longer contain Johnny's fidgeting limbs. He springs up and starts walking in circles around me and Eddie.

"You must have some idea who my actual father might be," he says, arms flailing. "Someone has to know who Aunt Rachel was going out with back then. Gosh, my father might still be alive. I might have a dad out there who doesn't even know I exist. I might have another family with other brothers and sisters. I might—" he says, then stops in his orbit and looks down at me. "Is that why you didn't want to tell me?"

I lower my head. "I was worried you would find your other family, and they might take you away from me," I say, my voice shaking. "I don't know what my life would be like without you. I hope you can forgive me for not telling you sooner." Tears roll down my cheeks. These aren't tears for show or manipulation. These are real. These tears feel thick and heavy as if they've been waiting to fall for a long time.

Johnny takes a seat next to me at the picnic table. "Look, I'm pretty sure I'm gonna want to try to find my real father someday, but I'm not going anywhere." Johnny puts his arm around me, and I lean against his shoulder. "Uncle Eddie was right," he says. "You're my mom in every way that matters."

CHAPTER THIRTY-SEVEN

Mrs. Henderson

SUNLIGHT BOUNCES OFF the cars in the church parking lot. I shield my eyes under the narrow brim of my hat. Frank and Bessie hold hands like a pair of young lovers—fingers interlaced, arms swinging back and forth. Judging by the strength of their colors, I'd say they grew even closer last night. A melody composed of adult chitchat and children's laughter serenades us, winding its way between families and automobiles before rising to the sky. It's a song of summer, praising God for this beautiful day and the promise of the lazy Sunday afternoon ahead.

"Do you think Eddie and Florence will beat us home from the hospital?" Bessie asks. "The Presbyterian service let out almost an hour ago."

"I doubt they're home yet. Getting discharged from the hospital takes time," Albert replies in his professorial tone.

The last time he joined us at church, on Easter Sunday, Albert sat closest to the aisle next to Edna's husband. This morning, he sat next to me in the middle of the pew, and we shared a hymnal. Albert can hold a hymnal open with one hand. I hoped he might put his available arm around me while we were singing. I thought about it so much, I kept losing my place in the music. I wonder what might have happened in the kitchen last night if Edna and Douglas hadn't stopped by with those blueberries.

I bring myself back to the conversation. "Well, I hope it takes a little time," I say. "We've got Florence's welcome-home party to organize."

"I don't want to rain on anybody's parade, but the doctor might not think she's ready to come home," Frank says.

"The nurse didn't give me any indication one way or the other when I dropped off her change of clothes," Bessie adds.

Her clear, bright pink pulses next to Frank's golden yellow. Once again, their colors reach out to one another, pulling this way and that in a playful game of tug-of-war.

"Oh, nonsense. I checked in with the house this morning, and it's gearing up for a celebration," I reply with a grand wave of my hand.

"A celebration?" Albert asks with a raised eyebrow.

"That's right, and I have a feeling it's gonna be a doozy," I say.

Albert offers me his arm. I link my elbow with his and keep walking.

"Edna and Douglas are already on their way back to the house to help us get organized. Everyone will be there to welcome Florence home. Bessie, I'll help you frost the cake before dinner."

"When did you two find time to bake a cake?" Frank asks.

"Oh, Mrs. Henderson and I were down in the kitchen mighty early," Bessie replies.

"Don't tell him we wiped out the first pot of coffee all by ourselves," I say. "I felt like a Mexican jumping bean during the service."

A happy, nervous energy ran through every wall, window, and floorboard of Henderson House this morning. Normally, my house feelings only pulse through me when I'm in the building, or at least on the property. Carrying the house's nerve-tingling anticipation right out the back door and into the sanctuary is a powerful sign of things to come.

"Let's get a move on," Frank says as we arrive at his car, "and get this celebration started."

Edna is already bustling in the kitchen when the four of us walk through the door. She's gotten the overnight French toast casserole out of the icebox and a skillet of bacon sizzling on the stove.

"Hey there, slowpokes," she greets us. "Douglas is in the dining room blowing up balloons. We had some left over from Dolly Tinker's eightieth birthday party."

"Balloons? How wonderful!" I exclaim, and the air crackles in agreement. The men head into the dining room, and Bessie and I trade our hats and gloves for aprons.

"The oven should be preheated by now," Edna says. "Are you sure that's a good idea?" She points the bacon tongs at Bessie wearing an apron.

"It's a fine idea because after I put the casserole in, Bessie is going to frost the cake," I say, sliding the enormous pan of batter-soaked bread and blueberries topped with a little brown sugar into the oven.

"What?" Edna jumps back from the range as if hot bacon grease just splattered her arm. "Why would you want her to do that?"

"Because she baked it."

"You baked that cake? The one on the counter?" Edna asks Bessie, raising her eyebrows.

"Yes, ma'am. Made it this morning," Bessie says with a wide grin and a slight blush of pride in her cheeks.

Edna looks around the kitchen, searching for signs of a cooking misadventure. Then she stares at the cake on the counter. "How can that be?" she asks.

"Turns out, Bessie Blackwell can cook, after all," I say, taking down the powdered sugar and vanilla for the frosting.

"Well, she's not the only one who's been cooking up surprises in the kitchen," Edna teases, shaking a finger at me.

"What does that mean?" Bessie asks.

"Do you want to tell her, or should I?" Edna asks.

"Oh, I'd love to hear your side of the story," I reply.

"Last night, when Douglas and I stopped by with the blueberries," Edna says to Bessie, "we walked in on Mrs. Henderson and the professor in a compromising position."

"No!" Bessie's eyes grow wide. She turns to me. "Is it true?"

"I'm not sure I'd call it a compromising position. We were talking at the table, and I got up to check on the casserole. When I turned around, I didn't realize Albert had followed me, and I bumped into him."

"So, it's *Albert* now, is it?" Edna says, drawing out Albert's name. "You're not telling us everything." She shakes her finger at me again.

"If you must know," I begin, and they both take a step closer, "the professor is considering returning to teaching in the fall. He might have a position at Princeton." Both Edna and Bessie put their hands over their mouths in surprise.

"Oh, and you're not just a teensy-weensy bit happy that you and Albert might be moving to the same town in New Jersey?" Edna asks, with a hand on her hip.

"I suppose I am pleased. I enjoy his company and it appears the feeling is . . ." I break off my sentence as the sound of tires crunching on the driveway drifts through the kitchen window. The three of us rush to peek out the screen door.

"They're here! Quick, hide the cake," Bessie says.

I pick up the cake plate and place it deep on the corner of the counter next to the icebox and slide the cannister of sugar in front of it.

"Make way for the queen's guard," Eddie announces as Johnny guides Florence into the kitchen.

She looks pale and even smaller than usual, but the color surrounding her head is a startling clear green. Florence shines like an emerald today.

"Welcome home," I say, moving to embrace her. "You gave us quite a scare."

"I scared myself," Florence says with a laugh.

"Hello, honey," Bessie says, taking her turn to hug her.

"Well, get over here," Edna says. "I want my hug, too."

Florence complies, and the two women wrap their arms around each other.

"We're under strict orders to make sure she takes it easy today," Eddie says. "Not too much activity."

"Dinner won't be ready for at least thirty minutes," I report.

"Let's sit in the front room," Florence says to Eddie. "That way I won't have far to walk to the table."

Eddie holds Florence's elbow as they creep toward the dining room. Johnny lingers near the door, leaning on a chair at the dinette. Poor boy, it must have scared him half to death to think his mother might be seriously ill. He doesn't look as relieved as I might have expected.

When Eddie pushes opens the door to the dining room, the balloon crew shouts, "Surprise!"

Edna, Bessie, and I crowd into the doorway. Colorful bunches of balloons hang from the chandelier and decorate the chairs around the table.

"Oh, this is perfect. Thank you all for such a festive welcome," Florence says with a weariness in her voice.

I can tell she's working overtime to sound cheerful. The door to the dining room swings closed, and I return to gathering the ingredients for the icing. Johnny hasn't moved from his spot next to the table. He's clutching a large brown paper sack with Florence's name on it.

"Does that bag have your mom's clothes from yesterday?" Edna asks, striding over to him.

Johnny gives Edna the strangest look of confusion before answering, "Yes, ma'am."

"Let's put it over here with the other laundry for tomorrow," Edna says, taking the bag from Johnny.

I examine Johnny's color. I've never been good at using color to determine young people's emotions. I can tell if they're hurt or ill, but not if they're troubled. Good old motherly intuition seems to work better in that department.

"Johnny, why don't you come out to the garden with me and help me snip some mint for the iced tea?" I say, picking up my kitchen shears.

Johnny nods, Louie gets up from his nap, and the three of us walk out back.

"Isn't it great to have your mom home?" I ask.

"Gosh, it sure is," he says, opening the gate for us. Louie and I walk under the arbor, but Johnny waits outside the garden. "Did you know?" he asks.

"Did I know what?"

"Mrs. Henderson, you always know everything about everybody, whether or not they tell you. Did you know about my mom and my aunt Rachel?" Johnny chews on his lip while he waits for my answer.

"Did your mom have a talk with you this morning?"

"Yup. We went to the park on the way home from the hospital. She told me and Uncle Eddie about how I'm really Aunt Rachel's baby, and when Aunt Rachel died, my mom raised me as her own."

He doesn't sound angry, but I hear uncertainty and discomfort in his voice.

Johnny walks under the arbor and pulls the gate closed behind him. The latch doesn't catch. He tries to close it again with no luck. I'm worried he might slam it shut out of frustration, but he gently lifts the gate handle, aligns the hardware, and clicks the latch into place.

"I didn't know, Johnny—not until yesterday. I overheard your mom speaking with Mr. Davis," I say.

"Wait, does Mr. Davis know, too?" he asks, bending down to pick up a stick. He runs the stick along the base of the fence, making a quiet *ka-thunk, ka-thunk* sound.

"I imagine he does, Johnny. There was a misunderstanding yesterday. For a short time, Mr. Davis thought Aunt Bessie was your mother."

Johnny looks up. "I didn't know about that! Boy, no wonder Aunt Bessie was in such a hurry to find him and sort things out." He returns to dragging the stick across the base of the pickets.

"Your head must be spinning."

"You can say that again." He blows air out through his mouth and lets his lips flap like a horse whinnying. "I'm not sure which way is up. In a lot of ways, everything is the same as before I knew about Aunt Rachel. She died the day I was born. It's not like she was ever really my mom. But in some ways, everything has changed. I can't stop thinking I might have a dad out there." He leans the stick on the fence and puts his hands in his pockets. "Do you remember how the Spencer twins gave me a hard time at the club?"

"I do."

"Do you think maybe the reason I look more Cherokee than the rest of the Blackwells is because maybe I *am* more Cherokee?" he asks.

"Anything is possible, Johnny. I hope you're able to find the other side of your family someday and get all your questions answered."

"Yeah, me too. It sure is easy to talk to you, Mrs. H. I'm gonna miss you and Louie something awful when we move."

I turn to snip some mint so Johnny can't see my tears. "We're going to miss you, too."

CHAPTER THIRTY-EIGHT

Bessie

WE'VE MANAGED TO put together quite a festive welcome-home party for my sister. I can't help but smile as I look at the cake in the center of the table—my very first cake. I was worried the icing might look uneven but, seeing it shining atop Mrs. Henderson's silver cake stand, I feel a real sense of accomplishment.

"Here's the last of it," Mrs. Henderson says, emerging from the kitchen with a steaming platter of scrambled eggs.

Strange to think I know how to make scrambled eggs now. Mrs. Henderson finds room for the platter on the table next to the blueberry French toast and takes her seat.

"Why don't you say grace, Johnny?" Mrs. Henderson asks.

We all bow our heads.

"Dear Heavenly Father, kind and good, we thank Thee for our daily food." Johnny begins his usual singsong blessing, then he pauses. "We also want to thank you for bringing my mom home safely from the hospital, and for family—not just the people related to us, but all the people we think of as family. We thank you for our Henderson House family most of all. Amen."

My throat tightens, and I worry I might cry. It's the first real prayer I've ever heard my nephew say. My heart is so full, I'm afraid it might burst. Florence dabs at her eyes with her napkin and kisses Johnny on the cheek. Frank squeezes my hand. Douglas puts an arm around Edna, and the professor smiles at Mrs. Henderson from the other end of the table. He's never sat at the head of the table before, but I like how it feels with the professor as Mrs. Henderson's counterpart.

As soon as everyone recovers from Johnny's beautiful blessing, we dive into the food. Frank shares more stories from our fishing expedition on Friday. Florence laughs when I recount how Kay almost fell into the lake trying to retrieve her new hat. My sister seems as happy and relaxed as I've ever seen her, even if she does look a little tired.

Dear Lord Jesus, thank you for your unconditional love and forgiveness. I pray that a weight has finally been lifted from my sister Florence. The Bible says the truth shall set you free, and I pray that Florence will embrace the freedom of an honest life from this day forward. Amen.

"Let's clear the plates," Edna says once everyone finishes eating. "And then it's time for the cake."

The moment Edna announces the cake, I'm nervous. What if my cake looks pretty but tastes terrible? There's no way to sample a finished cake like you can sample sausage gravy. I tasted the frosting, and it was fine, but I have no idea about the cake itself. My stomach tightens as I watch Edna take the dessert plates down from the glass shelves in the hutch above the sideboard and place them on the table.

"I have strict instructions from my doctor to change my diet," Florence says. "If this is my last cake for a while, I'm glad it's your homemade white cake with butter vanilla frosting, Mrs. H."

Mrs. Henderson looks at me and gives me a nod of encouragement.

"I have a confession," I say.

All the eyes around the table turn to me, and I'm surprised to see worried faces.

"Oh, it's about the cake."

"Phew," Johnny says. "I'm not sure I could handle another surprise today."

"Well, I don't know if this will come as a surprise or not," I say, "but Mrs. Henderson has been teaching me how to cook."

Eddie gasps, and my sister's mouth drops open.

"In fact, you've been eating my cooking in the mornings for the last week or so. The cheddar and chive biscuits yesterday, the scrambled eggs, sausage gravy, and blueberry muffins last week—all made, from scratch, by me."

A murmur of surprise runs around the table.

"And I baked this cake for you, Florence. Welcome home."

I push the cake stand toward my sister and hand her the cake knife. Florence looks petrified as to what might escape once she breaks the seal of the icing, and I can't blame her. She slides the knife through the moist layers and removes the first piece with trepidation.

"Do you want to sample it before we serve the rest of the table?" I ask. "Just in case it's awful?"

My heart races as Florence picks up her fork and takes a small bite. She rolls her eyes in delight. "If you hadn't told me that you baked this cake, Bessie, I would have sworn Mrs. Henderson did. It's delicious."

A round of applause fills the dining room, and I my cheeks warm before I sit back down next to Frank. He puts his hand on my knee under the table. Florence continues slicing the cake, and Eddie passes the dessert plates around the table.

"I can't imagine anyone else owning this house and enjoying dining in this room as much as we do," the professor says with a sigh.

"I can't imagine anyone else taking care of all this woodwork," Edna quips back.

Frank looks over at Mrs. Henderson and she gives him a "Why not?" shrug.

"Since we're making confessions," Frank says. He turns his attention to Edna's husband. "Douglas, I want you to know that when I first came to Henderson House, I assured Edna and Mrs. Henderson that I had no intention of living here as long as this other ragtag bunch of characters. But now it seems I've had a change of plans." He pauses and addresses the whole table. "I made Mrs. Henderson an offer to buy Henderson House, and she's accepted. Bessie and I are thinking about . . ." He stops. "Wait. Wait a minute. I'm getting things in the wrong order."

Frank stands, pushes his dining chair out of the way, and pulls something out of his jacket pocket. He gets down in front of me on one knee. My heart pounds in my throat, and I put my hands to my chest.

"I've been carrying this around in my pocket for the last twenty-four hours. I had it with me at the park, in the waiting room at the hospital, and out in the garden last night. But now feels like the perfect time to ask." He opens a small black ring box. "Elizabeth Clara Blackwell," Frank says, "will you marry me?"

"Oh, Frank," I murmur. "Yes, a thousand times, yes!"

He slips the diamond ring on my finger and kisses my hand. He hops up and pulls me close in a ballroom-dance position. Frank twirls me under his arm, and the room spins in a kaleidoscope of smiling faces and colors. I feel beautiful and graceful as he winds me back to him, and I can't help but giggle as he dips me toward the sideboard before returning me to my feet. Then we kiss. It's the first time we've ever kissed in front of an audience, and we must have done a pretty good job because the entire Henderson House family explodes into a standing ovation.

When we release our embrace, Eddie lets loose his "round up" whistle, and Louie zips around the dining table and out into the foyer and back into the dining room—the white tip of his tail waving like a flag. Johnny chases the dog, whooping and hollering as he goes. Florence, Edna, and Mrs. Henderson make their way around the table to admire my ring. Eddie, Douglas, and the professor congratulate Frank. Over the barking, congratulations, and backslapping, I hear something. It sounds like a large, contented cat purring in the background, but we don't have a cat, and you would never hear one over all this commotion. I glance up into the corners of the room. The sound is coming from above us. I look out into the foyer. Or is it coming from out front?

"What are you looking for?" Mrs. Henderson asks me.

"I'm trying to figure out where that sound is coming from," I say.

Mrs. Henderson puts a hand on my arm and smiles. "What sound?"

"That purring sound, it's almost like—" I break off my sentence and stare into Mrs. Henderson's eyes.

"Bessie, can you hear the house?" she asks, taking my hands in hers.

I close my eyes and realize the sound is everywhere, celebrating with us. "Yes," I say, as my eyes brim with tears. "Henderson House is humming."

THE END

AUTHOR'S NOTE

My great-aunt, Beulah Taylor Allen, was the inspiration for Henderson House. Aunt "Boo Boo" was born in Oologah Indian Territory in 1896, she worked at Phillips Petroleum in Bartlesville for most of her life, and she was an old maid living in a boarding house when a divorced man moved in and they fell in love. She was a member of First Baptist Church and never missed a Wednesday Night Supper. One member of the congregation I spoke to said, "Anytime the doors were unlocked, Beulah was in that church." Aunt Boo Boo continued to teach Sunday School even after she went blind—quoting Scripture from memory. She lived to be ninety-nine years old.

Aunt Boo Boo was the inspiration for Henderson House, but the novel is a work of fiction. I created a boarding house, filled it with characters from my imagination, and let those characters play out the story they wanted to tell. Mrs. Henderson, in particular, was a driving force in the completion of this novel. Mrs. H woke me up in the middle of the night. She demanded a larger role in the narrative. She told me how she wanted the novel to end. I have heard writers talk about their characters taking over the reins, but this was the first time I experienced it for myself. It was truly exhilarating.

Thank you for reading *Henderson House*. I hope these characters stay with you long after the final page. Mrs. Henderson would want it that way.

ACKNOWLEDGMENTS

I started this novel at the Atlanta airport during a flight delay in November 2017. It's been quite a journey to get it into your hands, and I am truly grateful to everyone who helped me along the way. My first official round of thanks goes to my husband, Joe, and my children, Sam and Charlie, for sticking with me through this multiyear process. *Henderson House* never would have been completed without your love, support, laughter, and excellent playlist suggestions.

Special thanks to my alpha and omega: Jane LoBrutto, the first person to ever meet these characters in an early September 2018 draft, and Kimerer LaMothe, the last person to guide me through the challenging developmental editing phase in 2022. In between, I was blessed with wonderful beta readers. Thanks to Maureen Chaffee, Elisa Croft, Betsy Dickie, Skip and Derry Dickenson, Jennifer Jacobs, Christie K. Kelly, Kim Kowanko, Jane LoBrutto, Joe McVicker, Kim Ploetz, Tom Salmon, Cathy Sowers, David Shehadi Jr., Sarah Stefanak, Sanfra Weiss, and Pam Williams for your honest feedback and encouragement.

A round of applause to Mary Jo Gourd for coordinating my first ever book group with Carolyn Brogan, Julie Citron,

Terry Findeisen, and Julie Ragaishis. And gratitude to my pandemic writing group partners, Gemma Lury and Kathryn Holzman, for helping me continue to grow as a writer via Zoom. Heartfelt thanks to the late Yvonne Daley and everyone at the Green Mountain Writers Conference for all your guidance and support.

Shout out to the team at The Bartlesville Public Library and Vicki Evans at Evans Nursery in Bartlesville for helping with my research when I couldn't travel during lockdown. Thanks to Mary Dezember for letting me know about the Inkshares 2020 All Genre Contest. The kindness and generosity of fellow writers has been inspiring throughout this process. Cheers to everyone who helped me win the contest by preordering the novel, engaging with my page, and reading draft chapters. Thank you for believing in me and for being so patient during the publishing process—well, everyone except Art McKenna, who was supportive but not exactly patient.

Many thanks to Noah Broyles, Avalon Radys, and the whole team at Inkshares for giving me the editorial feedback necessary to take *Henderson House* to the next level. And kudos to Tim Barber for my beautiful cover design.

This novel would not exist if my late father, Charles Simpson, had not dragged me on all those Memorial Day trips to the cemetery in Claremore, Oklahoma, with Aunt Boo Boo and Grandma Simpson. And I probably wouldn't be writing these acknowledgments if my mother, Shirley Simpson, hadn't read all the Laura Ingalls Wilder books to me when I was little, thus igniting my lifelong love affair with books and writing.

Last but not least, I want to honor the late Coach Lola, who was the best office dog ever. I miss seeing her perched on the stairs every morning, gently growling at me to get to work. June Bug is doing a great job following in her paw prints. Thanks, Lola, for showing her the way.

ABOUT THE AUTHOR

Born in Oklahoma, Caren Simpson McVicker is an enrolled member of the Cherokee Nation. She currently lives in Vermont with her hubby, a rescue pup, and a barn cat turned happy house kitty. Caren is also a mom to two incredible humans. *Henderson House* is her first novel.

GRAND PATRONS

INKSHARES

INKSHARES is a community, publisher, and producer for debut writers. Our books are selected not just by a group of editors, but also by readers worldwide. Our aim is to find and develop the most captivating and intelligent new voices in fiction. We have no genre—our genre is debut.

Previously unknown Inkshares authors have received starred reviews in every trade publication. They have been featured in every major review, including on the front page of the *New York Times*. Their books are on the front tables of booksellers worldwide, topping bestseller lists. They have been translated in major markets by the world's biggest publishers. And they are being adapted at the biggest studios and networks.

Interested in making your own story a reality? Visit Inkshares.com to start your own project, connect with other writers, and find other great books.